I0598147

IN THE FLESH

Paul Nelson

BooksForABuck.com
October 2009

IN THE FLESH

Paul Nelson

Published by BooksForABuck.com

ISBN: 978-1-60215-105-5

DEDICATION

This book is dedicated to the love of my life, my wife Sissy.
She put up with me through the endless re-writes and frustrations
and always believed my books would happen.
Sissy, I love you, very much.

Paul

In the Flesh

CHAPTER ONE

Fools say in their hearts, "There is no God".
Their deeds are loathsome and corrupt.
Not one does what is right.
Psalms, 53:2

"Please boss. Just see her one time. Just for me? O.K.? She hasn't got anywhere else to go."

Josephine was pleading now, imploring me while making her big black eyes seem even larger. Almost pure Filipino, Josephine had a virtually flawless face. Long black hair surrounded a light olive countenance featuring a petite nose and a generous mouth with just enough oriental emphasis to add a little mystique to her attractive appearance. Her five-foot frame probably did not weigh over 100 lbs., but it could pack a lot of energy and right now all of it was devoted to convincing me to see a prospective client.

Josephine, or "Joe," was my chief screening paralegal responsible for sorting through the masses of prospective clients and weeding out the ones we would not handle. As a lawyer who specializes in personal injury lawsuits, I get a lot of kooks and frauds looking for a fast buck. Joe was usually pretty good at cutting through the chafe and getting rid of those prospective clients who were obvious bad risks, phonies or just plain crazies. As a part of this weeding process, Joe also referred out prospective clients whose needs fell outside our realm of practice but whose cases could be handled by other firms.

However, the client Joe wanted me to meet with on this particular morning was a different matter entirely. As far as I was concerned, she was a kook of the weirdest type. I wanted nothing to do with her.

Having attempted to get me to meet with this woman twice before, Joe refused to give up and here she was, back for a third time. I forgot to mention, Joe could be really stubborn when she wanted to and this was obviously one of those times.

As a PI lawyer, I don't like psychological mumbo jumbo. Broken bones and nasty scars are something to play show-and-tell with and sell to a jury. Paraplegics and quadriplegics can be wheeled in for jurors to see their discomfort and feel their pain.

But psychological pain? Physical pain and suffering brought about by mental stress? To top that off, this was a psychological trauma that science only recently accepted as real and was something I personally wasn't sure even existed. My level of excitement for taking this case was just about on par with retaking the Bar exam for kicks.

One thing I do know—if a lawyer doesn't believe in what he's selling, the jury usually isn't buying!

But Joe wouldn't let go. Unusually obstinate, she continued pleading with me to interview a prospective client with Multiple Personality Disorder, something I considered mumbo jumbo of the highest order. Hell, my guess is that everybody has different personalities, it just depends on a given set of circumstances as to which one you feel like exhibiting. But you controlled them, not the other way around. Just as in the courtroom, you wore the hat that fit the image you needed to convey.

Regardless of my personal reservations, it didn't take psychic powers to recognize that Josephine was cloaked in her most endearing, pleading and stubborn personality.

Well, I didn't want to start a war and I was sure that Joe wouldn't quit until she wrangled an interview out of me or I got upset and ordered her to cease and desist, which would then set the mood for several days of silent Asian sullenness. Not a fair choice, but a real one.

"O.K., O.K. Set up a conference; I'll give her 15 minutes and not a minute more. We'll do it in our library, not my office. I don't want her back here." I knew from experience that it was much easier to get away from an unwanted client by walking away from him or her than by having them escorted out of my personal office.

"And make sure she has that quack, I mean psyche with her, Dr. what's his name."

"Dr. Felton Trey," Joe responded, her face beaming while she tried unsuccessfully to hide an impish grin.

"Just like you want, boss. I'll set it all up in the law library. No problem." Joe was already backing out of my office. Having gotten exactly what she wanted, she knew better than to spoil it by hanging around.

"And wipe that silly grin off your face! It's just an interview. I did *not* say I'd take the case!" I thundered the last at her in mock severity, knowing full well who had won this battle.

"Yes boss, I know." Joe flung the words back over her shoulder as she bolted from my office.

* * * *

They were there, already seated at my conference table.

I had two actual conference rooms, but I liked the law library. I designed it myself, and it did look impressive. Rows of books lined three full walls in built-in shelving. A divider, consisting of more bookshelves, crossed the center of the room, and on either end were more books in recessed shelving and seating for comfort while perusing. To my immediate left in the far corner was an alcove that contained a couch, table and chairs where one could sit quietly while looking out through the windows over the Hillsborough River leading into greater Tampa Bay.

In the center of the space between the divider and the door entrance was a long rectangular conference table. Originally it had been one solid top, but after I purchased it I found that we could not get it up the six flights and into the zlibrary, so, I had it cut in half and reassembled. It was professionally done and looked great, but I had really hated to have it cut.

The conference table was ringed with eighteen chairs, and, as I entered the library, a man and a woman were seated in the two chairs at the end of the table on my right. Joe was seated in the second chair to my left, across from the woman, leaving an open chair next to her, directly across from the man at the end seat.

"Mr. Newton," (that's me), "meet Dr. Felton Trey and Judith Hoople," Joe said in introduction as I approached the table.

"Pleased to meet you." I shook hands with both of them.

Felton Trey was a trim man, about five foot six with dark eyes and a shock of black hair combed straight back. He wore tinted glasses, the kind that get lighter or darker as one goes from darkness to light, and they gave the impression of a man trying to couch his expressions behind them. Dr. Trey had an O.K. handshake, not as firm as I liked, but not as limp as a wet dish rag anyway.

"Mr. Newton," Dr. Trey acknowledged in a slightly high-pitched voice with definite nasal intonations.

Shaking hands with Judith, I noticed her warm hands and a slightly damp but surprisingly firm grip accompanied by a bright smile. "Pleased," she said in a throaty smoker's voice. I further noticed her brown hair was shoulder length with natural curls falling down over an otherwise unremarkable face. Not unattractive, but no raving beauty either. Female jurors wouldn't feel threatened and males would find her acceptable. She had big blue eyes and was dressed in a black, knee length dress and black pumps. Simple but nice. Her blue eyes were steady as she gazed through long lashes, watching me in an attentive fashion.

I dropped my legal pad on the table in front of my chair, looking from one to the other deciding the best approach to the interview. I needn't have worried, because as I took my seat, Dr. Trey cleared his throat. "Thank you for agreeing to meet with us about Judith's problem. She asked me to come along with her today and sort of speak on her behalf. You see, I've been Judith's psychotherapist for about a year now and I know all about what happened to her".

Shifting in his chair, he continued. "Judith can well speak for herself, and will answer any questions you ask her, but to put things into perspective, I will try to lay the initial groundwork.

"Judith is thirty-four years old, and until recently, she led a normal life. She was working as a T.V. reporter for the local news station, part-time, and also for the Hillsborough Crisis Counseling Center, specifically for the crisis hotline.

"She is a divorced mother of two children, both girls; one eight and one twelve. Even though divorced, she is on good terms with her former husband and since the divorce they have shared homes on more than one occasion.

"Judith is a heavy smoker and so are most of her co-workers at the Rape Crisis Center. A couple years ago, a hypnotist came to Clearwater selling hypnosis as a cure for smoking. Some of Judith's co-workers signed up for the sessions. Judith also intended to, but could not get into a session that did not conflict with her schedule. In fact, several of her co-workers found themselves in the same boat—desire but no ability.

"Hearing of their problem, one of the psychologists at the Center offered that he was studying hypnosis and volunteered to treat this group for free. His name was Red Greely, and Judith and some of the others decided to take him up on his offer. They began a series of sessions, each one in private.

"At first things proceeded rather benignly, with Judith feeling little difference before or after a session. She was a willing subject and readily slipped into a hypnotic trance under Red's tutelage. In fact, after only a couple of sessions Red had only to say a few words and Judith was under."

Dr. Trey wiped his mouth with a handkerchief and continued. "After a few sessions, strange things began to happen. Strange things not connected to smoking cessation. Judith began having frightening dreams, waking up in bed while drenched in sweat and filled with almost paralyzing fear. Her nightmares invoked scenes of child rapes and blood sacrifices. More importantly, Red began to notice major changes in Judith's personality when she was under hypnosis.

"While under, Judith's voice and demeanor would change, and she would talk and act like a child. Sometimes, the effect was still present at the end of a session and she would be disoriented and not understand where she was.

"On the job, Judith became forgetful, unable to communicate, ill-tempered and physically exhausted. Her whole life was turning topsy-turvy. She did not and could not understand what was going on.

"Finally, Red sat her down after one session and told her that he suspected she suffered from Multiple Personality Disorder, MPD. He said he had some training in treating MPD and offered to treat Judith. He agreed to bill her group insurance company and accept what they paid and waive the difference. Since he had a private practice as well as his practice at the center, he could treat and bill her in a way that would not bring her under the scrutiny of her peers at the center.

"Desperately wanting to end this confusion and fear, Judith agreed to immediate treatment and the sessions began in earnest. Over time, Judith attended sessions in Red's office and in a trailer at the center. After many, many sessions, Red identified what he claimed were forty different personalities living in Judith's body."

Dr. Trey must have noticed my eyes rolling, for he stopped, looked hard at me. "How much do you know about MPD?"

"Other than watching the movie about the different faces of Eve, absolutely nothing." I replied. "In fact", I said, "I'm not at all sure that I believe in MPD. For all I know it's nothing more than psychological hocus pocus."

At this astute pronouncement, Joe rolled her eyes and let out a loud sigh. To his credit, Dr. Trey only smiled. Judith said nothing, and did not react at all to my statement, only sat there looking demure and waiting for Dr. Trey to get on with it.

"MPD is a very real psychological phenomenon and is recognized by the American Board of Psychiatry. Numerous cases have been diagnosed and subjected to in-depth studies. Thousands of cases are treated each year throughout the U.S. Almost all of the true MPD cases develop as a result of physical and psychological trauma of such a magnitude that the mind cannot cope with the problem head on. And, almost all of these traumas occur at a very early age, even as early as one year old or less.

"Generally, as the trauma develops, the young child, unable to cope with reality, develops a separate area of the mind that is devoted to assimilating the traumatic data. This isolated area of the mind preserves the data and keeps it secret from the rest of the mind, thus allowing the remainder of the mind and body to function in a normal state as though nothing untoward were occurring.

"There are different levels of importance with these personalities. The core personality is the primary personality of the individual. Picture, if you will, a large oak tree. The trunk of the tree is the core personality. The main branches are strong alternate personalities with the twigs and leaves being minor or insignificant personalities.

"Most MPDs have only two or three different personalities or *alter egos*, if you feel more comfortable with that. Judith has more. Although we have tentatively named and identified about thirty, probably between six and eight actual personalities truly exist. The rest are individual segments in time; leaves of the tree, if you will."

"Wait a minute," I said. "You're saying that this lady across the table from me has over thirty personalities, six or eight of which are actually other persons than the one I am looking at?"

"Exactly!" said Dr. Trey. "I know it may sound far-fetched, but bear with me and I'll try to resolve your doubts."

I looked at my watch. My fifteen minutes was long gone. However, in spite of the doctor's preposterous claims, I was curious. I had no idea how in the hell he'd try to resolve my doubts, but I was going to give him a few more minutes to try.

Seeing the look in my eyes, the doctor continued. "What we now know is that Judith was subjected to a series of rape incidences and devil worship at a very early age. Even, she believes, as an infant in diapers in her crib. As is often the case, these were by family members, Judith's father and uncle."

"The most dysfunctional personality of Judith's multiple personalities we call Baby Judy. Baby Judy was "born" as a result of the child Judith being repeatedly raped while in her crib. Her father would take off her diapers. Having dropped the side-rail of the crib, he'd pull her to him and, while he was standing there, he would force her to lie down while he spread her tiny legs and enter her. While raping her in this position, he would hold her down with her buttocks hanging over the rail of the crib with the rest of her little body pressed into the mattress. This placed the small of her back against the crib rail and the resulting pain was excruciating. Either her father failed to realize the pain, or, most probably, he didn't care.

"In any event, the young Judith, with a mind that was just beginning to develop, was unable to mentally cope with the reality of the situation. The pain, from the lower back down, was completely intolerable. So, Baby Judy was created. She was a separate baby, if you will, with a mind and a body all her own. Baby Judy absorbed all the pain and actually became a paraplegic and arthritic. When daddy struck to satisfy his demented sexual desires, Judith went to sleep and Baby Judy took the pain. A solid wall developed in Judith's mind, completely separating the two personalities. Judith was totally unaware of Baby Judy or of the despicable acts of her own father.

"There are many, many other episodes of abuse in Judith's young life, and several other personalities developed as a result of that abuse. All of them remained secret for over twenty years, until Red. Red, through his experimentation with hypnotherapy on Judith, all highly unprofessional and unethical, poked holes through the mental barriers awakening Judith's conscious mind to more reality than she could deal with.

"At first Red just plundered. Like a thief who has broken into a grocery store expecting to find a few hundred dollars and instead finding millions, Red was overwhelmed. He couldn't keep from going back, over and over. Not offering any solutions or resolving problems, just experimenting and leaving painful residue in his wake.

"Meanwhile, Judith became less and less able to cope with reality and daily living. She lost her job with the T.V. station, had to reduce her hours at the Center, and became irritable with her children. Worse yet, she became totally dependent upon Red. Her children personalities began to treat Red as the loving father they never had.

"In complete disregard of ethical considerations, Red encouraged the dependency of these childlike personalities. He often told them that he would never leave them and that, unlike their real father, he loved them deeply. Red's sessions became the highlights of their newly blossoming childhood lives. The children often sat on his lap and squealed with childish delight."

"Hold on just a minute, Doc. If I understand this, you're saying that a full-grown woman, Judith, sat in this doctor's lap squealing and playing like a young child?"

"Yes, yes. And much more, but I'm coming to that. As a part of his treatment of Judith, Red attempted many unorthodox and disastrous experiments. None was successful and many were highly detrimental. Two of the most controversial methods are worth noting at this point. First, in one period of treatment, Red had Judith mentally gather together all of the memories of all the personalities, forcing them in front of the core personality in a sort of fast forward fashion. Picture loading up your VCR and running it continuously on fast forward, through to the end.

"The result proposed by Red was to lead to a desensitization of the core personality, leaving Judith able to cope with the total reality of all that had happened to her. The actual result was just the opposite. Judith was totally traumatized and descended into a state of shock so severe that it took weeks to recover, and then only by realignment of all the original separate personalities; i.e., reinstating all the original barriers to avoid reality. Only now these barriers were fraught with holes and shadows.

"The second of Red's highly unorthodox treatments was an attempt to integrate all the personalities into the core personality. This would be considered a valid MPD treatment, but not through the use of regressive hypnosis, which is what Red fixated upon. In attempting to merge Baby Judy with Judith, Red crippled Judith. For weeks she was in severe pain, and required a wheelchair and then a walker. She was confined to bed for days at a time and still suffers intermittent pain, almost crippling at times. Once again, Red's treatment was a complete failure. He attempted to return to square one, only this time, as on his first experiment, he was only able to bring her part of the way back. Each time Judith wound up further depressed and less able to cope with life.

"Even with the horrible results of Red's experiments, the children's dependence upon Red continued to grow. Red began to include experiments where he would take the children on outings—for pizza, rides, park outings and visits to the zoo. Can you imagine, a thirty-four year old woman cavorting around the zoo squealing and laughing like an eight year old? "Daddy, look at that one! Can I have some popcorn, Daddy? Can you buy me one of those, Daddy?

"Red had his own living laboratory experiment going. Obviously he thought he had something in Judith that would eventually make him famous in the eyes of his peers.

"Then more disturbing things began to occur. Keep in mind that Judith had no immediate recollection of the children's visits, *etc.* When Judith would come out of her trance at the end of a session, she would find herself sitting in Red's lap. Sometimes her blouse was open and unbuttoned, sometimes her bra was off and, at other times, her panties were disheveled. Soon it was obvious that sex had become part of the 'therapy,' with different personalities competing for and becoming jealous of the amount of attention and affection Red dispensed to each.

"Still, Judith kept coming back to Red. She literally had no choice. Besides the dependency she had developed for Red, the children drove her crazy when she stayed away too long. Remember, Red was the Daddy who would never hurt or leave them.

"Finally, the inevitable happened. Unable to affect a cure and realizing that the psychiatric profession would never condone his outrageous treatments, Red tired of the game. At least part of this can be blamed upon the insurance policy running out of coverage. In any event, Red announced that he would no longer treat Judith nor visit the children.

"The children and Judith were devastated. One of the child alters got a gun and threatened to kill the body in front of Red. Another took glass and sliced the body on the arms, legs and face. Suicide and disfigurement were the desires of the children who had been hurt all over again.

"Today, Judith is literally a wreck. She has been to several doctors over the last year and a half. I have counseled her for several months myself. It will take years, if ever, to undo the damage Red caused. All of his treatment was unprofessional, unorthodox, unethical, incompetent, inappropriate and, in some cases, illegal. This is as clear a case of psychological malpractice as I have ever encountered."

With that, the doctor sat back in his chair and looked at me rather expectantly, waiting for my questions. It was only when I looked at my legal pad that I realized it was still blank. I hadn't written a thing. I looked at Joe's pad, and although not blank, it was almost bare as well. Joe normally took copious notes thus allowing me to pay close attention to the speaker. This time, she'd been as engrossed as I.

Obviously there was something wrong here, but how it could be resolved or prosecuted through the legal system was something I wasn't ready to commit to yet. I had some research to do, but first, I had some curiosity to satisfy.

Looking at Judith I asked, "Judith, is everything Dr. Trey recited accurate?"

"Oh yes," she said. "Of course there is a lot more to it than that. But that gives you enough of the basics to allow you to see what is going on. I also brought some things for you to look at."

Judith reached down alongside her chair and brought up a large folded poster sized paper and a file folder full of what looked to be handwritten pages, children's crayon pictures, drawings and writings.

Opening the large poster paper first, I could see a family tree, sort of. Only this family was all Judith, with the various members representing the various personalities.

Judith explained, "Dr. Trey and I have been trying to identify all the personalities by name and rank, using the tree we explained earlier. We think we have all of them, but I can never be sure."

"What do you mean, 'you can't be sure?'" I asked. "You think there may be more?" There were over thirty names on the tree. I met some folks from India once with eight to ten names each, but thirty names representing thirty different people sharing one body? My short spurt of enthusiasm was once again on the wane. How in the hell could you sell this to a jury?

Perhaps sensing my change of heart, Dr, Trey spoke up. "See this name here? We only discovered her two weeks ago. We also don't know if Red created any more. He did cause two that we are aware of, this one, Judy R., a record keeper, and Judith, here" he pointed his finger at the poster tree.

"Wait a minute," I said. "I thought Judith was the real person?"

"Judith is real," Dr. Trey said. "So are the others. But there are presently two Judiths. One is Mommy Judith, the one you are talking to, *i.e.*, the woman you see before you, and the other is simply Judith. She was created by Red to be the supreme personality."

"How can you tell the difference?" I asked.

"You and I can't. But Judith knows. Sometimes I can, but not always."

Geeze! I'm beginning to feel like Jimmy Stewart in "Vertigo."

"Maybe this will help." Judith pulled out some of the paperwork from the file folder. These are some of the drawings and writings from the children."

When I looked at the colorful pictures and drawings, it was obvious that this was children's work, and equally obvious that it was the work of several different children. I pulled out one page and studied it for a moment. It was a child's drawing of a young girl with brown hair, standing outside in the bright yellow sun. Lots of colors and a bright smile on the child's face made this a happy picture. It was signed in neat childlike writing, Judy R.

"I take it this was drawn and colored by the five year old record keeper, Judy R.?" I asked.

"That's right." Judith and Dr. Trey answered jointly.

"Is there anything written by her in this file?" I asked.

"Oh sure, she is a very prolific writer," Judith said while sorting through the file, looking for samples of Judy R's writings. She extracted a half dozen more pages of writing, some with drawings and some without.

I spent a couple minutes looking at them. *They all look the same to me.* I compared one against the other, but they all looked as though they had been written by the same young child.

"Dr. Trey, can you get Judy R. to appear, call her up or whatever it is you do to see her?" I asked.

"Certainly, but why don't you ask her yourself?"

"Funny, but I don't know how to hypnotize anyone. It was left out of my law school training."

Ignoring my sarcasm, Dr. Trey said, "With Judith, it is no longer necessary to use hypnosis, especially if the personality you are asking for is already in the light."

By now he had me truly confused. "What's this about the light? Not well lit enough in here for you or what?"

Judith spoke up "Since we have been treating with Dr. Trey, we have learned a lot about coping with so many people occupying one body. There are three principle areas we reside in at any given time. The one who is talking to you now, Judith, is where we call 'In The Flesh.' The ones who are hardest to get to right now are actually in their own private rooms in our mental mansion. In between the mansion and the flesh are always three to six others at any given time. We call them 'In The Light,' because they are conscious of what is going on and may be called up by the person in the flesh or they may ask to come up on their own at a moment's notice. Sometimes they actually fight to get out and it is a real battle, but usually they just wait."

A brief pause then. "Except for Jude, the only male. He's the protector of the body. He never comes out unless there is a physical threat to the body by an outsider. Then he takes over, all on his own."

Hoo boy!! Got a man in there too! Oh well, in for a penny, in for a pound.

"Is Judy R. in the light now?" I asked.

"Yes she is."

"May I talk to her?"

Judith closed her eyes and sat still for a moment. Then, as if shot from a cannon, her eyes sprang open. Right in front of my eyes, a grown woman turned into a little five year old kid. One foot shoeless, she literally bounced onto the chair and sat in a very unladylike fashion, with her dress askew. She was energetic. Her eyes flashed and she had a big smile on her lips. Her hands and gestures took on the actual outer appearance of a small child.

Hell, put her in a bonnet and high collared dress and she would be nothing but an oversized kid.

Gallantly struggling to avert my eyes from below this *child's* waist, I said, "Hi. I'm Paul Newton. Who am I talking to?" *Nothing but veritable words of wisdom flow from the mouth of this great orator. Especially when talking to a child in an adult's body.*

"Silly, I know who you are, I was watching. And you know who I am, cause you asked for me...Judy R. Remember?"

The voice sounded utterly childlike and utterly without pretense.

"Yes, I forgot you had been waiting. Tell me, how old are you?"

"Five." She held up five fingers of her right hand fully opened. *Just like any little girl proud of her age.*

"Aah, five. What do you like to do, Judy R?"

"Oh, I like to write and draw and color and play. I used to play with Daddy Red lots of times. That was fun. But he don't love me any more. He's gone now. But I still love him." The last was said in a sad monotone.

"What kind of games did Daddy Red play with you?"

"He played riding horse on his leg and on his back. Not on his shoulders though. His beard tickled. He took me to the swings and to eat and even to the zoo. We got to play and feed the animals and a goat jumped right up on me. I got knocked down, but Daddy Red picked me up and brushed me off and kissed me all well." All was spoken in a great gush of words, one right after another.

Turning the handwritten papers and drawings face down on the table in true Columbo style, I asked Judy R. "Can you draw me a picture of the sun, and a little girl, and then write your name in the bottom of it for me?"

"Sure, I'd like that. Mommy says I'm the best writer of all. That's why I'm the records keeper, cause I'm so smart."

I gave her my legal pad and a pen and watched her begin to draw. Using her right hand she drew a sun in the middle of the paper, at the top. The top in this case being the center of the page as she was holding the legal pad lengthwise. After drawing the rays coming off the sun, she moved down to the little girl. A stick figure with curly hair, a dress, five fingered hands and shoes for feet. Then, satisfied with the drawing, she took the pen and wrote in block letters, JUDY R. on the bottom of the sheet.

"How's that?" She asked, obviously expecting praise for a job well done.

"Very good, very good. May I keep it?"

"Sure. You can keep it. I can always make more," she told me.

Just then the library door opened and Michelle, my secretary, interrupted. "Excuse me," she said, obviously flustered and blushing as she took in the scene and Judith's sitting posture and appearance as a child. "You have your telephonic hearing with the Special Master in the Marwick case in fifteen minutes and I need to know what you need for it."

I looked at my watch. *My God, where had the time gone?*

"O.K. Pull the file and I'll be right out."

"Judy R., I have to go now. So I'll have to say goodbye and ask you to let Judith come back. Will you do that for me?"

"Well, O.K. But I like you. Can you come again? Next time I'll bring my crayons and do a real good picture, with swings and everything. Bye."

And, with that short "bye," the eyes closed and moments later Judith returned, quickly straightening out her dress and sitting up ladylike.

Before she could say anything, I said, "I have a hearing in a few minutes and it will last for a couple hours. Would you mind if I had Joe make another appointment for you both? Also, I need you to leave the file folder and poster with me until you return."

"Does that mean you are taking us as your clients?" Judith asked.

"What it means is that I'm more interested than I thought I'd be and I want some time to do some research and think about it. I'll let you know when you come back next week." As I said that I couldn't help but see Josephine's smirk. *I told you so* was written all over her face. So much for the inscrutable oriental countenance.

With everyone in agreement, I shook hands and left the room, leaving Joe to take care of the details. I was not too fast to miss Judith putting her things together. No question; she was definitely left-handed.

* * * *

Late that evening when everyone else was gone, I retrieved Judith's file from Joe's office. Going back into the library, I spread out the colored drawings and writings of Judy R. and lay them face up in a row on the table. Then I took the new pen drawing from the legal pad and carefully placed it under each of the old drawings, comparing the style and handwriting of the new against the old.

In some instances, I could almost place one over the other, as far as the writing was concerned. The drawings were different, but the suns were the same and the shape of the little girl was quite similar to two others.

I'm no handwriting expert, but if there is any difference between these, I can't see it. I have used handwriting experts before and I know how much difficulty is associated with reproducing writings freehand, especially after extended periods with nothing in front of you to copy from. *And yet, earlier today I watched as a five year old right handed girl did exactly that in the body of a thirty-five year old left handed woman.*

* * * *

The next day I went over all the documents in the Judith file. I looked at photos of Judith at a younger age, probably as a teenager; childhood drawings in a different form than that of Judy R.; photos of Judith's two children; a bill from Dr. Greely for over two thousand dollars noting various visits, insurance exhaustion and past due bills; and copies of payroll checks from Channel 8 T.V. and the Hillsborough Crisis Counseling Center. Finally, a copy of a letter sent to the State Medical Association which was copied, certified to and accompanied by a demand letter to the Albatross Insurance Co. alleging improprieties by Dr. Greely.

I read the letter three times. She listed several sexual actions committed by Dr. Greely to Judith and the children alters. Fondling, kissing, petting, genital exposure of Dr. Greely to Judith and, finally, intercourse. *Well, that covers the entire spectrum.*

Another intriguing aspect of the demand letter was the charge that Dr. Greely failed to effect *closing* prior to terminating his *professional* relationship with Judith. Obviously, Judith had received some sort of professional help in drafting this letter. Cunning lawyer that I am, I could tell that this was no mere layman's demand. But it was not the best demand letter I had ever seen—probably something that Dr. Trey helped put together. At least I now knew who the insurance carrier was for Dr. Greely. More importantly, I knew that there *was* insurance.

Having satisfied myself that I had the basics of a malpractice action, a tort, a target and someone to pay for the damages, I began pulling the books on professional malpractice. I had previously handled both medical and legal malpractice cases, but never one based strictly on psychological malfeasance. *Oh well,* I mused, *if one accepts a role as a professional, one accepts the benefits and the liabilities. Screw up someone's life in the process and you get called up to pay the piper.*

By the end of the first hour of research, I was convinced of three things. First: psychological malpractice was handled basically the same as any other medical malpractice. Second: the statute of limitations was two years from the date one *knew or should have known* of the malpractice, leaving plenty of time before the statute ran out. Third: Red had definitely committed malpractice.

I also knew one more thing. I was the lawyer who was going to hang Red. I was taking the case.

CHAPTER TWO

We planned the next client meeting for a full half-day and, just like the first meeting, it ran well past the allotted time frame.

The first thing I did was to sign Judith up as a client. She had no money and I expected none from her. I signed her up on a contingency contract where I accepted the risk and cost of the litigation. In return, I was to receive forty percent of any recovery on Judith's behalf, as well as reimbursement of my cost advances. If, however, there was no recovery, I bit the bullet and Judith walked away owing nothing. That last part is why I insisted on research before accepting a case. If I had a crystal ball, I would have walked away right then, but then I've always been a sucker for the underdog.

While going through the file I had seen a drawing signed by an alter named Anne. It was dated from several months earlier. I inquired as to who Anne was and I learned that Anne was a very precocious four-year old. I called her up, just as I had Judy R., and she came out in much the same fashion as had Judy R.

Fortunately for all of us, Judith had worn slacks on this visit, and it was with a much more relaxed frame of mind that I interviewed this child in a woman's body. As I told you, she was even younger than Judy R. The first thing this child did was to pull her foot to her face and suck on her big toe. I doubted the adult Judith could get that toe within a foot of her face, but Anne did it as naturally as if she were scratching her head. Just watching her made my leg ache.

We talked, with me doing most of the talking and Anne giggling. As she warmed up to me, I asked her to draw a picture for me and sign it. I'm nothing if I'm not consistent. I watched as she drew a sun and a little stick figure, and noticed that this child used her left hand, just as the adult Judith did.

When I compared the new drawing with the old drawing, it was a perfect match, once again.

Then Dr. Trey brought something else to my attention. As different personalities emerged, real physical changes occurred, not just appearances. Judith's pulse rate and blood pressure would change, sometimes dramatically, depending upon the alter taking charge of the body.

Also, Judith's body temperature fluctuated between alters and her eyes changed to different shades of blue.

As Alice said, "Curiouser and Curiouser."

By the time the meeting had gone on for thirty-five minutes or so, I had resolved that there was definitely something weird and wrong with Judith. And, whatever it was, it was real, at least to her. Nothing phony. If this was a con job, it was the best I'd ever seen, and I didn't believe I could be conned that easily.

I told Judith and Dr. Trey the hard facts of litigation. "In order to have a valid malpractice action we have various obstacles to overcome. Always remember, as the plaintiffs in the lawsuit, we have the burden of proof. Red has nothing to prove; only to refute, and then, only if we have done a good enough job to preliminarily convince the judge that we have a case to put on."

"We must establish that there is a medical, or in this case psychological, problem that Red was attempting to resolve. Then we must show that the treatment rendered by Red fell below the acceptable level of care in the medical/psychological community. After that has been established, we get to offer damages that we can show as proximately related to his malpractice and caused by it. *Proximate causation* is a fancy legal term that means you must establish a causal relationship between the act and the damage which could or should have been foreseen by the one who is alleged to have caused the damage."

Having put both Judith and Dr. Trey on notice as to where I was headed, I began a truly in- depth examination of Judith's childhood. This time both Joe and I took serious notes and I did not hesitate to ask for clarification as needed. As the sordid details of Judith's childhood emerged, a picture developed. Often aided by the appearance of the various alters, Judith came to light as a beautiful young child with an apparently loving family and the outward appearance of an ideal childhood. However, inside the family circle, degradation, sexual depravity and satanic worship was the primary bond. The depravity involved was sickening to hear. *MPD or not, no child could be subjected to this kind of garbage and not be mentally affected.*

As an infant, Judith was repeatedly raped her own father. As she grew into a little girl, she became a sexual target for a favorite uncle, who sexually abused her on a regular basis.

By the time little Judith was five years old, her parents had become involved with a satanic cult in Miami and Judith was one of several children offered by the cult for sexual gratification of the high priest and its members. She specifically recalled having a mixture of urine and wine (referred to as blood by the high priest) poured over her body prior to and during the sexual assaults.

By age eight, the family was no longer involved with the satanic cult and her father had other interests. Her uncle had left Florida and Judith's life was becoming *normal* for all intents and purposes.

Then, she was brutally raped by a street bum at ten years old while bicycling home, causing another serious mental trauma.

Finally, another rape came close to pushing Judith over the edge at the age of fifteen. However, once again Judith's ability to compartmentalize these episodes as if happening to someone else was her saving grace. Within days of each episode, Judith would have absolutely no recollection of the event. Her little world refused to acknowledge anything out of the ordinary and Judith floated through life loving the world and her parents just as millions of kids do every day.

All her life Judith felt drawn to help others in need. In school she took psychology and media classes as her primary interests. After graduation, she worked as a T.V. news reporter who looked into *women in trouble* types of stories. She also worked as a rape crisis counselor at the crisis center. I had already guessed and, psychologists later confirmed that these occupations were inspired by Judith's early traumatic experiences.

Having established Judith's childhood problems, I then began to get details of Red's treatments. Who was he? What was his relationship to the center? Who approached whom about treating Judith? Where did treatments take place and how often? Who else knew of them? Etc. etc.

And then details. How often was she fondled? Which child alters were fondled? How many times did Red have intercourse with her? What other sexual activities took place?

As we talked, I began to get a picture of an older, obese man, kind of like Burle Ives, whom Judith and the child alters trusted and idolized. Red turned that trust into a sure-fire fountain of sexual gratification. He would have the children sit on his lap and play with his *purple,* as he had them call it. They came to him willingly, ready to please their loving Daddy, and he took every advantage he could. Finally, Judith herself was drawn into his web, ultimately competing with the children for his attention.

Dr. Red's noble agreement to cure Judith of a smoking habit had evolved into a dirty game of sexual exploitation until Red tired of it, and then he dumped them.

Then I turned to Dr. Trey and elicited information on MPD itself. I needed to know how long it had been an accepted medical condition. Who were the best experts in the field? What were the best sources of information on the subject?

I then went back to Judith to see how many counselors she had gone to for help, post Red. I was surprised to learn that Judith had seen six other doctors in search of help, and that all of them had concurred in the primary diagnosis of MPD. All that is, but one. He had leaned toward a primary finding of schizophrenia, but could not rule out MPD. He only saw her on one occasion.

By late evening, Joe and I together had compiled four legal pads of notes. We had also learned quite a bit about Dr. Felton Trey.

Dr. Trey's real calling in life was as a pastor of a church in west Tampa. He was not a native of Tampa, but was from Arkansas. He had two doctorates, both in divinity. Although he considered himself highly knowledgeable in psychological areas, he had no degrees to back up his claims of expertise. He had headed up some statewide programs when Bill Clinton was governor, and his license as a minister allowed him to counsel others under the laws of most states, including Florida.

It was becoming clear that Dr. Trey would be a fact witness and a good source of assistance, but he would never qualify as an expert in the case. But he would serve temporarily as an expert to provide an affidavit to satisfy the notice requirements of Florida's malpractice statutes.

Finally, I asked Judith how she had determined who Red's malpractice insurance carrier was. She told me that most of the counselors at the Center had private practices as well as their Center work, and many of the Center's patients were referred to these practitioners. Because of this, it was Center policy to have all counselors list their professional insurance carriers, with policy numbers and renewal dates, and keep them on file at the Center. Judith merely copied the info from Red's file.

Judith also said that neither the carrier nor the state medical association had ever answered her complaint. She also remembered that the insurance liability limit on Red's policy was one million dollars. Additionally, the Center carried a two million dollar liability policy.

In my astute lawyerly fashion, I concluded that linking the Center to Red's liability would be pretty nigh impossible, but Red would be a piece of cake, provided we could prove he treated Judith in the alleged fashion. *Damn, this thing might really work. If it flies, Josephine is in for a substantial bonus!*

* * * *

Over the next few weeks, I put together a comprehensive plan of attack. The first thing I did was the obvious. I filed a new demand letter. I didn't really expect the carrier to jump at the chance to part with a million dollars, but I figured I could give them something to chew on while I put together the actual lawsuit. Besides, under Florida's malpractice statutes, you must give the other side ninety days to proceed with *informal discovery* prior to filing a lawsuit. This allows them to test the waters and ascertain just how much their liability is hanging out. Some carriers actually use this time to do discovery and make an offer to settle the case. Most, though, just use the time to cover their assets.

I mailed the Notice of Intent and the demand letter, and included a laundry list of unethical charges against Dr. Red that would make a professional wrestler blush. Since Judith had already let the cat out of the bag regarding Dr. Red's sexual proclivities, I held nothing back. My normal practice would have been to go light on the sexual aspect of Dr. Red's case until pushed, giving him something to try to keep hidden, but as I said, the cat was already out of the bag.

Along with the nasty demand, I included several doctors' notes and medical records from Judith's extensive medical file. The more I looked at the material and the medical records back up, the more I became convinced that settlement was a distinct possibility without the necessity of filing suit. It was a good demand. It lay in my file for ninety days without any response. Go figure?

* * * *

In Florida, a written lawsuit filed with the court is called a complaint. It consists of the names of the parties and all allegations against each. The party bringing the suit in a civil lawsuit is called the plaintiff and the plaintiff carries the burden of proof, much like the State in a criminal suit. The parties being sued in a civil suit are called the defendants. They have to show up, and in the event that the plaintiff survives all motions to dismiss and presents what is called a *Prima Facie* case, they must offer a defense to the plaintiff's allegations.

The complaint itself is divided into *counts*, with each count specifying a separate charge, or allegation against a named defendant, including separate damages stemming from each allegation. Often, one or more counts of a complaint may be dismissed, but since each count stands on its own merits, the suit itself survives.

When I put the complaint together in Judith's case, I included two separate negligence counts and one deliberate tort count against Dr. Red. Insurance companies are not generally liable for deliberate violations of law on behalf of their clients, but I wanted to be sure the jury would hear the whole sordid story. The insurance company had the deep pockets for the negligence counts, but Dr. Red's scumbag activities held the keys to the vault. In addition, I threw in a count for negligent supervision against Hillsborough Crisis center, but it was more for show than for remuneration expectations.

I filed the suit on Friday, and on Monday the proverbial dung had hit the fan. The press had a field day over the weekend, and Monday's phone service was answering mode only. My operator was swamped and all my staff were picking up phones and issuing *no comments.* It was past three in the afternoon before things began to settle down. Meanwhile, my other clients had to call several times to get through. It seems that all the weirdoes had been waiting for a case just like this one, and now they felt obligated to speak out.

Tuesday was a normal day with only the usual three or four emergencies that go with my type of practice. But Wednesday was another matter.

Judith came in, hardly pausing with my receptionist to allow herself to be announced. She literally bounced into my office, face flushed, excited and happy. I expected to see champagne bubbles begin to flow around her.

"Come on in and have a seat; you look like you're about to bust." I said.

"Wait 'til I tell you!" Judith said. "My phone has been ringing off the hook. You remember that I told you someday when this is all over I want to write a book?"

I nodded. A real lawyer would have paid more attention to details.

"Well guess who's calling? *Inside Edition*! They want to do a story. Also Maury Povich and Sally Jessie Raphael have left messages. Isn't that super?"

My mind raced. Publicity is good for business, but only if controlled. My first impulse was to say absolutely not, at least not until the case had been resolved. I could tell, however, that Judith wouldn't be buying that approach.

I decided to utilize my charm. "Judith, you know that Red's carrier denied our claim and at this time we are looking at a trial. Adverse publicity can hurt us, especially if it is close to trial. I guess we've still got a year or more to trial, but we don't want to do anything to jeopardize that outcome.

"I don't trust daytime talk show hosts. They are completely governed by ratings and they could care less who they hurt. If, and I mean *if*, we get involved with a talk show, it will have to be set up very carefully. As to *Inside Edition*, they are like the *National Enquirer* of the T.V. news castors. We will have to be extremely careful."

"O.K." Judith said, still on her euphoric cloud. "I'll leave it all up to you. When they call back, I'll refer them to you. You just set it up however you think it should be."

I nodded, figuring that was as good as I would get and then watched as Judith bounced over to Josephine's office. I could hear them through the wall for the next half hour, sounding like two teenagers talking about the prom.

* * * *

Getting expert witnesses lined up and committed is always one of the hardest parts of a malpractice case. You need someone who is a true expert in a given field, but who is also relatively unscathed in the courtroom. This is far more difficult for plaintiffs than for defendants, because the medical community on the whole hates lawyers and a sure-fire way for one doctor to earn the disdain of his peers is for him to testify against another doctor. More than once I have entered a doctor's office to find Shakespeare's famous quote from King Henry VI hanging on the wall, "First thing we do, let's kill all the lawyers."

Of course, one can always hire a *Rent-A-Doc*, or paid medical whore, but that was a last resort only. These were doctors, usually retired from practice, who would agree to testify as an expert for a price. Their expertise was usually questionable and their results predictable.

Since this was a relatively new branch of malpractice litigation, I sure wasn't aware of any other MPD malpractice lawsuits, and, since Dr. Red's actions were so completely egregious, I was hopeful of snagging a bona fide leader in the field as my expert.

As for damages, those were easy. My psych experts could probably cover everything, but if we needed them, I had a couple of economic experts who were totally unflappable. Harvey Mulish could sit on the stand and swear that a person who worked part-time and had a partial disability could lose more income over a twenty-five year period of time than a fully employed non-disabled worker over the same period of time. And jurors believed him!

But for the medical/psychological expertise, I wanted the best. There was too much at stake to do otherwise. It wouldn't be cheap, but I figured it would be worth it.

After consulting with Dr. Trey and a psychiatric friend of mine, Dr. Wallace Enfield, I arrived at two possibilities. One was the recognized guru of MPD with an office in Maryland. He had literally written the book on MPD. Dr. Eric Lofton was his name and he was impossible to get hold of. We tried for over a week before going to the second choice, Dr. Frank Ames.

It took Joe three days to arrange a phone conference with Dr. Ames. He had offices in Atlanta and Chicago and was licensed in both states. After a few minutes of pleasantries, I got down to business. After giving a brief overview of the case, I said, "In short, Dr. Ames, I need someone who is willing to examine the records, examine my client and then testify as to a diagnosis of MPD. Further, I will need testimony relating to Dr. Greely's grossly negligent treatment of Judith and testimony outlining future treatment necessitated by Dr. Greely's negligence, the possibility of a cure and the cost of such treatment and if a complete cure is not in the offing, what type of life Judith can expect to be able to lead following treatment."

"Well Mr. Newton, based solely upon your representations of the facts as related to me at this time, I would say that I am your man. That presumes, of course, that my examination of your client proves out your hypothesis of a diagnosis of MPD, and the records substantiate your allegations.

"I can offer no more until I have examined your client. When I have seen her, I will tell you if I can help you and what it will cost. If you are comfortable with that, I will leave the making of the arrangements to our secretaries and I'll get back to you when I have something."

"Thank you Dr. Ames; that sounds fine to me. I look forward to working with you."

I had been speaking on the conference phone in Joe's office, and now I turned the rest over to Joe. Like the pro that she was, Joe soon had Dr. Ames's secretary eating out of her hand.

Ten days later, Judith was in Atlanta undergoing two full days of psychiatric interviews and examinations with Dr. Ames.

* * * *

The period of time between the filing of a lawsuit and the pre-trial hearing is called discovery. This is when both sides file requests to obtain information, documents, oral examinations, you name it. I had filed my initial request for copies of all of Dr. Red's records relative to his treatment of Judith, with the complaint. As I said, we call this discovery. However, the pile of documents lying in front of me on my desk labeled Response to Discovery Request was exceedingly meager.

From eighteen months of treatment, Red amassed only two pages of miscellaneous notes. Two pages for eighteen months? That was ludicrous. They didn't even contain any serious notes about care and treatment of Judith, just random statements. "Saw Judith today," and a collection of billings for insurance payments. Even with Red's (I no longer considered him a doctor) earlier professional intransigence, this was a joke.

Also included in the discovery response was a legible copy of Red's malpractice insurance. I quickly scanned the coverage: a million maximum liability per covered incident or patient. Usual exemptions, all normal. I just about set the policy aside when I noticed a small rider attached to the back of the policy. One clause in particular caught my eye. I read it twice as the impact sunk in. In order to reduce his premiums, Red had added this rider to his contract, limiting coverage to $25,000.00 in the event that a claimant alleges sexual misconduct at any time, prior to or following a lawsuit.

"Damn, damn, damn it!" I was livid. A $25,000.00 cap on damages. I grabbed a copy of the complaint, and then just as quickly, dropped it. It didn't matter. From day one, Judith had filed her demand full of allegations of sexual improprieties. Three letters in all, part of the formal complaints against Red.

Two days later I held in my hand a certified letter containing the Offer of Judgment and a tender of the policy limits of $25,000.00 from Albatross Insurance Co. Albatross was bailing out.

The next day, the Center's motion to dismiss arrived. The motion was set for hearing in ten days. The Center, with little recognizable liability, wanted out also.

That afternoon, Judge Brando's clerk called. Presuming the case survived the Motion to Dismiss, the Judge was setting it for mediation two days after the hearing. Anything left, it was thought, could be resolved at mediation without the necessity of a trial.

My three million dollar case was headed down a steep slope lined with twenty-five thousand banana peels.

CHAPTER THREE

"Good morning gentlemen." (Judge Brando was looking directly at Jim Angel.)

"Good morning Your Honor," Bill Handell, Jim Angel and I replied in unison. Bill was counsel for the Center and Jim represented Red. Both were paid by their respective insurance carriers.

"I trust everyone is ready to go this morning," Judge Brando asked pleasantly. "Let's see, this is case number 93-2079, Judith Hoople vs. Dr. Red Greely and Hillsborough Crisis Counseling Center, Defendants in their individual capacity. Correct?"

"Yes Your Honor"

And this is the Defendant Hillsborough Crisis Counseling Center's Motion to Dismiss, correct?"

"Yes, Your Honor."

"Which of you is here today representing the Crisis Center."

"That would be me, Your Honor, Bill Handell"

"And who represents the Plaintiff, Hoople?"

"That's me, Your Honor, Paul Newton."

"I assume you represent Dr. Greely then." He spoke to Angel.

"Yes Your Honor, although I have no interest in this motion, my carrier asked me to come along for the ride. We have already tendered our limits and intend to offer no more than an appearance should the plaintiff refuse to accept our Offer of Judgment."

"Mr. Newton, you have received their offer?"

"Yes Your Honor. We have it under consideration at this time."

"What's to consider? Limits are limits, are they not?"

"It's not quite that simple, Your Honor. But with all due respect, that's not at issue here this morning."

"Quite right, I suppose you have your reasons for delay, though I can't imagine what. Very well, since this is your motion Mr. Handell, the floor is yours."

"Your Honor, the plaintiff has alleged that Dr. Greely was affiliated with or employed by the Center and therefore his alleged negligence should be imputed to my client..."

Bill went on for about ten minutes, and his argument was a good one. However, desperation breeds intensity, and I had gone all out in my research of any way to keep the Center in.

"...And for these reasons, we respectfully request this Court dismiss the case against the Center, with prejudice."

"A reply, Mr. Newton?"

"Yes, thank you Your Honor. May it please the court, Mr. Handell's argument seems valid at first blush, but it is lacking in substance. The plaintiff has alleged that she was drawn to Dr. Greely, not by his employment by the center, but by his apparent authority conferred upon him by the Center, and the respect accorded him by that authority. There is ample case law to support the Doctrine of Apparent Authority as alleged in the complaint." I cited several cases in support of my argument, and then concluded, "Based upon the foregoing case law, the court cannot dismiss the case. I respectfully request this honorable court deny the Defendant's motion in its entirety."

"Rebuttal, Mr. Handell?"

"Your Honor, we believe that Dr. Greely's independent contractor status with the Center nullifies any so called Apparent Authority Doctrine and Mr. Newton's argument is nothing short of legal clap-trap. We stand on the merits of our motion."

"Very well. This Court finds merit in Mr. Newton's argument, and without substantial legal authority to the contrary, of which you have provided nothing, the Court has no choice but to deny the motion. The Defendant's motion is denied. This hearing is dismissed. Thank you gentlemen."

* * * *

Back at the office, I was still trying to find a way around the $25,000.00 cap.

When you run out of legal options, the last resort is equity. Equity is a legal doctrine that attempts to resolve conflicts that money cannot resolve. As an example, if your neighbor has a loud noisy party going on every Friday night, a court in equity would resolve the problem by ordering the neighbor to either quiet down or quit partying.

Equity dictates fairness, and the $25,000.00 cap on Red's policy simply wasn't fair. Think about it. When you go to a doctor for help, you assume that if he abuses his trust and hurts you, you will have recourse. I kept hammering away at the unfairness, until I stumbled into the little used area of law where laws and rules can be set aside if found by a court to be against public policy. Public policy being that which is best for the common good of the people.

By now it was after six, and I had the whole place to myself. Having decided on the public policy approach, I went into my office and poured myself a stiff drink. I took a good swallow, and then carried my drink back to the library and started my research. By 10 P.M. I had found two cases directly on point, and both were directly against my argument.

It seemed that the Florida Supreme Court had already decided the issue as it applies to the ability of the purchaser of an insurance contract to voluntarily exclude allegations of sexual misconduct, especially malpractice contracts, and especially by psychologists.

The only card left in the deck, and it turned out to be a duce.

* * * *

The blade was at her throat, pressing point first up into the space between the front of her jaw and her neck. She felt the tip break through her skin. She felt the weight of his body pressing down upon her chest where his hand held the knife handle. With his other hand, he pulled at the top of her cheerleading outfit. It was tight and would not tear easily, so he reached behind her and found the zipper, pulling it down, pinching her flesh in the process. Once the zipper had reached the bottom, he grasped the suit from the front, gathering the bra piece, stomach area and her panties in his grip. When he snatched down, his fingers ripped out several pubic hairs, while the blade point pierced her throat. Judith screamed at the top of her lungs, wetting herself and loosening her bowels as she desperately fought her way to consciousness.

Sitting up in bed, soaked in her own sweat and waste, Judith gasped for air while her two children cried with her, scared near to death of something they did not understand.

* * * *

"Let's introduce ourselves. I'm John Horne, the mediator for this court appointed mediation. Would the plaintiff like to go first?"

"I'm Paul Newton, counsel for the plaintiff, Judith Hoople," I said as I pointed to Judith on my right. "Next to Judith are her daughters, Lorna and Sherry, co-plaintiffs, and Dr. Felton Trey, a current treating counselor for Judith."

I was smiling, not a big grin or anything, but a small smile, trying to get my clients to loosen up. They had come in this morning looking tired and withdrawn and I was concerned that things would go downhill in a hurry if I couldn't get them to loosen up. Obviously, something was wrong, but I was not privy to what it was.

"I'm Jim Angel, representing Dr. Red Greely." Angel indicated Red with his right hand as he continued. "And this is Evelyn Ducasson, the representative of Albatross Insurance Company."

"I'm Dirk Summers, from Bill Handell's office, representing the Hillsborough Community Crisis Center, and this is the director of the Center, Tim Snead."

Greetings, nods and handshakes went around the conference table, then John Horn continued. "O.K. for those of you who are not familiar with the mediation process, I have been selected out of several court approved mediators by your respective attorneys to act as the mediator at this session. I am not for or against anyone or any party in this matter. I have no interest in this matter, other than to do my dead level best to see if this matter can be resolved, or settled, if you will, short of proceeding with the law suit."

"To that end, we will conduct this first meeting together. Then we will break up into parties and I will go from one party to the other, conveying offers and messages. I will only reveal to the other side, that which you authorize me to reveal. Anything you tell me in confidence will remain confidential.

"We will start with each side's attorney opening with a brief statement of the facts as he sees them, and what he is asking to be done to settle this matter. The plaintiff will go first, followed by defendant Dr. Greely and then by defendant Hillsborough Crisis Counseling Center. The spotlight is on you, Mr. Newton."

I laid out the basis of our claims against each defendant, the tremendous horrors experienced by Judith since her *treatment* by Dr. Greely, and the foundations on which we placed liability on each defendant. I was short, sweet and to the point. The opening statements were for the benefit of the clients, as the attorneys had all heard the song and dance many times before.

The defense attorneys were even more brief, with Jim Angel denying the allegations as they related to his client, but none-the-less, tendering the $25,000.00 limits of his insurance liability.

On behalf of the Center, Dirk Summers merely denied liability and stated they had no intentions of offering one penny to the plaintiff and were attending this function only because the Court had ordered them to be present.

Once the preliminaries were over, John Horne took the defendants to separate rooms then returned to talk with us.

"All right now. Let's get to it. Mr. Newton, what say you and your clients? I'm not asking you to bid against yourself, but do you and your clients have anything to offer in the way of a settlement proposition at this time?"

"To start with, we'll go on record as stating that the acts of the defendant, Dr. Greely, are so onerous and the fact that he was so negligently supervised by the Center as to allow these acts to occur with regularity on their own premises, that nothing less than the full limits of liability on each defendant will satisfy the plaintiffs demand for damages. Obviously, between you and me, we are willing to negotiate, but I want them to make the first offers."

Not one to mince words, John Horn said, "I understand fully, and basically, I concur with you in this regard. I'll be back after I talk with the others."

John left to chat with the others and I killed the next few minutes twiddling my thumbs and talking small talk with my clients. I say clients, because even though Judith had the primary case, under Florida law, each child had a consortium claim, sort of a loss of services cause of action.

After a few minutes John returned. He did not look happy.

"Well, I had assumed from the charges in the complaint that some substantial sums of money would be placed on the tablet to try and resolve the situation. However, I was in for an awakening. First, the Crisis Center is offering one dollar, not a penny more. Dirk Summers told me they had another Motion to Dismiss in the works and they expect to be out of the case soon.

"To continue with the less than prime time news, Greely's carrier says they have already tendered their limits to you and will be petitioning the court to accept their offer and hold you responsible for any additional defense necessitated by your failure to accept their tender."

"I'm sure you were aware of their positions, so what do you propose we do now?"

"I think you need to get them back in here. I've got another argument they haven't heard yet."

"That's not my normal style, but at this point, what have we got to lose? I'll be back shortly with the others."

Once everyone was back together, Dirk Summers spoke up and said: "We were ordered here by the Court and offered everything we can in good conscience. I believe anything further on our part is a complete waste of our time, so we are leaving. We will, of course, still pay our full share of the total mediation cost when it is concluded. Just send us the bill."

He nodded to the table and he and Tim Snead walked out of the room.

As soon as they departed, Jim Angel stated, "We have already tendered our limits and I really see no need to prolong this any further. Either you accept our offer, or we will tender our limits to the Court. Period!"

"Jim, before you get too carried away, your carrier might want to hear this. I intend to get an excess judgment against Red, and move for a bad faith action on the part of your client, Albatross. With the facts of this case, you know I can do it. The damages will far exceed your maximum policy limits of one mil. As for the $25,000.00 cap, I firmly believe it is against the public policy of this state to allow doctors who are otherwise obligated by law to carry a quarter million dollar bond against malpractice claims, to beat the statute and exempt out coverage of the most despicable acts a practitioner can be accused of. I believe that when carriers allow this to occur, they are guilty of aiding and abetting an attempt by the practitioner to subvert the laws of the State of Florida to the detriment of the public good. I spent several hours in research on this subject, and I have found absolutely no case that has challenged the public policy argument on these grounds.

"Jim, I think I can win it, and I know it's going to cost Albatross a mint to find out."

"My advice to my client is still..." At this point, Evelyn Ducasson stood up, cutting Jim off and telling him they would go back to their other room and discuss this turn of events.

When they left, John Horn looked pleasantly surprised. "At least you brought one of them back to the table. I'll go see what they have to offer and get back to you."

John was gone for about five minutes and he came back with a big smile on his face.

"Well, more money on the table. In fact, double, $50,000.00. You must have hit a nerve. Do you really think that public policy argument will fly?"

"As long as it flies for the rest of this session, that's all I'm asking for. All right, to show good faith, lets make a jump. We really only have $25,000.00 available, so anything above that is pure gravy. Asset checks showed nothing on Red but a heavily mortgaged home, a car with an eighty percent loan and a bank account balance below four figures. If we get anything from Red's direct liability, it will have to come from Albatross. Let them know we are serious about settling, but not ready to choke. Go back to them with $300,000.00."

Two more trips to the opponents' conference room and twenty minutes time, and we had $100,000.00 on the table. Then, while John and I were discussing a rebuttal figure, there was a knock at the door and Jim and Evelyn came in.

It was clear that they had been arguing. Jim was red faced with barely concealed anger, and Evelyn was avoiding eye contact with him. Apparently

Evelyn was negotiating against his advice and Jim did not appreciate her going over his head. He could still see no reason to go above $25,000.00.

Evelyn looked at me and said "$100,000.00, take it. That's it, there is no more. Take it or leave it."

"I'll take it, for Judith's part. There is still a matter of the two girls."

"Are you crazy?" Jim exploded. "This is a single incident. Their claims are derivative consortium claims. They don't impact on the $25,000.00 limit."

"How much do you want for the girls?" Evelyn interrupted displaying a look that said she was tired of bickering and we would either end it now or go to court, but discussion was almost over.

"$10 K"

"For both?"

"For both. $5 K each, keeping it below necessary court approval. We can settle this right here, right now."

Not a million, but over four times the policy limits. Not good, but not bad at all. Now all I have to do is keep the Center in and convince a judge and jury that the center was responsible for Judith's problems. Piece of cake. Yeah, right.

CHAPTER FOUR

As predicted, the Crisis Center filed another motion to dismiss, and lost again. I tried not to let it go to my head. After this attempt, Judge Brando gave us a trial date and now discovery would heat up.

Dr. Ames had come through like a champ, giving me an outstanding report with everything we needed to hold in the Center and confirming Judith's MPD diagnosis and Red's malpractice. He had also given us the requisite figures and disability ratings for my economic experts to rely on to formulate their estimates for damages, i.e., past and future loss of income, past and future medical/psychiatric losses, etc. I still had not met the gentleman, but that was about to change. Bill was setting Dr. Ames for a deposition and I wasn't about to let that take place without me having spent some time with the good doctor. Ames was my high card and no one would sit him down for a deposition before he and I had covered every possible question and outlined the best possible answers.

My problem was that my schedule was becoming real tight. While this case was heating up, I also had a major product liability case against Honda Motor Company coming to a head. The week before Dr. Ames' scheduled deposition, I was scheduled to be in California with Julie, my other paralegal, going through mountains of documents at Honda's Torrance depository. Honda played hardball, and it had taken too long to get this scheduled to change it now.

Fortunately, Josephine was able to schedule a meeting with Dr. Ames on Friday, prior to the Saturday Julie and I were to fly to California. We rearranged the schedules to fly all three of us to Atlanta early Friday morning. I would spend the day with Dr. Ames and then on Saturday morning, Julie and I would continue on to Torrance and Joe would fly back to Tampa. Meanwhile, Friday night I would be in Atlanta with two very attractive women on my arm. What a plan.

* * * *

Arriving in Atlanta mid morning, I grabbed a rental car from Hertz and headed straight for the hotel. We had eaten Delta's brunch, such as it was, and needed only to get checked in and then scoot over to Dr. Ames' office. Dr. Ames' secretary had faxed directions to Joe so that we would have no problem getting from the hotel to his office.

Arriving at the hotel, I slipped the doorman a five and asked him to make sure the car was not parked far away as I needed to leave in a few minutes. As he called over a bellhop to take our baggage he assured me there would be no problem. The car would be waiting when I was ready. He gave Joe and Julie the once over and smiled, as did several others in the hotel lobby. I just smiled to myself and headed to the reservations desk.

We checked in, the girls sharing a room a few doors down on the same floor as me. Both rooms were spacious with mini-bars and all the comforts of home. After hanging up my bag and freshening up, I buzzed the girls.

"Ready to go?

"Meet you downstairs in five minutes," Julie said.

Five minutes later we met in the lobby and headed for the car. True to his word, the doorman had the car waiting right in front and we piled in, Julie in front with me. Joe sat in the back. The rental was a brand new Lincoln Town Car with a moon roof. That's my *roughing it* speed.

With Julie reading directions, it did not take long to reach Dr. Ames' office. I'd expected class. Instead, it was a small dingy looking single story older home, made of mottled brick and nestled in a few oaks, surrounded by newer office buildings. Parking was in the dirt and the whole place seemed unkempt and unprofessional.

Inside wasn't any better. The lighting was dim to nonexistent. *Maybe that's the way these psycho doctors like to practice?* The carpet was threadbare and the living room furniture would have sold at special reduced rates at the Salvation Army Gift Store.

I was becoming more nervous by the moment.

Letty, Dr. Ames' secretary, stepped from around a recess in the wall and introduced herself to us. Joe immediately reciprocated and in seconds the two of them were going on like long-lost friends. Joe had that kind of knack with people. They had become allies over the past few months.

I watched as Letty and Joe carried on. Letty was thin and her actions were bird-like. Quick little jerks here and there never really settling down long enough to call her still. She was not at all unattractive for an older woman. She looked to me to be in her mid sixties, dark hair turning to gray, fashionably framed glasses that sat on a roman nose. A touch of rouge and delicately applied lipstick complimented her five and a half foot frame. She didn't strike me as a runner or one of those obnoxious seven day a week work out fanatics, so she must have been one of those blessed with a metabolism I would kill for.

Pausing in her interaction with Joe, she looked at me and said: "The doctor will be with you in just a few minutes. Meanwhile, I just put on a fresh pot of coffee. How do you like it?"

I had to give her credit; she fixed it just as I like it. Black and strong.

She had just finished serving coffee when the Doctor buzzed us in. As Letty ushered us in to Dr. Ames' inner sanctum, I was shocked even more than before. It wasn't just the mountains of paper stacked on the beat up, old desk, *I swear some of that paper at the bottom is positively yellow,* nor the ratty furniture, but the doctor himself.

Dr. Ames was seated at his desk, pipe in hand, looking every bit like an eighty-five year old, dotty professor whose students had long since quit attending his adjunct classes. A face with the unhealthy pallor of someone who never visited the outdoors was resplendent in pasty white with a full complement of liver spots. Thin hair of a peculiar deep rusty yellow color lay akimbo on a shiny pate. Overgrown eyebrows of the same dirty yellow color seemed to curl outward and in, aiming directly at his opaque, lifeless eyes. When he looked up and smiled, he displayed a set of worn-down yellow and brown stained teeth of the old English variety. Although seated at his desk, he was wearing his suit coat and it was old, stained, dirty and full of yellow hair and piles and piles of dandruff. I was astounded. I could not possibly fathom how that much dandruff could fall from so little hair.

I have to tell you, I was going through a major emotional conflict. This pile of rags and dandruff held the keys to my client's recovery of two million dollars. How in God's name had he sounded so competent on the phone? Better yet, how was I ever going to present him to a jury?

Mustering up more control than I knew I possessed, I held out my hand and said, "Hello Dr. Ames, I'm Paul Newton and these are my paralegals, Josephine and Julie. I believe you have spoken to Joe on the phone."

Dr. Ames took my hand in his damp, cold, clammy, limp fleshy hand and squeezed with the enthusiasm of a snail dropping slime across the sidewalk. *My God, can this get any worse?*

Since there were not enough chairs in the office, we all adjourned to pre-antique furniture of the living room. Joe, Julie and I sat on the sofa and tried to wriggle until we had at least one spring per cheek. Dr. Ames and Letty, far more experienced in the art of sitting in psychotherapists' offices than we, sat in separate wing back chairs from some early colonial era. They didn't wriggle. I was jealous.

As the discussions went on, I started feeling somewhat better. Regardless of how he looked, the old geezer seemed to be mentally competent and he was adamant about his diagnosis and opinions. Having decided that with a little help, hairdresser, new clothes and tooth bleaching, I could make a decent expert witness out of Dr. Ames, I was unprepared for his final statement after I thought we had basically completed our discussions.

"I would be remiss if I did not tell you about a couple of things."

I waited as he gathered his thoughts.

"It seems as though a couple of my patients have reported me to the Georgia Medical/Psychiatric Board for disciplinary action. Their claim is that I seduced them and had sex with them while they were under my influence during hypnotic sessions."

Clearing his throat he continued. "There is nothing to these allegations, of course, and my attorney is confident we will ultimately prevail when everything is checked out. But I thought you should know."

This has got to be a joke! I'm supposed to walk into a courtroom with an expert who is charged with the same sexual misconduct as the defendant he is testifying against? And my expert looks even more despicable than the defendant!

Trying to hide my thoughts, I panned, "Thank you for sharing that with me, Dr. Ames. I do need to know this in order to plan accordingly." *I don't need to throw away a lot of my client's money on this randy old goat.*

"We will talk again just prior to your deposition. In the meantime, please keep me informed as your case progresses with the Georgia Medical Association. I need to know of any movement on their part. Especially the disposition of these charges. I also wonder if you would have your attorney contact me at his convenience. That would help."

"I'll take care of it first thing next week. Good to see you. I look forward to us working together on Judith's behalf." Dr. Ames offered his hand once again, and as I shook the limp wet dishrag-feeling mound of flesh, I felt as if I had been kicked in the stomach.

Were all of these psychologists' sexual deviates?

* * * *

Back at the hotel, we had plenty of time before dinner. Joe had made reservations for three at a restaurant partially owned by a friend of the firm. It was currently on the *in crowd* list of hot places in Atlanta, and offered good food as well. We planned on doing the town, but first the girls needed to freshen up, and I needed a stiff drink.

I pulled two miniature bottles of Crown Royal from the mini-bar and poured them both over a glass of ice. I sat down on the edge of the bed. *So far I've spent about $10 K on this expert. About $20 more to go. But can I still use him? I hired him because of his impeccable credentials. No one can overrule him on his knowledge of the diagnosis and treatment of MPD. But his ethics? The success or failure of this whole case, as well as its monetary value, turns around ethical values and violations. A lustful man ignoring the canons of his profession and giving in to his own prurient cravings? Every woman on the jury can place herself in that position of betrayal and feel hate and contempt toward the perpetrator. That's when they get mad. That's when they go for the deep pockets.*

But if that contempt is divided between the defendant and the plaintiff's own expert? Bye bye deep pockets. Well, the good Doctor's deposition is coming up in two weeks. Let's see if Bill Handell has done his homework.

My phone rang, jolting me from my reverie.

The girls were dressed and ready to go. Was I ready? As before, I agreed to meet them in the lobby in five minutes.

I quickly pulled off my shirt and tie, splashed on some aftershave, pulled on a sport shirt and grabbed my sport coat, transferring my billfold from one to the other and began to hum to myself. It had been a hell of a day. Time to forget business and have some fun.

I was already in the lobby when the girls' elevator arrived. As the door opened and Josephine stepped out, every eye in the place turned to her.

Josephine wore a shimmering, white form-fitting slip of a dress that stopped excitingly high on the thighs and began at the top of her breasts. Her fully sized chest (recent additions) strained at the top of the garment as if trying to break free of their gravitational hold. Her perfectly shaped legs were encased in sheer nylons, the kind that caught the light and added attention, as if it was needed. The dress was trimmed in black and emphasized her tiny waist. Joe's long black hair was combed out, dropping down her shoulders and back like an ebony velvet waterfall. She wore only enough mascara, lipstick and makeup to enhance her natural oriental beauty. She was a knockout.

Behind her, Julie followed. Not as opulent as Joe, but every bit as beautiful. Dressed in a simple blue pullover dress with a single zipper down the front, all of her womanly features were emphasized at their best. Her light brown hair, luxuriously soft and boasting just a hint of natural curl, cascaded down over her shoulders, caressing her body like a soft silk mantel. Her full lips and natural lashes needed minimal make up. Deep brown eyes gazed out of a face displaying a natural radiance more mature than Joe's and equally flawless. A light tan added a healthy glow to her entire body. Her blue dress was zipped provocatively to her breast line, the zipper trail plunging invitingly from her breast straight to the bottom hemline, which rested about mid thigh. Full, beautifully shaped legs naturally tanned and ensconced in sheer natural panty hose tucked into matching blue pumps completed the ensemble.

Two women, totally different, and, each in her own way, totally beautiful. *Tonight, wherever we go, I'll be the most envied man in Atlanta.*

When the doorman held the car door for the girls, I noticed that under Joe's micro mini dress she wore a matching pair of Lycra shorts. They were totally unnoticeable until she was in an awkward position. Apparently this was her one concession to chasteness. Didn't bother me.

The restaurant was as good as its billing, and equally as expensive. Joe and I had steaks, while Julie opted for pasta. I wanted to strangle Joe for her numerous aspersions to Julie's method of eating pasta, the wine she liked, etc. The worst was when the pasta came and Julie began to cut it and Joe, getting louder all the time, began to instruct her to twirl it, not cut it. I was afraid one of them might wind up wearing it instead of eating it. My money was on Julie, if it came down to a catfight.

Once the meal was over, the tension died down and things returned to normal. Julie had been a good sport about Joe's picking but I could tell it had bothered her.

Warmed by the wine and feeling a slight glow, we hit the various clubs. One of Joe's friends had given her a list of what were supposed to be the hottest nightclubs in town.

It was soon apparent that Julie was by far the best dancer. Josephine had absolutely no rhythm. Even with the multitude of dance steps available to the heavy beat, she was immediately out of step with the music.

Julie, on the other hand, floated with the music. Simple steps that seemed to conform to whatever moves her partner made. I enjoyed dancing with her.

We all turned in about 2 A.M. I had managed, temporarily, to forget about Judith and the problems with her case. Tomorrow it was on to California, and then back to Florida and Dr. Ames' deposition. What a mess!

* * * *

Bill Handell had rescheduled Dr. Ames's deposition to take place in the Delta Crown Room of the Atlanta airport. Bill had tried to put together a couple of cases and not have to stay overnight in Atlanta.

Since the depo was at 2 P.M., I had Joe arrange for Dr. Ames to meet with me two hours ahead of time. I wanted to go over everything once more, and particularly, to make sure nothing else had come up on Dr. Ames' sexual proclivities agenda. I also wanted to make sure that Dr. Ames would not volunteer anything about this problem unless put directly on the spot, and then only what was absolutely necessary to answer the question.

The meeting went well, with me trying my best to educate Dr. Ames on how to best answer questions at his deposition. Depositions are weird animals, and the questions are to be answered differently depending upon the actual purpose of the deposition. Usually, I want my witnesses to answer only what is asked, and then, only with as limited an answer as is necessary to satisfy the question. No volunteering of information. Make the other side work for anything they get.

One exception to the rule is in the case of expert witnesses. With these people, I generally tend to have them make sure that there is enough information in the record to insure that we have established a prima facie case in their area of expertise. This precludes having to scramble around filing last minute affidavits to defeat motions to dismiss, or motions *in limini*, etc.

Luckily, at the deposition, Bill Handell seemed preoccupied. He had allowed himself to be caught in a time deadline between flights, not the best setting in which to conduct a deposition. His primary intent was to establish, for the record, Dr. Ames' opinions and the basis for them, as well as to ascertain that Dr. Ames had actually seen, tested and spent time with Judith prior to rendering his opinions.

Although Bill did spend time establishing Dr. Ames' credentials, he did not attempt to inquire into any current licensing problems in Dr. Ames' life. At the end of the depo, we all shook hands and went our separate ways.

With a little luck, these charges will be resolved soon and we will be O.K.

I flew back to Tampa feeling somewhat relieved. Shows how much I knew.

* * * *

Inside Edition had never given up in their quest for an interview, and they finally agreed to my terms for Judith's participation. Her interview was to be conducted in my office and I was to be present at all times. We both understood that I would call a halt if anything came up that I felt would jeopardize the lawsuit.

Judith arrived early, and so did the camera crew. While the camera crew worked in the library, setting up the bright lights and microphones, I worked in my office, setting up Judith.

These last few weeks she had overcome whatever had been dogging her at the mediation, and today she seemed flushed and excited. She was ready to enjoy her moment of fame. My main concern was to calm her down so she would be thinking clearly and not over-react, or say anything that could be detrimental to her case. Although I could jump in at any time, once Judith said something to the camera, it was history.

"You must remember, no matter how you feel, or how many times they ask, no switching. It is too dangerous for your case. You can now do it easily, almost instantly. But people don't understand that. If they believe it at all, they think it must be induced through hypnosis or trauma of some sort. Or, they saw the Faces of Eve and expect some slut to slink out and have sex with the first man she sees. We will have time to educate the jury at the trial, but not the entire national audience of Inside Edition and not in one or two minutes. So, no switching. Got it?"

"That's O.K. with me. I don't need the headaches anyway. But what can I tell them about the alters? About my past?"

"That's all fair game," I told her. "We know that these altars can never be tripped up as to what they know or what they remember. That is permanently implanted and cannot change. They can never forget, even if they want to. Let the newsmen ask whatever they will, and you can answer whatever you actually know."

I knew from talking with my experts, my own research, and from what I had observed with Judith, she had little direct knowledge of her own memories. Her knowledge was third hand, just as mine or the doctors'. In fact, it was when these memories surfaced that Judith had her problems. So what she knew and could relate to the news crew was limited.

I also knew that what the alters knew they would always know, they could never forget. Their entire life consisted of living in a moment in time. The five-year old would always be a five-year old, etc. They had a complete and perfect photographic memory of the event or events that caused their being. If you needed information, it was always available, just get the right alter.

I also had observed that switching caused Judith headaches. Rapid switching caused migraines that could only be relieved by hours or even days in bed in a dark room. It had taken many months of meetings to find out as much as I had about Judith and her past lives. I really knew far more about her than she did, or ever could, barring a cure for her condition.

They took Judith first, and I had to admit she did a good job. Josephine had taken her shopping for clothes and then primped and fussed with Judith until she really looked good. Then the show's professionals added their touch and the woman on camera was Judith at her best.

The questions were fair and well thought out. Judith took her time and provided clear and reasonable answers, while keeping eye contact with the reporter and displaying a natural sincerity that came through well on camera.

I had recognized the reporter as soon as he had come in. I had seen him often on national T.V. The T.V. screen, however, had not adequately prepared me for this guy's size. He stood a good 14 inches taller than I was. He was young and masculine and I could see why women would be attracted to him. He had an easy, successful way of talking, and a bright smile displayed a million dollar row of pearly whites that were flashed often, whenever appropriate. I wondered if I could get Dr. Ames to his orthodontist.

When they finished with Judith, it was my turn. They asked a lot of questions and I had a lot of fun taking pot shots at Red and the Center. I came on strong and offered no apologies for my statements.

I thought it went well, and after the filming, we all stood around talking as they put up their equipment. I learned that they had tried to interview Red earlier in the day, but he had holed up in his house and refused to come out. When they pretended to leave, Red drove out and they followed him to a red light. They pulled up alongside and pushed a camera and mike at him and he bolted up on the interstate to escape. A wild ten-minute ride ensued until Red careened off the interstate at an exit they couldn't make. They had it all on tape and would edit what they wanted to show with Judith's interview.

The spokesperson at the Center had merely referred them to Bill Handell's office, where they received the typical "no comment" responses.

After a couple minutes, I sent Judith off, accompanied by Josephine, to insure no last minute changes to the agenda. A few minutes later, the office cleared out and I went into my private office and poured a shot of Crown Royal. *Not a bad taping. Judith handled herself really well. Red blew it. A little favorable pre-trial education for the public. Not bad. Not bad at all.*

* * * *

A few days later, Maury Povich's producer also agreed to the conditions I laid out. I had misgivings about a national talk show on live T.V., but Judith was adamant, and, she had the Inside Edition experience to point to as evidence of how well these things could go.

The show agreed to pay plane fare for Judith, Dr. Trey, Judith's older daughter, Lorna, and myself. They would also pay Judith $1,000.00 and they would foot the bill for all of our hotel rooms. I would advance Joe's monies. I wasn't about to let Judith run wild in New York without Joe.

When we got to the hotel, it was obvious that we didn't rate star status. The Plaza is one of New York's older hotels, and cheapest.

As I unpacked in my room, I thought about the last time I had been here at the Plaza. I was still in law school then, and a member of Moot Court. We were sent here to represent the school in a national competition, me and a beautiful young black lady named Dallastine Yates. Dallastine was my partner and we did well, scoring in the top five contestants in the oral arguments. We should have progressed to the next level and the finals, but the local law school that sponsored the competition also scored the briefs. They needed to insure that their teams and the local competitors moved up and they had to score down several teams to pull it off. Dallastine and I subsequently missed the cut by 1/13th of a point. All New York teams, although scoring poorly on the orals, received extremely high grades on the briefs and advanced to the finals. It was a total New York style rip off and everyone knew it.

The one good thing about losing was that it left Dallastine and me with two free days in New York. I took her to Sardis and a Broadway Play, *A Chorus Line.* We also went to the Atrium Club where Dallastine and a very talented piano player sang duet for two hours. We had a great time. Nothing intimate, just two good friends on a holiday.

Checking into my room now, I knew I would never stay here by choice. However, when in Rome...

That evening I took everyone out to dinner and then to drinks at Rockefeller Square. Lorna had never seen ice-skating before and it was fun to watch the excitement in her eyes as some of the better skaters pirouetted and spun about upon the ice. She was a bright young girl and she was having a blast in the Big Apple.

On the way back to the hotel, with a full stomach and three drinks in her, Josephine fell asleep in the cab. Judith had to hold her to keep her from slobbering on herself in her sleep, and we all had a good laugh.

The next day was total disaster.

* * * *

The day started out nice enough. We all had a good breakfast and then piled into the limo supplied by the studio. When we arrived, they were expecting us and we were ushered into dressing rooms. I didn't like the notion of being separated from Judith, but I was assured it was just for makeup purposes and the men and women all had to be in separate dressing rooms. It made sense, but I still didn't like it.

I should have listened to my instincts. The producer came by and introduced herself, chatted for a few moments and then handed me a release form to sign on Judith's behalf. I read it and, much to her chagrin, made a few changes and then signed it, initialing each change.

Next, Maury himself came by, shaking hands with all the guests and posing for pictures with each guest as he went through. I allowed Joe to take a shot of me and Maury, like Mutt and Jeff. Me at 5'7" and Maury at 6'5" or so.

When he left, we were ushered into the area just behind the stage where the filming took place. Joe was given a front row seat off stage, but the rest of us would appear on stage in couches and chairs with Maury.

Before I knew what had happened, Maury had taken Judith and was on stage with her, alone! I was livid. The producer said Judith wanted it this way, but I knew we had been had. I could do nothing but sit backstage and watch the monitor as Judith and Maury chatted away in front of millions of people.

Maury was good, very good. He started on Judith at once, projecting a fatherly figure, kind and sincere. He dripped with it. He was someone truly interested in her tale of woe. But nothing really about the bad times that caused her problems. More of the lighter moments. Judith explaining how it feels to go to the closet in the morning while twelve or so people decide how one person will dress for the day. Or how Judith would sometimes allow the child alters to come out and play with her two daughters. Or how her daughters would sometimes trick her at the mall, having one of the child alters emerge so they could take Judith's charge cards and buy something special that Judith might not otherwise allow.

Before long, Judith was relaxed and confident. Trusting. Way too trusting for my comfort. I could feel the pressure building in my head as all the alarms went off. I did not trust Maury. He did not build his ratings up just sitting out there being nice.

The first fifteen minutes had run and it was break time. It wasn't really fifteen minutes, commercials took five of fifteen, but it was the end of the segment. We were then rushed out on stage and seated in our chairs. Judith was still talking quietly with Maury and I wasn't able to speak with her before the next segment started.

Maury introduced the rest of us, allowing me a couple of minutes to explain the legal aspects of Judith's case, and Dr. Trey to explain MPD itself. Then Maury announced that Judith had consented to allow one of the children alters to come out!

Before anything else could be said, Judy R. popped out. She was beaming and seemed to enjoy every moment in the spotlight. Immediately there were boos and cat calls being yelled from one segment of the audience. They called Judith a phony, fake, and all sorts of nasty names. The blip button must have been going wild. It was easy to see that this section of the audience had been handpicked to respond negatively.

And, through it all, there was Maury, right in the middle. Judy R. became scared and then subdued, more so with each passing moment. Maury allowed the audience to ask questions, and each of Judy R.'s answers elicited more catcalls and hoots.

Time seemed frozen as if the next break would never arrive. Finally, though, the break came.

During the break, without the constant jeering and questioning, Judy R relaxed and Judith came back. Having regained the flesh, she put her shoes back on and no longer trembled. Even the act of putting her shoes back on was challenged by the brutal audience.

The next segment began with Maury bringing out his ringer. The hatchet man was a New York psychiatrist with an impressive sounding list of credentials.

I wish my expert looked this good.

The doctor immediately denounced Judith as a fraud, basing his opinion on his training and his viewing of a 15-minute tape of Judith in session with one of her earlier counselors.

I was burning up and could stand no more of this farce.

I jumped up and shouted above the noise, "Doctor, have you ever met Judith?"

"No, of course not"

"Have you reviewed her extensive medical and psychological charts and history?"

"No, I have not had the opportunity, but that would not affect my diagnosis."

"Do you specialize in MPD?"

"No, general Psychiatry, but MPD is a psychiatric problem and I am a psychiatrist."

"Dr., do you have patients?"

"Of course, many patients."

"Do you commonly diagnose your patients based upon a review of a three year old video tape, never having met your patients nor reviewed their medical history?"

"Well, no, but I was asked to—"

Raising my voice I interrupted. "Isn't it true you were hired to do exactly what you have done, denounce Judith and label her as a fake?"

"Well, no," the Doctor sputtered.

I interrupted again. "Your diagnosis is nothing but quackery and you, Doctor, are nothing but a quack!" I literally shouted the last statement at the Doctor, standing not more that two feet away from his face, probably spraying him with spittle.

The rest of the segment was bedlam, with me calling the doctor a quack, a fake and a charlatan. Dr. Trey tried to get his two cents in on Judith's behalf and Maury played at restoring calm. It was a halfhearted attempt at best. Maury's ratings were soaring.

The final segment started out on another bad note when Maury took the mike over to Lorna and began to question her. She did well, until he hit on the money questions.

"Oh? And how much do you expect to get out of this lawsuit, Lorna?" Maury asked in a very innocent manner.

"Well, were asking for a million dollars each for me and my sister," she replied.

"A million dollars! That's a lot of money, Lorna. Do you think it's fair for you to get a million dollars when you haven't been hurt?"

I groaned inside. Lorna was a smart kid. She must have read the complaint and knew what had been filed. She was smart, but she wasn't up to this kind of interrogation. She couldn't possibly know the reasons why we had filed what we had filed. Nor had I prepared her for these questions, not knowing she had read the complaint.

Lorna was shot down in flames over the money aspect, but later, when the quack was attempting to explain some aspect of MPD, Lorna jumped in and leveled him.

"You don't know anything about MPD," she shouted. "That's totally wrong. I know lots more about MPD than you."

I wanted to congratulate her, but I was too busy battling the quack myself. He was the proverbial tar baby, hit him hard and you were stuck in black yuck.

Finally, the show was over. The curtains were pulled and the audience was gone. Maury immediately disappeared and his producer reappeared, congratulating everyone on a job well done. Thanking all of us and acting for all the world as if this was all prearranged and we had all passed the test. Some minor apologies were offered to insure no one's feelings were hurt too badly, and then we were all in a limo, headed back to the hotel.

It was a very subdued group that arrived back at the hotel. Judith had a migraine, and could not talk. Lorna was still mad at her encounters with Maury and the psychiatric quack and wanted to be left to fume and fret on her own. Josephine and Dr. Trey were simply exhausted and needed nothing more than to sleep, as if, like a hangover, the whole thing might go away if they slept soon enough and long enough.

I just wanted a stiff drink and a willing woman. I settled for three stiff drinks and a lumpy mattress in a dingy old hotel.

CHAPTER FIVE

Our staffs arranged that Judith's deposition would take place in Bill's office, in his conference room. Let me tell you, Bill's firm was a major defense firm and their office was exceptional. I'm proud of my office, but it is peanuts compared with the kind of opulence old Tampa defense money generates.

As a condition of the depo, Dr. Trey was allowed to be present, but not to participate in any way. He was like a safety feature as far as I was concerned. If something went wrong with Judith, I wanted help available. Even after all this time, I never knew what to expect when Judith came under pressure.

I spent several hours with Judith the day before her depo, going over her testimony and trying to insure that she answered only the question asked, and then, only to the extent absolutely necessary.

"Always remember, Judith, that this is a discovery deposition. It is not intended to be a forum for us to present our case. It is a time for the defense to probe our strengths and discover our weaknesses.

"We are not trying to establish a record through Bill Handell's questioning. If I think that something is lacking, or something needs to be placed in the record, I will ask you the questions myself, after Bill is finished. But as far as his questions are concerned, if you can answer with a yes or no, do so.

"Never elaborate your answers. As an example, if he asks you if you saw a car, don't say 'do you mean the blue car with the white sidewalls?' Simply say yes if you are sure you saw a car, and no if you sure you did not see a car. If you are in doubt, tell him so. Just say 'I'm sorry, I don't know,' or, 'would you repeat the question, please.'

"Never answer a question unless you are sure you understand it. Remember, the deposition itself can never be used in court, except for one purpose. To impeach you, to call you a liar. That means that the more you put on the record, or the more general your answers are, the easier it is for a good attorney to find something you said that will appear to contradict what you say in court.

"Especially, do not let Bill's easy-going demeanor fool you. He is an excellent attorney. If he acts puzzled, don't believe it. He always knows exactly what he is doing, and why. Even if you don't. He has tried hundreds of cases and conducted thousands of depositions. Be wary of him."

On the day of the depo, we arrived right on time, me, Joe, Dr. Trey and Judith. I had spent a few more minutes with Judith, last minute prep, and then, not wanting her to have time to get any more nervous, I had declared her fit, ready and able for her first deposition. I told her to relax and that we would get the show on the road.

We did not have to wait at Bill's office, but instead were ushered right in to the conference room. High above and looking out over the city, it was a beautiful room with a breathtaking view. The furnishings were impressive, highly polished antiques with ornate trim; the conference table stretched the full length of the room. Picture windows filled one side of the room, and floral prints in gilded frames adorned the wainscoting and wallpaper on the opposite side.

Coffee and pastries were present, on real china, cups and saucers on silver trays with real cream in miniature silver pitchers.

It was set up to impress, and it did.

The court reporter was already present and set up, and Bill and his Paralegal, Heidi came into the room immediately behind us. The initial introductions went smoothly, and then Judith was sworn in.

"Do you swear or affirm to tell the truth, the whole truth and nothing but the truth, so help you God?" The court reporter asked the question as she had done thousands of times before.

"We do." Judith said in a strong voice, especially given the circumstances,

Judith always referred to herself in the plural, reflecting her numerous entities. I was used to it, but it did not sit right with Bill.

"Mrs. Hooper," Bill said, "You understand that this is your deposition and that you are required to answer, under penalty of perjury, the questions put to you?"

"Yes sir."

"Then, I will ask the court reporter to swear you in, one more time."

Picking up her cue, the court reporter repeated, "Do you swear or affirm to tell the truth, the whole truth and nothing but the truth, so help you God."

"We do."

"Mrs. Hooper," Bill intoned in an exasperated voice, "I thought we just established that I am here, and you are here, for the purpose of my taking *your* deposition. I do not want or intend to talk to any person other than you. I only want and expect answers from *you.* I also expect *you* to take the oath and be sworn in. Do we understand each other?"

"Objection, argumentative" I stated.

"It's your client who's being argumentative." Bill said. "Not me. I'm entitled to a proper affirmation of the oath and a proper answer to my questions."

"Well she has taken the oath, and she is prepared to and will answer your questions, but if you don't like the answers, that's tough. You can take it up with the judge if you want to, but I will not allow you to become abusive to my client." I had no idea how Judge Brando might rule on this issue, but I wasn't going to let Bill overwhelm Judith.

Looking completely urbane and unflustered, as if we had not had our previous discussion, Bill asked Judith: "Very well, Mrs. Hooper, will you state your full name, for the record."

"Judith Amanda Hooper is *my* name."

"And you are the person who is answering my questions at this deposition, right Mrs. Hooper?"

"Right now, I am."

"Let's not start that again. I am conducting this deposition with, and have subpoenaed you, Judith Hooper, and no one else. Is that clear?"

"That is clear. Yes"

"Good, let's get on with it."

The rest of the deposition was spliced with more objections and complaints whenever Judith would answer in the plural, but we worked through it with Bill holding his exasperation to a minimum. I was somewhat surprised that Bill did not probe to deeply into Judith's childhood sexual abuse allegations, only asking enough to establish their existence. Quick questions, who was involved, who was present, who was in residence at her home, sisters, brothers, *etc.*?

Most of Bill's emphasis surrounded Judith's relationship with Red, her training at the center, and, particularly, her perception of Red's relationship with the Center.

It did not take a genius with acute legal acumen to see where Bill was headed. Under Florida law, if Judith worked for the Center, and was injured as a result of that employment, recovery would be limited to Workers Compensation. On the flip side, if he could establish no employment relationship between the Center and Red, and Red did all his dirty deeds in his capacity as an individual practitioner, the Center could claim it had no liability.

My theory cut right through the middle of Bills two competing theories. We admit that Red was not an employee of the center, but assert that Judith relied upon the Center's superior knowledge of Reds talents and the *apparent authority* bestowed upon him by the Center as a recommendation upon which Judith relied in making her decision to allow Red to treat her.

It was at best a sticky situation, liability wise, but so far we had withstood three attempts to dismiss the case. Besides, it was all we had, what with Red having been dismissed following mediation.

A major portion of my pre-depo conferences with Judith had gone into preparing her answers to insure our position would be sustained. Judith had answered all liability questions as well as I had a right to expect.

The depo lasted two hours. This was a surprise to me. I had expected five or six, at least. Throughout the depo, Bill had treated Judith with bare civility, and pronounced disdain. He exhibited a clear and absolute belief that Judith's MPD was nonexistent and that she was a gold digger wishing to exploit his client and get rich in the process. Frequently he was abusive in his questions, and just as frequently, I objected.

The battle lines had been drawn.

When the depo ended, I took our little troop back to the office for a quick conference. More than anything, I wanted to reassure Judith that she had done well and everything was O.K. When we were seated in the library, I said:

"Bill really surprised me. He is normally a very easygoing man. This case has really set him off. I've never seen him that abusive in a deposition

"I know it was getting to you, Judith. I could see you flinch several times when he jumped at you for answering in the plural."

"He came on strong. If you hadn't been there I might have been in tears. In fact, I almost was a couple of times." Judith was still on the verge of tears as she spoke.

"When we go to trial, I expect he will have you on the stand several hours." I told her. "You'll have to control yourself. We don't want him to drive you into a catatonic state right on the stand. You, slobbering and in a fetal state might be fine in the movies, but it would probably be grounds for a mistrial." Coming back to reality I said, "Don't worry. No matter how aggravated Bill might get, he's not that stupid. Besides, both the Judge and I wouldn't allow things to progress to that point."

At that, we all laughed and the tension seemed to drain out of our little group. Or so I thought at the time.

* * * *

Dr. Trey's deposition was scheduled for a week later. Just as I had with Dr. Ames, I spent time preparing my witness for his testimony.

The deposition took place in Dr. Trey's office off to the side of his church. It was a spacious office with ample seating and a surprisingly large library. The shelves were stocked with numerous books and all appeared to be well read.

At first things went smoothly enough. Bill was his normal, affable self, in charge of his deposition, but not abusive. However, as the depo progressed and Bill began to inquire deeper into Dr. Trey's credentials, Dr, Trey became very defensive. As is the case with many amateurs, Dr. Trey began to take personal offense to legitimate questions. He constantly shifted his eyes behind those dark glasses, looking shifty and untrustworthy. His nervousness and belligerence combined to make him a very poor witness.

His only apparent saving grace was that he really did know a lot about MPD, and he had the DMSO and related text available to back up his assertions. (The DMSO is the industry recognized bible on diagnoses, recognition, attributes and treatment of psychiatric disorders.)

However, even though Bill was somewhat impressed by this, both he and I knew that this witness would never be offered to establish Judith's psychological diagnosis of MPD.

Dr. Trey would be a fact witness and a counselor, but that was it. Now I was certain that I had to have Dr. Ames or I had no winnable case.

* * * *

With only a couple months to go prior to trial, things began to move rapidly. Several fact witnesses were set for depositions, all of whom played some small part in Judith's case.

A girlfriend of Judith had been in the hospital with them when Red displayed himself to Judith.

A family friend would testify that Judith appeared to be a normal child.

Police records custodian to introduce evidence of the one reported rape of Judith as a child.

Judith's other treating counselors, none of whom treated her for any appreciable length of time, but all of whom agreed with her current diagnosis and with the fact that they believed Judith was telling the truth.

One counselor, Dr. Sherrie Lyons, had quite extensive notes confirming

Judith's allegations against Red. Although in early treatment, Judith had not referred to him by name, the factual allegations all supported Judith's later claims.

During Dr. Lyons' deposition, Bill had gone into a new area of questioning. "Dr. Lyons, in your notes, and in your testimony, you state that Judith is 'quite manipulative,' is that correct?"

"Oh yes, very much so." Dr. Lyons answered. "But don't take that the wrong way. Manipulation is a well-recognized aspect of people with MPD. It is to be expected, not the other way around."

She continued, "When you have several members of the same body, all fighting over the right to be present, manipulation will take place. It's a natural. Judith has more than one strong personality, so, of necessity, manipulation and concession will take place."

"Would that extend beyond the personalities themselves, Doctor?"

"Objection, overbroad" I said. I didn't like the direction he was headed, but there was precious little I could do to stop him.

"With all do respect to Mr. Newton, Doctor, what I am asking is does Judith's manipulative nature extend beyond her dealings with her MPD problems and into her dealings with others?"

"Although that is possible, that is not what is intended by my notes.

"If you are asking for my professional opinion as to whether Judith is or could be a manipulative person in her daily life, of course she can. So can we all be, even you, In fact, manipulation is, I suspect, part and parcel of what makes you good at your trade, Mr. Handell."

A good laugh was had by all and I put an asterisk by Dr. Lyon's name. I would definitely call her as a witness at trial.

* * * *

Bill Handell had still not identified his expert witnesses, so I filed a motion to compel and set it for a hearing.

Bill cross-noticed the hearing, setting a hearing for a trial date, set certain. It had become apparent that this case would require two to three weeks for trial, so the normal trial week setting would not suffice.

Generally, trial week consisted of several cases set at the same time under the same judge. A calendar would be set up listing the various cases and their positions on the docket. In reality, only one or two cases could actually be heard in a given week. However, at two to three months out, each judge had anywhere from ten to twenty cases listed on his docket for each trial week. That way, if a given case settled, and most did, the week was not wasted. Those cases still pending on Monday morning would see their respective counsels in attendance at the cattle call.

It was an uncertain system, but it usually sufficed. However, in a case where the length of the trial was sure to exceed one week, the procedure was to apply to the court for a date certain. The problems with putting on a two or three week trial were substantial. Expert witnesses had to be on standby, at great expense to the parties responsible for calling them. Fact witnesses and depositions were kept handy to use as filler between experts, as no juror's time should be wasted. Woe to the lawyer who kept a jury cooling their heels while he waited for his witnesses. Resentment could taint verdicts.

At the hearing, I stipulated with Bill as to the necessity of a trial date certain. Judge Brando granted the motion and set the trial for a three week period, four months away. He also granted my motion to compel, (a motion to force Bill to name his witnesses) and gave Bill thirty days to produce his expert(s).

When Judge Brando inquired as to the possibility of settlement and whether or not a second mediation might resolve the case, Bill responded that his client was adamant. They would not offer one red cent to settle what they believed was a completely false claim.

Looking morally indignant, Bill stated, "We will not be subjected to blackmail by this person and her psycho mumbo jumbo. Not one penny, Judge, not one penny."

Not to be outshone, I responded, "We are not looking for pennies, Your Honor, but dollars. Real dollars to compensate for a real and legitimate injury."

Shaking his head and smiling, Judge Brando said, "I guess that answers my questions about settlement. You gentlemen have a nice day. I'll see you at the pre-trial hearing." He stepped out of his chambers, leaving Bill and I to pack up our brief cases and depart on our own.

* * * *

I was taking a last minute look in my briefcase before leaving for California for a depo in the Honda case when Joe buzzed me on the intercom.

"Boss, I think you need to take this call. It's Dr. Ames, and it's important!"

What now. Joe knows I'm leaving. I'm already cutting it close to the airport. Doesn't feel like good news to me.

As I picked up the receiver, I hit the blinking light. "Dr. Ames. Good morning, sir, how are you this morning?"

"I'm quite all right, thank you. I called because something has happened and I think you ought to know. The GMA has issued its preliminary report, finding in favor of these female charlatans and against me. On all charges! This isn't the final official record, but my lawyer says the prelims are usually followed pretty closely by formal findings. It's pretty much perfunctory from here on out.

"We are looking now at the sanctions and hoping that we can effect a settlement that will allow me to voluntarily relinquish my license in Georgia without affecting my license in Illinois.

"I don't quite know how this will affect your case, but I thought you should know."

You don't know how it will affect my case! You just blew a major hole all the way through it!

"Doctor, I appreciate your calling. I need some time to digest this and then get back to you. I'll be in California the rest of this week, co I'll call you next Monday morning, first thing, to work something out.

"Thank you again for calling me, and, good luck with your license."

"Yes, well, I just thought you should know. You did ask. I'll talk to you then."

As he hung up the phone Dr. Ames sounded thoroughly defeated.

I replaced the receiver, picked up my two briefcases and stepped into Joe's office.

"You know?"

"Yeah Boss." Joe looked like a little puppy who had just been scolded for wetting on the carpet.

"Let me think on this for a while. I'll call you from L.A. tomorrow. We'll think of something."

I headed out to the elevators and the airport.

What next? I sure as hell can't put him on the stand. He'd look worse than the flasher naked under the raincoat scaring old women in central park.

When I got on board, with only a minute to spare, the first class hostess asked if I wanted a drink.

"Yeah, make it a double." *It's a long flight.*

* * * *

We had too much money invested in Dr. Ames for me to give up on him easily. Besides, we were getting close to discovery cut off, and I could just hear Bill Handell screaming his objections to the court. That presumes I could even find a replacement for Dr. Ames at this late date anyhow.

I decided to try for a video deposition. We would notice it as a trial depo and take it subject to cross-examination. If it worked, and if the doctor's proclivities with female clients and the subsequent licensing problems did not come to light, I would never call the Doctor to the stand. We would just play the depo to the jury. The more I thought about it, the more I liked it. It just might work.

Might hell, it had to.

Josephine made the arraignments and set the depo. Dr. Ames had a condo near Jacksonville, on the beach, and she set up to take it there.

On the morning of the depo, I drove over with my video man, my brother and best friend. It was all the same man, Tip. While Tip set things up, I spent time with Dr. Ames. One of the first things I noticed was that even though this was a two bedroom condo, both Lettie and Dr. Ames had left their luggage in one bedroom, and only one bed had been slept in that night. He really was a randy old goat.

We sat down with coffee, and I started my prep.

"Dr. Ames, I will be conducting most of this deposition. I will take you through all the things I want, step by step. We will start with your credentials and establish your right to offer expert opinions on Judith's MPD, Red's deviations from the acceptable standards of care in his treatment of her, and the Center's liability in all of this.

"After that we will get into detail about your examination of Judith, her records, your appraisal of the treatment provided by her other practitioners and the psychological phenomenon of Multiple Personality Disorder. Once we have covered this to my satisfaction, I will ask you if you have an opinion, within a reasonable degree of medical probability, if Judith Hooper has medical and or psychological problems. You will answer yes. I will then ask you what that opinion is and you will tell me, MPD.

"I will then ask you if you are familiar with the canons governing professional treatment of patients by counselors and therapists relating to their psychological problems. You will answer that you are. I will then ask you if you have an opinion, based upon the records and the information available to you, and upon your own qualifications, as to whether Dr. Greely deviated from those canons. You will say yes, that in your professional opinion, within a reasonable degree of medical probability, Dr. Greely fell miserably below those standards, and that his conduct was completely unprofessional, unconscionable and reprehensible. You will then explain, in detail the reasons upon which you base that opinion, nailing Red to the cross of his own dirty deeds.

"O.K. up to this point, Doc?

"At no time will I ask you about any pending charges against you. You have not, at this time had any final findings of guilt, Correct?"

"That is true."

I will establish that you are being paid for your time, and for your honest opinions. I will not, and I expect you to insure that Bill does not trick you into saying that you are being paid to testify on behalf of the plaintiff. Clear?"

"Clear."

"Bill will have two opportunities to get into your charges. First when I tender you for cross after I establish your qualifications as an expert, and last when you are under cross for your opinions and statements. Don't act embarrassed about your charges. You are a highly qualified expert and the jury will expect you to charge for your expertise. Just act as if it is your right.

"As we sit here today, you have never been found guilty of any professional infractions, correct?"

"Yes, that is correct."

As we sit here today, you are licensed in Georgia and Illinois, correct?"

"Yes, that is true."

"I will ask and establish all your professional qualifications and licenses, when I go through your credentials. Afterward, on cross, be very careful of Bill Handell's questions. If he asks you if you have ever been convicted of, or if any board has ever rendered a formal finding of professional infractions, you can and must answer no! Understood?"

"Yes."

"Do not get cute. Do not volunteer any information along that line. If he doesn't ask the exact question that puts you on the spot, and I mean the exact question, you have no obligation to divulge your pending problems, and, in fact, you have a duty to your client/patient, Judith, not to volunteer anything that would hurt her. Understood?"

"All right, I understand."

As we walked upstairs and into the living room where things were set up, I figured one of two things would happen. He really was as good as he pretended, or we were in deep ca-ca. At least someone, probably Lettie, had shoveled the dandruff off his blue jacket. Teeth and hair were still gross, but you couldn't have everything. Besides, my brother was at the camera. He could help, hopefully.

As we came back into the living room, Lettie was serving coffee to Bill Handell and the court reporter. Tip already had a cup and Lettie asked if I still took mine black. I thanked her and nodded yes and walked over to shake hands with Bill.

The deposition began well. I sailed through the Doctors credentials and Bill decided to forgo challenging the Doctors claim to expertise until his total cross examination. That allowed me to keep the momentum at a steady pace and the Doctor was performing well. One by one, we covered all of the testimony I needed from the Doctor for my proofs.

We worked steadily for a little over an hour and a half, and then I turned Dr. Ames over to Bill for cross-examination. So far, there had been minimal objections from Bill, none that seriously undermined any of the Doctors opinions.

Bill opted for a 15 minute break while he reviewed his notes and we scrambled to divest our used coffee and freshen up our cups.

As Bill went through his cross, it became apparent that Dr. Ames was no pushover. He came across as extremely knowledgeable and he never once let Bill twist his testimony or trip him up as to how he had arrived at his opinions. I was elated.

Bill ended his cross-examination saying:

"Well, that's all I have, Dr. Ames." Then, almost as an afterthought, "By the way, one last question. "Have you ever been convicted of a felony or a crime involving moral turpitude?"

If that's it we're home free. Dr. Ames has never been convicted of anything, period!

To my total surprise, Dr. Ames said, "Well, not exactly convicted."

If I had been drinking coffee, I would have just spit it all over the good doctor. Instead, I just gaped, open mouthed as Bill's eyes lit up.

"Tell me, Doctor, what do you mean, not exactly convicted?"

The next ten minutes were a lifetime for me. A dozen lifetimes, all of them bad.

Under skillful questioning from Bill, Dr. Ames went into great detail about his current licensing problems, and the reasons for them, including the names of his two protagonists who claimed to have had sex with the Doctor upon the very couch we had sat on in his office.

No amount of objections on my part could stop the flood of verbal disaster from flowing. The dam was broken, the boat sunk, the Doctor was history.

I had no expert for the trial and discovery closed in one week.

CHAPTER SIX

Meanwhile, in the private office of Bill Handell:

Bill looked up from his notes. "It looks like something good is finally going our way. I called you in, Red, to go over your role in this whole mess and make sure we're on the right track. You say that Judith is a whore and a charlatan. I don't mind saying, those are pretty strong words, Mr. Greely."

"I'm telling you that this whole thing is a hoax." Red shot back. "This bitch enjoyed every single sexual tryst we had. She was an animal when it came to trying different things. On the desk, on the floor, in a chair. Hell, she almost killed both of us when the rope broke while she was dangling from the ceiling in the trailer. I couldn't walk straight for a week!"

"Enough with the sex already!" Face flushed and exasperated, Bill was fast approaching a serious dislike for his own best witness; he needed more reasons and less sexual enhancement from Red. "What about the book?"

"The book? Oh yeah". Red reluctantly came out of his reverie. Lightly sweating and with an obvious bulge in his pants, this dirty little man in the Burl Ives body grudgingly returned to Bill's questions.

"Judith already had inquired about a book with several publishers. One even talked about a pretty strong advance if she could produce quality writing along with her claims about MPD. Especially if she could get some kind of publicity prior to the publication." Red was back in the present and trying to give Bill what he needed.

"But you don't know what publishers or the names of anyone she talked to." Bill was fishing for anything he could use as concrete evidence to blow this fake out of the water, but all he could get were Red's words and dim recollections.

"No, but I can tell you that she was really happy with our arrangement, especially when she realized that I would get paid extra monies by the insurance companies while we had sex on the premises." Despite his efforts to the contrary, Red was quickly slipping back into his mental sexual reveries with Judith.

Sensing the direction his witness was once again headed and wanting no part of it, a disgusted Bill Handel quickly ushered Red out of his office.

Still feeling dirty after his conversation with Red, Bill walked to the men's room and began washing his hands with soap. As the warm water ran over his hands, and feeling somewhat like Pontius Pilot, Bill was once again confronted by the disgust he felt with both Red and his opponent, Judith. Like the noble Knights of old, stopping Judith from harming the center had become Bill's Holy Grail. *She really is nothing but a greedy bitch and she doesn't care who she hurts, as long as she gets what she wants. I will bring her down. I will not let her hurt this center which has helped so many women, good women who have been really injured.*

Without even intending to, Bill's mind slipped into the past where he could never forget the phone call that night. He and his wife, Clarisse, were home alone; Melissa was out, presumably with friends. She was eighteen then, and of late had been rather moody. She was their only child and from the day she had been born had been the light of their lives. Clarisse had taken the phone call and as Bill watched she seemed to implode from within, tearfully nodding, mumbling and looking crushed. She wordlessly handed him the phone.

"Melissa is O.K. now." The unknown woman's voice said, quickly continuing before any interruption could be broached. 'Since she's technically an adult we couldn't call you without her permission. She called us from the Holiday Inn where she had already taken over twenty sleeping pills. From what she has told us so far, she was a victim of a date rape about two months ago. She hid it, feeling very shamed and hurt, and not wanting to let anyone know. "Quite common reactions to these things these days," the voice went on, "Two days ago she found out for sure that she was pregnant and she went to another Doctor, feigned severe problems sleeping and received a prescription for narcotic sleeping pills. It was these pills she was taking when she saw our number flashed on the TV screen and called us.

We called 911 and had them request an emergency crew with a stomach pump and we met her at the ER. She is now resting comfortably and even though she doesn't wish to talk to you now, she is O.K. and will probably consent to see you tomorrow."

It had been a rough night for both Bill and Clarisse, but even rougher for Melissa. That night, in the hospital, Melissa's body naturally aborted the baby. When they saw her the next morning, Bill could not believe the change. Sunken eyes and a pasty white countenance had replaced the youthful shine he had known and loved for all these years. It left an impression that he could never forget.

Two days later she was home. The boy was picked up by the authorities, but it had been his first use of a drug to obtain sex and after hearing what his actions had caused, he was truly devastated. As an adult, Melissa had agreed not to press charges and the State had allowed community service. No record was ever formally made of the incident, but Bill would always be grateful and indebted to the center for saving his only child's life. From that day forward his firm had quietly but stalwartly represented the Center on all legal matters, free of charge.

I don't give a damn that Red may be scum; Judith will not be allowed to bring down this Center, not as long as I can still practice law!

Once again at peace with himself, Bill returned to his office to put together the best case possible to nail his opponent. He would truly enjoy smashing this fake!

* * * *

"The other one is in Maryland, just outside of D.C." Joe said. "His name is Dr. Eric Lofton, and he is a board certified psychiatrist."

"Get him on the phone for me. I don't care what it takes. Promise him your body, anything. I've got to have an expert.

I was fuming. Bill Handell would not agree to allow me to get a new expert. Surprise, surprise, right?

While Joe was trying to get in touch with our last hope, I was busy dictating an emergency motion to get court approval for a new, last minute expert. At least I was going for the top gun.

Hopefully this shrink isn't screwing his patients too.

As before, the good doctor did not come to the phone voluntarily. Joe had tried pleading in her best whine, and still nothing could get her past the doctor's secretary. Nor would the secretary budge when I talked to her.

"Get his fax number again." I told Joe.

I dictated two pages, explaining our plight and why it was crucial for us to enlist the doctor's aid. I then added Dr. Ames written findings, opinions, etc., and a copy of the complaint. A twelve-page fax package. I had Joe fax it and then we waited.

It took two hours for the doctor to call us. He agreed to make room for Judith on his busy schedule. He said he would need her for two days, starting day after tomorrow. She was to bring with her all of her past medical records, and her package of drawings, etc. Meanwhile, I was to overnight her deposition, Red's deposition, and any other depo's of treating physicians or counselors. Dr. Lofton would get back to me on the following Monday and let me know if he would take the case.

Hallelujah. We finally got a break!

* * * *

Dr. Lofton was even better than he had promised. On Monday morning a fax arrived with a list of opinions and an agreement to accept the case. The six page fax went into detail, positively diagnosing Judith as an MPD case, and acknowledging between four to six actual separate personalities, with an as yet undetermined number of splinter personalities.

He further found, in his professional opinion that Judith was truthful in her complaints against Dr. Greely and that Dr. Greely was completely unethical and although not the cause of her MPD, Greely was the cause of all of her current physical and mental distress.

As a surprise bonus, he also found that the Hillsborough Community Crisis Center had committed actionable negligence in its dealings with Red and its lack of supervision in giving Red such tremendous supervising authority when he had such a limited educational and occupational background.

We finally had a silver bullet. Now all I had to do was to convince Judge Brando to allow me to use him.

* * * *

"So you see, Your Honor, there was no way I could have known when I contracted with Dr. Ames that he would actually be guilty of the same depraved sexual misconduct as the defendant, Dr. Greely." We were in chambers with Judge Brando on my motion to allow for the addition of Dr, Lofton as my expert.

I continued. "I was completely surprised. Hillsborough Community Crisis Center will suffer no prejudice by this change. All of Dr. Lofton's opinions are in the file in front of Your Honor and there should be nothing new for the center."

"Mr. Handell, I assume you have a different opinion?"

"Yes, Your Honor, thank you. My client has already paid for, and I, in good faith, conducted two depositions of Mr. Newton's current expert, Dr. Ames. Mr. Newton hired him. He listed him as his expert and he alone had the responsibility to ensure that the expert he chose was what he claimed he was.

"That is not my client's responsibility, nor should my client suffer the additional economic *burden* of further depositions as a result of Mr. Newton's misfortune. Further, to change experts at this late date will impose an additional burden upon my expert as well, and that means even more costs to my client.

"Therefore, with all do respect to Mr. Newton, I must stridently oppose the addition to any new experts at this late date. Mr. Newton knew and agreed to the discovery cut off date and it should remain closed."

"Although I sympathize with both of you, I must lean toward allowing the plaintiff to present her claim in the light most favorable to her cause. However, this must also be tempered with the understanding the Rules of Court are to be followed and unnecessary costs cannot be arbitrarily imposed upon either side.

"I will allow the plaintiff to list Dr. Lofton as her expert witness at this time, subject to final approval by the trial court.

"I will not be your trial Judge, even though I must admit that it is a unique trial that should prove very interesting. However, we have two retired judges on call for that trial period to preside over these lengthy trials. Whichever of those two is your trial judge can make the final determination at that time. I will however, caution the defense, on the record, that if you choose not to depose Dr. Lofton, you do so at your own peril and I do not believe the trial court will look at that as a reason to disallow the witnesses testimony. Good day, gentlemen."

That's about as close as it gets. No home runs, but at least we are still in the ball game.

* * * *

Dr. Lofton was more than I had hoped for. When I flew up to Maryland to meet with the doctor prior to his deposition, I was impressed. We spent about three hours together going over everything.

Walking into his spacious, clean and well furnished waiting room, I was greeted by an attractive young lady in a white nurse's dress. She offered coffee while she buzzed the doctor, and no sooner had I received my coffee, than I was ushered into the doctor's office.

Dr. Lofton's office was impressive. A large desk sat in one corner with numerous certificates and diplomas on the right hand wall above the desk. The left side was a complete wall of books set on recessed shelving. These looked to be the most often referred-to books, as the entire remainder of office walls was comprised of full bookshelves also.

The furniture was modern overstuffed leather, expensive and comfortable. The man behind the desk blended well with his surroundings.

He looks like a real doctor is supposed to look.

Doctor Lofton appeared to be in his mid forties with a full head of dark brown hair, blue eyes, a well-trimmed mustache, and an intelligent face. He stood about six feet tall, was trim and obviously worked at keeping physically fit. He rose and held out his hand.

As I offered my hand I said: "Dr. Lofton, I'm Paul Newton."

"Glad to meet you, Paul. I'm Eric Lofton. Come in and have a seat, please."

As we shook hands he motioned to one of the overstuffed chairs in front of his desk.

My God. That's the first firm handshake I've had from a doctor since I took this case.

Over several cups of fresh coffee, 'Eric' and I went over Judith's case and his opinions, step by step. Dr. Lofton, Eric at his insistence, was bright, well spoken and completely sure of himself and his opinions. He knew his business and did not hesitate in his answers to my questions.

When I left his office I was given the name of a good seafood restaurant. Eric apologized for not being available to spend the evening with me, but he had other plans that had been made months before. I told him that was fine and that I hadn't expected him to show me the town, only save my case. He got a good laugh out of that.

That night, after a dinner of a half dozen cherrystone clams, one dozen Chesapeake bay oysters and a fillet of sole accompanied by a bottle of California Gamay Chardonnay, I was thinking that if the depo goes half a well as the visit and this meal, we really are back in the ball game.

The next morning started out well. It was a beautiful day and everyone was in fine spirits. However, once the deposition got underway, Bill was far more aggressive with Dr. Lofton than he had been with Dr. Ames. Obviously, this would be his only chance prior to a closely scheduled trial; Bill was intent upon making sure it was done right.

His examination of Dr. Lofton regarding his credentials was very thorough and left nothing to chance. Bill had come too close with Dr. Ames and it was clear that wasn't going to happen again.

Then Bill went into Judith's MPD, something he barely touched before.

"Dr. Lofton. You state in your opinion letter that Judith Hoople has between four to six separate personalities, correct?"

"Yes, that is correct."

"How do you explain the discrepancy between your findings and the fact that Judith Hoople and Dr. Trey have logged in almost forty 'personalities', if you will, and have named them?"

"You must first understand the basis of Multiple Personality Disorder, or MPD. MPD means just that. Multiple personalities, not multiple problems. A personality is something alive, something real. A personality is current and capable of acting on it's own, in the present and in whatever form it presents itself in."

Judith has at least four, and possibly five or six actual personalities. Where the confusion stems from is that she also has numerous incidences in her past life that are highly traumatic and locked away from her conscious being. These incidences are like snapshots, little fragments of one's life, locked into time and space, frozen in time, if you like. Like a snapshot or photo, they can be called out, looked at, remembered and dissected, but they do not think, or act, or exist other than as that specific fragment of time and space."

"Dr. Trey, although more knowledgeable than most in his field about MPD, has confused these mental snapshots with personalities. He and Judith spent a great deal of time naming these snapshots. They actually did a very good job of uncovering these hidden atrocious segments of Judith's life, but they mistook them for something other than what they really are.

"But don't misunderstand me, Judith does have a classic case of MPD."

"Dr. Lofton, Judith claims to remember having been raped by her father as an infant, while still in a crib. Truly now, isn't that absurd? I mean that it is not possible for a human being to remember things that began in infancy, now is it?

"Your assumption, although widely held, is invalid, Mr. Handell. First we must ascertain what is meant by infancy. One month? Three months? Twelve months? What I am assuming you are referring to is Judith's recollection of being raped while in a crib and while wearing diapers.

"The baby departments commonly sell diapers for infants and toddlers up to two or three years old or more. Exactly where Judith fits into this age bracket is open to speculation, but I can assure you that traumatic induced memory is common and has been documented numerous times in children as young as one year of age. The child at one, who gets bitten by a large group of ants and has a phobia about ants, even as an adult. Or the child who is scalded by steamy hot water and who, as an adult can't fly in airplanes because of a fear of being in the clouds which his memory associates with the steam of his childhood trauma. Through hypnosis we can go back in time and locate the reason for a person's unnatural fear and often, when it is understood, help the person to overcome the fear.

"In Judith's case, instead of hidden fears of phobias, she developed other persons to take the blunt of the trauma and relieve her of the terrible pain and suffering she was going through. These persons live with the complete knowledge of these traumatic incidences, and they have a really bad life. Emotions in these alters range from abject misery and pain to vengeance and mayhem.

"On the whole, if one of these personalities were allowed to become dominant, the real Judith would disappear and a far less desirable person would take her place. An example occurred when Red tried to integrate the personalities and nearly succeeded in allowing the arthritic cripple to control the body. A frightening result indeed. We can be thankful that it wasn't permanent, although Judith still shows signs of disability, and probably will for quite some time, if not forever.

"Judith's MPD is real, Mr. Handell. You can't laugh it away or sluff it off as imaginary. She is a very troubled individual. Dr. Greely's incredibly unprofessional and incompetent treatment of Judith has unleashed a torrent of horrors into this lady's consciousness that cannot be imagined by the normal human mind. Red's treatment alone was an unconscionable abuse of his authority over her, and I'm not even including his despicable sexual atrocities.

"Red dumped his client, Judith, the child alters, the whole scene when he was through playing around and got tired of them. He just dumped them.

"With psychiatric patients, a bond of dependency develops, even in appropriately handled cases. Before stopping treatment, or even referring the patient to another counselor, it is imperative that the treating therapist go through the period known as closure. The counselor prepares the patient for the separation and only after the patient accepts the change is the transfer or termination accomplished.

"This is a very necessary procedure to protect the patient and prevent additional trauma to the patient and to keep from erasing the positive effects of what is, in many cases, the result of years of treatment.

"I stress that this was even more important in Judith's case, as both she and the alters had been encouraged to rely upon Red not only as a therapist, but as a daddy, or father figure as well. When he cut them off, it was every bit as traumatic as if their own father had abandoned them.

"There was a series of unforgivable breach of protocol that caused irreparable damage. He not only hurt the existing alters, but the entire incident was so traumatic that a new and suicidal alter was created. This alter has apparently secreted a gun, hidden it away somewhere that no one knows about, and has obtained two bullets for it. It is this alters intent to blow the brains out of the body. This in no joke, but a real and present threat to Judith.

"This alter has used broken glass to disfigure the body, slicing Judith's legs and slicing her wrists on two occasions. She has not gained, nor do I hope she ever gains the strength to overpower the core personality for any extended length of time. Unless she does, she will not be able to accomplish her grisly task. But she is there. She is real. And, she exists solely because of Red.

"Dr. Greely is a disgrace to the profession, and your client is equally guilty of allowing him to achieve the stature and respect with which your client bestowed upon him by its recognition and acclaim of him in his exalted position of supervisory status. They allowed him a completely free hand in running the place and dictating policy, even though he was uncertified, unqualified and possessed nothing more than a fifty-dollar license and no degrees or diplomas above a bachelors degree in Fine Arts.

"I apologize if I got a little off track with my answers, Mr. Handell, but I have absolutely no respect for Red nor for any other parasite like him. He is nothing more than a charlatan and a menace to society in general and the medical profession in particular."

Bill made a few more attempts to attack Judith's credibility, but they were halfhearted at best. Dr. Lofton could not be shaken.

* * * *

In accordance with Judge Brando's order, Bill finally named his expert witness. He was Dr. Charles Krauff, an imminent and well respected psychiatrist in the Tampa Bay area.

I had met the doctor before. Dr. Krauff did some work for the defense bar, however, he was not widely held in disdain as were many of the experts frequently used by the defense lawyers in the area. He was regarded in the legal community as pretty much a straight shooter. A no-nonsense psych who told it like he saw it.

I immediately set his deposition.

* * * *

I looked around at the lush furnishings in Dr. Krauff's office. I think I liked it better each time I came here. Familiarity breeds appreciation or something like that. Numerous medical books and magazines filled the bookshelves behind Dr. Krauff's desk. Volumes of respected psychiatric journals filled over half the shelves, all of them neatly and numerically filed in order of the volume number.

I recognized several of them, especially the latest DSMO volume. He had each edition, not just the latest one. Knowing the price of some of this stuff, I mentally calculated over fifty thousand dollars in books. Not as much as my law library, but impressive.

Dr. Krauff was already seated in what I considered his power seat, behind his desk with lots of space between himself and the deposers, and lots of power diplomas and certificates behind him. It was especially effective in video depositions, but that wasn't happening today. We all knew this was just for discovery. He would be live, in court. I just needed to know what he would say. I could handle almost anything if I knew about it in advance, but surprises could kill you. I wanted no surprises from Dr. Krauff. He was too good.

After the swearing in and the initial record identities were completed, I chose to skip the qualifications and get straight to the point. Hell, I already knew his qualifications and they were excellent, although he was not a world recognized MPD diagnostician. I already owned the best in the field.

"Dr. Krauff, have you been retained to review the records of Judith Hoople and to offer opinions as to her physical and psychological being?"

"Yes, I have been asked to do that."

"Please tell me, Doctor, exactly what have you reviewed as a part of your employment in this case."

"First, I interviewed Mrs. Hoople, here in my office for approximately four hours. I have also read the depositions of Dr. Ames, Dr. Lofton, a counselor, Red Greely who calls himself Doctor, but for whom I have seen no medical reason for such title, Dr. Trey, and Dr. Sherrie Levin. I read all of the medical records supplied to me, which was the full complement of what you supplied in response to a request to produce. Finally, I reviewed volumes of the American Psychiatric Quarterly and the two latest DMSO volumes as it relates to Multiple Personality Disorder."

I painfully waded through each of these sources, questioning Dr. Krauff as to what he had gleaned from each source. He was, as expected, vague about anything he did not agree with, which was most of the reports that favored Judith.

On the question of his examination of Judith, he became specific.

"Dr. Krauff, you examined my client, Judith Hoople?"

"Yes. As I stated earlier, she spent about four hours here, in my office. We administered several tests, and conducted quite an extensive examination of Mrs. Hoople."

After going through the various tests and examinations, I asked, "Based upon your examination of my client, were you able to arrive at an opinion as to her mental and/or psychological health?"

"Yes, I was."

"And what was, or were those opinions, Dr.?"

"To begin with, Judith struck me as a very willful and manipulative person. The kind of person who will do whatever it takes to get her way, as long as it doesn't require too much hard labor.

"She is well-read and opinionated. She is a very capable person when it comes to providing herself with her own creature comforts.

"She is self centered and incapable of caring too much for others, even her own family.

"She professes to have MPD in order to gain the attention she craves and possibly monetary rewards as well.

"Those are my opinions."

"You *really* didn't like her, did you Doc?"

"This isn't about likes or dislikes, but professional opinion. You asked and I answered."

"Believe me, Doc. I'll never ask your professional opinion of what you think about me.

"You said, I believe, that 'she professes to be MPD.' I take it then that one of your unannounced opinions is that she doesn't have MPD?"

"That is correct."

"You think she is lying then?"

"No, I never said that."

"Come again? You lost me, Doc?"

"Oh, I think Judith believes she has MPD. I think she has firmly convinced herself that this is a fact. However, just because she believes it, for whatever reason, does not make it so. In essence, using her own natural manipulative personality she's convinced herself that she actually suffers from MPD."

"I see, I think. Dr., have you ever treated anyone that you believe actually suffered from MPD?"

"Personally, no, I have not."

"Have you ever treated anyone, or had a patient referred to you who claimed to be suffering from MPD?"

"Yes, a few times. But they didn't stay long."

"You didn't cure them?"

"No, of course not."

"Doctor, do you, personally, believe in MPD as a real condition?"

"I have never actually seen anyone who I believe suffered from MPD. I would have to say that if it exists, it must be extremely rare."

'You ever treated anyone with Mad Cow Disease before, Doc?"

"No, I have not."

"Does it exist?"

"I suppose it does."

"How about, ah, *Munchouser's* disease."

"Your pronunciation threw me off a bit. You are referring to inflection of illness on another for attention by proxy?"

"That's right"

"No, I've never treated anyone for that."

"Does it exist?"

"Once again, I suppose so."

"The DSMO on the shelf behind you. The most recent edition. That's kind of the Bible in psychiatric and psychosomatic problems and their diagnosis and existence, isn't it?"

"Well, I don't know that I'd refer to it as a Bible, but it is a widely respective diagnostic tool."

"Kind of like Merc's Manual for medical diagnosis and treatment?"

"Yes, like that."

"And it lists many of the symptoms and signs to look for, does it not?"

"Yes, it does."

"A manipulative personality, such as you described for Judith is listed as occurring in most MPD patients, isn't it Doc?"

"I believe that is correct, yes."

"In fact, all the personality traits you told me about regarding your opinions of Mrs. Hoople are listed as possible personality traits of persons suffering from MPD, aren't they Doc?"

"Well, I think that's correct, yes."

"And, once again, as you have already stated, your professional opinion is that Mrs. Hoople is not lying about her condition or her various traumatic experiences?"

"That's correct."

"Do you have an opinion about her counselor, Red Greely?"

"No, I was not asked to form an opinion about Red Greely."

"You read the medical reports and the allegations against Red Greely?"

"Yes, I did?"

"And, being a licensed psychiatrist yourself, you are aware of the ethical and legal obligations of a mental health counselor to his patients, are you not?"

"Yes, I am,"

"Assume that the allegations are true and tell me, Doc, would Red's treatment of Mrs. Hoople be allowed or condoned by the AMA or any other legitimate governing body of the medical profession."

"Absolutely not."

"Not under any circumstances?"

"Again, absolutely not."

"Would you refer your patients to Red for counseling?"

"Of course not

"Should Hillsborough Community Crisis Center have the supervisory position of its staff and patients to be held by Dr. Greely without supervision of any kind?"

Bill had taken as much as he could of my use of his expert to bolster my case.

"Objection. Argumentative, assumes facts not in evidence at this time and requires an expert opinion of my witness which is not within the realm of his assigned employment. I will not sit by while you use my witness for your own benefit, nor do the rules necessitate it."

"Very good, counselor, your objections are noted. However, this is a discovery deposition and this is all fair game. You may answer the question, Doc."

Bill was livid, but there was nothing he could do under the rules of civil procedure. Although I would not use the depo in trial as an introduction of evidence, I would certainly have a mound of information that I could use to keep Dr. Krauff in check while he was on the stand.

Dr. Krauff answered, "Obviously, if they were aware of the problems, they would not have had him in that position. But my understanding is that they had no knowledge of any inappropriate behavior on the part of Dr. Greely while he was in charge of the Center."

"But Doctor, that begs the question, does it not, should they have been aware? Should they have inspected? Should they have supervised their own system? Should they have at least monitored the situation?"

Retreating, again, Dr. Krauff offered, "I really haven't researched that and I am currently not prepared to answer that question without a clear knowledge of all the pertinent facts."

"Well then, do you intend to offer an opinion whether or not the Center was negligent in their supervision of Red?"

"Based upon the facts currently available to me in that regard, I am."

"And what is that opinion?"

"HCCC was not negligent.

I rolled my eyes. "You might want to reconsider that opinion, using all the facts, Doc.

"Getting back to Judith Hooper, Doc. You read her deposition and the various sources of information on her physical and psychological condition prior to being treated by Red?"

"Yes, I read quite a bit of information in that regard."

"With everything you read, and anything you learned in your discussions with Judith, or anything at all you obtained from any other source, is there anything that leads you to believe that Judith was not a healthy, active, normal appearing person, productive and a caring parent prior to Dr. Greely's treatment?"

"No, not in the way you have phrased the question."

"And all of the problems she has now, reaction to MPD, physical infirmities, whatever, came into being at the time of and in conjunction with Dr. Greely's treatment of her at the Center, correct?"

"Yes, again, as you have posed the question."

"Are there any other factors on the record that would account for the activation of Judith's problems, other than her treatment by Red that you are aware of?"

"No, none that I am aware of."

"Then would you agree with me that it is more likely than not that Dr. Greely's treatment of Judith was causally related to Judith's physical and psychological breakdown?"

"Under the framework you have presented, I would have to agree."

God, he hates to have to give me anything. Tough!

"Is there anything in the record to support any other presentation, Doc?"

"No."

"And your opinion is that, to her, Judith's injuries are real, whether you believe she has MPD ore some other mental problem, correct?"

"Well, yes, she believes they are real."

"Then, whether or nor she has MPD, she has been severally injured by Dr. Greely, correct?"

"If you put it that way, I guess so."

"I do put it that way Doc. And it's no guess. Thank you for your time."

"That's it?"

"No further questions."

I told the court reporter, "I'll take the original."

"Read or waive Doc?" My question to the doctor referred to the rule that allowed a deponent to read the original transcript to check for perceived inaccuracies and note any such perceptions for the record.

"I'll read, thank you."

"O.K. Madam reporter, I'll take my copy as soon as you complete the transcript. Then send me the original, complete with any errata sheets generated by the Doctor after you and he get together. That suit you?"

"Will do, counselor."

CHAPTER SEVEN

The young girl lay trembling—partly from the cold of the air conditioner blowing over her naked body, partly from fear. She knew what was coming. As in the past, she had been disrobed by her parents and forced to lie on her ceremonial "altar". Actually an army cot, it was one of six that had been draped with white sheets for the ceremony. Five other cots held young children as well, three girls and two boys, all naked and all trembling.

A large building in an abandoned shopping center housed the ongoing activities. Old strip malls abounded in the suburbs of Miami and this was just one of many and, therefore, totally unremarkable. With windows covered by plywood, the inside was completely hidden from view. Further enhancing the aura of isolation and abandonment, the Children of Satan cult members parked their cars on side streets in the surrounding neighborhood. Absolutely nothing encouraged onlookers to give the area a second glance.

As the young girl watched, the high priest began the sacrilegious rite at the main altar, a makeshift affair consisting of grouping three large orange packing crates; two on the bottom, one on top and all covered with white sheets. Hanging upside down, a black cross of the crucified Christ was prominently displayed in the center of the altar. Two groups of candles burned at each end of the altar providing a flickering, eerie light that added to the tension in the room. Wearing a red robe held together by only a single black silk belt, the high or dark priest, as he was called was otherwise naked, except for a ragged pair of brown slippers.

Pouring wine into a chalice the dark priest held it up above the candles while the cult members, each with his or her own candle, and each dressed only in a robe (white for women, black for men) lined up to approach the altar. As each stepped up, the dark priest took a sip of the wine, gave them a sip, and then allowed the member to light his or her candle from the altar candles.

When everyone had drunk from the chalice and lighted their candle, the dark priest poured more wine into the chalice, filling it about half way. Then, placing his penis in the cup, he urinated into it, bringing it to almost full. Taking the newly filled chalice in both hands, he poured a line of the mixture across the altar, splashing the crucifix deliberately three times in the process.

Stepping away from the main altar, the dark priest approached each of the children, beginning with the first boy and ending with the young girl. As he came to the cots, he liberally poured the chalice mixture over each child. Nearing Judith's cot, the dark priest's countenance turned menacing and lustful as he grinned in anticipation.

Watching through the slits of her mostly closed eyes, the innocent, young Judith trembled violently. When the priest splashed the remaining chalice mixture on her, she lost control of her bladder and a large wet spot appeared between her little legs.

Having used the last of the mixture on Judith, the dark priest now set the empty chalice down, away from her cot.

She watched as he leaned down over her, his acne-scarred face with full mustache and dirty yellow teeth smiling at her in anticipation. Trying her best to look away, her small body nonetheless cringed when she noticed that his robe was parted and his erection protruded.

Cult members watching in anticipation swayed back and forth, caressing and playing with each other's genitalia as the dark priest leaned down and pulled Judith's small legs apart.

She began to cry. Although she knew from experience that it would do no good to scream, she still couldn't hold back the large tears that streaked down her cheeks. As the dark priest callously and forcefully entered Judith, she felt her young body being ripped and torn apart. However, before she could physically react to the intense pain something almost spiritual happened. A glowing aura covered all she could perceive and, as if from the appearance of a guardian angel, in Judith's mind another girl took Judith's physical place. Judith no longer felt the searing pain of sexual abuse but was spirited away to a playground somewhere in her own mind where she could have fun and be the loved and cherished little girl she wished she truly was.

In the throes of his demonic passion, the dark priest never noticed that the little girl's tears had stopped running down her now peaceful face.

Dr. Lofton looked at his notes concerning Judith. He was preparing for trial, making sure he had not forgotten anything. He thought back to when, under deep hypnosis, Judith had revealed her experiences with the dark priest and his cult. Her entire body had trembled so violently that Dr. Lofton was amazed. Judith had suffered from incontinence and, upon awakening, was extremely embarrassed. Dr. Lofton had his nurse work with Judith, getting her some clean underwear and slacks from the nearby mall. They had all worked to reassure Judith that it was nothing to be embarrassed about. It had taken quite a while to calm her down, but finally, she was O.K.

Dr. Lofton wasn't completely sure about his beliefs in God or a supreme being. But he was sure of one thing. If there was a just God, then there must also be a special place in hell for the dark priest and his depraved band of followers.

* * * *

The first day of trial began promptly at 8:30 A.M. Monday morning. Judge Julius Midder had been selected to preside over the case.

Judge Midder was a medium sized, somewhat rotund man with very thin white hair and a round, florid face that had a habit of turning bright red whenever the Judge was angered, which was usually quite often.

I remembered my last case in front of Judge Midder, several years ago before the Judge retired. I was trying a case against a cab company, and an attorney named John Duff was defending. John had attempted to save his client money by not hiring a court reporter until after jury selection, a tactic frowned upon by Judges, but used in smaller cases by some attorneys whose clients were cost conscious.

John had gotten carried away with his own rhetoric and overstepped the bounds of professional courtesy, referring to my client in a highly unflattering fashion. I strongly objected and Judge Midder had sustained the objection, giving John a very dark look in the process and telling him to be more careful.

The second time it happened, I objected again and Judge Midder called both of us to the bench and issued a strong warning to John not to let it happen or the Judge would consider serious sanctions. Judge Midder's face had been bright red and I recognized the clear warning signs, but apparently, John missed them.

The third time it happened, Judge Midder exploded. His face was livid and he did not even wait for me to object, nor did he call us to the bench. Instead, he openly and loudly chastised John in front of the jurors, most of whom had already been selected.

The Judge delivered a wilting discourse on John's lack of professionalism and his failure to follow the rules of court, and in particular, the direct order of the Judge himself. Although it boded well for my case, I was embarrassed for John.

John attempted to resume *voir dire*, but it was clear he had lost all respect with the jury and had suffered a severe blow for his client. Turning back to Judge Midder John asked:

"May we approach the bench, Your Honor?"

Judge Midder honored John's request, and when we were in front of the bench, John began his argument.

"Since the Court has openly and severely criticized me in front of the jury, I do not believe that my client can receive a fair trial. Therefore, Your Honor, I respectfully request the court declare a mistrial."

I rolled my eyes. Obviously, John was entitled to a mistrial, even though it would cost his client a couple thousand dollars to get back in court. It could probably be done today, since not much time had elapsed and there were still plenty of prospects in the jury pool. John was more than willing to forgo the cost of a mistrial then to go on with the trial and this tainted jury.

Without consulting me, or asking for my objections, Judge Midder replied to John, "Since you specifically requested that no court reporter be present, sir, there is no record of any open rebuke by this court. No record means it never happened. Now I suggest, counselor that you get back in front of this panel and finish selecting your jury."

A no nonsense judge who can cop an attitude in a heartbeat. As long as I am on the right side, it might be the best thing for Judith.

Bill and I were in Judge Midder's chambers, ironing out the last minute details prior to trial. *Housekeeping chores* as they were commonly referred to. Both Bill and I had filed several *Motions in Limini*, motions designed to cover any disputed legal or factual issues remaining prior to presentation of our cases to the jurors.

Judge Midder had requested that we both submit our proposed jury instructions at this Hearing. These would include a statement of the case as well as directions to the jurors as to how to listen to evidence, etc. We would go over them in advance with each side filing our objections as we won or lost an argument. This was always done outside the presence of the jury.

"I have seen your *Motions in Limini*, and denied all but two."

Like I said, no nonsense and cut right to the chaff.

"Mr. Handell. You have resubmitted your most recent Motion to Dismiss for reconsideration by this court. As you are both aware, I did not rule on your motion earlier, Judge Brando did. I will tell you that if I had been sitting on this case back from the beginning, I might very well have ruled differently. However, I was not.

"I am not going to grant your motion at this time, however, neither am I inclined to dismiss it outright, as my colleague did. Instead, I will reserve ruling on the motion, giving you the right to raise it again at the close of the plaintiff's case in chief."

Brother. What a cheap shot. In other words, I must put on a case of absolute liability or he is going to let the Center off the hook. Come to think of it, he probably won't rule then, either. This way he can let it go to a jury and then, if he doesn't like their finding, i.e., I win, he'll grant the motion and throw out the case. Unless, of course, I blow it first and miss-try it.

"On your second motion, Mr. Handell, regarding your objections to the testimony of Dr. Lofton, I presume you did take the doctor's deposition?"

"Yes, Your Honor."

"Please make sure a copy of it is on my desk by the end of court today."

"Yes, Your Honor."

"Mr. Newton. Do the deposition of Dr. Lofton and the interrogatory answers provided by you contain all the opinions you intend to exact from the Doctor's testimony on the stand?"

"As we sit here that would be a 'yes,' Your Honor; however, I reserve the right to include anything that this witness is qualified to answer too, should something come up at trial which is not anticipated at this time."

"Very well then. Mr. Handell, as to your motion argument of surprise, I find that to be without merit. However, as to your argument regarding the cumulative nature of Dr. Lofton's testimony, I will reserve ruling on that at this time."

"Mr. Newton, I know that all attorneys like to, and should be free to, orchestrate and present their cases in their own fashion within the established rules of court. However, in this case, I will ask you to hold Dr. Lofton until your final expert witness. I will then rule as to whether or not to allow his testimony, or as to whatever restrictions I may put on his testimony, if I perceive them to be warranted."

"All right, gentlemen." Judge Midder began to rise to end the hearing and meet us in the courtroom.

"Your Honor! For the record I most strongly object to the Court's imposition of the restrictions regarding the testimony of Dr. Lofton. As to surprise, the Court has already ruled there is none. As to perceived cumulative testimony, that can and should be addressed if and when it occurs. This would be in the normal course of the trial. Further, I object to this court's interference in any way as to how I present my case, my offers of proof and the order of my witnesses."

"Spoken like a true advocate, Mr. Newton, but my ruling still stands. Let's pick a jury now gentlemen, shall we?"

* * * *

Back in the courtroom, the players were already seated. The two large counsel tables were still clean on top, as evidentiary materials and the normally accumulated materials of trial had not yet been revealed.

Seated at the Plaintiff's table were Judith and her daughters. Once the jury had been selected and had seen the girls, they would disappear and only be back occasionally. Kids tended to get bored and fidget a lot, a distraction I did not want. With them, but back at the end of the table where she could readily access the boxes of evidence and testimony, sat Josephine.

At the defense table were Tom Snead, the Center's rep, and Bill's paralegal, Heidi.

Both the tables held empty chairs for the attorneys.

Neither Red, nor anyone representing him would appear at counsel table, for his part had already played out as a party. However, he was under subpoena from both sides as a witness.

The jury box was filled with the first 18 prospective jurors, with 22 more prospects sitting in the part of the general seating area reserved for the jury pool, roped off from the rest of the spectators.

Court T.V. had applied for permission to televise the entire trial, but Judge Midder had flatly refused. Their representatives were there, however, along with media representatives from numerous sources. Judge Midder had ordered extra bailiffs for this trial and all were present in the courtroom. Judge Midder was not going to allow the case to become unruly.

As soon as the lawyers sat down at their respective tables, the clerk brought them copies of the juror questionnaires. These are a one page series of questions which each prospective juror was required to fill out under penalty of perjury. They consist of names, birth dates, relatives, occupations and numerous general questions which reveal facts about which attorneys can base their decisions on whom to choose in their quest to bias the jury in their clients favor. Questions regarding occupations and dealings with law enforcement officials and the courts are two primary areas of interest to attorneys. Injuries and illnesses are not listed, but like some other subjects, would be dealt with by the attorneys in *voir dire.*

As I completed reading through each form, taking notes and familiarizing myself with each juror and his questionnaire, I passed them on to Judith. I had given her a legal pad and a pen, and instructed her to write any objections, negative or positive vibes, or anything out of the ordinary she noticed about each juror. I especially wanted to know if she knew any of them, or if she recognized them from some other time or place.

Normally, each side is awarded three peremptory challenges per defendant in a case, *i.e.*, three in this case since Red was out. However, because of the nature of the case, Judge Midder had given us an extra. So, Bill and I would each be allowed four peremptory challenges, and of course, an unlimited number of challenges for cause. A peremptory challenge is one in which the attorney is allowed to excuse a juror without having to offer a reason or get court approval. One just has to say that you are excusing juror number so and so, and he or she is gone. Period. Challenges for cause are different. To get one of those, you must demonstrate that the juror has shown that he or she cannot be fair and impartial in deliberating the outcome of the trial. With most judges, getting these are like pulling teeth. The exception is where it appears that an appeal might show prejudice, the juror's testimony to the contrary not withstanding.

Obviously, with only four guaranteed exclusions apiece, Bill and I would be very particular as to how we exercised them.

We would, however, be awarded another peremptory when it came to the jury alternates. These were jurors who would never deliberate nor vote on the outcome of the trial unless one of the original six jurors had been excused prior to the conclusion of the trial, usually through illness. These alternates would be chosen in sequence, following the selection of the original six.

I had two inherent prejudices, which I had developed over the years when it came to jury selection. Both of them had become ingrained as a result of bitter experiences on the occasions I had not followed my instincts.

First, I *always* excluded defense lawyers and any employees of defense firms, secretaries, paralegals, maintenance workers: you name it. They are either naturally pre-disposed toward the defense, or they want to impress their employer by assuring a defense verdict. Invariably, other jurors deferred to them, they wound up as jury forepersons and always held out for a verdict for whomever the defendant happened to be.

The other hard and fast rule was no bookkeepers. They were way to conservative and rarely sympathetic. They would never sit on my jury. They were out.

As Bill and I did our paperwork, Judge Midder addressed the prospective jurors. He gave them the standard lines describing the purpose of *voir dire* and let them know that we lawyers would be asking them a lot of questions, some of a personal nature, but for them not to take it personally. The questions, he assured them, were not for our own gratification, nor to embarrass them, but to insure that each attorney would be able to select the jury panel he believed would be the most fair to his client.

Yeah, right. What Bill Handell and I both want is a totally biased jury. Totally biased to our own clients.

Judge Midder then introduced me to the panel and turned over the *voir dire* to me. In state court the lawyers are given a lot of leeway with the amount of time to conduct *voir dire*, as well as the types of questions. Federal judges usually place serious restrictions on both the time allowed and the questions asked. Federal judges require written questions to be submitted in advance by the attorneys, and then give the lawyers about ten percent approval of what they ask to be allowed to inquire into with the panel. These judges ask most of the questions themselves, and hold a tight rein on the lawyers when they are conducting *voir dire.*

As was the custom in state court, Judge Midder had merely inquired whether the prospective jurors had any physical impediments that would interfere with their ability to serve if impaneled. He had asked similarly if their jobs or family responsibilities would prohibit them from being here, possibly as long as three weeks.

It was customary for the plaintiff to go first in most procedures, because, after all, we had the burden of proof. As I walked to the podium, I carried a legal pad and the juror inquiry forms. I hated taking paperwork to the podium, choosing instead, most of the time, to wing it. A good memory and the ability to look the jury in the eye without notes were more important to me. However, during *voir dire*, I needed to take notes to record my own findings and impressions.

I had already drawn in three lines of boxes, six across and three deep, with the currently seated jurors named in each box. Additionally, I included anything outstanding which I felt might bear looking into, based on the information either already asked by Judge Midder, or contained in the juror questionnaire.

"Good morning, ladies and gentlemen. As Judge Midder told you, I am Paul Newton. Behind me at counsel table are the plaintiffs, Judith, Lorna and Trish Hoople, my clients. With them is my paralegal, Josephine Schaeffer."

Facing the table, I said, "Please stand up."

Turning back to the jury, I asked, "Do any of you recognize either myself or anyone standing at the table?"

A plump, older lady on the back row held up her hand.

Glancing at my pad I said. "Yes, Mrs. Brown, isn't it? Mrs. Mollie Brown, just like on the Titanic?"

"Yes sir. Although my maiden name wasn't Brown, when I married my second husband I became an adopted member of the Unsinkable Mollie Brown fan club."

Everyone chuckled, including Mrs. Brown. She continued: "I caught the tail end of a Maury Povich show and I believe you and your client were on it."

I motioned for those at the table to sit down and then I addressed Mrs. Brown: "Thank you for that, Mrs. Brown. We will address that again in just a few minutes."

"Anyone else?"

No one else indicated any recognition, so I moved on to Bill Handell's table. An older trial lawyer had told me many years ago that the more introductions a lawyer could make in a courtroom at the very beginning of trial, the more the jurors would presume him to be in charge. I always used any advantage I could get.

"At this table, we have the Defendant's attorney, Bill Handell and his paralegal, Heidi Snook as well as Mr. Tim Snead, representing the Defendant,

Hillsborough Community Crisis Center. Do any of you recognize any of these individuals, or have you had any dealings with either Bill Handell's office or the Defendant Crisis Center?"

This time there were no hands.

"Thank you. Now, back to you Mrs. Brown. You indicated that you saw a T.V. program with my client and myself on it."

"Yes, Maury Povich."

"Without going into any detail at this point, was there anything about what you saw that might in any way influence you if you were selected to sit on this jury?"

"Well, possibly."

I then turned to the courtroom and faced the rest of the jury pool and asked:

Have any of you sitting out here in the waiting area, seen the program we are discussing?"

Three more prospective jurors raised their hands. I asked each one her name, and then turned to Judge Midder.

"Your honor, may we approach the bench?"

Judge Midder nodded and Bill and I went to sidebar.

"Your Honor, there are a total of four prospective jurors who admit to having seen the Maury Povich show, and one of them admits that it might have influenced her enough to have a bearing on her ability to sit on this jury. I need to be able to question each of them, but not in front of each other, and certainly not in front of the rest of the panel. I don't want to taint the rest of the panel with their answers, or, for that matter, my questions. I respectfully request that you allow individual questioning of these four prospective jurors."

"Mr. Handell?"

"Your honor, I'm afraid I'll have to agree with counsel. Although I expect that the testimony might well inure to my benefit, it may well save us from having to impanel an entirely new group from the jury pool."

"Very well, rather than drag this out, the Court, on its own motion, excuses these four jurors for cause."

"But Your Honor! That might not be necessary. We don't yet know what effect the show may have had on these jurors." *Damn! I liked Molly Brown!*

"I have ruled, Mr. Newton. Gentlemen return to your places."

"Ladies and gentlemen. An issue has arisen involving what we call pre-trial publicity. Four of you have honestly stepped forward and alerted us to the fact that you have witnessed a program involving the plaintiff. Has anyone else had any advance knowledge, T.V. or otherwise regarding the plaintiff or this lawsuit?"

No other hands were raised.

"Very well. The four of you are excused from this jury selection and the Bailiff will escort you back to central jury pooling. Thank you for your honesty."

"Bailiff, if you please."

As our bailiff walked the four excused jurors to the central pool another bailiff had the remaining jurors shift in to fill the empty slot were Molly Brown had sat. The courtside jurors did the same thing, and by removing the specific questionnaires we now had a complete pool again. I scratched off the Molly Brown box on my pad and added one at top and everything flowed again.

Damn. I really felt good about Molly Brown. Oh well, I'll never know. But I think someone is holding out. I think more saw that program than raised their hands. I'm going to ask for extra alternates, just in case.

"Well now, back to business folks. You may continue, Mr. Newton."

I nodded to the judge. "May it please the Court."

Then, to the Jury, " This case centers around a psychiatric condition known as Multiple Personality Disorder, commonly referred to as MPD, and the treatment of it. How many of you are familiar with MPD. Please give me a show of hands.

Over half of the pool raised their hands.

"Good, good." I checked off the boxes of the jurors with raised hands.

"Has anyone of you ever been diagnosed with MPD?"

No hands this time.

"How about anyone who has had a relative or close friend diagnosed with or treated for MPD?"

Again, no hands.

I then went down my list and asked each juror who was aware of MPD exactly how they had become aware of MPD, and, generally, what they knew of it.

Several had seen the movie, *Three Faces of Eve* and the rest had all heard of it in a vague fashion, all that is but one. Juror number 14 was a psych major at the University of South Florida.

Without asking her whether she did or not believe in MPD, I quickly ascertained that her knowledge would impact upon her ability to be otherwise fair and impartial. Judge Midder excused her for cause.

Five jurors down, and so far, neither side had to use a peremptory. Unusual, especially for a no-nonsense judge like Midder. We still had our guns fully loaded.

"Have any of you ever been treated by a psychiatrist, a psychologist or a mental health counselor of any kind?" I continued.

Several jurors looked around uncomfortably and one finally raised his hand.

"Mr. Albert Olsen?" I said

"Can you briefly describe to me what the problem was that caused you to seek treatment?"

"When my first wife died, we had been married for 28 years. She passed, with cancer. It ate her up. There was nothing we could do. It was slow and horrible. There was nothing we could do.

"After she was gone, I became very depressed and went into a dark hole. My sister finally convinced me to seek help. When I did, it was the best advice I ever took. I thank God every day that I listened to my sister. Otherwise, I might not be here today, married six years and enjoying life and all it has to give, even sitting on this jury, if it comes to that."

"Thank you Mr. Olsen. Mr. Smith, I thought I saw you put your hand up." I lied. I had seen his look of embarrassment when Mr. Olsen spoke up and I knew he wasn't going to volunteer what I needed to know. I put him on the hot seat.

"Well no, I mean yes, I mean I was going to raise..." Letting out a deep breath he continued. "What I'm trying to say is that I was treated for depression. I'm a Viet Nam vet, and about two and a half years after I got back, I was in pretty bad shape. Drugs, alcohol, the whole nine yards. I went to the V.A. Hospital, but it did not help. Finally, I just about drug myself to a public clinic in Baltimore. I got some relief. It took a while but I was able to move on in life, drug free."

He's outta here. Public clinic in Baltimore, now cured. He owes the system. No way he sits on this jury. Especially since he didn't want me to know.

"Thank you very much, Mr. Smith."

No one else had responded to my psyche treatment question, so I moved on. However I did not believe no one else had ever been treated by any kind of psyche. Hell, there were thirty-three more people here. The odds were too much against it. I could tell by the look on Judge Midder's face he didn't believe it either.

Hell, that red faced old goat had probably been to one himself.

I went on with *voir dire* for another two hours, probing each juror about his answers to the questionnaires and anything else that seemed fruitful. Nothing was sacred. I was especially interested in past jobs, family relatives jobs, police involvement of any kind, involvement in any other lawsuit, prior jury status, and in particular, whether they admitted to using mental therapy themselves or not, their beliefs in its validity.

Finally, I got to the conclusion of my initial *voir dire.*

"Most of you have seen *Perry Mason*, or Matlock, haven't you?"

The jurors all nodded and smiled, not just agreeing with me, but also glad I was back to group questions, especially easy ones.

"I'm going to have to ask you to forget everything you ever saw and learned on those T.V. shows. There will be no last minute saving witness to rush in as in Perry Mason. There will be no guilty or not guilty parties in this case. Nor will you be asked to render a guilty or not guilty verdict.

"This is a civil trial. It does not find guilt or innocence, but liability. And, most importantly, the burden of proof is quite different. Judge Midder will explain the burden of proof to you. It is called a preponderance of evidence standard."

The Judge was allowing me some leeway and I was taking all he would allow.

"In a criminal trial, like on Perry Mason, you would be instructed to base your verdict upon a finding beyond and to the exclusion of any reasonable doubt. Ever hear Perry Mason or Ben Mattlock say 'Beyond a shadow of a doubt?'"

A show of hands by all the jurors.

"Now I have to ask you to forget that term. To put all those pre-conceived notions aside. You must put them completely out of your mind. You must tell me, each of you, can you do that? Can you base your deliberations and findings using the burden of proof that Judge Midder instructs you to use, not on the Perry Mason standard?"

I polled each prospective juror independently, making each one proclaim out loud that he or she could do so.

"You can think of a preponderance of the evidence in this way. Picture a set of scales, like those of the Statue of Liberty." I held out my arms, wide. "Evenly balanced. Then, a feather drops on one side and it causes a slight tilt." I moved my arms accordingly.

"Ladies and gentlemen, that is a preponderance of evidence. Not even 51%. Just a featherweight over even, just a featherweight."

"Do each and every one of you agree to follow Judge Midder's instructions, using the court ordered standard of burden of proof as your ruler in your judgment, if you are selected to serve on this jury? I'll start with you, Mrs. Rosen."

One by one, row by row, each juror promised, out loud, to follow the standard imposed by Judge Midder.

"Thank you. Do each one of you agree to wait until all the evidence is in and you begin deliberations before you make up your mind about the case?" Usually, this was a line the defense used, but I wanted to go there first, especially in this case. Jumping to conclusions could be devastating to Judith.

Once again, they all agreed.

"Finally I need to address damages. Some of us find it difficult to talk about money. Especially what we may consider large amounts of money. However, we have a system in America that provides that when a person is injured by the negligence of another, he or she has a right to sue for damages. Damages, in such a case, refer to money. It may sound crass. It may not be perfect, but it is the only remedy we have. It is what the founders of our country provided. Not an eye for an eye, not a battle royal, but money damages.

"Can each of you agree that if you find for the plaintiff, you will follow the law as the court instructs you and award money damages to my client, the plaintiff?"

Although all agreed, I noticed that juror numbers six and eleven showed obvious discomfort to the forced agreement. Conversely, eight and nine seemed relieved at the idea of awarding money. I was sure that Bill Handell had made his own notes about these jurors, also.

"Thank you very much, ladies and gentlemen. This concludes my *voir dire* at this time. I hope I did not embarrass anyone, but if I did, I hope you will hold it against me, and not my client. Thank you again for your time and courtesy."

"All right folks, this seems like a perfect time for a break. I'll see counsel in my chambers. Bailiff, escort the prospective jurors to the break rooms for a twenty minute break." With that, Judge Midder stepped down from the bench and through the door to his chambers.

After we were all seated in chambers, Judge Midder said, "Glad you finally wrapped it up, Mr. Newton. I didn't want to have to hurry you along."

"Sorry, Your Honor."

"No problem. Just keep it in mind. Mr. Handell, how long do you anticipate it will take for you to conclude your initial questions?"

"Well Judge, Mr. Newton covered most of the areas that need covering, but I still have a few questions left. I figure about forty-five minutes, max, Your Honor."

"O.K. Hopefully we will be able to find our jury from this pool and not have to start over with a new group. Now, how many alternates, gentlemen?"

"Standard is one or two, Judge. I propose at least two." Bill said.

"Your Honor, I propose we take four alternates. I have a feeling that some of these jurors might not have been quite candid about some of the things I asked. If we have to let them go later if it becomes apparent that I am right, then I would rather have someone standing in the wings than have to have a mistrial."

"I agree with your observations and logic, Mr. Newton, but four is too many. We can't deprive the central pool unnecessarily. We will go with three."

"Two peremptories each for the alternates O.K., gentlemen?"

"Fine." we both agreed.

"O.K. then. Let's be back in court in ten minutes."

* * * *

Standing at the podium, Bill Handell made an imposing figure. I had to admit, he was good. Tall, good looking, dressed in an impeccably tailored blue pinstripe suit accompanied by a red silk tie, he would stand out in any crowd.

"Good morning, ladies and gentlemen. I'm Bill Handell. As Mr. Newton told you earlier, I represent Hillsborough Community Crisis Center. Mr. Newton earlier covered quite a bit of ground, so I will promise to be briefer than he was, but in all fairness to my client, I must ask you some additional questions.

"To begin with, can you all agree with me that just because Mrs. Hoople filed this lawsuit and you are being interviewed as prospective a juror that does not mean that she has a case against my client?"

Some of the jurors nodded agreement, but some looked puzzled.

"This is the way our system of justice works. Anyone can walk through those doors downstairs and file a lawsuit. Anyone, with or without a valid cause. Whether it is real or not, valid or not, depends upon you, if you are chosen to sit on this jury. Can you all agree to withhold coming to a conclusion about the validity or strength of the case until all the evidence has been heard?"

This time, all the jurors nodded agreement.

"Throughout these proceedings, just as here, in *voir dire*, the plaintiff will go first, meaning, Mr. Newton. That is not because her cause, or her story or her witnesses are any better than ours, the defense, but because as the plaintiff, she has the burden of proof. Therefore, can you all agree that you will wait until you hear the witnesses' complete testimony, both direct examination and cross examination, and give each of us your same level of attention?"

Again, all nodded agreement.

Bill then launched into the individual jurors, asking many questions that had already been asked and many that had not, but primarily making sure that the jurors saw him and his client as equals to us in this battle. For him to rest too early might appear to some that we had more going for us than Bill and his client, and Bill would not let that happen.

Toward the end of his questions, Bill stated, "Mr. Newton and I have both done a lot of talking this morning. Now it is your turn. This will be the only time during this trial that you may ask questions of either myself or Mr. Newton. Mr. Newton has already concluded, bur I'm asking you right now, is there anything in any of this questioning that you don't understand, or wish to ask me about."

No nibbles here. I ought to be horse whipped for not asking the same question. Oh well, nobody's perfect. Here comes the biggie.

"We have asked you everything we believe is necessary in seeking to do our jobs for our clients. However, sometimes we miss something. I can only ask you, right now, is there anything you think might be important for us to know about that we have not asked you about?"

A hand came up. Juror number five, a small older man that worked in a bicycle repair shop. He was one of the jurors I liked.

"Earlier, Mr. Newton and then the Judge asked if anybody had watched the Maury Povich show. Well, I didn't watch it, but I heard it. We got a T.V. in the shop and it stays on all day long. Where I was working that day, was off to the side of the T.V., so I couldn't see it. But I heard most of the whole show. Sounded to me like Mrs. Hoople got railroaded. She..."

"That's quite all right Mr. Sexton." Bill quickly interrupted him.

"Mr. Sexton." Judge Midder's voice rang out. "I appreciate your honesty and I thank you for haven spoken up. "Is there *anyone* else who knows about, heard or saw the plaintiff on the Maury Povich show?"

One more hand went up from the prospective jurors in the front row, courtroom section.

"I listen to daytime T.V. in my car sometimes when I go from call to call on my route. I heard about half of the show."

"Once again, thank you for your honesty. You are excused for cause. Bailiff, please escort these men back to the central jury pool. The rest of you move over to fill in the gaps. That's right. Thank you.

"Continue, Mr. Handell."

"Thank you, Your Honor."

"I'm just about to wrap it up. Will you all agree that you will hold Mr. Newton to his promise? His promise to you and to the system, that when he brought this lawsuit, he would satisfy the burden of proof?"

Heads nodded affirmatively.

"And will you also agree that if Mr. Newton does not keep his promise, if he does not satisfy that burden, if he does not prove his case, you won't hesitate to find in favor of the defense as required by law?"

Again, all heads nodded affirmatively.

"Finally, will you all remember your promise to me that you will withhold from making any decision until all the evidence is in and you are retired to the jury room to deliberate and decide your verdict?"

Again, all heads nodded affirmatively.

"Thank you." And with that he walked back to counsel table, a slight smile on his face, hidden from the jurors.

"Counselors, please let me know when you're ready." Judge Midder said to Bill and me.

"Yes, Your Honor." Bill and I parroted together.

Approximately ten minutes went by while Bill and I went over our notes with our clients. Then, we both looked up at Judge Midder and nodded.

"Are both counsels ready to proceed?"

"Yes, Your Honor."

"Approach the bench, both of you."

Bill and I walked to the bench and stood, one on each side of the court reporter where the three of us could talk to each other without the jurors hearing what was said.

"First, are there any requests to strike for cause; Mr. Newton first?"

Voir dire had been pretty clear cut, the potential cause jurors already stricken by Judge Midder, so neither Bill nor I advanced any argument for cause challenges.

"All right, then, Mr. Newton do you wish to strike a juror at this time?" Judge Midder was smiling. With only four peremptory challenges apiece, the current pool would make up our panel without having to go back to the central pool for additional jurors. Although it was possible for that to change, it was now very unlikely.

"Judge, let me make sure I understand your procedure. We are selecting from the current first row of six jurors only. Then, after we excuse whomever, those from the next row will fill in the empty seats, with everyone moving forward. We continue this through the current eighteen jurors in the jury box. After that, we fill in from the pool still in the courtroom, and only if we run out of these too will we resort to the central jury pool, if necessary?"

Judge Midder said, "That is correct."

"What about back striking?" I asked, referring to the practice of some judges to not-allow striking a juror once he had been passed over by both counselors, even if they still had peremptories left.

"I allow back striking," he said. "You may use all of your peremptories or not, as you choose, until you run out or cede. Your choice."

Although I fully intended to strike the current number five juror, I decided to let Bill make the first move. He might remove him for me. You never knew. Jury selection was a mixture of poker and dice rolling.

"I'll pass, Your Honor."

"All right, the plaintiff passes. What say you, Mr. Handell?" Judge Midder was speaking low, but forcefully enough to ensure the court reporter did not miss a word.

"The defense strikes juror number four, Your Honor."

"Juror number four is excused. The current jury is 1-2-3-5-6-7. What says the plaintiff?"

"The plaintiff strikes juror number five, Your Honor."

"Juror number five is out. The panel now consists of 1-2-3-6-7-8. What says the defense?"

"The defense strikes juror number seven, Your Honor."

"Juror number seven is excused. Our panel is now, numbers 1-2-3-6-8-9. What says the plaintiff?"

We continued the game until all our peremptories were exhausted, each of us attempting to get the other to use a peremptory on someone we did not want, but neither of us really got what we wanted. We both wanted a panel that was best for our clients, or to put it another way, a panel that was the least adverse to our respective clients.

Our jury was a not a true cross-section, but it was a varied one. All white, except for one person. Bill had excluded all the blacks he could from the jury. Blacks were notoriously pro plaintiff and tended to allow larger cash awards than whites.

Mostly women and non professionals. Non professional was my choice. However, I still had my doubts about two jurors. Number three, Jim Blood, an engineer, and number four, Lila DePaul, an old maid school teacher. Engineers by lot tended toward conservatism, a natural plus for the defense. As for Lila DePaul, you can't get much more conservative than an old maid, Jewish school marm. I'd be willing to bet the mortgage on my house that Jim Blood would be elected the jury foreman.

However, when it came down to it, they were better than the alternates. The luck of the draw had placed solid conservatives as alternates. One was even a bookkeeper. Hopefully, no one would get sick and they would be sent home prior to deliberations, thereby not tainting the rest of the jurors with their ultra conservative beliefs. They would merely listen and observe, and then be dismissed at the end of the trial. A thankless job, but necessary to prevent a mistrial.

I had once stared into the prospect of a conservative group of alternates, and instead of choosing, agreed to be bound by the decision of five if one of the regular jurors became incapacitated. Since all but one juror were elderly and the one young juror was very pro plaintiff, and very healthy in appearance, I figured it was a win-win situation. Until, that is, the young juror turned out to be severe epileptic, had a fit, went into convulsions and was *saved* by the defense expert, a Doctor who was testifying at the time of the onset. The juror was dismissed, the doctor was a hero and my case was lost. Never again.

All in all, if I had my way, I would send them all back to central and choose the next six blind. But the choices had been made, the die cast, so to speak.

* * * *

Judge Midder discharged all but our panel and our alternates, sending them back to the central jury pool after thanking them. He then addressed the remaining jurors.

"Ladies and gentlemen, you have been chosen to sit as the jury in the case of Judith Hoople, Lorna Hoople and Trish Hoople, Plaintiffs versus Hillsborough Community Crisis Center.

"If you will stand and raise your right hand, the clerk will administer the oath and swear you in."

"Madam Clerk, if you will."

After they were sworn in, Judge Midder admonished them not to talk with anyone about the case. Not husbands, wives, friends, lovers, no one. He told them to be especially careful around lawyers and people from the news media. They were not allowed to discuss the case among themselves and they were to make no decisions until after they deliberated the case at the end of the trial.

"You will now retire to the jury room where you will select a jury foreperson to represent you. After you have done so, knock on the door and the bailiff will come in and issue you new I.D. buttons identifying you as jurors. You are to wear them at all times while in the courthouse until the end of this trial.

"The bailiff will then escort you to the cafeteria where you have a section reserved for you in which to eat. The court admonishes you, once again, that you are not to discuss this case among yourselves or with anyone else.

"Lunch will go from the time you leave this courtroom until 1:00 P.M. It is now 11:35 A.M.

"Are there any questions?"

There were no questions.

"Very well. Bailiff, please escort the jury to the jury room. I'll see counsel in my chambers in fifteen minutes."

"All rise," the bailiff intoned while everyone rose and the judge exited the courtroom.

I turned to Judith: "It looks like you will probably go on about 3:00 P.M. I was hoping to start you when we would have a full day for your testimony, but all we have left are opening statements, about forty-five minutes apiece for Bill and me. Then you go on. I'm going to ask for more, but it is doubtful. Forty-five is about all this judge normally allows. We'll see. That's what this next session in chambers is about.

"Joe will take you across the street to a cafe and sandwich shop. Eat light, but eat something. Do not joke, laugh or display any emotions where a juror may see you. If they catch you laughing, they may interpret it as a sign that you think you are putting something over on them. If you come across any jurors, just give a slight smile, nod your head and keep going.

"Joe, if I'm not over there with you by the time you have to come back, bring me a candy bar and a pack of crackers, or something. O.K.?"

"Sure boss," Joe said, knowing full well that I would probably be right here the whole time after I came out of chambers, getting ready for opening statements. She also knew she wouldn't be bringing back any candy bars and crackers. I am a type II diabetic, although few people know it. Josephine knows, and she would be bringing back a sandwich, already cut into bite sizes, and an orange juice or something like that.

I slipped Joe some money and sent them on their way. I then headed to the men's room for a much needed break, and then to chambers.

"Gentlemen. My secretary informs me that your offices have both supplied me with your initial proposed jury instructions and the related other materials I had requested. Thank you for your promptness.

"There has been a change in plans for today's activities. The chief judge has assigned me to preside over, and if possible, issue warrants requested by the sheriff's department. Apparently they need them by late today. Therefore, I will send everyone home no later than 4:00 PM."

"Now, Mr. Newton. How long do you need for opening statements?"

"Your Honor, I am requesting at least one and a half hours for opening statements. I know that may seem a little long, but this is a complex case with several issues and I don't feel that I can cover them all in any less time. After all, Your Honor, the complexity involved was the main reason we were granted a three week trial schedule."

Let's see how far that gets me.

"Actually, Mr. Newton, I am hoping to keep this to a two week trial, if possible. But I do get your meaning."

"Mr. Handell, how much time do you require?"

"Not that much Your Honor. I think one hour would be just fine, and I probably won't use all of it."

"Very well, gentlemen. I'm going to be somewhat expansive here, do to this rather unique situation. I will allow you each one hour and fifteen minutes for opening statements."

"I know, Mr. Handell that you said you didn't need that much time, but I imagine that's somewhat of a strategic move on your part. I've never yet met a good trial lawyer that wouldn't use every minute I gave him in front of a jury.

"We will break between your statements, let the jury wake up for you, Mr. Handell, and then after both statements are in the record, we will call it a day so I can get on with my warrants.

"Any questions?

"Good. I'll see you both at 1:00 PM."

CHAPTER EIGHT

I was sitting at counsel table, going over my opening statement issues, when Josephine arrived with my sandwich and juice. Not saying a word, she took my briefcase and positioned the sandwich in it, out of sight in the open briefcase where I could just reach in and take out the bite sized pieces with practiced ease.

I mumbled a quiet "thanks," reaching in and grabbing a bite while continuing to peruse my notes. Joe opened the top of the orange juice and placed it next to the sandwich. She then walked back out of the courtroom to chaperone her charges for the next few minutes. There are several hiding spots throughout the courthouse where she could go and be at very low risk of the clients being seen by the jurors. Joe knew them all.

At precisely five 'til one, Joe shepherded Judith and the girls back to the table. I had finished my lunch and my review and had placed two sheets of legal paper strategically at the far corner of the counsel table. These contained bold printed words and names to remind me to cover all the issues and people I needed to cover in my opening statement. I also had a final checklist, including liability areas and all my primary points that would be left at my seat at the table and which I would refer to when I was almost through with my statement.

I never liked to use notes, preferring instead to go with the flow, so to speak. I like to look the jurors in the eye and feel my way through the statement, reacting to the jurors' signals rather than written notes. I already know what I want to say before I get started. However, sometimes in the course of discourse, I would be at a loss for a word, usually a name. That was why I lay the papers or my 'cue cards' on the table, basically out of sight of the jury. They did not look like notes, but they were arranged where I could see them if I needed to. Before I wrapped up, I would ask for a moment to consult my notes to insure nothing important had been overlooked. This also added a little humility to my presentation.

Although our styles were different, I knew Bill would be equally as prepared. He was a good lawyer and a stalwart adversary.

The court clerk and court reporter came in and set up their desk areas. The court reporter was a cute little redhead named Stacy. Pretty-faced, she wore a short skirt over a pair of long shapely legs and I had to be sure to avert my eyes in order to keep from losing my concentration. The burdens of being a trial lawyer.

I put my coat back on just as the bailiff inquired if everyone was ready. Joe gave me a quick once over, straightening out my tie just before the bailiff intoned, "All rise. Court is now in session; the Honorable Judge Julius Midder presiding."

There was a pause while Judge Midder took his seat behind the bench, then the Judge said, "You may be seated."

Glancing at Bill and me he asked, "You gentlemen ready to go?"

"Yes, Your Honor."

"Bailiff, please bring in the jury."

When the jury was seated, it was with the first three jurors in row one, the next three in row two, directly behind the first three, and the alternates in row three. That way each juror was as close to the witness stand as possible.

Judge Midder addressed them, "Welcome back, ladies and gentlemen. I hope you had a nice lunch. In the future, you will usually be asked to use the courthouse cafeteria only. However, if you will agree to a restaurant within a block of the courthouse, on Mondays and Fridays, time and weather permitting, I will allow the bailiff to accompany you there. He will supply you with a list of acceptable restaurants."

"Occasionally, it may be necessary for you to eat in the jury room. Especially once you have begun your deliberations. When that happens, the bailiff will do everything possible to make your accommodations as comfortable as is prudent.

"Were you able to arrive at a jury foreperson?"

"Yes, Your Honor." Some spoke, while others just nodded.

"Will the jury foreperson please identify yourself to the court clerk."

The engineer, Jim Blood stood up and identified himself, as requested.

Bingo! I knew it. Too bad I didn't have anyone to bet with. The engineer! Damn, damn, damn!! Sometimes I really hate it when I am right.

"Ladies and gentlemen. The attorneys are now going to address you with their opening statements. They will tell you what they believe the evidence in the case will be. They will outline for you how the case will be presented. The information they give you is not evidence. The only evidence you will hear will come from the witness stand. However, what they say is important, and I request that you give them your complete attention."

"Mr. Newton, are you ready to proceed?"

Standing, I nodded: "Yes, Your Honor. May it please the Court."

I then walked to the podium, completely empty-handed.

I was wearing a conservative blue pin stripe suit (common apparel for trial lawyers), Allen-Edmonds black wing tip loafers, white shirt, button covers on the cuffs, monogram on the left sleeve and a simple watch. I never wore my Rolex in court. I also wore a muted red silk tie, designed for empathy.

Like most attorneys, I have a wardrobe full of ties designed to elicit different responses from those I face in court. Red for empathy, yellow for power, *etc., etc.* Each time I buy a new suit I get new mood ties to go with it. When I'm not in trial, I select a tie that I like. When I am in trial, my tie is chosen depending on the type of witness, *etc.*, I intend to face that day. Today was a jury day, therefore, empathy for the client and her cause, muted red.

"Good afternoon, ladies and gentlemen. I hope you all had a good lunch. I know that sometimes, after lunch, it is easy to get drowsy, or just plain tired. Should that happen, if you will just alert the court, a break will be provided to allow you to stand up and stretch.

"The reason I bring this up is that I know that we lawyers are sometimes long winded. There are times when we must cover areas and subjects that are important, but boring. It is important to both my client, and to the cause of justice, that you remain attentive during the trial.

"As the Judge informed you, what I tell you next is not evidence. Instead it is what I believe the evidence you will hear is going to tell you. You may use it as a road map to guide you through this trial.

"If you consider the trial as a jig saw puzzle, right now you know a little about what is coming up, but I will give you the pieces, and put them together for you so that you will be aware of the big picture as we progress through the trial. Obviously, my picture and Mr. Handell's picture will be somewhat different, but nonetheless, they will have much in common.

"Judith Hoople was victimized. As an infant, she was repeatedly raped and sodomized by her own father. Her own mother knew of it and did nothing to help. In fact, later on she actually assisted her husband and others, and even participated in helping her husband and others engage in satanic rituals and group sex with her own daughter, Judith. *Her own daughter!*

"You will all learn that Judith, even as a little girl, had no place to go for help. She was still in diapers when the rape and sodomization began. The rapes were particularly brutal, in that her father took her with force, pulling her to him to attack her both vaginally and anally. It depended on his mood. In the vaginal position, little Judith was pulled, on her back, to the edge of the crib in order to meet with her father's vicious thrusts. Her tiny back would be placed over the crib railing which had been let down next to the mattress to allow her father access to his bestial, inhumane, brutal and evil pleasures of the flesh.

"You will learn that like others before her, the young infant, with nowhere to go, turned inward. Too young to seek help from God, or any mortal, Judith had only herself. The pain was too great to bear, and yet, she did not know of suicide or of the things that might have appealed to an older child. She only knew that she could not handle what was happening to her.

"The young Judith's mind literally split. Unable to survive in the present, she unconsciously developed another person to take the punishment for her. Someone who could feel the pain. Take all the hurt. Absorb it all, and then go away. Just disappear as if nothing ever happened. The little girl could still love mommy and daddy. Still live. Her device, her escape route, if you will, literally saved her life.

"Without this escape mechanism, Judith could not have survived. She most certainly would never have become, for all intents and purposes, and in her own mind, a functioning, normal child; much less, a functional adult.

"*But she did! She really did!* The mind, ladies and gentlemen, is a wonderful instrument. It works for us both consciously and sub-consciously. In other words, sometimes it works for us, does what is best for us, before we know what is necessary to enable us to survive. Judith's mind, even at this early age, came to her rescue. Her mind did not know of a thing called M. P. D. Her mind was too young to register psychosomatic abnormalities as what it was going through. But her mind did know that by herself, little baby Judith could not handle the obscene abuse being pummeled upon her by her own flesh and blood. Her own father. The man supposed to be her protector. The man she was supposed to love all her natural life. The man little girls snuggle up to. Whisper their dreams to. Confess their fears to. Look up to with adoring eyes.

"Scum, scum, scum. That's what little Judith had. *Scum*!" My eyes blazed and my voice punctuated the air with loud hissing noises as I repeated the word scum, all the while watching as the jurors literally shrank in their seats.

"But even that depravity is not enough. You will hear of other episodes of abuse by this man and his companions. Devil worshipers. Members of a satanic cult who enjoyed defiling young girls and young boys. Yes, girls *and* boys. These people were truly evil incarnate.

"Judith survived. She grew up and, for all outward appearances, she was a normal, healthy loving child.

"Along the way, she suffered from two additional traumatic experiences. This is not unusual. The psychological experts will tell you that there is something about a traumatized victim that victimizers recognize and these people are more likely than the rest of us to become victims again. She was brutally raped by persons unknown, twice. And, for a while, as a six year old, she was molested by her uncle, her father's brother.

"Through it all, Judith had only one protector, one person she could turn to.

"Herself.

"Herself, in the form of another person in her mind. The one who came forward in her mind. The one who came forward when all hope was gone. The one who took all the pain away.

"Her alter ego.

"Her split personality, for lack of a better concept.

"Away from her parents, Judith excelled. She was an outgoing, engaging young lady. She liked to dance. Liked to have fun and was looking and studying for a career in public media. She married the love of her life and had two girls, and was a good mother.

"She divorced at age twenty-eight, but remained close friends with her former husband, and her children's father. There were no custody battles and each parent took an active interest in raising the girls. They were both loving parents. Judith believed she knew the value of a loving father and wanted to insure that her daughters knew and loved their father.

"Judith, for reasons not consciously known to her, found that she had a natural affinity for abused women. In school she took classes designed to aid individuals in assisting battered and/or abused women. She got a job with the Hillsborough Community Crisis Center. She wound up working as a rape crises counselor, taking incoming calls from injured women, helping them through their traumatic experiences, helping them survive. She was good at what she did. Very good.

"Judith also worked part time as a T.V. news reporter for Channel 8. She covered social events and various local happenings. She was well received by the viewing public. She was a good reporter, conscientious and ready to roll at a moment's notice.

"You will hear that the people where Judith worked, the Center, were a tight knit group of people. They worked together, as a team, often under severe crisis-like conditions. Then, as friends, they socialized with each other. After hours they were as close as during working hours.

"The Center has two types of workers. Employees, like Judith, and others like *Dr. Red Greely* who were essentially independent contractors. These people usually had private practices independent of the center and worked for the center on a per session basis. They derived many of their private patients from the Center. It was a super referral service for counselors. These people held supervisory positions with the Center. Chief among these independents was Red Greely, a former defendant in this case.

"It was well known by all Center employees that whatever Red said was gospel. It was the law. The Center had empowered him with virtually absolute authority. It was therefore assumed he must be pretty darn good. Certainly Judith never heard anything but good about him, and the director of the Center afforded Greely with complete deference.

"Judith and several of her co-workers smoked and had discussed breaking the habit. However, as most of those who enjoy a bad habit or two, they never did anything about actually quitting. Never, that is, until one of them saw an ad in the Tampa Tribune. A hypnotist was selling smoking secession classes at Ruth Eckard Hall in Clearwater. He advertised that in three sessions, you would be rid of the habit of smoking. Several co-workers decided to attend, but others, like Judith couldn't. Their work schedule wouldn't permit it.

"When Red Greely heard about this, he approached Judith and those who were unable to attend the group therapy in Clearwater with a proposition. As the evidence will show, Red, with the actual or apparent authority of the Center, solicited the employees to allow him to hypnotize them to help them to control or quit smoking. His only reward was to supposedly improve his hypnosis techniques.

"After a few hypnotic treatments, Judith began to sleep only in restless spurts. No more peaceful night's sleep. Weird dreams began to invade her night's rest. She began to wake up disturbed, drenched in sweat, sometimes panicked, occasionally hyperventilating. At this point, she still could not remember the dreams, only snippets, bits and pieces of something horrid.

"At this same time, Red began to notice that Judith was starting to use various childlike words and actions while under hypnosis, sometimes even lingering for a few moments following a session. By about the tenth treatment, these were a regular occurrence.

"Now, unknown to Judith, Red began to explore these happenings and found a little girl who was willing to talk to him. Even without the benefit of training, Red recognized something highly significant had happened. Red was never a real doctor, not an M.D., not a Ph.D., not a Master's Degree, nothing but a Bachelor's and a Psychologist license. But he was smart enough to realize he was on to something, even if he did not understand it.

"But he did not want to share it. No sir!

"So he went to the books and discovered a clear cut case of Multiple Personality Disorder. MPD. Red was excited. This was for him, a dream come true. A dream case. A client or patient who trusted him completely and didn't even know what she had been living with all her life. Red knew. This could be big. Really big. This one case could put him over the top in this area of his profession.

"A trusting patient. A rare psychological disorder. Insurance money to pay him for his work. Approval from the Center to do his thing. Rooms in the Center to use when he did not have time, or Judith was too pressed to conduct sessions at his private office. All this and the case that could make him an icon at the top of his profession. Hell, the books would be worth millions!

"What more could one ask for?

"Judith, on the other hand, was totally distraught. Her life was turning upside down. She needed help. She trusted Red. She knew the high esteem in which he was held by the Center. She was convinced that she couldn't ask for or find a better referral or recommendation. She allowed Red to become her primary, and at that time, only psychiatric counselor for her MPD.

"You will hear how Red took advantage of Judith. Despicable acts. How he experimented with various techniques on her while she was under his control. How he used Judith in his effort to make a name for himself. How he abused her trust. How he broke every ethical rule in the book in his treatment of Judith.

"Judith had several personalities buried in the recesses of her mind. Buried because she couldn't handle the knowledge they possessed. Red unleashed all of them into her conscious mind, driving her to the brink of insanity. She could not cope. Could not accept the knowledge. She became physically disabled, mentally dispirited and depressed. Her days became foggy. She lost all enthusiasm for her work. She lost her job at the T.V. station and had to reduce her hours at the Center. She would sleep in until nine or ten every morning, and still not get enough rest. She smoked cigarettes incessantly.

"Under hypnosis, Red began to perform despicable acts with the child alters. At first, he was only petting and caressing. Then Red began to have the children play with his 'purple,' as he taught them to call it. Then it became intercourse with the child alters. Finally, intercourse with Judith as well. Red had his own little harem. Depending on his mood, he could have sex with a four-year old, a five-year old or a thirty-four year old. They were all willing to please the one man they thought loved them and whom they believed they could trust. Any one of them would do *anything* for Red. Depending upon how he felt, he needed only to call up his sexual pleasure for the day.

"And he did it while they were working! With complete and absolute authority he would commandeer a room for his 'treatment' sessions, right at the Center. He was never supervised, questioned or in any way restricted in his pleasures by the Center. And he billed the insurance policy of Judith and the Center for his trysts.

"Judith will tell you more about his 'treatments.'

"Judith began desperately seeking help after Red finally tired of his little sex menagerie and cut Judith and the alters off. Stone cold. No closure. As complete an abandonment as if a father had walked out of their lives. Not surprisingly, this abandonment occurred at precisely the same time as Judith's insurance hit its limits. Her coverage and treatment expired simultaneously.

"Dr. Felton Trey, A mental health counselor and ordained minister was Judith's next long term counselor.

"You will also hear from Dr. Sherrie Lyons, another treating counselor of Judith's. In fact, you will hear from five treating Doctors and counselors, all of whom will testify as to Judith's problems and the various treatments she underwent.

"Dr. Trey, whom I mentioned a moment ago, has treated Judith longer than any of the others. He has helped her to regain some semblance of normalcy. He will tell you she still has a long way to go."

"It was Dr. Trey who first suggested that Judith seek legal help to try and offset these devastating losses by Judith and her two children.

"You will hear that Dr. Trey was the key figure in developing and instituting the widely acclaimed rehabilitation program for the care and treatment of sexually abused children in the state of Arkansas. He worked directly for and was accountable to then governor, Bill Clinton. It was that experience and depth of knowledge that enabled him to understand and to help Judith.

"You will also hear from the undisputed, peer recognized world expert in the field of Multiple Personality Disorder, Dr. Eric Lofton. He is a psychiatrist with an impeccable reputation. He will tell you that Judith is a classical victim of MPD. That she has between four and six separate distinct personalities. Separate people, if you will, all living in the same body. All fighting for the right to be heard and to live. Control is now extremely difficult for the real Judith.

"Most importantly, Dr. Lofton will tell you that Judith is not a freak. Rather, she is a product of survival. The ingenious part of the human brain has come to the rescue in Judith's mind at a time of extreme distress. Rather than allowing circumstances of uncontrollable and unspeakable horror to destroy her sanity, her mind fashioned a means of circumventing the tragedy. These workings of the human mind will be explained to you by the nation's leading expert in the field.

"He will also tell you how truly despicable, evil and utterly wrong Red's treatment of Judith was. How Red almost destroyed her, made her revert to an invalid. He will tell you that Red almost caused Judith to be driven totally insane. He will explain to you how Red's unorthodox and invalid treatments not only did not help Judith, mentally or physically, but instead, actually caused the creation of an additional personality. This one is suicidal. This one wants to kill the whole of them. This one still haunts Judith and lies in wait to complete her deadly ambition.

"The testimony will show that Red himself was evil. There is no other word for it. It will also show that the Center, the defendant in this case, was not evil. But it was wrong. The Center's directors were wrong. Wrong to allow Red to practice unsupervised. Wrong to endow him with unimpeachable authority and esteem. Wrong to present him as a man of honor and integrity. HCCC. was derelict in their duties to their staff and to their clients, most of whom, like Judith, looked to HCCC. for guidance. In other words, the testimony will show that the Clinic was negligent, and that their negligence caused or contributed to the horrendous damage inflicted upon Judith Hoople by Red Greely.

"On behalf of my client, I thank you for your patience and your attention these last few minutes. Thank you ladies and gentlemen."

I walked back to the counsel table and sat down. The courtroom was completely silent for a few moments, then, "Thank you Mr. Newton. Ladies and gentlemen, we will take a twenty minute recess. Bailiff."

"All rise." The bailiff said in a loud voice. Those in attendance stood as one as the Judge left the courtroom, then the bailiff said, "Court is now in recess. Ladies and gentlemen of the jury, step right this way, please."

Everyone at both counsel tables remained standing as the jury filed out of the courtroom. I noticed several jurors looking at Judith, women especially with sympathetic expressions on their faces.

Good. At least they see her as a victim, not a freak.

Judith seemed somewhat more relaxed. Lorna seemed intrigued by the whole thing. Trish just seemed bored.

I once again admonished them about being caught out in the hall, and especially, not to talk to anyone when they took a break. Then we all headed to the restrooms. On the way out, Bill Handell said to me, "Nice going, counselor, but I still think, no, I *know*, she's a phony." He smiled as he moved on with his client.

* * * *

Outside the courtroom, T.V. reporters gathered around the litigants and as we came into the hall. Since I was ahead of Bill, they came at me first.

I stopped and held up my hands. "Hold on now, hold on. We have only a limited break time, and certain basic functions must be met. Today is a short trial day and we will break early. I promise you that I'll give you some time then. Until then, thank you for your understanding and patience."

I then moved the others off in the direction of the restrooms, me along with them.

Bill had already moved through the crowd. He wanted to get back for the finishing touch on his opening statement.

* * * *

"All rise." The bailiff intoned as Judge Midder re-took the bench. "Court is now in session, the Honorable Judge Julius Midder presiding."

"Be seated, please. Are we ready to bring in the jury, gentlemen?" Judge Midder asked.

I rose. "Not quite, Your Honor. I have a matter that I think would be better raised now than later."

"You have the floor counselor."

"Thank you, Your Honor. I appreciate Mr. Handell not interrupting me during my opening statement with objections, even though I'm sure he had some. That is why I requested this moment. I'm afraid that Mr. Handell may try to bring up the Maury Povich show in his opening statement. I noted the tape is included in his evidence list, and as yet this court has made no ruling as to whether it will be allowed in as evidence. I strenuously object to any mention of the show or any of its content. I believe the tape to be totally inadmissible. It contains rank hearsay and unsworn comments, some of them slanderous, and has absolutely no place in a court of law. It would do nothing but detract from the decorum of this court and any minute value it might be said to have would be far outweighed by the overwhelming prejudice to my client."

"What says the defense, Mr. Handell? Do you intend to mention the show during your opening statement?"

"Well, Your Honor, I do intend to cover a couple scenes with the jury. I believe the tape represents a good picture of Mrs. Hoople in her more natural appearance, and I believe it should be admissible as evidence. Actually, it is prejudicial. I wouldn't want to use it if it weren't. All evidence is prejudicial, if it is of any value at all. That does not make it objectionable."

"Mr. Handell, the Court has not had an opportunity to view this tape, nor will I with the tight schedule we have today. Let me tell you, with all candor, that I am persuaded by Mr. Newton's objection, and unless this tape shows otherwise, I most likely will not allow it to be entered as evidence. So, if you mention it, you do so at your own risk. Do I make myself clear?"

"Understood, Your Honor."

"That's it then. O.K. bailiff, bring in the jury."

As soon as the jury was seated Judge Midder said, "Mr. Handell, you may proceed. Ladies and gentlemen, I remind you that what Mr. Handell is about to say is not evidence, but I admonish you to listen closely, giving him the same attention you gave Mr. Newton."

"Mr. Handell."

"Thank you Your Honor. May it please the court?

"Good afternoon ladies and gentlemen. As you already know, my name is Bill Handell. Mr. Newton painted you quite a picture of my client, Hillsborough Community Crisis Center; as well as Mr. Greely and his own client, Mrs. Hoople. Quite a picture.

"However, I believe the evidence that you will see will paint an entirely different picture. The real picture that will evolve from the evidence will point to a manipulative, deceitful woman who has problems all right, many problems. Oh, she may well be mentally different from you and I, but she is not the victim that she pretends to be.

"The evidence will show that every single medical or psychological provider that appears before you, or who ever examined Mrs. Hoople, has one common term that can be attributed to Mrs. Hoople. *Manipulative*! Every one. No exceptions. Even the great hocus pocus guru, Dr. Eric Lofton, the plaintiff's most revered expert, if he actually appears, will agree. Manipulative!"

Well, Bill sure took the gloves off and came out punching.

"Anyone and everyone who hears her sob story about all this infant rape and childhood satanic rituals would have to feel sorry for her. *Have to!* If it were true. But the evidence will show that this is nothing more than the product of an overly imaginative mind seeking to manipulate people into feeling sorry for her so that eventually she can ask you to award her a large sum of money. A 'green' cure, so to speak.

"You will hear the depositions of Judith Hoople's mother, Ruth Benefield. She lives far away in Anchorage Alaska, in a rest home. She is an invalid, and therefore cannot attend this proceeding in person. But make no mistake, her testimony is an adamant statement that none of these fictitious accounts of molestation of Judith by her father ever occurred. She will deny any accusations that she or her husband ever belonged to or attended any satanic or occult practices. She is a Christian lady. She will tell you that her name, Ruth, and her daughter's name, Judith, were both chosen out of the Bible. They certainly are not names that a satanic worshiper would choose to name a daughter.

"Judith's father and uncle are conveniently deceased, so they cannot defend their good names against these rank and slanderous accusations. Her brother cannot be found to ask him about these allegations, but the mother's testimony is such that you will need nothing else.

"Although there is evidence of two reported rapes occurring during Judith's childhood, no actual perpetrators were ever charged. Not one single suspect. Not one. Unless maybe you were to look at Judith Hoople as suspect. Like Chicken Little, when you holler the sky is falling often enough, people stop listening.

"Like a sweater that begins to unravel with just one string, the evidence will unravel Judith Hoople's story, piece by piece, until there is nothing left, except just that. A story, nothing else.

"Dr. Red Greely has been branded a sexual deviate, a menace to his patients, a liar, a child molester and God knows what else by this woman. Humbled so much and persecuted so much as a result of Mrs. Hoople's accusations that he settled her claim against him in absolute fear."

"*Objection*! Your Honor." I was almost screaming.

"Sustained! You know the rules, Mr. Handell. You may proceed, but watch yourself." Judge Midder was almost as angry as I was. We were getting close to a mistrial argument and the trial was just starting.

Bill Handell continued as if nothing had happened.

"Red Greely will tell you that it was Judith who approached him and asked to be hypnotized, not the other way around. It was Judith who wanted to have a sexual relationship with him, and it was Judith who finally dropped him, not the reversal."

Bill is really going out on a limb on this one. I'll tear Red apart if he tries to pull that crap. The insurance billings will bury him, as well as his own notes, few as they are.

"She tried every way possible to manipulate him. She played the mental hocus pocus, mumbo jumbo, psycho jumbo on him, almost convincing him she really had something. But then he caught on. That's when he decided to get out. That's when Judith Hoople threatened him.

"Oh yes. I said threatened him. But it was not an empty threat. Oh no. That's why we are here today. Judith Hoople is a manipulative, vindictive woman. Hell hath no furry like that of a scorned woman is nothing like the truth of Judith Hoople. She has ruined Red Greely, professionally and personally. His reputation in both is shot. He is a broken man."

My God. He wouldn't go this far out on a limb unless he already had something from Red to substantiate it. What the hell have they got?

"Now, this manipulative woman, this Jezebel, is trying to do the same thing to a great community asset, the Hillsborough Community Crisis Center. An institution revered for their tireless work to help those who truly need it, even when they have no insurance and cannot afford it. They are there for anyone, at least they are now. But Judith Hoople is going to ask you to award her millions of dollars. That's right; I said millions of dollars from the Center. From my client.

"Ladies and gentlemen. Even if all this nonsense was true, which the evidence will show clearly is not the case, my client was not to blame. The Crisis Center did nothing but offer Judith Hoople a chance to make a decent living helping others in a decent environment.

"As far as Red's relationship with the Clinic, he was at all times what is known as an independent contractor. He was never employed by the Clinic. He came to my client with impeccable credentials and assisted people who had problems. Some of them became his clients. Others did not. Any relationship between Red and Judith was of their own doing. It was not known of, sanctioned or in any way imposed by Hillsborough Community Crisis Center. In fact, the evidence will show that the only reason my client is in this law suit at all is because Judith Hoople needs some deep pockets to realize her dreams of becoming a millionaire without working for it.

"Forget the garbage. Forget the smoke and mirrors. That is what the evidence will show.

"Thank you ladies and gentlemen."

On that note, Bill Handell went back to the counsel table and joined his client. Tim Snead gave him a big smile as he sat down.

The women jurors were not looking happy, or sympathetic. The men looked at Judith as if she had the plague. Bill had scored some heavy points. Now, it was my turn, I hoped.

CHAPTER NINE

Back in my office, alone, I reflected on the day's events. True to his word, Judge Midder had dismissed us immediately following opening statements. Outside the courtroom, it was bedlam.

The press now sensed a true Donnybrook. A knock down drag out, no holds barred fight. Bill had certainly left no other option. He had called my client a liar and worse, a potential thief. He had left no middle ground. There would be no settlement options in this case. It was a fight for the jury verdict all the way.

After the impromptu press report, I had come back to the office. I sat down with Judith and the girls and reassured them. Everything was O.K., and moving as expected. I briefly touched on Judith's testimony tomorrow, but I saw no need to go into it in depth. Tonight, the only assignment I gave Judith was to go over her deposition testimony and then to get a good night's sleep. At least a good night's rest.

I had a mock courtroom in my office and we had already spent several hours prepping Judith. Either she was ready, or she was not. But tonight I needed her to relax. Tomorrow she would be on the stand, probably all day, maybe the next as well.

I knew that if I could get six hours of testimony out of her tomorrow, Midder would call it a day. You could only work one witness so much, and Judge Midder was no tyrant, at least with non-lawyers.

I had Josephine line up the next four witnesses, guessing that none of them would be needed before Wednesday afternoon at the earliest. I would then go to Judith's treating counselors, starting with Dr. Trey and ending with Dr. Sherrie Lyons.

I decided that my next move would be one to shake up Bill Handell. I would call Tim Snead to the stand. It would be quick, merely to establish the relationships of Judith and Red to the Clinic. But it would shake up Snead. He thought he was only here to smile and look prominent in front of the jury, not to testify. This part would be fun.

My last witness, by judicial fiat, would be Dr. Lofton. If I had my way I would put him on first, even before Judith. However, Judge Midder had made it clear that if he was allowed on, it would be under whatever restrictions the judge imposed after all the other witnesses had testified. I would have to be careful indeed not to let the other experts steal any of Dr. Lofton's thunder. No explanations of MPD would be allowed. Diagnosis only as necessary to explain treatment options, not to explain the diagnosis itself. It would be tricky, but I could handle it. All I had to do was walk a tightrope between now and next Monday or Tuesday when he was offered.

I poured myself a strong Crown Royal, took a couple sips and relaxed. I would go home soon, eat a quick bite and then go over tomorrow's testimony. Might as well. I never slept more than a couple hours a night in trial.

I finished my drink just as the cleaning crew came in. I nodded a goodnight to them, none of them spoke English, and caught the elevator to my car.

* * * *

"Good morning, ladies and gentlemen. Glad to see you all made it back. Mr. Newton, Is the plaintiff ready?"

"Yes, Your Honor."

"Mr. Handell, is the defense ready?"

"Yes, Your Honor."

"Very well then. Mr. Newton, call your first witness."

Aannnddd they're offff.

"Your Honor, I call Judith Hoople to the stand."

"Mrs. Hoople, would you please approach the clerk and be sworn in?"

On her way to the witness stand Judith stopped in front of the Clerk.

"Would you raise your right hand, please?"

"Do you swear to tell the truth, the whole truth and nothing but the truth, so help you God?"

"We do." Judith replied.

"Objection!" Bill was out of his seat almost before Judith finished her oath. "The plaintiff has not..."

That was as far as Bill got before the judge spoke. "Silence! Mr. Handell, I will not tolerate jury speeches with objections. You will both approach the bench in a moment. First, however, Mrs. Hoople, will you kindly step up and be seated in the witness box?"

Judith complied.

"Now, both of you gentlemen approach the bench."

As we approached the bench, I smiled. Mutt and Jeff. Short and tall. Both of us dressed in similar blue pin stripes, red ties, and wing tip shoes. The jury probably thought we both had the same tailor. Maybe we did. Hell, I don't know. I'd have to ask Richard sometime.

"Now, Mr. Handell, what can be so important as to rile you up this early in the trial? She hasn't even begun to testify yet?"

"Your Honor, this was an improper swearing in. Mrs. Hoople is being sworn in, a single person. The correct answer is "I do", not "we do". This is just a crazy stunt of hers to gain attention to this phony psychic business. It is improper."

"Interesting observation. Mr. Newton?"

"Your Honor, Mrs. Hoople has a *bona fide* documented psychotic condition that is in total juxtaposition with Mr. Handell's position. She has more than one person in her psyche. Her oath binds all the words that flow from her lips, regardless of which personality is speaking. That is a far more binding and appropriate oath response than the one Mr. Handell suggests. This is a unique case Your Honor. If only Judith Hoople, in that form, swore to the oath, and one of the other alters spoke in response to a question, would she be bound? Or, if one of the alters spoke up and did not tell the truth, would that be perjury if they were not bound by the individual oath? Her current answer binds them all: no tricks, no excuses. In this unique case, that is the appropriate response."

"Since neither of you has any case law to support your arguments, I will treat this as a case of first impression. First, I will ask the witness what she means by her answer."

He turned to Judith. "Mrs. Hoople, when you answered under oath that we would tell the truth, to whom were you referring?"

"All of us, Your Honor. Myself and the various alters."

"Thank you. The oath will stand as taken and recorded. I'll hear no more argument on the subject. Back to your places, gentlemen. Continue, Mr. Newton."

"Would you tell the jury your full name, please?"

"My name is Judith Amanda Hoople."

"How old are you, Mrs. Hoople?"

"Thirty-five."

"And your address?"

"6214 Beechnut Street, Tampa Florida."

I spent about ten minutes on the easy, non-contentious questions, old addresses, jobs, etc. I wanted to get Judith to relax and get into the flow of questions and answers. She was doing well, but I knew that it would get rough soon enough.

Judith had worn an attractive pant-suit, feminine and nice. Nothing that might distract the jury from her testimony. Soft shoes, low heels; sensible. I wanted to be sure she didn't trip on the way to the witness stand. I learned that lesson years before.

"Judith, I need to ask you about your early childhood. Will you be able to answer my questions in your present form or will you need to switch?"

I had already told Judith that under no circumstances was she to switch personalities, unless I instructed her to do so, and that was not going to happen. I would just let the jury wonder. Switching was far too risky. If I changed my mind I would let her know beforehand, and I had no intentions of doing so.

"No, over the last few months, with Dr. Trey's help, I've become able to handle a lot. I think I can handle it."

"O.K. If it gets to hard to handle, just let me know.

"Judith, tell the jury of your earliest childhood recollection."

Judith sat there for a moment as if composing herself for an ordeal of fire.

The Jury was intent and every juror's eyes were riveted on Judith. It was as if the whole courtroom was holding its breath. A collective suspense.

Judith leaned into the microphone, looked straight at the jurors and, in a husky voice, began. "Thrusting. Pain. Rough hands. A crib. I am on my back as rough hands hold me and pull at my diapers. One hand on my chest, holding me, pushing me into the mattress, while the other hand pulls at my diapers. Thrusting. The diapers come off and then rough fingers on my thighs. Hands that wrap completely around my legs. The diaper comes off, then fingers, or thumbs, I don't know, between my legs, pulling me apart. Hurting.

"I am crying; no, screaming. Scared. I can smell his body. No longer a safe smell. Body odor and alcohol. Harsh. Then a white hot, searing pain explodes between my legs, filling me with intense agony."

Judith's voice was only a hoarse whisper now, but no one missed a word. There was absolute silence in the courtroom. The only noise was Judith's agonizing, hoarse whisper.

"Then a slight withdrawal, and then more pain. More pain as he begins to thrust himself into me. Harder and harder. Blinding flashes of pain. Endless.

"Suddenly he pulls me further into him, allowing him to push himself deeper into me, while at the same time placing the rail of the crib under the small of my back. The pain was unbearable. I scream, clenching and unclenching my hands, waving them everywhere."

Tears were flowing slowly and steadily down Judith's face as she continued with her story. Her voice unwavering, soft, husky and yet intense.

"Then peace comes over me. I become as an observer. Not exactly gone, but no longer in pain. Father finished, lying on top of me for a moment, then pulling out."

"That's all I remember of the first episode."

"Who took care of cleaning you up? Pulling up the crib rail or tending to your needs when he finished?"

"I'm not really sure. I have a vague recollection of, or awareness of, it possibly being my mother, but I can't really say."

"Was that the only such incident?"

"No, it became a routine thing. It lasted for a long time."

"Were there any changes in the routine?"

"Yes. After a while. I remember he was thrusting. Thrusting. The pain wasn't as bad now, but still there. Then he pulled out of me, picked me up and rolled me over on my stomach. I remember my face hitting the mattress. Then more pain than ever before. This time it felt like my insides were tearing completely apart. He kept shoving further and further inside me. Then he began to withdraw, then back in, further. More and more. The pain was too much to bear, and then, all at once it went away and I was an observer again. Oh, he was still going on, but there was no more pain. I actually felt as though I was watching my little body being jerked around by this big man and it was all happening to someone else. Not me. Then, as before, it was over."

"Did this type of assault occur again?"

"Yes, many times."

"How long did this go on?"

"It seemed like forever." Judith leaned back, wiping her face with a tissue the clerk had handed her.

Judge Midder glanced at his watch. Judith had been on the stand over an hour. "I know it's a bit early, but I think this would be a good time for a break. We'll recess for fifteen minutes."

"All rise." The bailiff intoned. "Court is now in recess."

I watched as the jury filed out and noticed tears in the eyes of several of the jurors. As soon as they were all out of the courtroom, I helped Judith off the stand and let her know she was doing a good job. Then, we took a break also.

* * * *

Back on the stand, Judith looked composed.

"Judith. Can you tell the jury how long this treatment by your father went on?"

"No. I thought about it over the break, but I can't think of it in a relative time frame. I don't know how long, only that it happened several times."

"O.K. Tell me, what is your next childhood recollection?"

"Oh, we had some happy times. I remember my fifth birthday party. I remember ribbons, bows, presents and cake and ice cream. Lots of other kids, too."

"Any particular present come to mind?"

"No, just presents. Pretty packages with bright paper, bows and ribbons, that sort of thing."

"I remember Easter, going to Grandma's for an Easter egg hunt and a big lunch with ham. Pretty dresses and new shoes. And candy, lots of candy.

"I remember hiding an egg in my closet. It was real pretty and I wanted to save it. I forgot about it and after a while it began to stink. When mama found it she was pretty mad. She scolded me good."

"Are there any more not so pleasant things you remember about that time?"

"Yes. Red and white. White sheets over a big table. Candles and a man in a red robe."

Once more her voice lowered and became husky.

"I now know that he was some sort of high priest of a satanic cult. He was real big. Not just tall, but fat too."

You could see that Judith was trying to recall. Her face was tense and her look was one of concentration, and fear.

"What else, Judith?"

"It was in an old building in a run down shopping center in Miami. It was all locked up and dark. The only lights were candles. Mommy and daddy would park a block away in a seedy movie parking lot. We would walk to the storefront. They always dressed me the same. A little short pullover skirt, panties and sandals. I hated that dress.

"When we got there everyone would hug and kiss a lot. Always whispering, touching me and feeling me all over. Daddy would make me pull off the dress and sandals, putting them in a chair. Then, for a while, I would walk around in my panties.

"There were other kids too. Usually four to six of us. Boys too, not just girls. Then everyone would start humming. Just mmmmmmmm, that sort of thing. The priest would fill the goblet with wine and everyone would drink from it. Then he would urinate in it and re-fill it with wine. The priest would splash it on the altar and then over us kids.

"Then the people would put on their robes, men in black and women in white, no clothes under the robes. They would take off the rest of our clothes; the kids I mean. All of our underwear. There were cots with sheets on them and they would make us kids lie down on them, naked. Then the priest would pour the wine mixture over us. Then the adults would have sex with the kids. The priest usually took me first, but the adults would mix around with each other and then with all the kids."

Judith was back down to a whisper now, her husky voice literally breathing into the microphone. Her eyes were not actually crying, just tearful, sad. Like an embarrassed child recalling something truly shameful.

"It seemed to go on for a long time, but it probably only lasted an hour or two."

I knew that even though she thought she knew everything the alters knew, Judith herself did not know the real extent of what had gone on in the storefront. Dr. Lofton had told me that Judith was only able to remember small segments of most of her traumatic episodes. But that was enough. No way was I going to call up any of Judith's alters. No way.

"Was it painful?"

"Yes, but not like earlier. Not like when daddy took me in the crib. It hurt, but I also remember the stink and the nastiness. They would pour the wine and urine on us, calling it the blood of the universe. Then when the men would mount me their sweat and body odor would mix with the wine. Sometimes they would spill themselves on me and mix it too. It was gross, nasty. Just nasty and stinky. I would feel dirty for days."

Judith began to weep, now. Her shoulders shaking as the memories flooded her senses, slamming into her consciousness.

Without being asked, the clerk handed Judith a box of tissues and a glass of water.

Judith nodded her thanks and blew her nose.

The jurors wore mixed expressions of disgust and pity. Most of them had wet eyes, and jurors number four and six wept openly.

Bill Handell had a tight smile on his face, clearly wishing this part were over, but knowing he could do nothing but wait it out.

After a moment, I continued.

"How long did these meetings continue, Judith?"

"Several months, maybe a year or more. I can't really be sure. Then one day when we went there the place was burned to the ground. Mommy and daddy took one look and we almost ran back to the car. We never went back. I don't know what happened to the group, but my dad never touched me again in a sexual way after that day. Never."

"Was there anyone else touching you that way, in your childhood?"

"Yes, my uncle Bob, my father's brother. For a while he came to the house after I got out of school. I was in the first grade. He had been my favorite relative, always playing with me and bringing me presents. He would hold them behind his back and make me guess which hand they were in.

"Then he became just like the others. He hurt me. Not as bad as the others, but he hurt me. For a couple weeks he had sex with me after school, when we were alone. He made me promise not to tell, or something bad would happen to me.

"Then one day mama came home early and caught him. They had a talk and he left and it never happened again. He never did that again."

I bit my tongue to keep from letting out a smart remark about her protective parent.

Judge Midder looked at me and said, "Counselor, if this is a convenient stopping point for you, I think it is about time for lunch?"

"Certainly, Your Honor, it's as good a time as any."

"Ladies and gentlemen. It's only 11:30 and I normally go till noon, but this has been an unusually tense morning, I think you will all agree. The court will allow a longer lunch break than normal, today. Court will be in recess until 1:15."

"All rise," the bailiff stated.

Judge Midder exited the courtroom and the bailiff took the jurors out through the jury room.

I turned around and caught Bill looking at Judith with undisguised contempt. As I looked at him, Bill saw me and carefully put his tight little smile back on, nodded to me, and escorted his client from the courtroom. Tim Snead looked pale and somewhat shaken. He looked like he needed a drink.

* * * *

Over lunch I talked to Judith, assuring her she was doing fine. I had Joe order sandwiches brought to the office. Judge Midder had given us plenty of time and my runner would drive us back to the courtroom. My office was a place the press could not get in, and it was also away from accidental contact with the jury.

When Judith went to the restroom, I talked to Joe.

"It's going well, boss. The jury was eating her up. The only one who seemed skeptical was Bill Handell. Even the Judge had tears in his eyes. I saw Tim Snead blow his nose three times!"

"Yeah, I think so too. And that scares the hell out of me. I don't want to get overconfident. We've still got a long way to go. I intended to move much faster than this, but Judith seems to have developed her own pace. I don't want to push her. She's doing too well right now to try to change. However, we may not finish by tonight. We'll see how it goes. I'll try to make sure we leave the jury with plenty to think about tonight."

Just then Julie came in.

"Boss, I hate to interrupt you, but this is important."

"Go ahead, we've got some time. What's up?"

"Mike Bilmore called from the U.S. Claims Court. He's ready to concede liability in Ashcroft, and wants to get with you to schedule a hearing on damages."

I'll have to get a life care report drawn up. Then, submit it to Mike. Then the justice department will have their own plan drawn up, then hearing and compromise, etc. etc.

"Julie. Call Mike back and tell him we'll have our report to him in three weeks. Ask him to prepare a joint stipulation on liability and set it for a hearing with the Special Master, A.S.A.P. Then let him pick a time for a hearing on damages. Tell him he's welcome to tell the Special Master that our courtroom is available for the hearing. Tell him I'm sorry I can't get back to him personally, but I'm in the middle of a trial. He'll understand."

"You want me to go ahead and get the info over to Watson, Boss?"

Tom Watson was our primary life care planner in these vaccine cases. Usually, you had to wait for an order from the Special Master before hiring the life care planner. If you ordered it on your own and liability was denied, you would have to eat the cost yourself. However, since Mike was conceding liability, it would present no problem.

"Yes, put it all together for him. Medicals, mother's statement, petition and the video of the child. Tell him it's not a rush, but not to drag his heels on it either."

"You got it. Anything else?"

"Nope. Just hold down the fort while we are in court."

* * * *

Back in court, Judith took the stand and I moved back to the podium. I had no notes, just my checklist back on the top of the counsel table.

"All rise."

Judge Midder entered the courtroom and nodded to the bailiff.

"Court is now in session, the Honorable Judge Julius Midder presiding. You may be seated."

"Good afternoon, Mrs. Hoople, counsel. I trust you had a good lunch break and are ready to proceed?"

"Yes, Your Honor." I said.

"One thing, Your Honor," Bill said. "I realize this may seem a bit cold, but if Your Honor would instruct the witness to back off on the theatrics a bit, we could move forward a lot faster."

Judge Midder's face turned bright crimson. Before I could even object to Bill's self-serving statement, the judge waved me down as his eyes narrowed as he glared at Bill Handell.

"Mr. Handell. This Court is satisfied that the witness is doing a good job considering the testimony she has had to endure. I assure you that the Court is well aware of what goes on in this courtroom and if I see anything resembling theatrics, I will address the problem. Meanwhile, Mr. Handell, you would be well advised to watch your comments. You are extremely close to contempt with that last remark. Do I make myself clear?"

"Yes, Your Honor." Bill said, looking not at all apologetic.

"Very well, bring in the jury."

As the jury filed in, I noticed that all of them looked at Judith with respect, and some with a touch of pity.

"Good afternoon, ladies and gentlemen. Did everyone get enough to eat?" Judge Midder had a smile on his face as a few of the jurors rolled their eyes.

All nodded affirmatively.

"Then we will resume where we left off. Mr. Newton, you may proceed."

"Thank you, Your Honor."

"Mrs. Hooper. We were talking about your childhood in Miami. Now I have a question to help clear things up a bit. Up to the points that we have covered, were you aware of these things as you were growing up? I mean, in your childhood and early teens?"

"Not in the normal sense of awareness, no sir."

"How did you live, or function? At least as far as anyone else knew?"

"Well, I think that for all intents and purposes, I was a normal child. You see, I had no recollections of these happenings. Even my early onset of periods did not surprise anyone, because of the rape."

"What rape is that, Mrs. Hoople?"

"I was in grade school, almost eight years old. I walked home from school every day. It was about twelve blocks to my house from school. The neighborhood wasn't too bad and I knew all the corners to cross on. Most had crossing lights and some even had school crossing guards."

"Exactly what happened?"

Judith sat straighter, now. Her body was tensing up as the memories came back.

In a strong voice, she continued. "I was walking home in the afternoon. About half way home, on a corner of the block was a liquor store. It always had some rough looking people around, but usually there was a crossing guard there and no one ever tried anything. I just scooted through, keeping a steady pace.

"This time there was no crossing guard. But the liquor store seemed deserted. I walked on by, but as I walked to the corner of the store, where the ally led into the parking lot and through the block, a man reached out and grabbed my arm. He scared me, bad. He was so nasty."

Judith had slowed down, and now seemed to fall back into herself, like a child who is afraid in a confrontation with an adult. I prodded her along. "What else, Judith?"

She continued, her voice once again falling into that low, throaty hoarse sound. "He had on a raggedy old long sleeve shirt and a pair of dirty pants that were held up by a piece of rope.

"He was so dirty. He had a beard and long filthy hair. His fingernails were long and yellow, and they were biting into my arm. He had real bad body odor."

Judith continued in her near whisper. Although she was looking at the jury, she gave the appearance of looking inward, at her inner self. "His face was splotchy and he was missing several teeth. When he spoke to me his breath smelled of liquor and rot.

"He was big, real big. I couldn't have weighed over 40 or 45 pounds.

"He yanked me behind the store, almost dragging me. I couldn't do anything. He had his other hand over my mouth.

"There was a trash dumpster behind the store with a hedge behind it. He pulled me back there, between the dumpster and the hedge.

"I had on a white blouse and a pleated skirt. He pulled up my skirt and ripped my panties off. Then he pulled the rope and his pants fell down. He was not wearing any underwear. He was already hard. He was huge.

"He pulled my legs apart and raped me. He hurt me bad. Real bad."

Judith's voice was faltering, now. In her mind the stinking wino was lunging at her all over again. Her voice although husky, was almost childlike as she continued:

"It felt like he was tearing me up, inside. With each thrust he kept tearing into me. Nothing before or since has ever hurt me like that. He didn't care that I was sobbing through his filthy hand. He just stared at me. Leering and drooling on me. He was raised up on me, with a lot of pressure on my mouth with one hand and his arm across my chest, his elbow jamming into my left rib cage and arm. I remember his drool kept falling in my face, and up my nose a couple times.

"I gagged into his hand but he held on so tight that I couldn't vomit, I just choked it back, along with my screams that wouldn't come out either.

"Finally, he finished. He wiped himself off on my shirt. He removed his hand and told me that if I hollered he would hurt me worse. Then he tied his pants back up and left. He was smiling and had a weird, sharp giggle. High pitched, like an ally cat. He didn't even run. Just shuffled off.

"I lay there for a while, all bloody and hurt. I vomited until nothing would come up, but I couldn't stop for a long time. I was ashamed. I wanted to die. I did not know much about God, but I wondered why he wouldn't take me away.

"After a while the pain subsided. My panties were torn and my dress was all bloody and slimy. In a daze, I walked back to the front of the store. The manager saw me and ran out to me."

"What happened then?" I asked.

"When I told him what happened, he called the police. The police and an ambulance came. The store man gave me a cold soda to rinse out my mouth with, and drink. But he wouldn't let me wash. He kept saying the police needed to see me just like I was.

"It was a nightmare. The police. The ambulance people. Everyone was nice, but they just kept asking the same questions. Then the doctor put things inside me, then finally cleaned me up. They gave me stitches, inside, internal, as well as external. Then my mother took me home."

Judith took a drink of water and a deep breath. Judge Midder asked if she needed a break, but she declined.

"What happened then, Judith?"

"They sent me to a psychiatrist. By the second time I went to him, the only thing I remembered was the liquor store. I knew it was a bad place."

"After a few more sessions the psyche said I had amnesia and it was just as well. He called it selective, protective amnesia. Whatever that really meant."

"O.K. Judith. Were there any other incidences as a child?"

"No. Not as a child, not real young."

"How about later?"

"Yes, when I was 15."

"Tell us about that incident."

"We were still in Miami, but we had moved to the south side. I had just turned 15 and was in junior high. I was riding my bike home after cheerleading practice. I had on my cheerleading jersey and shirt with the matching overpants.

"A man pulled out of a side street right in front of me. I braked hard, but still hit him and fell off my bike. I was scratched up a little, but not hurt bad.

"The man kept saying, over and over, how sorry he was. He insisted on taking me home. My front wheel was bent out of shape, so I agreed to let him take me home.

"He put my bike in the trunk and we headed home. However, he didn't go to my house. He said he had a quick stop to make on the way. Then he pulled into an ally behind some abandoned homes. He pulled out a long knife and told me to get in the back seat. He said we could do it the easy way or the hard way: my choice.

"He shoved me into the back seat and I pulled off my jersey and was working on my bra when he got too impatient. He put the knife under my chin and grabbed the overpants and my panties and pulled them down, tearing them as he did so.

"When he took me, I still had on my sneakers. He was rough, but he did not hurt me bad. Not like the other big men. I just lay there, staring at the roof of the car praying, "God, Please don't let him cut me.

"When he finished, he pulled up his pants and helped me out of the car. "While I was putting my clothes back on, he took my bike out of the trunk, taking an oily rag and wiping it down.

"Then he told me he bet I never had it so good, and he laughed. Then he said, "See you around," and he left."

"What did you do after that?"

"Well, I knew about where I was, so I pushed and pulled the bike till I got home. No one was home, so I went in and washed. I showered until there was no hot water left, and still stayed in. I douched three times. I just felt so violated. At that time I had no recollection of the other problems, so it was all new.

"When mama got home I told her what happened. She was real mad that I had showered and douched. She called the cops and they took a statement. Since I had erased the evidence, and I did not have a tag number or anything except a description that would fit thousands of Hispanics in the Miami area, they didn't even bother to take me in to the station.

"To the best of my knowledge, nothing was ever done about it. Over time I just quit thinking about it. I got on with my life, especially once we were sure I was not pregnant."

"Counselor, it is 3:30. Let's take a 15 minute recess."

"All rise, court is now in recess."

* * * *

The break was uneventful and I quickly resumed questioning when we got back. I had a breaking time frame in mind for the evening recess, and I needed to get there. Judge Midder wouldn't go past five.

"Judith, I want you to tell the jury about the other Judith. Not the person you know. Not the one with all the pain and problems you go through each day, but the Judith your kids love and your friends knew before your current problems. The normal Judith, if you will.

"Begin with high school. Did you complete it?"

"Oh yes, I liked school. I was a cheerleader my last four years of junior high and high school. I was also in the school newspaper and we were the ones who set up the newspaper and the annual. I was also good at gymnastics and I graduated with honors."

"After you graduated from high school, did you get any additional education?"

"Yes, I enrolled in Miami-Dade Community College. I took the mandatory generic courses, and also emphasized media courses and psychology/social courses. I wanted to be a T.V. reporter or a newscaster."

"Did you finish college?"

"I received an A.A. degree from Miami-Dade, but I never went further than that. That's when I met my husband to be, David Hoople."

"Tell the jury of your relationship with David."

"He was an airline mechanic. He worked for Delta Air Lines at Miami International Airport. He was taking some night classes at Miami-Dade, and I met him there. Some of my classes were evening classes, too. We were in English Lit when we met.

"We talked a lot and after about a month, well really, twenty eight days later, he asked me out. He was kind of shy, and I liked him a lot. We dated for about eight months, and then I graduated. He asked me to marry him, and I said yes.

"Ten months later, Lorna was born."

"Tell the jury about Lorna, Judith."

"She was a beautiful baby. Big, deep green eyes and curly hair. Cute as a button. We adored her. Dave couldn't wait to get home to play with her. He would hold her a lot, even while he ate supper, or watched T.V.

"We were a happy trio. Lots of love." This last was said very wistfully.

"Did you go back to school again?" I asked this while looking to see how the jurors were reacting to the other side of Judith. I liked what I saw.

"I had intended to, but I didn't get around to it. Money was a little tight and I would have needed a part time job if I went back to college. That, plus school and studies would have been too much time away from David and Lorna. So, at that time I was essentially a housewife and mother."

"How long did you stay in Miami?"

"We were happy in Miami. And probably would have stayed there forever, but Delta needed Dave in Tampa. They offered a nice raise and paid our moving expenses, so, Tampa was our new home. This was two years after we were married. We moved into a nice little home in Town and Country and I promptly got pregnant again. Nine months later, Trish was born."

"Tell us a little about Trish, Judith."

"Trish was a happy child, also, but she wasn't as healthy as Lorna. She was colicky quite a bit of the time and had a severe case of thrush mouth. As soon as one case would heal up, another would begin. At night she cried a lot. Only because she felt bad, not because she was a problem child or anything like that." Judith was very protective in her last statement. A caring mother.

"I don't think that is what caused it, but things became strained between Dave and me. He started stopping off at the bars at night. Coming home later and later at night. We did not go out anymore on the weekends. Our happy family was becoming less happy every day. It did not seem like anything I did pleased David. We began to argue a lot. I cried a lot at night, usually by myself.

"When Trish was two, we got a divorce. It was friendly enough, as divorces go. I got the house and primary responsibility for the girls. He agreed to pay child support and house payments. He had joint custody. After we were separated for a while, ever so slowly, David and I became friends again.

"It was funny. For the first few weeks, he didn't come around much. Then, he started spending more and more time with the girls. Especially when I got my first job."

"What was your first job?"

"I went to work as a part time news reporter, a very junior reporter, with T.V. 8 News Room. I did community interest items, things like that.

"I really was excited about it. I just knew this was a fun way to work. I could picture myself as the first female Walter Cronkite, you know. 'And that's the way it is,'" Judith said with a smile.

I quickly glanced at the jurors and they were smiling too. A good sign.

"It was a good assignment. I was home most of the time. I would go into the station two or three mornings a week, get my assignments and report when necessary. I was given a base salary, with extra pay which depended upon the number of assignments. However, no insurance. It really wasn't enough money, either, but it was a help, and fun. Dave pitched in when he could, to reduce the babysitting cost. The girls were too young to stay by themselves."

I glanced at my watch. It was getting close to five and I knew Judge Midder wasn't going to allow us to continue much longer. I wanted to get the issue of the Crisis Center in before the jury was sent home. A connecting hook between her early miseries and the later problems in Judith's life. Oh well. When all else fails, use the direct approach.

"Judith, how did you become involved with Hillsborough Community Crisis Center?"

"Actually, it was through an assignment by T.V. 8. I was sent to do a story on the Crisis Hot Line.

"As a part of their community relations program, T.V. 10 spotlights various help agencies throughout the year. I was sent to do a story on the crisis hotline at the Center.

"While doing the story, I became really interested in their work. It just seemed so right. I knew that with a little training, I could be one of the people on the end of that phone line. I could help. *I knew it.* So, I looked into getting a job with them."

"You were given a job, then?"

"Yes, I got the job as a phone crisis counselor; however, I was told it would be up to me to learn and observe for a while before I could actually work the phones. Then I would be tightly supervised until I was given my certification. Then, I would be on my own.

"The first day I reported to work, I met Red Greely, the man who was to ruin my life."

"Counselor, it is now five after five. I think this is as good a time as any to break for the day," Judge Midder broke in.

I choked back a smile. "Yes, Your Honor."

Actually, this is a perfect time for a break.

"Ladies and gentlemen of the jury, I am about to send you home for the evening. I hope this has not been too trying a day for you. I remind you that you are to speak to no one about this case. Not your husband, wife, boyfriend, girlfriend, mother or anyone else. You are not to watch anything about this case on T.V., nor listen about it on the radio nor read about it in the paper. If anyone approaches you about this case you tell them you can't discuss it. It they insist, you report it to me."

"I am sorry for this imposition, but it is better than sequestration. You are all honor bound upon your oath to follow these instructions. It is your duty. I don't think I need remind you of the consequences were you to deliberately disobey these orders."

"Does anyone have any questions?"

All the jurors nodded negatively.

"Very well then. I have a couple hearings in the morning, one at eight and one at 8:30. We will begin at 9:00 A.M. Please check in here promptly at 8:45 with the bailiff. Court is now adjourned."

"All rise." As soon as the judge departed, the bailiff continued: "Court will be in recess until 9:00 A.M. tomorrow morning. Ladies and gentlemen of the jury, please be good enough to come with me into the jury room where I will collect your badges."

Judith, the girls, Joe and I remained until the jury left the courtroom. Then I used the clerk's phone to call my office and have the runner bring the car around to the back of the courthouse to pick us up.

Before we got out, though, Judge Midder came back into the courtroom and called Bill and me up to the bench.

"Gentlemen. I suspect that after that testimony today, the press will be eager indeed to hear from each of you. However, I do not want this case to be tried in the media any more than necessary. Therefore, I am enjoining you from discussing this case with the press, from this moment until we have a verdict. Feel free to tell them that I have prohibited you from commenting, but that is all you are free to say about this case. Do I make myself clear?"

"Yes, Your Honor." Bill and I parroted.

"Good. I'll see you both at nine tomorrow. Good evening, gentlemen."

"Good evening, Your Honor," we responded in unison.

As I joined the girls I said, "The judge just did us a favor. He placed a gag order on Bill and me, and of course that includes you as well. If the press wants to use anything at all, it will have to be from your testimony, Judith.

"Now, let's get out of here." I grabbed the briefcases, which Joe had already packed and we walked out of the courtroom. For just a moment, I once again saw the look of disdain on Bills face. When he noticed me looking at him, he wiped it off and replaced it with his tight smile.

Bill really has a case going against Judith. Well, he better damn well get rid of it. I'm getting tired of his attitude.

Outside the courtroom, the hall was packed with the press. I raised my hands and held them up until everyone quieted down.

"Ladies and gentlemen. I had quite a speech prepared and was ready to spend an hour or two with you." With this last, the press members rolled their eyes, recognizing the bold-faced lie for what it was. I continued. "But, Judge Midder has placed a gag order on both myself and Mr. Handell."

More rolling of the eyes and several groans as the press reacted to the news.

"So, I'm sorry. But all I can say is, 'No Comment.'"

I took Judith and Joe in tow and we pushed ourselves through the crowd and down stairs to the rear exit where my car was waiting for us.

Back at the office, I spent about an hour with Judith and Joe.

Julie stepped in the library and told me everything had gone well with the Ashcroft case and the damage hearing was set. She had also set a hearing in federal court on the Honda case, as per court instructions. Then she asked me how this case was going.

"At this point, it has been almost too smooth. You know me; I get worried when things go too well. The jury is listening carefully. No one has fallen asleep. No one looks overly incredulous. The only real mystery is Bill Handell. He really seems to be taking this thing personally. I have never seen him act this antagonistic before on a case."

Julie patted me on the shoulder saying: "Well, I'm sure you can handle him. Sounds like things are going O. K. See you tomorrow, Boss."

"Good night. See you tomorrow. Have a good evening."

I turned back to Judith: "I know we have a hell of a lot of testimony left, but I'm not sure if we have a full day's worth, or not. How do you feel about what you've done so far?"

"As far as my testimony, I feel pretty good. I'm considerably more confident now than I was before we started. But how do you feel about it? I mean, really?"

"As I told Julie, I think you are doing fine. Hell, I haven't had to do any work yet. You're carrying the ball like a champ. We just have to keep the ball moving up court.

"Tomorrow we will get into your relationship with the Center, and the most important part of tomorrow's testimony will not even be recognized as such by the jury. Your understanding of the faith and trust the Center placed on Red. The high esteem they held him in. Your reliance on the Center for their superior knowledge of Red and his abilities and qualifications.

"Don't hold back. We need to establish, once and for all, that without the Center lauding him as they did, giving him the absolute authority that they did, you would not have allowed Red to attempt to treat you. Not for smoking discontinuance, and certainly not for M.P.D. That is the most crucial part of your testimony tomorrow."

"I understand, but what about the alters? The sex and all that?"

"That is also important, but it doesn't do any good to vilify Red, no matter how he earned it, if we can't also bring in the Center with him. Let's face it. If HCCC. had done a half way decent job of investigating Red before enthroning him as their chief guru, they would have insisted he carry a better insurance policy. It is unconscionable of them to allow a man who has such a position of trust to be able to ruin someone's life and have no liability beyond twenty-five thousand dollars. That's just plain wrong."

"I understand. It's just that sometimes I get so upset with Red and what harm he has done to me that I forget about the Center. After all, I think that they do a pretty good service. They just screwed up with Red."

"That's why it is called negligence." I told her. "It's not that they intentionally did anything against you, like Red, but that their negligence put Red in the position to do what he did to you, without making sure he would be responsible for his own actions.

"Tomorrow we will move into the Clinic right off the bat. We'll get all that out of the way before you get into Red's actual treatment and all the sexual stuff."

"O.K. I can handle it. Right now, I'm drained."

Judith looked as if she had aged ten years in the last ten minutes. I knew she was about to crash, and she needed to rest and be fresh tomorrow.

"You go on home and get a good night's rest," I told her. "David is waiting in the lobby to drive you home. Sleep well and be back here at 8:15 tomorrow morning. We'll ride to the courthouse together. O.K. with you?"

"Sounds good to me. See you both tomorrow. Goodnight." Totally exhausted, she walked through the door and off to her ex for a ride home. Funny how he still cared for her and she for him, so much. And yet, they were apart. Go figure.

Joe looked at me, a questioning look in her eyes.

"She'll be O.K." I told her. "She's just had a rough day. Speaking of which, you better get home to your hubby. We start early tomorrow."

"Gotcha, Boss. I'm on my way. You need anything else?"

"Nope. Just a little peace and quiet. I'll sleep well tonight."

"Yeah, right." Joe rolled her eyes and made a face. She knew me well enough to know that was a load of malarkey.

"See you in the morning."

"Good night, Joe. See you then."

I went back to my office, taking a small glass of ice with me. I poured a double Crown Royal over the ice and sipped it while I sifted through the mail. Terry had made sure it was all opened, in order of importance. Three of them had little yellow stickies on them with particular notes for my immediate attention.

Terry was my bookkeeper, office manager and friend. She was a dream come true. She was a hard worker and completely loyal. God had really blessed me with a good crew, I mused as I riffled through the mail.

I finished the mail and poured a final Crown Royal.

Judith was as good as I could expect. But there is still a lot she does not know about herself. Only Red and Dr. Lofton, and through them, me, know how depraved Judith had really been treated. She is by no means well enough and able to know and accept all the truth. In a way, I wish I could have been there while she was in deep hypnosis with Lofton. He is still concerned that if she ever learns the full truth and experiences it, she will never come out of it. Probably regress to a cowed child. Damn Red Greely anyhow. Hell, now I'm getting as bad as Bill. Too personally involved. Must be the profession. Sometimes, it sucks.

CHAPTER TEN

"Good morning, Ladies and gentlemen," Judge Midder said, addressing the jury.

It was 9:20 and the jury had just been seated. Judge Midder was behind in his hearings and we were starting slightly off schedule.

"I trust you all had a good night's rest?"

The jurors nodded affirmatively.

"Now I need to know if anyone here saw, heard or discussed anything at all about this case while you were out last night."

As I watched, all the jurors nodded negatively. Juror number two, however, seemed uncomfortable with the question, casting a quick furtive glance at one of her neighbors, even while she was nodding to the judge.

She's lying, or at least being evasive.

I am well aware that jurors often discuss their cases with their spouse or read articles in the newspaper without divulging it to the court. Since the juror wasn't married, it was probably a newscast or maybe a talk with a boyfriend. Every local station, as well as court T.V. had something on about the case yesterday and last night.

It wouldn't surprise me if all the jurors had seen something about the case last night. No one lives in a vacuum, no matter what the judge tells them. Just so long as it wasn't against us.

I also knew that the jurors would discuss the case among themselves at each opportunity, again, regardless of what the court ordered. They would start, tentatively at first, one on one, then in small groups, and finally, all together. It just happens, period.

"Mr. Newton, is the plaintiff ready to proceed?"

"Yes, Your Honor. I ask Judith Hoople to resume her place on the stand."

"Mrs. Hoople, please resume your seat in the witness box. I remind you that you are still under oath."

"Yes, Your Honor," Judith replied while stepping up and in to the witness box.

She looked at the judge and nodded slightly, just as I had instructed her to. Then, on cue, she looked at each juror with a somewhat tremulous smile. I had spent quite a bit of time with Judith in my own courtroom, going over the courtroom mannerisms which I expected her to use. One thing I had taught her was never to look a juror in the eye, but instead, just above the eyes, the bottom of the forehead. That way it would appear to each person that she was looking directly at them, but she would not be distracted by direct eye contact, nor get pulled into one of those *who turns away first* type of deals.

"Mrs. Hoople, yesterday you had begun to tell the jury about your employment with Hillsborough Community Crisis Center. Let's return to that discussion.

"Nuts and bolts, how did you come to be employed at the Center?"

"Well, as I said yesterday, I first went there on assignment. I was impressed with the type work they did. They were an independent agency, catering to the needs of women in trouble. Oh, I guess there was an occasional man, but mostly women.

"After the story was finished, I came back to the Center. The very next day, in fact. I inquired as to employment as a phone counselor, and was given an employment form to fill out. It was extensive, so I took it home so I could verify dates, addresses, that sort of thing."

"Let me stop you here. The application, did it contain any questions regarding past sexual or physical assaults?"

"Yes, it had a section where it asked for any sexual assaults or physical violence, spousal abuse or otherwise, including any rape experiences."

"And what was your response to those questions?"

"At that time, the only assault that I was aware of was the rape that occurred in the vehicle, in the alleyway behind the deserted old houses. It was only a vague recollection, more like a bad date sort of thing than what it really was. I wasn't even sure it was a rape."

Judith stopped and sort of shivered, then continued. "I had no recollection of any other sexual abuse."

"Not even the rape at the liquor store, the one that had the police report written up for documentation?"

"No. Not even that. It was completely gone from my mind."

"O.K. After filling out the application, then what?"

"Well, I took it back to the center and was told that they would review the application and get back to me for an appointment with the personal director, if they wanted to proceed further with my prospective employment. If not, I would be notified within a week.

"The next day I got a call to set up an appointment. I went down and met with Steve Robinson, the personnel director. He remembered me from the T.V. interview, and we had a very pleasant conversation. He was mainly concerned with my lack of experience, but he conceded that my reporting experience and my own 'date rape' would go a long way toward helping me understand and counsel others in trouble.

"He hired me on the spot.

"I was then introduced to the office manager, Jeanie, and she got all the pertinent information for my employment out of the way. She told me that the Center operated in three shifts, and that I would start out by monitoring the heaviest shift, the night shift.

"Jeanie introduced me to everyone who was there, many of whom I had already met because of the T.V. interviews. Most of them were surprised to learn that I was only part time with the station and would be working full time with them. Kind of like surprised that I was a real person too, like them."

"And did you meet Red Greely at this time?"

"Yes, he was across the hall in a counseling room, standing in front of and talking with the Director and two other counselors. This was a group counseling room, one of four large counseling rooms at the Center.

"Jeanie introduced me to all four of the men, first the Director, then Red, then the others. When she finished the introductions, the Director told me how happy he was that a person as bright, outgoing and openly friendly as I was would be working with his 'team.' He told me to think of the Center as one big family, and if I ever had a problem, he or Dr. Greely would always be available to help. Of course, he said, the others were there for me and each other also, but if it was something they couldn't handle, he or Red would make sure it was taken care of."

"Was there any hesitation or reservation in his remarks about Red?"

"Absolutely none. He expressed supreme confidence in Red Greely. Dr. Greely was second only to the Director himself. I later found out that he had used Red's services himself, several times for counseling when he had family problems.

"Ben that was his name, Benjamin Ayer. He knew every mental health counselor, divorce counselor, psychiatrist, psychologist, etc. in the Bay area that was any good at all. When he needed help, he had turned to Red, and he advised others to do the same.

"The entire time I was at the Center, Red was held in the utmost esteem. He could alter or directly change Center policy if he desired. He had the authority to assign patients to other counselors. He could reassign employees at will. Most importantly, if we had any questions or problems regarding a victim or a patient, we were to go to Red. He was, without question, the ultimate authority. That was both the written and unwritten policy of the Center. When it came to operational or mental health problems, Red was God."

Unable to constrain himself any longer, and knowing that Judith had a good flow going and was clearly in control and making points with the jury, Bill Handell had to try and break up the flow.

"Objection, Your Honor, this is clearly repetition—"

Cutting him off in mid sentence, Judge Midder said, "Overruled, Mr. Handell. Please control yourself. Continue please, Counselor." Looking at me.

Hoping to continue the established rhythm I looked at Judith. "How did your job progress, Mrs. Hoople?"

"Well, for the first few weeks, I just monitored the incoming calls and the phone counselor's response to them. We got all kinds of calls. Suicide calls, abused wives, school kids needing help...and rape victims. Lots of rape victims. Everything from date rapes to group rapes, or gang bangs in the teenage vernacular.

"It was our task to sort them out, getting the right victim with the right phone counselor. Then, talking them through their immediate crisis. Sometimes we would access the situation and know that the police or EMT's needed to be on the scene, and we would have to find out the address or location and get them to respond while we kept the victim on the phone.

"Other times, it was a matter of getting the victim through the crisis and then having them come to the Center for counseling and follow through. Some victims wouldn't come in, but became sort of regulars, calling in once a week or so."

"It sounds like you phone counselors had a lot of responsibility on your shoulders," I said.

"Yes, sometimes it was bad. Sometimes you wondered if you had made the right choice. Sometimes a counselor did not prevent a tragedy. It would be real bad. We all really cared about the victims. If you lost one, it was bad. Real bad."

"What did you counselors do, when you lost one?"

"Go see Red. If necessary, several times until you got it straight in your mind. Red was the one we were instructed to see in any Center crisis."

"Did you ever have to see Red?"

"Not in that sense, no. But I did see him. Oh boy, did I see him."

"Counselor, I think this is a good time for a break if that is O.K. with you." Judge Midder looked at me as he glanced back from the clock.

"Yes, Your Honor. My eyes are getting a bit watery, too." Several jurors smiled at my remark and nodded in agreement.

"Let's take a 15 minute break." Judge Midder brought down his gavel and left the courtroom.

"All rise, court is now in recess." Looking at the jury, the bailiff intoned, "Please follow me."

* * * *

Well, so far so good. Judith is doing well. Good rapport with the jury. The record is now clear about Red's apparent authority.

I know Bill didn't really expect to be sustained, but I was pleased to see the way the Judge cut off his water. Zap! Didn't even let him finish. Instead of breaking up Judith's rhythm, he got her even more attendance. Any effect at all was not detrimental.

Well, the next step is the biggie.

* * * *

When court was back in session and Judith had returned to the stand, I continued in my best Perry Mason imitation.

"Mrs. Hoople, please tell the jury about your first treatments with Red. How did you approach him? How did it come about?"

"I did not approach Red. He approached me. It started when some of us got talking about quitting smoking. One of the girls brought in a newspaper article about a hypnotist who would be in Clearwater, at Ruth Eckerd Hall. For a fee, I don't remember how much, you could attend group hypnotic sessions to quit smoking.

"With my schedule, I couldn't go, nor could several of us. But a couple girls did attend, and it seemed to help them at least reduce their smoking. However, it would cost them the same amount each time they went. They were told it would take at least three or four more sessions before they would reach the final stage of total abstinence.

"Red heard about the treatments. He came to us. He offered to treat any of us who wanted to quit smoking. For free. He said that it would allow him to work on his hypnotic techniques while allowing us to become non-smokers. It seemed like the perfect solution."

"And did you begin treatment with Red?"

"Well, sure. It seemed harmless enough. After all, remember who Red Greely was. He was the chief guru. The man in charge. Why go to someone you know nothing about and pay money for a service when the man your own employers recommend is willing to give you the service for free?"

Lowering my tone and voice, I asked, "What happened when Red began treating you, Judith?"

"At first, nothing that I noticed. We would go into a private counseling room right there at the center. One of Red's favorites was a little trailer separate from the main building. Red would have me relax and he would begin talking, real low and peaceful. Next thing I knew, 15 or 20 minutes had gone and I would feel fresh and alert."

"Did you quit smoking?"

"No. At first I think I may have cut back some, especially for an hour or two after a given session. But nothing permanent."

"You mentioned that you felt refreshed after the session, was that all the time?"

"Oh, yes. At first. After number one, the next five or six sessions, I really looked forward to it. It was almost as good as taking a dip in the pool, or a fresh shower during break. It really felt good."

"You said at first, then what happened?"

"Gradually, things began to fall apart. First at the sessions, but then, at home also.

"I began to feel funny and tired at the end of the sessions. Not peppy any more. And, a couple of times after a session, my voice was not my own when I first woke up. It was kind of like looking through a cloudy window, listening to someone else talk to Red. Someone young, a little girl. It was weird. It was scary."

"What about at home?"

"I began to toss and turn a lot at night. No really sound sleep. When I did sleep, I had bad dreams. Frightening dreams. I could not remember what the dreams were about when I woke up, only that I was scared out of my wits. Sometimes I would be wet and clammy, covered with perspiration.

"I began to sleep fitfully, and later into the morning, not getting up in time to get the girls ready for school. Late for their breakfast and such. One morning, after eight or nine sessions, Lorna woke me suddenly and I heard a young girl talking to Lorna. It took me a moment to realize, it was *me*! I was the young girl talking to my daughter.

"That pretty well scared both Lorna and me. She asked if I was all right. She even wanted to know if she shouldn't stay home from school to be with me. It took a few minutes before either of us was convinced that I was O.K."

"What happened next?"

"After about the tenth session, I was really upset. I knew then that something was really wrong. I had come out of hypnosis, babbling like a little girl. I heard it. I knew it was me, but it wasn't. It was almost like I had lost complete control of my mind and body. I was an outsider, looking in.

"Red, once I was finally me again, told me we had to talk. He told me that for the last few sessions he had noticed something very peculiar about me. He said he had studied my behavior and he was now convinced that I had MPD. Multiple Personality Disorder."

"How did you react to his diagnosis, Judith?"

"I was stunned. I literally couldn't breathe. I began to hyperventilate. I think I scared Red for a moment. Once I calmed down, Red began to tell me it wasn't all that bad. Obviously, I had lived with this condition for quite some time and it would be good for me, in the long run, to learn about it and control it. He told me to think of it as a mental fever blister. It only showed up once in a while, but once you knew of it, you could control it."

"Were you consoled by his analogy?"

"Absolutely not. I was scared. I had seen the movie *Three Faces of Eve*, and I could envision another me in a slinky dress and fishnet stockings, frequenting bars and sleeping with strangers. Nightmares, on and on and on. It was horrible." Judith had begun to shake and she let out a little sob as she uttered, "horrible."

In a low soft voice, I asked her, "What happened next, Judith?"

Judith hesitated, visibly willing herself back in control.

"It took a few minutes for Red to calm me down and convince me that things would get better. I knew things were no longer O.K., but at least he offered hope that things could get better. He talked about treating me on a long time basis. He said it was necessary to get into my subconscious mind and find the root of the problem. Once he had done that, he could integrate the personalities and I would be cured.

"He actually said it as if he knew what he was talking about. I knew how much trust the Center put in him. I never even questioned him or his abilities or knowledge. If these people, who knew so much more than I did, trusted him, who was I to question him?

"He also told me that he would bill my insurance company and he would accept what they paid and waive the co-payment, meaning my part of the bill."

"Did you accept his offer?"

"I had no choice that I could see. We began sessions the next day. Actually, looking back now, I believe that Red had already started treatment, I just hadn't known about it. But we started as doctor/patient the next day. That is when he started billing my insurance carrier, and I went to his office for the first time."

"You did not treat at the Center any more?"

"Sure, sometimes. But he said it was better, when we could, to meet at his office. That way my co-workers would not know of the problem and the fact that I was in regular treatment."

"Then what happened?"

"Well, of course I was devastated. In shock. But in a couple of days, I adjusted. I just sort of accepted that I had a problem and I would have to work on it. For a while, the nightmares receded.

"Little by little I came to accept that I had several children alters. Especially, early in the morning, Judy R would be in the flesh and Lorna and Trish would be in my room, sometimes laughing and playing as I watched."

"Judith. Tell the jury what you mean by 'In the flesh,' and explain how you can watch someone else in your own body."

"Well, I'm actually getting ahead of myself a little. I did not have or know those terms back then. But I recognize them now, looking back at that time.

"'In the flesh' means exactly that, the personality that is actually in control at that time. The person in control of the body.

"'In the light' refers to the other personalities who are watching what is going on and are ready to assume control of the body if given the opportunity."

"So, when you were talking of the morning games with Judy R, and your children, that's what you meant. She had control and you were an onlooker?"

"That's right."

"O.K. now, let's get back to your treatments. What happened next?"

"Well, for several months Red explored me while I was under hypnosis. He began to converse in depth with the children alters. He told me that he had to first gain their confidence. He sure did that. He began playing with the children, little games like rocking horse on his knees and pony rides on his back."

"What happened next?"

"Well, several things happened, all in the same time frame. In talking to the children alters, Red first learned of the severe abuse I told you about earlier."

"Let me stop you for a moment. At this point, were you aware of those problems? I mean you, Judith, aware of them?"

"No, absolutely not. Even my bad dreams were not known, or remembered by me. The fact that they were horrible, that I knew. But the content, what they actually were, that I did not know."

"Continue, please."

"I began to notice things. Little things after our sessions." Judith's voice dropped at this revelation.

"Like what?"

"Oh, buttons unbuttoned on my blouse. Bra straps loosened or undone. Things like that."

"Did you say anything to Red?"

"No, not at first. I was afraid that maybe I was wrong. Maybe I was already that way, you know? I honestly did not know if I was losing my mind."

"O.K., Judith. What happened next?"

"Red told me he had been studying a new treatment to cure my problem, once and for all. He had identified several alters by now, and under hypnosis, he would call them up and have them release their knowledge to me. One by one, only in rapid succession. Like fast-forwarding a videotape. I would then be able to know and accept what had happened to me and the multiples would no longer be necessary."

"Did Red actually try this instant replay deal?"

"Yes, he did," Judith said in a very subdued voice.

"Did it work?"

"Good lord in heaven, no! I almost lost my mind.

"Oh the flooding part worked. All of a sudden the images that I had never been able to cope with came flooding into my mind. I couldn't look away. I tried to get away. I actually tried to run. I tried to scream, but I was trapped."

Judith was wide eyed now, flushed and scared, clearly upset by the memories of the episode.

"And then the pain came. The thrusting and splitting. I was on a couch in an air-conditioned office, but I was being torn apart in my mind. My insides were being pummeled and gored by an unimaginable instrument of pain. A hot searing poker was being forced into me, but it was too large to be contained by my body. I was literally being torn apart.

"Then the pain in my back. It was like a large animal had hold of the small of my back and was ripping into my backbone. Gnawing and grinding. He wouldn't stop. Wouldn't let go."

Judith paused for a breath. Sweat was heavy on her brow. Tears glistened in her eyes and her breath came in silent but noticeable gasps.

"Oh the thrusting, harder and harder. And then all of a sudden the driveling face of the wino. His putrid face, his slobber drooling on my face, his hand on my chest. The hard hurtful thrusting, over and over, on and on. Then, sticky wine all over my body. A young body, not even into puberty. A little body, but it was me. I was the one who was sticky with the smelly wine. The wino then turned into a large man in a red robe and a mustache and rotten teeth and a mean smile and more thrusting, thrusting, pain, tearing, searing pain."

Judith stopped. Tears ran freely down her face and her breathing was now nothing more than low sobs of breath.

I looked at the jury. They were all affected, stricken. Wet eyes, heads shaking.

"Counselor, I believe it is time for a break.

"Ladies and gentlemen, we will break for lunch. It is almost noon, so let's be back at 1:15 and start promptly at 1:30." So saying, Judge Midder left the courtroom.

Damn, even the judge was crying!

"All rise, court is now in recess."

* * * *

Back at the office I told Judith it was going well. I did not compliment her too much because I did not want her to get overconfident. But I tell you, even though we had been over all this numerous times in my office, today she was making me catch my breath while she was on the stand.

"Joe, call Dr. Trey and tell him we won't need him till tomorrow. Move everyone else back as well. Judith will take the rest of the day. Maybe even into tomorrow with cross."

"Sure Boss," Joe said, going to her secretary to make sure it got done.

Then we tackled our sandwiches, Judith eating sparingly and me downing mine too fast. What the hell, a man's got to eat and it had been a long morning.

* * * *

"You may proceed, Counselor."

"Thank you, Your Honor."

Judith was back on the stand and the jury was seated and ready.

"We were discussing the integration session, Judith; please tell the jury what happened as a result of this session."

"I was a total wreck. Red tried to console me, but it was impossible. My father. The man I thought I had loved and whom I thought loved me. Love. What a monstrous word. My mother, knowing what he did. It was more than I could handle. I cried and cried. I was weak and sick. I vomited several times until only dry heaves came up. I kept wiping my face. I could taste and feel the wino's drool.

"I couldn't drive home. Red spent two hours with me, trying to console me. I think he was afraid. Not for me, but for himself. Possibly for his reputation. I had to leave my car at his place. My ex came to pick me up. I couldn't even talk to him. I couldn't tell him what happened. I just sobbed and curled up in the back seat, all the way home.

"I didn't eat for two days. I didn't go back to work for a week. I lost ten pounds. I was smoking two to three packs of cigarettes a day. My back hurt all the time. Like it was in a vice.

"On the fourth day, I went all through the house to get the photos of my mother and father. I took a metal wastebasket and I sat in a chair and one by one, I burned every photo of my parents and my uncle.

"I took sleeping pills, so I could not dream. Real knockout pills. After that, I was as close to normal as I could get. Whatever normal means. I knew then and I know now that I'll never again be the same normal, happy person who first applied for a job at the Clinic. But at least I was functional again.

"I realized that I could not live the rest of my life, zonked out on sleeping pills every night and hung over the next day. So, when Red told me he thought it was time to resume treatment, I went back to him."

"What happened when you went back to Red for treatment, Judith?"

"We went back to the basics again. Red talked to the alters, playing with the kids, the same things as before the attempt at integration. It was a happier time, no confrontations. At least not until the next integration attempt."

"Tell the jury about integration attempt number two. How did that come about?"

"Once we were back, functioning reasonably well, Red told me that since the video integration concept had not worked, there was only one other primary relief available. It would not be as traumatic as the earlier attempt, but it was considered the cutting edge for the cure of MPD. He called it integration. I said 'that's what I thought we had earlier attempted,' and he said 'no, that was the goal, not the treatment.' This was the actual treatment for integration."

"Did Red explain what he meant to do to you?"

"Yes. I know I must have looked puzzled. He explained that he would take the most hard suffering of the alters and integrate them into my core personality. This would be done under hypnosis. Since I already knew what their problems were, I could absorb them all and feel nothing.

"It sounded too good to be true, but Red insisted. More than that, he was adamant. He even had a book he said was on point that explained all of what I had to go through to be cured.

"At this point, Red was the only hope I had. I was completely dependent upon him. I agreed to go through with the treatment. Had I known that the last video integration treatment was nothing but an attempt by Red to use me as a guinea pig to try to get a name for himself as having invented a new treatment form, I would have walked away right then. No, ran away. But, as I said, he was all I knew and I depended on his knowledge.

"Red began the process, all under hypnosis. I still don't know exactly what transpired, but soon I could not get around. I was in constant back pain. Severe. Pretty quick I needed a walker to get around. I thought I was coming down with muscular dystrophy. At first I did not associate it with Red's therapy.

"Red sent me to a medical doctor to get some pain medication, and a complete physical."

"What was the result of the medical examination?"

"I had some muscle spasms of unknown cause, but that was the only physical problem. I was prescribed some pain medication and muscle relaxers, but they did little good. I was soon in a wheel chair. That lasted a couple weeks.

"Eventually Red realized that he had actually allowed the initial alter, the child whom my father repeatedly raped, and who was virtually crippled, to become the dominant physical personality. She had a major role in our lives, all day long. It was an impossible arrangement.

"I don't know the details because all of this therapy was conducted while I was under deep hypnosis. But Red must have begun to reverse his treatment, because after a couple of months, I was able to resume walking without aid. I literally threw the walker out. I was so scared. I thought that if I kept it around, I would revert back to needing it. It was awful."

"Judith, have you ever fully recovered from Red's treatment?"

"Absolutely not. I have been told it will take years, if ever, before I can expect to be normal, whatever that is."

"What happened next, in your treatment by Red?"

"We continued treatment, and things got a little better. Then one day I realized that I was not imagining that things were happening under hypnosis."

"How is that?"

"Something must have happened to bring me out of the trance before Red was ready. I just woke up quickly and there I was. Sitting on his knee. My right hand was around his neck, over his shoulder. My left hand was in his lap. My blouse was open and my brassiere was pulled down over my left breast. Red was still clothed, but obviously aroused.

"I stood up and began to pull myself back together, buttoning up, *etcetera.* Red turned away from me and quickly got behind his desk so that his arousal was hidden.

"Red then made a comment about Judy R being a naughty little girl."

"It was a turning point in our relationship. I no longer trusted him as I had before. But at the same time, he was the primary focal point in my life. I could not imagine living without him. Every night he called me on the phone at bedtime. We had a system were he would talk to me for a few minutes, then I would go under. Then he would call up each of the child alters, or children if you wish, and talk to them. He would wish them peaceful dreams and end with each of them by telling them how much he loved them and would always be there for them.

"I and they had become totally dependent upon Red. He was the father they needed in their lives. I could not go to sleep at night until he called. Pills or no, if he didn't call, I couldn't sleep. He even called when he was out of town on seminars and things. It was a seven day a week happening.

"More than once I had noticed stained underwear following a session. It became more frequent, and I understood something wrong, very wrong, was going on. I knew I needed to get away from Red. But then something weird happened. Instead of my getting away from Red, another Judith was being born. A mirror image of myself. Not fully independent, like the other alters, but greatly at odds with me. A part of me that was in love with Red.

"Even though I knew it was wrong, I watched as a part of me succumbed to Red's sexual advances. Now, Red had sex with an adult Judith when he wanted adult sex and with the children when he preferred to have sex with a child. He literally had a one-body harem going for him.

"I found out later that he could set the stage by making his plans the night before, on the phone, and then follow through the next day."

Judith's face was red, somber, and it was easy to see that she was embarrassed. Her voice was low, but clear as she continued with her story.

"What happened next, Judith?"

"It got to be a frequent thing. Sex, that is. Red could come in at any time and take me for a break out to the trailer. There, he could have the children play with his 'purple,' as they called it, or have me. All he had to do was ask. I knew it was wrong, but I couldn't stop. Even though he still used hypnosis in the treatments, I knew what he was doing. I was ashamed, but I needed him. And the children loved him. I didn't know it then, but he had convinced me, under hypnosis, that I loved him too.

"One time he got mad when I questioned him about the moral aspect of our relationship. With the children and all. He said I shouldn't be concerning myself so much. After all, no matter what my mind said, it was all sex with consenting adults, at least physically."

"Objection, this is all hearsay, Your Honor."

I was amazed that Bill had waited so long to object. But I didn't think it would do him any good. Sure it was hearsay, but there are exceptions to every rule and dozens of hearsay exceptions.

"Exception, admission against interest, Your Honor," I replied.

Under the laws of most states, when a party or one of its agents says something detrimental to the party, it is called an admission against interest and therefore probably truthful, thus, it rates an exception to the rule against allowing hearsay evidence. Red was an agent of the Clinic, therefore, anything detrimental to him was also detrimental to the center. Ergo, exception. *Damn I'm good, sometimes.*

"Overruled, continue Counselor."

"What was the outcome of this confrontation, Judith?"

"I was upset, and Red said that if that was the way I felt, he wouldn't call any more. It was ten days before I apologized. The children were completely torn apart. I got no sleep, even though I was taking so much sleep medicine I was a zombie. Once again, I lost several pounds.

"I just couldn't keep going like that. I cried and apologized, and Red forgave me. We had sex in the trailer that afternoon. Just quick, oral sex, for Red. He said it was so I could show that I was sincere about my apology.

"I felt like a street prostitute. A whore, giving a blowjob, only it wasn't for money."

"Red called that night, at bedtime, and for several weeks after, things were 'normal.'

"Then, disaster struck."

"What do you mean by disaster, Judith?"

"Red dropped us. He just flat out dropped us. He said he was through being nursemaid to a woman and a houseful of kids and he did not want to see us any more. No more treatment, no sessions, no nighttime phone calls, no nothing. Just over."

'What happened as a result of this surprise?"

"At first I begged him, even on my knees. Time after time. I told him we couldn't live without him. Somehow, inside, I knew he had broken all his promises, not only with me, but with the children as well."

"You still did not know what Red said or did with the children?"

"No. Red always had me under hypnosis when he brought them out. Because of the hypnosis, I never knew about the 'light' area, as the alters did. They knew and saw everything, but not me. I was kept in the dark."

"What happened next?"

"I was a walking skeleton. I couldn't eat or sleep. Even the pills did nothing. No help. One morning, when I did doze off, I woke up and I was bleeding all over my stomach and thighs. A piece of broken glass was in my hand. I had been stabbing and slicing myself with it.

"I did not know it then, but because of Red, a new alter had risen. One with one specific intent, to kill the body. To commit suicide. She most wanted to do it in front of Red in as messy a way as possible, but she would do it any way she could. Hopefully at his home."

"At his home? You knew were he lived?"

"Yes, we had been there many times."

Judith appeared tired, now. Tired and listless. She had been telling nine strangers embarrassing and personal parts of her life and the strain was showing.

"Counselor, it is time for the mid afternoon break. Court is in recess for 15 minutes."

"Thank you, Your Honor." I said.

* * * *

Over the break, I saw the woman again. She was in the very back of the courtroom, pretty much out of sight. Until she stepped out in the hallway and spoke to Bill Handell. This was the second time she had done it, and so I was sure. She had to be the claims representative for St. Phillips Mutual, the Center's liability carrier. I thought so earlier, but this cemented it.

Sure wish I could sit in on the conversation. So far, all they have offered is a joke. Wonder if they still feel the same way. I'm damn sure the jury doesn't think it's a joke. Nor the judge, for that matter. Oh well, only time will tell.

* * * *

Back on the stand, after the break, Judith looked a little better. But I could tell that these last two days had taken their toll. If she could hang on one more day, the worst would be over.

"Mrs. Hoople, did Red Greely ever treat you again?"

"No sir, he did not. He cut us out, completely. Just like cutting off a finger, or a limb.

"He did, however, send us a bill. A bill for over two thousand dollars."

"What in the world was the bill for, Mrs. Hoople?"

"He said this was the amount due that the insurance did not pay."

"My God," I said. "After telling you he wasn't going to charge you, and never before sending you a bill, he actually sent you a bill for his services?" I managed to put quite a bit if incredulity into my voice.

"Yes sir. Apparently our 'services' weren't enough to offset his charges for his services."

Several jurors were shaking their heads, glancing over at the empty chair at the other defense table. They did not look happy.

"So, what did you do, after Red dropped you?"

"Well, we knew we had to have help, so we went to several doctors. We knew we couldn't see any other counselors at the center. Red would deny everything, and we would be fired."

Well, she's dropped back into the 'we' mode. I don't know if that is good or bad. I know we did not plan it this way.

"We went downtown to a psychiatrist, Dr. Arthur, first. All he did was to prescribe lots of drugs. He didn't believe in MPD, and he thought that we were schizophrenic. We only went back twice."

"Then we went to see Dr. Sherrie Lyons, and she was somewhat helpful. She insisted that we file a complaint with the Florida Medical Association about Red's treatments. We went to her several times. She also referred us to a counselor in Brandon, but even though he was nice, and we liked him, it was too far to drive back and forth. We only went there twice."

"Were there any more cutting or stabbing episodes during this time?"

"Yes, one more cutting incidence. This time with broken glass, just as before. Only this time, it was our wrist, here."

Judith held up her wrist for the jury to see. Several slash marks were visible, scars that looked nasty. Not clean, like a knife, but jagged. A little more depth and they might have done the job.

As I watched, juror number four gave a little shudder as she looked at the scars.

Bill Handell merely shook his head and looked down at his counsel table. He acted like he was disgusted.

I didn't look back to the rear of the courtroom, but I was willing to bet the adjuster was watching.

"Did you continue to treat with Dr. Lyons?"

"Yes, and she mentioned a counselor, Dr. Trey. We went to see him. He was a pastor at a Westshore church. I think God sent us to him. We certainly thank God for finding him."

"I take it, then, that Dr. Trey was able to help you?"

"Yes, he had worked with multiples before, and he was a big help. Right from the beginning."

"Tell the jury some of the ways Dr. Trey helped you, Judith."

"First, he taught us that it was unnecessary for me, Judith, to be hypnotized in order to alter personalities. This allowed me to be in the light, consciously standing by and witnessing what was going on at all times. No more will I be kept in the dark in my own mind, even when I am not in the flesh.

"He taught me about the light, and the flesh and the rooms where the little ones are.

"I, Judith, learned how to communicate with the other alters. To learn about them, first hand. I now know and love them, and they love me. Instead of opposing each other, and fighting for recognition, we are a team. At least most of us."

"Why do you say, most of us?"

"Well, there are still some others I don't know about. Alters so deep we can't contact them yet. And then, of course, there is the suicidal alter. She is on her own and we deliberately try to keep her away.

"She won't communicate, even through hypnosis. Dr. Trey has talked with her twice, only. She is a very purposeful alter. Very controlling. She only comes out in the morning time when she can gain full control and shut the rest of us out. No light, no consciousness, nothing."

"Objection, Your Honor. These are nothing more than pure fantasies and are clearly irrelevant, immaterial, inadmissible and outright untruths. Further..."

"Enough, Mr. Handell! Approach the bench, both of you!" A clearly irate Judge was not happy with the objection.

"Mr. Handell. In my courtroom we do not engage in jury posturing. If you have an objection, you state it, clearly, without self-serving rhetoric. I will not tolerate this type of grandstanding. And I certainly will not allow you or any other lawyer to cast aspersions upon a witness. If you had gone the final step and called her a liar, you would be cooling off in a cell right now. Do I make myself clear, Counselor?"

"Yes, Your Honor, but this is absurd. She is taking the time of the jury pool with these rambling idiocies—"

Once again, Judge Midder cut Bill off mid-sentence.

"Counselor, you are a lawyer and I expect you to act like one. Do you have a valid objection or not? If not, then let's return to our seats.

"Continue, please, Mr. Newton."

"Thank you, Your Honor."

As I started back in my questioning, I noticed, for the first time, that Bill's skepticism might have struck a sympathetic note with two male jurors. Not good.

"Judith, you were talking of the suicidal alter. Does she frighten you?"

"Of course. She scares the hell out of us. Wouldn't you be frightened if you had someone hidden inside you that wanted to kill you?"

"Objection, Your Honor." Bill bounced up, right on cue. At last he had a legitimate reason.

"Sustained. Mrs. Hoople, you cannot answer a question with a question, especially one that attempts to put the other party in your shoes. Do I make myself clear?"

"Sorry, Your Honor."

"That's O.K. Just keep it in line. Continue, Counselor."

"Mrs. Hoople. Has Dr. Trey helped you in any other way?"

"Yes. He has helped us to make friends. Me, the girls, David, all of us. We go to church each Sunday and Sunday school for the girls. I am in the choir. Lorna and Trish are in youth groups. We are getting a life. But it is hard—very, very hard.

"People know about us. My friends at the Clinic are scared to associate with us. New friends often are not friends, only people who are curious about the new weirdo. They call us freaks behind our back. People can be mean and cruel."

"How are you now, as compared to before you met and treated with Red?"

"Oh boy." Judith took a deep breath. "That's a toughie. I guess I'm about fifty percent as healthy, at best, physically. The body hurts all the time. We only get two or three hours sleep a night, sometimes none at all. But we still stay in bed till eight or nine o'clock. It is often very hard to get out of bed. Both physically and mentally.

"We don't enjoy exercise any more. As a girl, I, Judith, was a cheerleader, a gymnast, active in various sports, a bike rider and track competitor. Now, I have a hard time moving about, especially after being in bed a few hours.

"On bad days, we take a lot of pills. Muscle relaxers and pain pills. We know they are not good for us, but the pain gets intense and they are the only thing that helps."

"Do you work anymore?"

"No. We can't hold down a job. That's a laugh. We can't even get a job to hold down. Nobody will touch us. I don't know what kind of reference the Clinic has given out, but no one will invite me back for a follow-up interview, so it must not be a very good one.

"For the first time in my life, I am on the dole. First it was welfare, then social security disability and S.S.I. It is not much, but Dave still helps too. We just get by.

"Lorna is doing real well in school, so we are hoping she will get a scholarship."

"You mentioned Social Security Disability. What percentage of disability is that, Judith?"

"100%."

"How old are you, Judith?"

"35 years old."

"35 years old and totally disabled from work. Just because you wanted to quit smoking. Judith, tell the jury, is there anything that you really, desperately want?"

"Yes." Judith answered in a very low voice.

"And what is that?"

Judith turned her head and looked straight at the jury. "To be normal again. Normal and pain free."

As she said this, she continued to look straight at the jurors, tears running quietly down her cheeks.

I looked at the Judge. "No more questions, Your Honor."

Judge Midder looked at the courtroom clock. It was 4:40 P.M. "Ladies and gentlemen. This seems like a perfect place to break. It's a little early, but we ran late yesterday. Once again, I admonish you, no talking with anyone about this case, no news, no nothing. You are dismissed until 8:55 tomorrow morning. I'll see counsel in my chambers."

"All rise; court is now in recess."

* * * *

I instructed Joe to get the car sent to the back of the courthouse and then wait for me. She took one briefcase and I took the other one with me into Judge Midder's chambers.

Bill and I took seats across from one another at the table that jutted out from the Judge's desk. Almost as we sat down, Judge Midder came in, removing his robe as he came through the side door.

"Stay seated, gentlemen." He took his seat behind his desk.

Under his robes the Judge had been wearing a white shirt with a paisley tie, but his coat was on the rack in the corner. The coat was light blue.

That will certainly show off his ruddy complexion.

"Mr. Newton, I assume that was your longest witness?"

"Yes, Your Honor. The rest will be considerably shorter."

"How many more witnesses do you intend to call?"

"Well, sir, I have 14 witnesses listed, but I don't believe all of them will be necessary. At least at this time. But I am reluctant to limit myself, in case something happens and I find it necessary to call any particular one."

"I understand, Counselor. I'm just trying to get an idea of our schedule. If you two gentlemen finish early, Judge Arness wants me to handle a three or four day trial in your last week space, assuming you don't need it."

"With all due respect to the Court, it is too early for me to limit my witnesses yet," I told a rather impatient judge.

"Yes. Yes, of course. Mr. Handell, do you plan on being very long with Mrs. Hoople in the morning?"

"Your Honor, I can't really see that I have any choice. I expect to spend most of the day with Mrs. Hoople on the stand." Bill answered.

"Well, then. It appears that our little session has been for naught. O.K. gentlemen. I'll see you in the morning."

As we left, I saw the adjuster and Tim Snead waiting for Bill.

* * * *

Back at my office, people were still milling about. It was only a little after five, and everyone was waiting to see how the trial was going. I told them that Judith was doing very well, and things were right on schedule. Everything was at least as well as I had expected them to be.

Sitting down with Judith, I told her, "Judith, you did well the last two days. But I won't kid you. Tomorrow is the key. Right now, tonight, the jury loves you. They feel sorry for you and they can't believe that Red Greely isn't even man enough to be here to defend himself.

"Tomorrow will either make or break your testimony. We practiced a lot on cross-examination. You know the way things can be thrown at you. Just remember everything you learned. Especially, keep your cool and make sure you let him finish his question. That way you only answer what he asks, not what you think he is going to ask. He is a good lawyer and if you aren't careful, he will trip you up: especially if you try to anticipate his questions.

"Just relax as much as possible and wait for his questions.

"I think you are ready. I'm going to send you home for a good night's rest, unless you think you need something else. How about it? Are you ready?"

"Yes, we are." Judith said. "Even if we weren't, we are too tired to concentrate any more."

"Good enough. Go home and I'll see you in the morning."

With a wan smile, Judith said her goodbyes and David led her out to the elevator.

I then told Joe to have Dr. Trey ready at about ten, tomorrow morning. I did not believe Bill would take all day on cross. I figured he was sandbagging, trying to catch me with my pants down. I wasn't going to be caught with a full day of trial left, and no witnesses. Dr. Trey would fill in the rest of the day and then the next witnesses would go faster; I really only planned on five more witnesses, but I wasn't going to let Bill know that. Not now, anyway.

"Joe. I think you should call Red Greely and have him stand by in the courthouse the next three days. He won't like it, but that's tough. He's under subpoena and I intend to let the jury watch this scum squirm. I'll use him when I need a fill in witness, or after Dr. Lofton, one or the other."

"Sure, Boss. Anything else?"

Before I could answer her, Julie and Terry came in to see how everything was going and if they could do anything to help. I knew that they both had several things they needed to talk to me about, other cases, *etc.* But they were too good to bring those things up right now. Good people are hard to find, and they were two of the best.

I filled them in on the trial, and then sent them all home. When they had gone, I poured myself a stiff Crown Royal and thumbed through the ever-growing stack of mail on my desk. Dropping the mail back on my desk, I pulled out the sideboard and leaned back in my chair, propping my feet up on the sideboard. It was still light outside and I could see down the Hillsborough River, to the University of Tampa campus. Two sculling teams were rowing in the river, while a man in a small motorboat and wielding a megaphone shouted directions at the coxmen and crews.

My thoughts drifted. I was still back in the courtroom, still listening to every word that was said. I was still wound up. 100% on alert. That's the way it was when I was in trial. Hard to come down at the end of the day. But slowly, ever so slowly as I sipped my drink and watched the sculling crews, I began to relax. It was like coming down off a high. Being in court was a high. Being in trial. It was a 100% effort in the courtroom. There was no room for error. No time for second questioning. Once the jury saw or heard something, no instruction in the world would erase it. It was history. Reactions had to be instinctive and instantaneous. Objections must be made now, not later.

It always took a while to unwind. As the trial progressed, each day it would take me a little longer to unwind. It always did. That was part of being a trial lawyer. The nature of the beast. I wouldn't have it any other way.

CHAPTER ELEVEN

Cautiously as if preparing to repel an attack, Red Greely opened his front door and peered at the stranger standing on his front porch.

"Mr. Red Greely?" The stranger asked.

"Yes, that's me." Red started before the stranger shoved a packet of papers into his hands.

"You've been served," the stranger announced, quickly backing away and almost running toward his car parked just a few feet from the porch.

Closing the door behind him, Red padded back to his lounge chair as he opened up the documents the stranger had given him.

Now the bitch's lawyer wants to bring me back into this mess.

Red remembered the first time he had been questioned by big bad lawyer Newton.

Looked down on me like I was scum! Like he never would have gotten a little piece of the action. Holier than thou he was in his fancy suit and silk tie.

All the years I put into this business and finally had it going; I mean really going. And now this bitch and her fancy attorney are going to take it all away.

Remembering his first encounter with the Center's attorney Red wasn't too sure he particularly liked him any better. He had met with him on several occasions since and each time Red had come away feeling slighted. At least he seemed to understand that this was all the bitch's fault. All her lies and excuses.

I really pumped his ass full of lead. He really thinks this fruitcake lady is at fault. Hell, if she hadn't gone so far off the deep end I might have kept her around longer. She sure was willing once she was under hypnosis. Too bad I never figured this hypnosis thing out years ago. Wow! What a harem I could have had!

Still looking at the paperwork in his hand Red Greely came back to the moment.

Well, if that bitch's lawyer wants to talk to me at trial, I've got a surprise or two in store for him. My lawyer says the only way the state doesn't come after me for criminal charges is if she loses. Well guess what… she loses!!

Thinking about Judith and his own ability to break her reminded Red of the better times he had enjoyed with her, in his own perverted way and that led him to realize he was getting excited.

I wonder who's lap dancing at the Playhouse tonight. It won't take much more than a twenty the way this boy's jumping.

With those thoughts in mind, Red headed to his bedroom to find some loose fitting jeans to wear to the Playhouse. Something dark that wouldn't show stains.

* * * *

"Mr. Handell." Judge Midder queried after the jury had been seated. "Do you wish to cross-examine the witness?"

"Oh, definitely, Your Honor. But not at this time. I would like to reserve the right to cross-examine the witness at a later time and let's get on with this case."

"Objection, your Honor. There is no provision in the rules for reserving an entire block of cross-examination. It is..."

"Hold it, Counselor. Both of you approach the bench."

When we were at the bench and the court reporter was set up, the Judge said, "All right, Mr. Handell. What the hell are you trying to pull? Last night in chambers you indicated you would take most of the day with this lady's cross-examination and now you are telling this court that was not true?"

Judge Midder was obviously upset; his facial color approached deep purple as he glared down at Bill.

"No, Your Honor, that is not what I'm telling the court. Your Honor, with all due respect to this court, my trial strategy is my own, and as an attorney, I am bound to do the best for my client in the best way I can see to try this case. As we spoke last night, I felt that I had no choice but to continue this witness and cross her today. However, my paralegal was able to find ample precedent to allow this court to follow in ruling upon my request."

With that, Bill quoted from several cases where the trial judge's discretion was upheld when he allowed cross-examination of a witness to be deferred at the request of counsel.

"So you see, Your Honor, this is not something unprecedented, nor even unusual. I have the right to call Mrs. Hoople in my own case in chief, and to treat her as a hostile witness if that is the only way to defer her testimony. But that is my client's right, and as his counsel, I intend to exercise it."

Still not looking happy, Judge Midder turned to me. "What say you, Mr. Newton?"

"First, Your Honor, even though this may not be unprecedented, it is certainly unusual. I have been in hundreds of trials and never seen it before. Second, based upon counsel's representations in chambers, I planned to call my next witness much later in the day, and have no one standing by at this time. Finally, although as Mr. Handell stated, he does have the right to call Mrs. Hoople in his case in chief; he has no such right to have her called as a hostile witness. That is always the court's prerogative, and then only after the witness has expressed hostilities in the way she answers the defendant's questions."

I was sweating. I really didn't have anyone waiting, and that was my own error. You try not to make anyone mad, especially your own witness, but you must have someone or something waiting. If not, the Judge could force you to end your case, or more likely, tell the jury that the reason they drove all the way to the courthouse was to cool their heels while you went out and found a witness because you were unprepared. Not a good alternative.

Also, if Bill was able to call Judith as a hostile witness in his case in chief, he could ask leading questions and be pretty nasty, without fear of judicial reprimand. I did not want that.

"Point well taken, Mr. Newton. At this time, Mrs. Hoople would be considered an adverse witness, allowing you some latitude, Mr. Handell. But not a hostile witness. Not yet anyway. As to your reliance upon Mr. Handell's assertions in chambers, that troubles me. If I thought that you had truly been set up, I would take action. However, giving Mr. Handell the benefit of the doubt, if he only found his supporting case law last night, he couldn't have done otherwise.

"Now, Mr. Newton. You are an experienced trial lawyer. You know it is your burden to have your witnesses standing by. Period. You know the consequences. I cannot force counsel to take the testimony of your client until he is ready. That is his choice. However, precedent or not, Mr. Handell, all the cases you cited upheld the trial court's decision to allow for deferment of cross examination. Nothing mandated that the court rule in favor of such deference.

"Gentlemen, my ruling is as follows: First, as to allowing you to reserve cross-examination of the witness; that is denied without prejudice to your subsequently calling the witness on direct examination in your case in chief, as an adverse witness. Second, the court finds that it is the plaintiff's obligation to have her witnesses ready to proceed, and when you leave the bench, Counselor, I will expect you to call your next witness, or pay the consequences. Unless, of course, Mr. Handell wishes to cross your client.

"Unless you have some other objections, all of your current arguments are on the record."

Neither Bill nor I said anything, so the Judge continued, "Gentlemen, return to your places."

As soon as we were in place, Judge Midder turned to Bill. "Counselor, do you wish to cross-examine this witness?"

"No, Your Honor. Subject to our bench conference, not at this time."

"Very well, Counselor. Let the record reflect that you have forgone the opportunity to cross examine this witness unless she is recalled to the stand, and then only within the scope of recall testimony."

I'll be damned. He really did it. Now he's trying to get me fried. If I can't call a witness, the jury ain't going to be happy.

"Mr. Newton, call your next witness."

"The plaintiff calls Mr. Tim Snead to the stand, Your Honor."

"Objection! This is obviously nothing but a retaliatory action on the part..."

"Silence!" Judge Midder roared at Bill while looking at me with a look that could have withered a stalk of corn. "Both of you approach the bench. Bailiff, take the jury out."

"Yes,Your Honor. Ladies and gentlemen. Please follow me to the jury room for a few minute's break."

The jury was led out while Bill and I stood in front of the bench, and in front of a very unhappy Judge.

"Now gentlemen and I use that word sparingly, would you like to tell the court what is going on? You first, Mr. Newton. Are you looking for a contempt citation or what, Counselor?"

"Absolutely not, Your Honor. In the first place, Mr. Snead represents a party, and therefore, is subject to being called to the stand at any time. Secondly, he was deposed, was subpoenaed, and is a listed witness. The plaintiff has every right to call him at any time."

"Mr. Handell?"

"Your Honor, Mr. Snead is only a representative here, not the party itself. Mr. Newton has given us no advance warning of any expected testimony and it is unconscionable for Mr. Newton to pull a stunt like this, just because he lost his earlier argument in front of the court."

"Well, Counselor, it appears to the court that Mr. Newton is doing just what he was ordered to do, i.e., calling his next witness. If you need a moment to prep him, I'll give you five minutes. Then we call the jury back in. You have five minutes, Counselor."

Judge Midder left the bench and I went back and sat down, wiping my brow as I went. Joe was the one who remembered to subpoena Snead, two weeks prior to trial. It was only routine, but it had saved the day.

* * * *

"Is the plaintiff ready to proceed?"

"Yes, Your Honor."

"Is the defense ready?"

"Yes, Your Honor."

"Call your next witness, Mr. Newton."

"May it please the court; the plaintiff calls Tim Snead, Your Honor."

"Mr. Snead, approach the Clerk and be sworn in, and then please take a seat in the witness box."

Yes, Judge," Tim Snead answered as he stepped up to be sworn in.

After he was sworn in and seated, I put him through the preliminaries, occupation, education, marital status etc. He had two masters' degrees, one in psychology and one in sociology. He was divorced and had a steady girlfriend. He had two kids from his former marriage, and was still paying alimony and child support. He was the director of Hillsborough Community Crisis Center.

"Mr. Snead, do you know Red Greely?"

"Yes, I do. He is, or was, the chief counselor at the Center."

Well, maybe they have canned the SOB. Good for them.

"When did you first come in contact with Red Greely?"

"He was already at the Center when I was hired on as the director. That was when I met him for the first time."

"And how was he introduced to you?"

"The outgoing director introduced us and told me that Red was a one-in-a-million find. A good counselor, a good supervisor, an excellent politician and, I was assured, a man who would become my right hand in the running of the Center."

"Was he introduced with a title?"

"Yes, he was introduced as Dr. Red Greely."

"Was he a doctor, or is he now a doctor?"

"No, although I did not know that at that time."

"When did you first learn that Red was not a doctor?"

"Well, you have to understand, we are not talking about a medical doctor, only a doctorate title. One can effectively operate in the position of chief counselor without the necessity of a doctorate."

"I repeat, sir, when did you first learn that Red was not a doctor?"

"It was probably a little over a year ago."

"Strange, that's about the same time this lawsuit was filed. Did you learn of this fact before Judith brought charges against Red, or after?"

"I really don't think..."

"Before or after?" I interrupted.

"After."

"So what you are telling this jury is that for years you had a man running around, in charge of the Center, calling himself Doctor Red Greely, and no one ever bothered to check and see if he had even graduated from high school?"

"Objection, Your Honor. Mr. Newton is putting words in the witness's mouth. Improper direct."

"I'll re-phrase the question, Your Honor." I said.

"Continue then, Counselor."

"Did you, Mr. Snead?"

"Did I what?" Snead retorted with a grin on his smug little face.

"Did you ever check to see if he had graduated from high school?" I asked, wiping the smirk right back off his face.

"Well, no. You see that isn't really necessary. You are taking this whole thing out of context."

"Sorry. I certainly would not want to do that. So, correct me if I am wrong, but did you just tell this jury that it is not necessary for Red to have a high school graduation in order to be employed in his capacity as the chief counselor of the Center?"

"No, no. I never said that. Obviously only a well educated person could be placed in that capacity."

"Then a high school degree is necessary?"

"Yes, of course."

"Well, did he?"

"Did he what?" An exasperated Tim Snead almost shouted.

"Did Red Greely have a high school diploma?"

"Certainly. I mean, he must have. I know. I remember it is in his recent resume."

"A resume printed after you found out that he was not a doctor, true?"

"Well, yes, but it was done many years ago."

"Yes sir. But you did not know that. In fact, you never checked on Red's credentials the entire time you ran the Center, did you, sir?"

"As I told you, he was there when I came on board. I just assumed he was as advertised."

"Did you feel no obligation to the people who came to the Center to insure that they received proper treatment from qualified counselors?"

"Of course we were very careful about who we hired. We have all sorts of regulations, state guidelines, insurance guidelines all kinds of guidelines and regulations which we follow religiously."

I looked over at Bill who looked like he was about to choke. He was afraid to object, because he did not want to point out his client's mistake and make it even more noticeable. His client had just brought up insurance, a big no-no. But that was his problem, not mine.

"So you religiously follow all these regulations, but you still allowed an undereducated man to pass himself off as a doctor and virtually run your clinic. Is that right, sir?"

"I wouldn't put it that way."

"Well then, put it your own way. Tell this jury in your own words how you allowed this to go on for years."

"Objection; improper question!" Bill was almost apoplectic.

"Sustained. Move on, Counselor."

"Sorry, Your Honor. Just trying to let the man talk."

"His own counsel can take care of that, Mr. Newton. Now I won't tell you again. Move on."

"Yes, Your Honor. Mr. Snead, Red conducted group training sessions with other staff members, did he not?"

"Yes."

"How often did you sit in on these sessions?"

"I didn't. It was not part of my job."

"But you are the director, the top dog, so to speak. Correct?"

"Yes, but I did not consider it good business to sit in on other people's territories. Step on their toes if you will."

"Red also conducted group therapy sessions at the Center, did he not?"

"Yes. Two or three times a week."

"How many of those did you sit in on?"

"I went to one or two when I first came on board. That's it."

"And, if I am correct, you never sat in on private therapy sessions, other than your own. True?"

"Yes, that is correct."

"Well sir, then who did it. Who supervised Red Greely? Who checked to see if his methods were acceptable in the community? Who checked to insure that he was doing a decent job? Who checked to see if he was hurting people with his treatments? Who, sir?"

"Objection. Multiple question, capable of more than one answer."

"Overruled, Counselor. I think the question can be answered. The witness will answer the question."

"No one. But there was no reason to believe anything was wrong."

"Isn't that what checks and balances are all about? To insure that things don't go wrong?"

"Certainly. But nothing did go wrong, at least not until this."

It's his hole, let him dig.

"And this time something did go wrong, didn't it. Something terribly, terribly wrong, didn't it?"

"If you believe that woman."

The cardinal rule of examining witnesses is for a lawyer never to ask a question he doesn't already know the answer to. Up to now, I had followed the rule, however I was about to break that rule. I couldn't let him go with that answer.

"If, by 'that woman,' you are referring to the plaintiff, what has she ever done to cause you to not believe her?"

"I know she is just after money. That's all, just a money grubber."

Well idiot. You violated the cardinal rule, now get out of it.

"And on what do you base that statement, sir?"

"I just know, that's all. I've read the depositions and things, and I talked to Red. I know."

"You talked to Red Greely? The man who lied to you about his credentials. The man who broke every ethical rule in the book and slept with his client while she was hypnotized. The man who won't even come to court in his own behalf. And because of that, you know Judith Hoople is just after money?" I had allowed my voice to become louder and more indignant with each sentence.

"Just what did this man tell you that would cause you to believe him now?"

"Objection; calls for speculation. The answer can only be hearsay. Also, it invades the psychotherapist privilege."

"Privilege?" I sputtered. "Whose privilege? Who was the patient, Red Greely or Tim Snead?"

"Besides, anything said would be an admission, exception to the hearsay rule."

"Gentlemen, approach the bench."

On the way to the bench, Bill and I puffed up like a couple of professional boxers, ready to do battle. Bill's client was running off at the mouth and he wanted to stop it. I wanted to let the man keep hanging himself. Besides, there was no other way to find out what Red would say except through this man."

"Gentlemen, and, once again I use that word sparingly, I am not going to allow courtroom theatrics to become the norm. Mr. Newton. Where are you going with this line of questions? Seems to me that you are treading in pretty deep water?"

"Your Honor, it was his client who opened the door. Now I feel that I must proceed in order not to prejudice my client. I deliberately avoided comment on the insurance issue and only followed up on what is allowable under the rules."

"And what rules are those, Mr. Newton?"

"There is no valid privilege objection to what Red told Mr. Snead, unless it actually was during therapy, and even then, it is a qualified privilege. There is no valid hearsay objection, because anything said would be an admission against interest, and that is an exception to the rule against hearsay."

"What say you, Mr. Handell?"

"What I say, Your Honor, is that this whole line of questioning is improper. It's like walking in a mud bog, surrounded at every step with quicksand.

Anything the witness says is subject to some kind of objection. Evidence is getting in that is improper, but cannot be objected to because the risk of making the objectionable evidence more noticeable to the jurors is too great. It's a Catch 22, and it is not a proper way to conduct direct examination of my client."

Bill was obviously still smarting from the fact that his client had been made to testify in the first place. Just as obviously, five minutes of coaching had not been enough to educate his witness in the art of giving good testimony. Bill wanted it over.

"Mr. Handell, I'm inclined to agree with everything you just said, but that does not rule out the fact that the witness currently belongs to Mr. Newton, and, if the questions are relevant and material and within the allowable scope of direct examination, I can't stop him from asking them."

"Now, Mr. Newton. What relevance do you expect to find in your questioning of the conversation between Greely and Snead?"

I could see Tim Snead out of the corner of my eye. He was only about three feet away from me, and I knew he could hear everything we were saying. Only the jury and those in the main courtroom could not hear us. I have always coached my witnesses to listen closely to arguments at the bench when they were on the stand. The arguments and subsequent rulings can tell a witness how to get his information across, or not. Depending on the circumstances. I was hoping Bill's five minute session did not cover this part of direct examination.

"I expect to find confirmation of the sexual violation of my client by an admission by Red to Snead."

"Very well then, proceed. But I warn you, I will not tolerate grandstanding, and you are on a very thin wire. Understood?"

"Yes, Your Honor."

"The first thing you have to do is to eliminate the privilege objection."

"Yes, Your Honor."

"O. K. gentlemen, back to work."

"Mr. Newton, you may continue."

"May it please the court?" I nodded to the judge and then faced Tim Snead.

"Mr. Snead, you mentioned a conversation with Red Greely in which he told you some things that influenced your mind as to Judith Hoople's relationship with Red. My question, sir, is in what context did this conversation take place?"

"Mr. Greely had come to me for counseling and we were in a session at the time."

Damn that lying son of a bitch!! He heard every word and figured out how to stop this before it gets any worse for him.

"Objection, Your Honor, privilege." Bill was on his feet, doing his best to sound indignant and, at the same time, trying hard not to smile in relief.

"Sustained. The witness is instructed not to answer any questions regarding discussions held within the bounds of the patient/counselor relationship."

"Move on, Counselor."

"May we approach, Your Honor?"

"No, Mr. Newton, you may not. I have ruled. Now if you have anything further to ask this witness, do it."

"But, Your Honor, even if it was in consultation, the rule of psychotherapist privilege is not absolute. It is limited and—"

"Enough, Mr. Newton. I have ruled. If you don't like my ruling, take it up with the appellate court when this trial is over. But for now, you will not go any farther with this line of questioning. One more word and I will hold you in contempt. Now get on with it."

Judge Midder's face was a rosy bright red, and I knew that even though all this had gone on in front of the jury, it was nothing compared to what would take place if I continued.

I smiled at the Judge, and then at the witness, even though I would have liked to smash in his lying face, and then in a somewhat disgusted tone said, "I have no more questions of this witness, Your Honor."

I walked back and sat down, fully expecting the Judge to slam me for my mannerisms, but he let it go.

"Mr. Handell, do you wish to cross-examine this witness?"

"Briefly, thank you, Your Honor."

"Mr. Snead, in the time that you have been associated with the Center, has Red Greely conducted himself appropriately?"

"To the best of my knowledge, absolutely."

"What is the necessary educational background to enable one to qualify for Red Greely's job?"

"A master's degree is required, just as what I have."

"A master's degree, not a doctorate?"

"That's right."

"And what level of academic achievement does Red Greely possess?"

"He has a master's degree in psychology."

"So he is qualified for the position he holds."

"Yes, definitely."

"Did anyone, anyone other than the plaintiff, ever file a complaint with the Center regarding sexual abuse by Red Greely?"

"No, of course not. We would have never kept a man in his position if such allegations had been filed and found valid."

"In fact, sir, there have never been any allegations of improper treatment by Red Greely from anyone for any reason during your tenure with the Center, isn't that true."

"Yes sir. Never any allegations of impropriety of any kind."

"And had there been, you would have looked into it, correct?"

"Yes sir. That's policy."

"No more questions, Your Honor."

"Thank you, Counselor. Mr. Newton? Any re-direct?"

"No, Your Honor."

"The witness may step down. It's time for a break, let's take twenty minutes."

As the Judge exited and the jury went out to their break, I tried to access the damage so far this morning. All in all, it wasn't too bad. But I was worried about Judith. She had been primed to go, and now she would have to wait. The break in her testimony would also work to allow the jurors to distance themselves from their earlier sympathetic emotions. Bill had taken a gamble, but I thought it was good strategy. I sure as hell hadn't expected it.

I went out of the courtroom and down the hall to the men's room, nodding to several reporters as I went. They had stopped trying to get me to say anything, and were now just taking notes and filing stories. The crowds had thinned considerably since Judge Midder's gag order was made known.

* * * *

"Dr. Trey's here, Boss." Joe was whispering to me as we regained our seats at counsel table. "He said he is ready when you are."

I did not have a lot of faith in Dr. Trey, but I needed him for some verification of Judith's condition and the hell she had been through to get this far in rehabilitation. My biggest problem would be to rein him in and not let him steal Dr. Lofton's thunder; or worse yet, accidentally prevent Lofton from getting on the stand.

"Is the plaintiff ready to proceed?" Judge Midder asked after the jury had been seated.

"Yes, Your Honor. The plaintiff calls Dr. Felton Trey to the stand."

"Bailiff, see if the witness is in the waiting room."

"Yes, Your Honor." The bailiff said as he went to the witness room, returning in a moment with Dr. Trey in tow.

Felton Trey was dressed in his best J. C. Penny sport coat and slacks. Light grey sport coat with dark grey slacks, black loafers, white shirt, tie and his shaded glasses that made him look as if he had something to hide. His hair was slicked back in 60's style, making his receding hairline even more pronounced.

"Dr. Trey, welcome to my courtroom. Please approach the clerk to be sworn in, and then take a seat in the witness box." Judge Midder smiled benevolently as he instructed the witness.

After he was sworn in, I approached the podium and began the introductions. Once I had covered his early education, I came to his doctorates. After establishing that both of them were divinity doctorates, I asked him what qualified him to counsel people like Judith for psychological problems.

"Well sir, experience. Experience and the law."

"Please explain what experience you have had that enabled you to assist Judith in her recovery." I hadn't really expected his cockiness to manifest itself so soon.

"I was the ramrod for the statewide program to assist children who had been sexually molested under then governor, Bill Clinton."

I couldn't help it, I had to join the jury in their laughter. Even Judge Midder laughed out loud at Dr. Trey's slip.

Dr. Trey turned as red as Judge Midder usually got when he realized his mistake. "What I meant to say was the statewide program instituted by Governor Clinton to assist victims of childhood sexual abuse." Trey was trying hard to keep from crying out loud as he explained his *faux pas*.

As the laughter subsided, I continued my questions, but not before Judge Midder instructed the jury that sometimes it was O.K. to laugh, but the courtroom and the administration of justice was a serious matter.

"Dr. Trey, approximately how many victims did you come in contact with during that tenure?"

"Well, I set up the program from scratch. We presented it to the legislature and then, when it got rolling, I supervised over three hundred counselors in their tasks."

You little twerp! Just answer the questions.

We had gone over this before, and I knew he had worked with over thirty victims personally. That is what I wanted him to tell the jury, not this self-serving crap he was dishing out.

"Thank you, Dr. Trey, I know you had numerous supervisory tasks as head of such an elite program, but please tell the jury how many individuals you personally assisted during this time. Individuals who had suffered greatly and whom you assisted in recovery." If that did not wake him up, nothing would.

"Yes, well, although that was not my primary responsibility, I did become personally involved and counseled over thirty individuals who were the victims of sexual abuse."

Thank you, God. "And you also indicated that there were legal reasons to support your administering to Judith?"

"Certainly. In the state of Florida, as in most states, pastors are licensed to counsel their flock."

A straight answer. How nice.

"Your Honor, may we approach the bench?" I really did not want to screw this up.

"Approach, gentlemen."

As soon as we got in front of the bench and the court reporter was set up the judge looked at me. "What's up, Counselor? Everything seems to be going O.K. Even your witness's goof didn't turn out too bad."

"Yes sir, but I am ready to tender him as a counseling expert. I want to be sure that the record is clear that he is being offered as a fact witness, and as an expert in psychological counseling, not diagnosis of any specific form of psychological problem nor its specific treatment. I will not ask him to diagnose Judith's condition as MPD, nor will I ask him about any expertise he may have in dealing with MPD. I will only ask him about his actual treatments and counseling. I want to be sure that if any of those doors are opened by Mr. Handell during his cross when I tender the witness, they will not impact on this Court's decision to allow Dr. Lofton to testify."

"Mr. Handell?"

"Judge, this is ridiculous. If this man can save us all a lot of time and take care of numerous questions at once, why waste this court's time? Not to mention this jury's time. If the man is qualified, let him talk!"

"Mr. Newton, I'm inclined to agree with Mr. Handell. Why waste time with multiple witnesses if one witness is qualified to do the job?"

"That's just it, Your Honor. This witness is not qualified to testify as an expert in MPD or any of the numerous problems suffered by the plaintiff. His credentials can be torn to shreds by any qualified psychiatrist, as Mr. Handell well knows. I will not offer him as a witness for something he is not qualified to do. But he is the one who treated her, and in his own way, he was eminently qualified to help her."

I knew that Trey was listening to every word. I didn't want to tee him off, but I had no choice but to make sure he would not keep Lofton off the stand. Right now he looked as if he had been slapped.

"I understand your position, Mr. Newton. Mr. Handell, you will confine your questions within the scope of direct, and only within that narrow scope. However, Mr. Newton, I caution you that your witness can affect this order, if he strays from his appointed role. "O.K. gentlemen, back to your posts.

"Mr. Newton?"

"Yes, Your Honor. At this time I would tender Dr. Trey as an expert in psychological counseling."

"Mr. Handell, Do you wish to examine the witness?"

"Yes, thank you Your Honor."

I sat down and Bill moved up to the podium. As usual, Bill was dressed impeccably, his suit coat buttoned and his cuff links shining. He had a large smile on his face, but his slate blue eyes were steady and cold.

"Good morning, Dr. Trey. It is doctor, isn't it?"

"Yes, actually I have two doctorates." Trey smiled, oblivious to the fact that he was being set up by a pro.

"Oh. Two doctorates. That's quite impressive, Doctor Trey. Must have taken quite a lot of study on your part."

"Yes, quite a bit. But I'm a hard worker and a fast learner, thank you."

"I see that, Doctor. Now, please tell the jury which one of those doctorates is in psychology, Doctor?"

"Neither one is actually in psychology, sir," A rather flustered Dr. Trey answered.

Feigning a surprised look, Bill went on:

"Oh, I must have misunderstood, Doctor. Which one is in psychiatry, then, Doctor?"

"Neither. As I explained to Mr. Newton earlier, they are both in divinity." Trey was getting angry, now, and it was showing.

"Well then, you must have obtained a masters degree in some psychiatric field. What would that be, Doctor?"

"My under grad was a Bachelor of Arts degree, and my masters and doctorates were all in divinity, sir." Dr. Trey was obviously straining to maintain control, and just as obviously losing the battle.

"My apologies, Doctor, but since you were being offered as an expert in psychological counseling, I'm trying to locate the source of that expertise."

There were a few chuckles and grins in the jury box, as Dr. Trey became red in the face and seemed as though he was going to choke.

"Objection, Your Honor, Counsel is badgering the witness."

"On the contrary, Your Honor," Bill began.

"Sustained. Move on, Counselor."

Still smiling, Bill went on. "I guess what I'm trying to find out here, Dr. Trey, is if you have anything other than a state license that qualifies you as an expert in psychological counseling?"

For God's sake, don't try to be cute, Doctor. He's going to eat you alive if you do.

"Yes, I do. I have over twenty years experience as a pastor and spiritual advisor to my flock. I also had four years in Arkansas running and participating in the program I mentioned earlier where we administered to the sexually abused children. Many of them suffered numerous psychological problems, including schizophrenia, bipolar disorders and multiple personality disorders."

Oh no! Here we go. That could throw this whole trial out the window.

"Then you are qualified, Doctor, to diagnose and treat people with multiple personality disorder?"

"My diagnostic capabilities, no matter how good they may be, are not what I was asked to do for Mrs. Hoople. Her diagnosis was concluded before I met her. I was asked to counsel her, and that is what I did. She was referred to me for that purpose."

Good for you, Doctor. You may not be such an ass after all.

Dr. Trey had not taken the bait and in destroying his credentials, Bill had made it easier for me to try to get Dr. Lofton on the stand.

"I have nothing further of this witness at this time, Your Honor."

"Very well, the witness is approved to testify as an expert in the field of psychological counseling. You may proceed on direct, Mr. Newton."

"Thank you, Your Honor."

"Dr. Trey, you indicated that Judith was referred to you by another practitioner, correct?"

"Yes sir, Dr. Lyons was the referring physician."

"And when you first began counseling with Mrs. Hoople, what kind of shape was she in, physically and mentally?"

"She was a total wreck. She had to be assisted in walking, and at times she even needed a wheelchair. She was often unkempt and appeared to get little if any sleep at night. She was underweight and malnourished. Very pale and dark eyed. Always rings around her eyes, like she never rested or slept. She was scared all the time. She cried a lot. Took lots of pain medication, but it didn't seem to help.

"She was very distrustful, and it took several sessions before she began to feel safe talking with me. Eventually, we began to tackle her root problems, but it was a difficult journey to get to that point."

"What were the primary problems that were confronting Judith at that time, Doctor?"

"Initially, the single most dominant problem was overcoming the devastation she felt after her betrayal at the hands of Red Greely. She had been sexually abused by him, of course, but that was only a minor part of the problems he caused in this lady. He had created a total dependency of Judith and the alters upon him. Then he dumped them, instantly and completely.

"Anyone with even a little psychological training knows that after a patient develops a dependency upon his or her counselor, a period of closure must be gone through prior to breaking up that relationship. Sometimes it only takes a session or two, sometimes a year or more. But it *must* be gone through or you stand to risk leaving the patient in worse condition than when you began treatment. When he violated that rule, Red broke the first and foremost rule of the Hippocratic Oath, i.e., 'I will come for the benefit of the sick, remaining free of all intentional injustice, of all mischief and in particular of sexual relations.'"

"Objection." Bill was out of his seat. "This witness is not a medical doctor and has never had to take the Hippocratic Oath."

My turn. "Your Honor, I don't understand counsel's objection. Did Dr. Trey misspeak or misquote the Oath?"

"Enough, I'm warning both of you." Judge Midder glared at each of us in return. "Overruled, get on with it counsel."

"Did you use hypnosis in your treatment of Judith, Doctor?"

"Yes, at first. It was necessary in order to get past the barriers she had set up for herself. But long-term hypnosis is never a good goal for therapy. After a few sessions, we evolved to a point that hypnosis was unnecessary. That's when we began to make progress."

"Why would it have been necessary for Red Greely to continue to hypnotize Judith for so long?"

"Objection, calls for speculation." Bill was up fast.

"Sustained. Rephrase the question, Counselor."

"Is there any valid reason that you are aware of, Doctor that would cause Red Greely to hypnotize Judith for such a long period of time?"

"Same objection, Your Honor."

"But not the same ruling, Counselor. Overruled. The witness may answer the question."

"There is no valid reason. He just wanted to be able to have sex with her without her knowing about it."

Way to go, Doctor. You get better all the time.

"Objection!" Bill literally jumped out of his chair, knocking it over in the process.

"Sustained. The jury will disregard the last part of the witness's statement. I caution you, Dr. Trey, not to add personal speculation to your answers. Just answer the question based upon your own first hand knowledge. Understood?"

"Yes; sorry, Your Honor."

Yeah, I'll bet you are. Good going. The jury won't forget it.

"Dr. Trey, were you able to call on the alters without the need of hypnosis?"

"Yes, after a few treatments. Now, Judith herself can *switch* personalities, and she can do so without being left out of the procedure. She can observe the alters as they take control of the body. Sometimes she can even make a game of it. Like five or six of them standing at the bedroom closet, choosing what to wear. That sort of thing.

"One of the principle ideas in my treatment of Judith is to lessen the fear of these alters so that eventually, integration can occur. Without integration, Judith can never be a normal person. That is the ultimate goal of everyone who treats her."

"You have been treating her for over a year now, correct?"

"Actually, a year and a half."

"And what do you believe will be the length of time it will take for Judith to achieve integration and become normal again?"

"Obviously, normal is a relative term. Bur time-wise, it will take years, if ever, for that to take place."

"When you first took Judith on, did you try to contact Red Greely?"

"Yes, I did. I needed to see what notes he had for his treatments of Judith. Obviously, this could be a tremendous help in her treatment."

"And what did Red Greely provide you with, Doctor?"

"Nothing, nada, absolutely zilch. He said he did not take any notes of his sessions with Judith."

"Is this unusual, not taking notes?"

"It's not unusual, it's unheard of. It is unconscionable. No practitioner would consider treating a patient, medical or psychological, without taking notes so that he can refer back to them for numerous reasons. Not the least of which is to offer the patient's next provider with an outline of where the patient has been and where she needs to go. If it wasn't for the fact that he billed the insurance company, we wouldn't even have a record of his treatments."

Yeah, but Greely got greedy, thank God. Otherwise it would only be Judith's word against his.

I spent another hour, going through Dr. Trey's counseling of Judith, his attempts to help her get back into the mainstream of society, Judith's position in the church community, anything I could ask that would bring the real Judith to light in the juror's eyes. Dr. Trey was turning out to be a pretty good witness.

"Doctor, we know from the records that prior to treatment by Red Greely, Judith was an energetic, outgoing, physically active young lady with the capability of holding down two jobs and raising a family. How long will it be until she can resume that position in life?"

"Probably, never. Although she has improved greatly over the last year, she still is nowhere near the point of normalcy. Heck, she isn't twenty percent of the way back, if that."

"How do you mean, 'twenty percent,' if that, Doctor?"

"Well, let's start by considering her ability to work. Assuming she could find someone willing to hire her at this point in her life, Judith could not be expected to keep regular hours, even on a part time basis. She never knows from one day to the next who will wake up in her body and what she will do when she wakes up. It's very difficult to imagine. Most of us are in complete control of our minds, and yet, sometimes it is harder than others to get out of bed in the morning.

"Judith, on the other hand, hurts all the time. Her body is at least sore and arthritic 100% of the time. Top that off with the morning problem of often having to take control of the body back from one of the alters and you can see what I mean. It may literally take her hours to be able to get out of bed and function. Not something conducive to gainful employment.

"Then, on those rare, thank God, occasions when the suicidal alter is in the flesh, even if Judith can regain control without damage to the body, the ordeal of regaining her control is enough to insure that the rest of her day is shot. And this is after a year and a half of therapy, drugs, counseling, etc., since Red's unethical and disastrous treatment."

"What kind of damage has this done to Lorna and Trish, Judith's two girls, Doctor?"

"Oh, it has hurt them badly. They have been ridiculed, been made the butt of numerous jokes, teased unmercifully about their wacko mother, you name it. But they are good kids, strong in their faith and in their love for their mother. They will survive, but it has been a real nightmare for them, as well. Not to mention the lack of material things they would otherwise have had. I wouldn't wish the shame they have had to endure on anyone. Red Greely hurt a lot more people than just Judith. He is an evil man."

"Objection; calls for speculation. Outside the realm of the Doctor's expertise."

Bill was mad. This simple preacher was coming off better than he or I had expected. He had to try to head off the flow. The jury was definitely sympathetic to Dr. Trey, and by association, Judith.

"Overruled, Counselor. It's not speculation; it is the Doctor's opinion. And, as you took pains to point out, the Doctor has two degrees in divinity. What better specialty to offer an opinion on evil is there? Continue, Mr. Newton."

"Thank you, Your Honor."

Well, Doc, the judge just put a halo on your head, let's see if I can capitalize on it.

"Doctor Trey, do you have an opinion, within a reasonable degree of psychological certainty, as to whether the treatment afforded Judith by Red Greely was at or below the acceptable level of care in the psychological community?"

"I do."

"And what is that opinion, Doctor?"

"Red Greely's treatment fell far below any acceptable level of care in this or any other psychological community. His 'care and treatment' was totally unprofessional, unorthodox, unethical, and without any saving merit. His 'care and treatment' could best be characterized as gross negligence, or, in another context, criminally negligent."

"Objection; this time the Doctor has definitely exceeded his realm of expertise."

"I will sustain the objection, but only as it applies to any criminal context, and I again warn counsel, no speeches in objections. The jury will disregard the witness's reference to criminality. Continue, Mr. Newton."

"Dr. Trey, foregoing any comments on whether or not Red's having sexual non-consensual intercourse with his patient while she was under his control in a deep hypnotic trance was in violation of any criminal statutes, do you have an opinion, within a reasonable degree of psychological certainty, as to Judith's chances of living a life again, free of any psychological counseling?"

"I do."

"And what is that opinion, Doctor?"

"Judith will never again be able to live without the aid of counseling and probably, medications as well."

"Thank you Doctor. I have no further questions."

"Thank you Mr. Newton. Mr. Handell, do you wish to cross-examine this witness?"

"Yes, Your Honor."

"Very well, let's see if we can finish this witness before the lunch break."

"Pastor Trey, it is all right if I call you that, isn't it Mr. Trey?"

Here we go. Bill is going to try to push the Doc's buttons and remind the jury of his minimal credentials. Come on, Doc. Don't bite.

"Certainly it's all right, Mr. Lawyer. I worked and studied many years to become the pastor of one of the finest churches in Tampa. I'm proud of my title and what it signifies."

Good for you.

"Well, Pastor Trey, I noticed that you forgot to mention whether you faulted the Hillsborough Community Crisis Center for its part in the hiring and supervision of Red Greely. Do you harbor any such opinion?"

You bastard.

"Objection. Outside the scope of cross examination."

"Your honor, this will just save time, after all, he is on my witness list also and there is no reason to recall him when with one or two questions, we can save the court and the jury a large amount of time."

"Mr. Newton, this seems like a reasonable request to me. What is so objectionable about it?"

"May we approach, Your Honor?"

"O. K., approach. I can see right now we may not make the lunch break without finishing with this witness."

Once we were there and the reporter was set up, the Judge intoned:

"O.K., Mr. Newton. What do you have against saving this court some badly needed time?"

"Not a thing, Your Honor. However, that's not what I see as happening here. Mr. Handell is attempting to open Pandora's Box. If he can get my witness, who is barely, if at all, qualified to render an expert opinion, to do so on the subject of the Center's negligence, then he can argue against me bringing in an eminently more qualified witness, Dr. Lofton, to offer the same testimony. I have not tendered this witness as qualified to answer this question, and I specifically refrained from broaching this area of questioning in its entirety. If Mr. Handell really wants to ask these questions of this witness, he can do so by calling him to the stand in his case in chief. But this is my witness, my dime, and my decision as to which witness is used to support which part of my burden of proof."

"Your Honor, this court has already expressed a concern for an early end to this trial so that the courtroom, and yourself, may be used to expedite another trial. I think it is beholden on Mr. Newton to forgo speculative and specious arguments and seriously attempt to assist the court in this matter."

"I suppose, Mr. Handell, that if I had this case from the beginning and had already ruled on your motion to exclude the testimony of Dr. Lofton, I would agree with you. However, it is not within the prerogative of this court to tell a lawyer how and in what order to present his evidence. I will sustain the objection, for now, and you can get on with whatever other questions you may have of this witness. Within the bounds of the scope of cross-examination, of course."

Back at the podium, Bill was not a happy camper. He bounced around Dr. Trey's credentials for a while, then changed tactics.

"Pastor Trey, I could not help but notice that in most of the medical and psychological records of Mrs. Hoople, she is noted to be quite manipulative. Could you expand upon that for me, please."

That was an objectionable question, and Bill knew it. However we both knew if I objected it would only make the manipulative aspect of the question stand out in the juror's minds. I decided to let it go and see where he was going. I figured I already knew, anyhow, brilliant trial lawyer that I am.

"If you are asking if Judith is manipulative, that is a common trait among multiples."

Uh oh. Easy Doc.

"A common trait among multiples, is it? I take it then that you have had experience in treating other MPD patients besides Judith?"

"Yes." Dr. Trey answered, apparently sensing the trap.

Backing off, a little, Bill asked: "Would you consider Judith more, or less manipulative than the other multiples you have treated, Pastor Trey?"

"Objection; calls for an answer capable of more than one interpretation." I had to try to re-direct his questions.

"Sustained. Tighten up the question, Counselor."

"Certainly, Your Honor. Pastor Trey," Bill continued just as if no objection had been discussed. "You agree with me, do you not, that Judith Hoople is a manipulative person?"

"Yes, as I explained before, that is one of the traits of MPD."

"And, people who are manipulative often lie to get the result they desire, do they not?"

"Yes, that is true in a general sense."

"And Judith Hoople can lie to get her way, as a part of that manipulative personality we are talking about, can she not?"

"Yes, but I don't—"

"Thank you Pastor. Just answer the question. Your counsel will ask you to add to it, if he desires when I am finished with my questions."

"Objection? Mr. Handell is attempting to limit the Doctor's answers. Dr. Trey is entitled to give a full and complete response to the questions."

"Overruled, Counselor. Dr. Trey, you will confine your answers to the questions, and only elaborate if you are asked."

"Yes, Your Honor," a contrite Dr. Trey responded.

"Is it possible that Mrs. Hoople has lied and exaggerated in her testimony, indeed in her activities concerning this entire event, in order to manipulate all of us, especially this jury, into feeling sorry for her, and ultimately effecting a sizable award of money?"

"Objection; there is not one shred of evidence—"

"Overruled. Sit down, Counselor. The witness will answer the question."

"Yes, I guess it is possible..."

"I did not ask you to guess, Pastor. I asked for an answer, not a guess."

"Yes, it is possible, but I don't think—"

"Thank you, Pastor." Bill cut in. "It is possible, is it not, that Mrs. Hoople could have you and all the other counselors fooled."

"Yes, it's possible, but again..."

"Thank you Pastor," Bill cut him off once more before he could elaborate. "Then, it is possible that this entire trial is based upon a huge hoax instigated by, in your own words, a 'manipulative' woman, Mrs. Judith Hoople?"

"Once again, yes, I guess anything is possible—"

"Don't guess!" Bill almost shouted. "Just answer the question in the manner the Judge instructed you to. I'm sorry if you don't like the question, but this jury is entitled to an honest and direct answer."

I was fit to be tied. I did not like Bill lecturing my witness, and I was sure an objection would be sustained, but it would only serve to emphasize this line of questioning. I sat it out.

"Yes, it is possible."

"Thank you, Pastor. That wasn't so hard, was it? Especially for a man of the cloth? It is also possible, is it not, that the sole reason for all of this manipulation by Mrs. Hoople is strictly money-oriented?"

"Objection; asked and answered." Sooner or later, I had to stop this line of questioning.

"I have a right to test the witness, Your Honor, especially in light of his earlier evasiveness." Bill responded.

"Overruled, this time. The witness will answer the question." Judge Midder was giving Bill some slack, but letting him know his rope length was shortening.

"Yes, it is possible."

"In spite of Mrs. Hoople's assertions, it is possible that all of the sexual activity that took place between Red Greely and Judith Hoople was consensual, isn't that true, Pastor."

"Yes, it's possible."

"And it is possible, is it not, that these 'children,' these alters that 'came out' to play with and have sex with Red Greely were nothing more than the manipulative concoctions of the manipulative mind of Judith Hoople. True, Pastor?" Bill continued to mock Judith's earlier testimony by making little quotation marks with his fingers as he asked his questions.

"Yes."

"And it is possible, is it not, that these children sex acts were originally nothing more then sex games which were later deliberately misconstrued by a rejected Mrs. Hoople as a way of getting back at the lover who walked off and left her when he got tired of their games. True, Pastor?"

"Yes."

"You've seen her lie?"

"Yes."

"Seen her manipulate you and others?"

"Yes."

"Lies, manipulation, overt sexual activity; not what you teach others to aspire to from the pulpit, is it Pastor?"

"No, but—"

"Thank you very much, Pastor. No further questions, Your Honor."

"Any re-direct, Counselor?"

I was in a very bad place. The rock and the hard place had nothing on me. If I said nothing, the jury had eaten up this lying and manipulation crap. No matter what passed before, that is all they would remember. The Pastor called her a liar and a manipulator. Like God himself had spoken. If I attempted to straighten it out, I would have to have Trey offer opinions, and that would open the door to stopping Lofton's admittance. Hell of a note. I passed.

"No questions, Your Honor.

"Thank you, Reverend, you may step down."

I can't believe it! He's even got the Judge listening to a preacher, not a professional psychiatric counselor. A preacher who is saying one of his flock is a liar and a manipulator who probably set this whole thing up. Damn, damn, damn.

"Ladies and gentlemen, it is past time for our lunch break. We will break for one and one half hours. Be back promptly at 1:45. Bailiff."

* * * *

"Boss, maybe it's not as bad as you think, I mean, it didn't seem that bad to me."

We were back at the office and Joe was trying to make me feel better. I didn't feel like eating, I was going through my notes and trying to figure out my witness list for the rest of my presentation of evidence. We were too close to losing our best ace, and I was scratching off the primary proofs that I knew we had already offered. Although I wanted to put several more witnesses on, each one could add to Judith's credibility, it was a mean game. If the witnesses were professionals, they could be attacked in the same way as Trey had been, and if they screwed up, Lofton wouldn't go on. Most of Bill's tactics had aimed toward that goal, and he had almost succeeded.

"You're probably right, Joe. It's not as bad as I think. It's probably worse than I think. We are talking about a condition that most people find hard to believe anyway, and this manipulation crap is in every one of the providers' notes. You can believe that Bill will capitalize on that, just as he did with Trey. And there is a good chance that if I put Dr. Lyons on, she will be forced to render her diagnosis of MPD, and if she does, there goes Lofton. With Trey, the Judge was aware that he is not qualified to combat Bill's witness, credential wise, so he let me get away with non-diagnosis. Lyons is a Board Certified Psychiatrist, so that dog won't hunt the second time around."

"Oh God, it is bad. He's using country metaphors!" Joe rolled her eyes as she almost shouted.

We all laughed and the tension broke. I ate about half of my sandwich and we headed back to court. I still had not made up my mind about the witnesses.

* * * *

"Mr. Newton, are you ready to proceed?"

About as ready as I'll ever be.

"Yes, Your Honor, the plaintiff is ready."

"Very well then, call your next witness."

"May it please the Court. The plaintiff calls Doctor Eric Lofton."

"Objection! Objection, Your Honor. This witness has not been allowed by this court."

"Hold it, Counselor. Both of you approach the bench."

Once we were set up, Judge Midder went right to the point: me. "All right,. Counselor, what is this all about?"

"Dr. Lofton is my next witness, Your Honor. I just called for him, as I am supposed to do, under the rules."

"Rules schmules, Your Honor. Mr. Newton knows full well that this Court has never ruled upon whether Dr. Lofton can appear. Mr. Newton is supposed to wait until the close of his evidence and then see if the Court will allow Dr. Lofton's testimony."

"Mr. Newton, I believe that Mr. Handell is correct. What are you trying to pull, Counselor? You want a contempt citation, or to lose your witness prematurely? Because that's what is about to happen; you want to choose between the two options?"

"Not at all, Your Honor. With all due respect to the court, I am following this court's order. I have exhausted my expert witnesses, and now I am calling up Dr. Lofton so that this court can rule on the pending Motion to Exclude."

"Your Honor, Mr. Newton has six other medical or psychological witnesses listed. He just wants to get Lofton on the stand before it becomes patently obvious to the court that Dr. Lofton's testimony is repetitious and cumulative. Then he can go on with his other witnesses, just as I warned about in my motion. This is nothing but a blatant ploy to enable Mr. Newton to circumvent this court's express order, and should not be allowed."

"Well, Mr. Newton, anything else you want to say before I slap you with contempt?"

Judge Midder was bathed in his famous crimson countenance, and I was sinking fast.

"Your Honor. There is obviously a misunderstanding here. I don't care how many witnesses are listed, as I told the court at the beginning of this trial, the number of witnesses I would use had not been decided yet. I have used all the expert witnesses I intend to call. With the exception of Dr. Lofton, I will call no more expert witnesses. I still have several issues of proof which need to be resolved, and rather than waste this court's time with six or seven unnecessary witnesses, I am tendering Dr. Lofton as the one witness that will resolve all of them."

"At this point, without Dr. Lofton's ability to testify, I believe it would take three or four days of additional testimony before we could resolve this issue, and then we would have to decide each of the issues Dr. Lofton would be allowed to testify to. By deciding not to use any other witnesses and proffer Dr. Lofton instead, we resolve the issues in advance and benefit judicial economy at the same time. It is no ploy, Your Honor. It is simply an attorney presenting his case as he sees fit, within the rules and using his best effort to insure that no time of this court or this jury is wasted."

Judge Midder's blood pressure was receding, while Bill's was reaching boil-over.

"Your Honor, despite all the clever words of Mr. Newton, this is still nothing but a ploy."

"No, Counselor I don't agree with you," Judge Midder interrupted. "Nor do I think the appellate court would either, based upon counsel's representation to this court that he intends to call no more expert witnesses. I have no authority to order him to call witnesses, only to insure that he calls only those which he is entitled to call."

"Let me send the jury out, and we will address the issue of your combined motions."

While the jury was being sent out, Bill and I both got our notes, case law and a copy of the motions. We then argued the same motions using the same case law supports and rules. Nothing had changed, except the facts. Now we knew that Dr. Lofton's testimony was not to be cumulative, nor conformation of anything already testified to by another expert witness.

"Mr. Newton, although I have already expressed the opinion that if I had been the one to rule on these motions to begin with, Dr. Lofton's testimony would never have been allowed, because I would never have allowed you to add him as an expert. That opinion has not changed. However, that is not the issue before us now. You were allowed to add him and, Mr. Handell, you were allowed to depose him and add any new witness you wished to correct any problems mandated by his late entry into the case. You did depose him and you did elect to remain with your expert.

"This court is persuaded that Dr. Lofton's testimony will not impede justice, and in fact, will expedite the conclusion of this trial. Therefore, it is the decision of this court to grant Mr. Newton's motion and allow Dr. Lofton to be called as an expert. By necessity, therefore, your motion, Mr. Handell, is denied.

"Bailiff, return the jury to the box."

Hot damn! We won one for the Gipper.

****

"Is the plaintiff ready?"

"Yes, Your Honor, the plaintiff calls Dr. Eric Lofton to the stand."

"Bailiff, please bring Dr. Lofton to the courtroom."

After Dr. Lofton was sworn in and had taken the stand, I proceeded to qualify him as an expert. His credentials were impeccable. We pointed out that he was the recognized expert in Multiple Personality Disorder, having written over sixty peer review papers on the subject, authoring three books on MPD, and being the writer of the chapters on MPD of the DMSO, the Psychological Diagnostic and Treatment Bible.

After qualifying him, I tendered him to Bill who had only minimal questions.

I then began my direct examination.

"Dr. Lofton, at my request, did you undertake to familiarize yourself with the plaintiff, Judith Hoople and prepare opinions based upon your findings?"

"Yes, I did. The first thing I did was to spend two days subjecting Mrs. Hoople to a battery of psychiatric tests, hypnosis and a thorough mental and physical examination.

"I then focused upon the medical and psychological records of Mrs. Hoople's treating physicians, psycho/analysts and counselors. After that, I read the transcripts of every witness and provider in this case. Finally, I referred to numerous ethical and legal manuals and statutes to refresh my recollection of the responsibilities and obligations of providers and supervisory regulations of institutions regarding the oversight of their professional staff."

"Dr. Lofton. Would you please tell the jury, which of these various avenues of information proved the most useful to you in arriving at your opinions, and how you used them?"

"Quite obviously, Mrs. Hoople's examination was the focal point around which everything else evolved. When I examined her, I was able to gain a solid foundation with which to go forward.

"I found Mrs. Hoople to be cooperative, honest, hurt, in severe need of psychological treatment, severely depressed, physically able to function at only 30 to 40% of her natural capacity, personable and an overall warm natured and spirited person.

"I found that earlier in her life, she had been able to focus 90% or more of her energy toward her own life and also toward the goal of assisting others, family, friends and victims seeking help. She had no difficulties in holding down employment, capably handling two jobs at one time. She was a happy, energetic person with plenty of love for her children and others in her life.

"I further found that she had several incidents in her childhood and young adult life that she had been unable to cope with at the time, but which had been successfully stored away in her mind, covered with several layers of deception to prevent having to cope with these incidents. She now has had these events ripped open and at least partially laid before her in such a violent fashion as to render her incapable of coping with the daily routine of her life."

"Dr. Lofton, you used the word 'partially,' referring to Mrs. Hoople's knowledge of these events. As I understand Mrs. Hoople's testimony, and the testimony of Dr. Trey, she is now able to access the minds of the alters in her psyche and can, through such access, know and understand what has happened to her?"

"Although it is accurate to say that she has access to the knowledge of these alters, it is still a limited knowledge. She is not now, and quite possibly never will be, capable of controlling the emotional impact of the full knowledge of what has hurt her. We are talking about physical and psychological abuse of a kind rarely seen. Despicable, cowardly acts were literally heaped upon this young child. Her ability to survive depended then, and now, upon the capability of her mind to bury the hurt and disgust, the pain and suffering, so deep in her psyche that it literally does not exist.

"Imagine, if you will, a young infant full of love and trust for the only person in her life, other than her mother—her father. Now imagine that same child looking into those eyes she so much adores, and then seeing her father brutally rip off her diapers, gouging her with diaper pins in the process, and then inflicting the most severe pain imaginable as he tore apart her hymen and forced his entry into her undeveloped vagina, ripping and tearing in a fury of sexual degradation usually reserved for savages raiding the camps of their worst enemies.

"Any child, confronted with such total trauma would respond with a reaction of death, severe psychosis, or some sort of complete mental blockage, so complete that the father would still be a father figure, not the despicable child rapist that he really was.

"No, Judith knows the essentials of what was done to her, but not the complete details. Each time she has gotten close to this knowledge, she has become a near invalid—in other words, totally dysfunctional."

"Dr. Lofton, during your examination of Judith and of her records, did you find her to be a manipulative person?"

"Of course she's manipulative. It's a benchmark of the true M.P.D. If they weren't manipulative, they could never do what is necessary to *fool* themselves into these states of unawareness. But manipulation is not necessarily a bad thing. Manipulation is merely using some facet of their personality to entice others to help them, or do for them. It also happens to be a trait of most people, especially professionals. Lawyers try to manipulate jurors. Doctors try to manipulate patients to achieve positive results. Manipulation can be good, or bad. In Judith's case I have found no evidence of any wrongful or bad manipulation, only necessary use of manipulation, for survival."

"We have also been told, Doctor , that Judith is a capable liar. Did you find this in your research?"

"Certainly. Once again, Judith would have to be an accomplished liar indeed, to completely fool herself. Think about it. We are talking about the mind selling itself on hiding something so powerful, and so evil, that she simply could not live with the knowledge.

"So, in answer to your question, yes, she is a capable liar. But I never found that she lied in any negative way, such as to hurt others, or to profit from a lie. She is quite the opposite. She is honest to the extreme. That is another natural trait of an MPD. Somehow, they know in their own psyche that the lies they told themselves are *good* lies, and that evil or bad lies might destroy the fabric necessary to hold the fantasy together. And that, of course, they can not allow. This not a conscious attribute they can act upon or ignore. It is an unconscious rule they must follow, or perish."

"Let's talk for a while about Red Greely, Doctor. Did you review any records to enable you to arrive at any opinions regarding Red's treatment of Judith?"

"Certainly. I first knew about this abomination to the psychiatric profession from Mrs. Hoople's statements, both while conscious and while under hypnosis. I then reviewed all the transcripts where he was mentioned several times. I then reviewed his single page of notes taken in the dozens of sessions he conducted. I studied his educational background and, I must admit, with much surprise, I looked into his rise to the controlling figure at the Hillsborough Community Crisis Center.

"Based upon these studies, my own knowledge, and my review of the ethical and legal rules as they apply to psychiatric counseling, I formulated my opinions."

"Before we get to your actual opinions, Doctor, will you please tell the jury the factual basis upon which you formulated these opinions?"

"To begin with I looked at Red Greely's position at the Center. He was an exalted ruler, with complete authority to exercise his own discretion in every aspect of administration, from hiring and firing to the actual rules and regulations pertaining to all the day-to-day operations of the clinic. He could also dictate the type and frequency of counseling sessions, both group and independent, that went on at the center. He was the person appointed by the center to guide and instruct other counselors, set protocols and handle all emergencies. Even though he reported to Tim Snead, he did so only as a courtesy, not as a mandate.

"Once I had ascertained his occupational functions, I then checked the Center protocols to see what kind of background was necessary to have such an important position. A Doctorate in an appropriate discipline was advocated, a Masters was mandated.

"I then followed through and checked up on Red Greely's credentials. He had a *bona fide* Bachelors degree, but his masters' thesis was never completed, even though somehow he obtained a certificate which proclaimed otherwise."

I glanced over to the defense table and saw Tim Snead worriedly lean over to talk in Bill's ear, but Bill was trying to keep him from letting the jury know this was a surprise. It was like trying to tell your kid you can't get off the freeway when he has to go. It doesn't stop him, it just makes him wriggle more.

"What did this tell you, Doctor?"

"As to Red Greely, it pointed out two specific problems. First, Red Greely was totally unqualified for his position under the Center's protocol. Second, one has to assume that Greely knew he was underqualified and deliberately misled the Clinic when he was hired."

"You said 'as to Red Greely,' Doctor. Was there something else on your mind?"

"Yes. If I could find this out in three or four inquires, the Center could have also. Therefore, the Center did not do a worthwhile investigation into the background of the man whom they hired to oversee and run the Center, and to whom they entrusted the lives and sanity of numerous victims who came in contact with the Center at the most vulnerable point in their lives."

"Please continue, factually, about the basis of your findings on Red, Doctor."

"He attempted to treat a person in a situation for which he had absolutely no expertise. He did not attempt to acquire the necessary knowledge, nor to refer the patient to someone who had the necessary expertise. He kept no notes upon which to build a referral treatment, or future basis for treatment by himself or any other practitioner. He attempted harmful and unprofessional treatments that not only produced no benefit to the patient, but which caused permanent and life threatening damages. He violated the canons and ethics of every branch of medical or psychiatric professionals by inducing his patient to satisfy his own sexual needs and desires while the patient was under the power of his hypnotic trance, and furthered that carnal ethical impropriety by inducing a state of dependence on his patient that insured repeated performances of sexual gratification for himself. I have sat on the Board of Inquiry for Psychiatrists and Psychologists of the State of Maryland for fifteen years, and I have never run across a situation as blatantly unethical as this one."

We continued in this vein for almost two hours, exploring every factual basis for the doctor's upcoming opinions. Bill fidgeted in his seat, but did not raise any objections. He already knew Doctor Lofton was no pushover, and any minor objection would only result in re-emphasizing whatever he objected to. As we approached the time for me to begin to get the actual opinions, Judge Midder decided it was time for a break.

* * * *

During the break, I saw the adjuster angrily approach Bill and Tim Snead. Probably a shock to her also. Good. Maybe they would start talking money.

I made a pit stop, and by the time I returned, everyone had calmed down. As I said, Bill is a good lawyer. It was time to put some more pressure on.

"Is the plaintiff ready to proceed?"

"Yes, Your Honor."

"Dr. Lofton, the court reminds you that you are still under oath. You may proceed, Mr. Newton."

"Thank you, Your Honor."

"Doctor Lofton, do you have an opinion, within a reasonable degree of medical probability, whether or not Mrs. Hoople suffers from Multiple Personality Disorder?"

"Yes, I do."

"And what is that opinion, Doctor?"

"Mrs. Hoople has a classic case of Multiple Personality Disorder, as defined in the DMSO, and she has between four and six different personalities, one of which is suicidal."

"Again, Doctor, do you have an opinion within a reasonable degree of medical probability what the cause of Mrs. Hoople's disorder was?"

"Yes, I do"

"And what is that opinion, Doctor?"

"For all but one personality, severe mental, physical emotional and sexual abuse as a very young child. This was caused primarily by her parents, especially her father. Once the dam was broken and an alternate personality had been formed, it was a more readily available form of punishment escape as further traumatic events occurred in Mrs. Hoople's life."

"You said all but one. What about that one, Doctor?"

"One alter was created as a direct result of the abusive and traumatic mistreatment, actual criminally negligent treatment by Red Greely."

"Objection!!" Bill was on his feet faster than a rattlesnake striking. "Dr. Lofton is not qualified to render legal opinions, only medical opinions, and Mr. Newton knows it."

Bill's really letting this get to him. Good!

"On the contrary, as a part of Doctor Lofton's time on the Regulatory Board, it was one of his duties to decide which practitioners should be turned over to the State Attorney's office for criminal prosecution. We covered that earlier in his credentials proffer, Your Honor, and Mr. Handell did not object at that time, nor challenge the Doctor's credibility in that arena."

Bill was livid. Judge Midder smiled and said: "Overruled, Counselor. You may continue, Mr. Newton."

"Doctor Lofton, do you have an opinion, within a reasonable degree of medical probability whether Mrs. Hoople was truthful in her testimony regarding her treatment by Red Greely?"

"Objection, Your Honor. If polygraph exams are considered too unscientific to be allowed in as evidence, surely, this fortune telling guesswork is just as objectionable."

Nice try, but it won't fly and you know it.

"Overruled, Counselor. Continue, Mr. Newton"

"Do you remember the question, Dr. Lofton?"

"Yes, I remember, and yes, I do."

"What is that opinion, Doctor?"

"She was telling the full truth. I examined her both in her natural state and while I had her under deep hypnosis. There were no discrepancies in her statements while in either state. The only thing I found remarkable about the two exams was that she tended to give Red Greely quite a bit less criticism while in a natural state than while under hypnosis. She still does not know or remember all the things, bad things that have happened to her."

"Doctor, do you have an opinion, within a reasonable degree of medical certainty, as to Mrs. Hoople's current medical and psychological state."

"Yes, I do."

"And what is that opinion, Doctor?"

"Physically, I agree with the social security evaluation that Mrs. Hoople is basically 100% disabled. Although she can get around and do things at times, she is subject to spurts of intense pain and total incapacitation at any moment. There is no way she could be expected to hold down a job at this time in her life.

"Mentally, or psychologically, she is equally impaired. She has little control of her mind after she is tired, stressed, or sleeping. She can be flooded with totally incapacitating thoughts at any time. Once again, she can not hold down a job or do anything too stressful without substantial fear of severe mental and physical pain and disability."

"Doctor, do you have an opinion, within a reasonable degree of medical probability whether Mrs. Hoople's MPD is the cause of her current physical and mental problems?"

"Yes, I do."

What is that opinion, Doctor?"

"Multiple Personality Disorder, although present and working in Mrs. Hoople, is not the cause of Mrs. Hoople's current medical and psychological condition."

I looked at the jurors, and most of them seemed genuinely puzzled at this pronouncement.

Good, keep them listening closely.

"Doctor, could you elaborate on this last statement of your opinions, please?"

"Certainly, it may sound a bit confusing. Judith Hoople has had MPD for thirty-four years or more. Yet, she was an energetic and vibrant woman, able to hold down two jobs and raise a family, and have fun in the process. Obviously, MPD did not interfere with her lifestyle, nor did it in anyway inhibit or disable her. It was just there, doing exactly what her mind had programmed as necessary to give balance and sanity to her life, in spite of the most horrible traumatic psychological injuries imaginable. MPD, in Judith's case, was nothing more than a benign tumor. It was non-malignant and non-invasive to Judith's sanity."

"Well then Doctor, do you have an opinion, within a reasonable degree of medical certainty, what caused Mrs. Hoople's current problems?"

Yes, I do."

"What is that, Doctor?"

"Red Greely and his unethical, unprofessional, criminally negligent treatment of Mrs. Hoople was the direct cause of her current problems. Hillsborough Community Crisis Center was also negligent and a contributing cause of Mrs. Hoople's problems."

"Would you please elaborate how, within a reasonable degree of medical certainty, the Crisis Center was a negligent and contributing cause of Mrs. Hoople's problems, Doctor?"

"The Crisis Center had a duty, under its own charter and protocol, as well as the rules and laws of ethical and professional conduct, to thoroughly investigate Red Greely prior to assigning him a position of such authority and autonomy and allowing him to actually set protocol in the Center. The Center had a duty to supervise Red Greely, check up on his practices, sit in, either through individuals at the center, or through outside independent agencies, on Red's counseling sessions, training sessions, routine practices, *etc.* No hospital or other agency entrusted with the responsibility that the Center had would allow unchecked and unrestrained authority to reign.

"The Center breached these duties, thereby allowing the mistreatment of Mrs. Hoople to take place. In other words, but for the negligence of the Center, Red's unscrupulous treatment of Mrs. Hoople never would have taken place."

"Thank you very much, Doctor. I have no further questions."

The timing was perfect. It was ten till five, and as I watched Judge Midder look at the clock, I knew we would break for the night.

The last thing this jury heard tonight is the only thing this trial is about.

"Gentlemen, please approach the bench."

When we were set, Judge Midder began. "Mr. Handell, I know you would like to take the Doctor's testimony right now. However, we both know it will take more than fifteen minutes and I am heading to chambers to autograph warrants for the Sheriff's department at that time. So, I'm sorry to do this to you, but we will break for the evening. Just wanted you to know why."

"Thank you, Your Honor." Bill said, but it was anything but thanks that sparked from his eyes.

* * * *

"See Boss. I told you that you were worried too much. Things are looking really good."

We were back at the office, Judith was on her way home and Joe, Eric and I were relaxing in my office. Dr. Lofton and I each held a drink, but Joe was getting ready to leave and was not drinking.

"I'm on my way out, Boss. You two have fun and don't work too late."

"See you tomorrow, Joe. Enjoy!"

As Joe left the office, Eric said: "Quite a gal you got there, Counselor. If she knew medicine, I'd try to steal her away from you."

"Fat chance, Doc. Every paralegal I have is both good at what she does, and loyal as well. I believe that if you treat someone with respect, they will do the same for you. You could try to steal her, but it would never happen."

"What's Mr. Handell going to do tomorrow, Paul? Despite the loyal optimism of your attractive paralegal, you and I both know things went too well for him to do nothing. What have I got to look out for on cross examination?"

"Unfortunately, Doc, I think you out-legalized Joe on this read. Bill cannot let this ride. This jury will have had all night to dwell on your testimony, which as I already told you, was excellent. If he can't put some doubts in their minds, he might as well ask the adjuster to get out her checkbook, and he can't do that."

"Interesting. Why can't he?"

"I'm not exactly sure why, but this has gotten personal to him. I'm convinced that he truly believes that Judith is a fraud, and my getting the judge to allow you in at the last minute is a direct affront to him as a lawyer. He is a good lawyer, and usually one of the most courteous as well."

"So, Counselor, back to my original question. What can I expect him to do?"

"I'm not sure. He has to attack, and there are only two areas open to attack. The actual evidence is pretty much unassailable. That leaves your credibility, or the validity of your opinions, and I'm damned if I can see any effective way to attack either one successfully. But you can bet, he's got to try."

"Well, I'm not going to let it worry me. I've got some patient notes and a few faxes to get out to my office before morning, so I'm heading back to the hotel. I thank you for the drink, and I'll see you first thing in the morning."

"O.K. Doc. By the way, when you get all your faxes ready, just bring them in with you in the morning and I'll have Terry make sure they get to your office."

"Thanks, I'll do that. Goodnight. Hope you can figure out where he's going."

"I'll sleep on it. Should have something on it by morning."

As Eric walked down the hall and out to the elevator bank, I leaned back in my chair.

Sleep on it. Yeah, right.

I poured myself another Crown on the rocks and opened my briefcase and dumped the file on my desk. Wouldn't be much sleep tonight.

* * * *

"Mr. Handell, is the defense ready to proceed?"

"The defense is ready, Your Honor."

It was nine in the morning, and we were back in court. I knew something had to happen, but I still didn't have a handle on it. Dr. Lofton was back in the witness box and had already been admonished that he was still under oath.

"You may proceed with your cross-examination of the witness, Counselor."

"Thank You, Your Honor. Doctor Lofton, have you ever appeared as an expert witness before?"

"Yes, I have."

"Ever been rejected as a qualified witness in any court of law?"

"No, never."

"Approximately how many times have you appeared in court as an expert witness, Doctor?"

"I don't actually know the exact number of times, but probably between twenty and thirty times."

"Twenty to thirty times. Wow. That's quite a few, Doctor. And, of course you get paid for your appearances don't you, Doctor?"

"I receive payment by the hour for the actual time I put on the case, and I also receive payment for my expenses."

"How much per hour do you charge, Doctor?"

"Two hundred and fifty dollars an hour."

"Two hundred and fifty dollars an hour! That's a lot of money for testimony, don't you think, Doctor?"

"No, actually I don't think that at all. I receive the same fees for my medical services, and am always booked full. Attending a trial like this requires me to block out a lot of time and I actually make less over a two or three day period than I would at my office."

"How much time have you invested in this case, Doctor?"

"I don't know for sure."

"Over fifty hours?"

"Oh, I'm sure it is over fifty hours."

"Over a hundred hours?"

"That, I don't know. Possible but I don't know."

"Well then, Doctor, it would be safe to say that you will earn at least a figure between $12,500 and $25,000 dollars, if not more in this case?"

"I guess so."

"No, doctor, you know so, correct?"

"Yes."

"And for that $25,000 you must offer expert testimony, correct?"

"That's part of it, correct."

"Part of it. Doctor, if you could not offer expert testimony you wouldn't be here, would you?"

"I suppose not."

"Doctor, what's with the supposes and guesses? You didn't suppose and guess with your expert testimony. Don't like talking about the money, huh?"

"No, I don't enjoy talking about money. It is not the controlling factor in whether or not I take a case, and I don't like to put too much emphasis on it."

"Oh, I see. Not the controlling factor. How many of the 25 to 30 cases you have testified in did you do so for free?"

That was a distortion. Doctor Lofton had said twenty to thirty and Bill and I both knew it. He also knew I wouldn't object, because that would only focus more attention to it.

"None."

"So, it's not the primary reason you take a case, but in 100% of the cases you have taken, you were paid. True?"

"Correct."

Bill gave a little throat clearance, and glanced knowingly at the jury. He and they were now sharing a moment of skepticism. Bill was good.

"Now doctor, when Mr. Newton asked you about your opinion, he used special terms, did he not?"

"I don't quite understand your question."

"The terms I am referring to are opinions within a reasonable degree of medical certainty. Remember those, Doctor?

"Certainly."

"Now, that sounds like pretty good stuff. But it doesn't really mean anything in lay terms, does it Doctor? It's actually a legal term, is it not?"

"You, sir, are the lawyer, not me. But I suppose that is true."

Don't start getting feisty, Doc. He'll burn you.

"Within a reasonable degree of medical certainty. What's that really mean, Doctor?"

"Well, it means that it's more likely than not that something is true."

"More likely than not. In other words, it doesn't even take fifty-one percent favor factors. Just a little more than fifty percent?"

"True, but—"

"And that means a little more favor in *your eyes*, right Doc? I mean you would have no empirical evidence to support the majority of your opinions, correct?"

"I believe one of the reasons they call it expert opinion is that the person rendering the opinion is qualified to offer such opinions based upon his or her recognized expertise in a given field, sir."

Way to go, doc. But be careful.

Bill continued as if Dr. Lofton hadn't said a thing.

"Is there any empirical evidence to support your opinion that Judith had sex with Red Greely?"

"If, by empirical you mean did anyone report observing Red Greely sexually abusing Judith, no; but you would have to ignore a tremendous amount of unchallenged testimony to believe otherwise."

"Doctor, please. I realize that you would like your opinions to rest unchallenged, but I am entitled to an uneditorialized answer. You have been here many times before and you know that.

"Once again, is there any empirical evidence to support your opinion that Judith had sex with Red Greely?"

"No."

"Thank you Doctor. Is there any empirical evidence to support your opinion that Judith was truthful in her assertions against Red Greely?"

"Other than a lifetime of study and experience, no."

"Your Honor, I have tried to encourage the witness to answer my questions properly, but I now have to ask the Court to instruct this witness to answer my questions in a manner consistent with the rules of court."

Bill was the epitome of a contrite, somewhat chastened lawyer, just looking for a little help from the court to straighten out an uncooperative witness.

"Doctor Lofton, this court instructs you to answer the defendant's questions with the same candor you answered Mr. Newton's questions. You understand?"

"Yes, Your Honor."

Damn, damn. Hang in there Doc. Don't blow it now. Your credibility is getting slammed, whether you know it or not. And I can't do a thing about it!

"Doctor, I ask you again, is there any empirical evidence to support your opinion that Judith was truthful in her assertions against Red Greely?"

"No."

"Doctor, is there any empirical evidence to support your opinion that Judith Hoople actually suffers from Multiple Personality Disorder?"

"No."

"In other words, Doctor, you can't tell this jury flat out that Judith Hoople is anything other than a woman with a story, which may or may not be true, and support it with any empirical evidence, isn't that true?"

"Well, I wouldn't—"

"Yes or no, Doc?" Bill had a definite edge in his voice now.

"Yes."

"It is entirely possible that this whole MPD thing, and all the accusations against Red are nothing but the actions of a vindictive woman looking to get even with a lover who spurned her and make a few bucks in the interim, isn't that true, Doc?"

"Anything—"

"Yes or no, Doc!" This time Bill jumped quickly and left no room for any mitigation. There was steel in his voice, and I could see it registered with the jury.

"Yes."

"Let's be clear here, Doc. You were hired by the plaintiff because you were willing to testify in her behalf, correct?"

"I'm not a mind reader, Counselor. I don't know exactly why I was hired."

"Well, I'm glad you admit you are not a mind reader. For a while there you had me convinced otherwise when it came to Mrs. Hoople."

"Objection."

"Sustained, the jury will disregard counsel's last statement. Be careful, Counselor. You're on the edge."

Acting for all the world as if the last exchange hadn't taken place, Bill continued.

"Doctor, are you telling this jury that you were not hired because your opinions were supportive of the plaintiff?"

Damn it Doc. You know better than to let him get to you. Quit playing with him. He's gonna eat you alive and I can't help you.

"I'm telling this jury that I don't know the exact reason why I was hired."

"Well, Doc, let's make it easy for them. In the last 25 to 30 cases in which your highly paid services were contracted, how many of them were contracted by a party with whom your opinions were at odds?"

"I'm not sure I understand your question, sir?"

"Geeze, Doc. I thought it was plain. How many people hire you and pay you $25,000 per case or more, to render your 'expert opinions' if those expensive opinions disagree with them?"

"Objection; misstates the witnesses earlier testimony."

"Overruled, Counselor. The Doctor can answer."

Damn it Doc. Now you got the judge on their side.

"None, Counselor."

"Now, Doc. I need you to tell me, how much of your testimonial work is done for the plaintiffs as opposed to the defendants in a law suit?"

"I'm not really sure about the percentages."

Look at me you idiot. He's reeling you in, hook line and sinker. He wouldn't ask if he didn't know.

"Well then, Doc, would you say it is more for the plaintiff or the defense?"

"Probably more for the plaintiff, but, again, I'm not sure of the percentages."

"Well Doc. According to my records, the percentages of your testimony are 100% in favor of the plaintiffs. 0% for the defense. That help your recollection?"

Don't bite! Tell the truth. All right already.

"As I told you, I'm not sure of the percentages, but I don't believe that those figures are accurate."

"Well Doc, I can certainly appreciate the confusion. After all, you were confused on the number of cases in which you testified also, weren't you?"

"I don't believe so, Counselor."

"I have a list here of forty-two cases in which you are listed as an expert witness, Doc. You want to look at it and tell me which ones my investigator messed up on?"

Shit, Shit, Shit.

"Objection; misstates the Doctor's earlier testimony."

"Overruled Counselor. If there is any misstatement, the Doctor can straighten it out with his answer. Please answer the question, Doctor."

"Obviously, I can't answer the question without the list."

Damn it Doc. Have you lost all your marbles? He's killing you and you are inviting it. Quit being so damn hardheaded. Bill's better than you are at this.

"May I approach the witness, Your Honor?"

"Certainly, Counselor."

Handing Dr. Lofton the list, Bill looked at me and smiled. I wanted to smack him in the mouth; the Doc too.

"Take your time Doctor. All I want to know now is which of these cases you were never an expert witness in?"

Like the mesmerized rookie expert he had let himself become, Dr. Lofton sat there and read each case before he answered. He was apparently quite unaware that the jury was now convinced that he was a paid whore.

Finishing his reading, Dr. Lofton handed the list back to Bill and said, "The list appears to be in order."

Without retrieving the list, Bill said:

"Hold on to that for a minute Doc. Now that we are in agreement as to the least number of cases in which you have rendered your highly priced expertise, look down the list and tell this jury which of these cases is the one, if any wherein you testified for the defense?"

Dutifully, even though everyone in the courtroom knew the answer, Dr. Lofton re-read every case. I wanted to crawl off somewhere to hide and lick my open wounds.

Eventually, Dr. Lofton looked up and answered. "It doesn't appear to me that any of these cases are the ones I testified in favor of the defense for."

No, no, no. You idiot.

"Oh, I'm sorry, Doc. You mean there are others that we missed. How many would that be, Doc?"

Finally realizing the trap he has set for himself, and also apparently realizing the mess he was in, Dr. Lofton said, "There are no others. The confusion lay in my regarding the role I played in prosecuting some of these unqualified practitioners on behalf of the state medical board as non-plaintiff cases. That is what I was looking for on your list."

Good answer Doc. Would have been great about a half hour ago, while you still had some credibility.

"Well I'll sure give you credit for a good imagination, but what—"

"Objection!"

"Sustained! Watch it Counselor. You're on thin ice."

"Sorry, Your Honor. No offense meant."

You lying SOB. You got your point to the jury, objection or not.

"Dr. Lofton, please clear up the confusion for me and the jury. Can you name a single case in which you testified in a civil matter were you were paid for your expertise in which you testified on the side of the defense?"

"No."

"Thank you Doctor. Now, getting back to my earlier question. It is entirely possible that this whole MPD thing and all the accusations against Red Greely by Mrs. Hoople are nothing but the actions of a vindictive woman looking to get even with a lover who spurned her and to make some serious money in the process isn't that true?"

"It is possible but—"

"Thank you Doc. Remember, no editorialization. One last question, and then Mr. Newton can clear up anything the two of you think needs clarifying. When you charge your $250.00 per hour, is that portal to portal?"

"Yes."

"So, from the time you leave your office in Maryland until you return, you get paid $250.00 per hour, even while you are sleeping at the hotel at the plaintiff's expense?"

"That's what portal to portal means, yes."

"But you weren't sure why they hired you." Bill shook his head as if in disbelief, looked at the jury, shrugged his shoulders and turned to Judge Midder and said, "I have no further questions of this witness, Your Honor."

As he walked back to his counsel table, Bill looked for all the world as if he had just completed a chore that left him with dirty hands and he needed to wash up.

"Any re-direct, Mr. Newton?"

I really wanted to scream no, what the hell good would it do, but instead I said: "Yes, thank you, Your Honor." I had to try to salvage something.

"Only one or two quick questions, Doctor."

"Explain, if you would, briefly, what the difference is between possibility and probability for the jury, Doctor?"

"Well, possibility means anything that is not impossible. Probability means something that is likely. Using the sun for an example, it is possible that when it goes down tonight, it may never come back up, in violation of all the known rules of the universe, but still possible. However, it is probable that it will be back tomorrow morning, and every morning as long as the earth survives."

"Thank you Doctor. Now, Mr. Handell asked you if it was possible that Judith was a vindictive person who made all this up, and you answered yes. What did you mean by that?"

"As I said, almost anything is possible. However, it is *probable* that what she has said happened really happened and what she has is a genuine case of MPD.

"In fact," he continued, "it would be highly improbable for it to be any other way."

"Dr., in the past have you been approached by any defense lawyers and asked to represent their clients in a civil action?"

"Yes, several times."

"Is there a reason why you haven't done so?"

"Yes, they all want the same thing, and they were all ready to pay top dollar for it."

"And what is that, Doctor?"

"They all wanted me to deny the existence of MPD, and to deny that the plaintiff had it. That I cannot do. MPD is a real, valid recognized condition, and Judith Hoople is a classic example of someone who has it. It may be insidious and hard to comprehend, but that does not make it any less real."

It was time to quit. We had been hurt, but this was the best I was likely to get, and if I pushed any harder, it would only open doors for Bill to tear down.

"Thank you, Doctor. No further questions, Your Honor."

"Any re-cross, Mr. Handell?"

"No thank you, Your Honor."

"The witness may step down. We'll take a fifteen minute break before the next witness. Bailiff."

* * * *

Over the break I made up my mind. One witness was all I had left that I intended to call. It was the only way I could figure that would possibly end the question of Judith's reliability, and there was no one else who could do it. I already knew what the answer to each question would be. Welcome to Fifth

Amendment time.

* * * *

"Is the plaintiff ready to call her next witness?"

"Yes, thank you, Your Honor. The plaintiff calls Red Greely to the stand."

There was a murmur that ran through the courtroom. Even Bill looked puzzled. We both knew all Red would say would be to invoke the Fifth Amendment, but he still hadn't figured how it would benefit Judith. Well, he would soon find out, or so I thought. With an adverse, or even better, hostile witness, a good lawyer was able to frame all questions as leading and leave only the possibility of a yes or no answer. Additionally, with a person on the hook, a perjury charge hanging over his head and a criminal charge pending, the only possible answer would be for him to plead the Fifth, leaving the lawyer to give a series of good speeches, uncontested by the witness and leaving the witness looking like scum. At least that's the way it went in theory.

After he was sworn in and took the stand, Judge Midder said, "You may proceed with direct, Counselor."

"Thank you, Your Honor."

"Mr. Greely, and so that I am sure that I am not demeaning you, sir, the title is Mister, is it not?"

"That is correct."

"It's not doctor or anything like that?"

"Mister is fine."

"I'm sorry; I must not have made my question clear. You are not a doctor, in other words, No M.D. or Doctorate, or anything that designates or bestows upon you the title of doctor, correct?"

"Yes, that is correct."

Good. Start sweating, sucker. I ain't even started yet.

"For the last few years you have worked for the Hillsborough Community Crisis Center, correct?"

"Yes, however...." Unsure of himself, Red looked over at the defense table. No help there. Bill is not his lawyer. His lawyer left after the settlement. I broke into his reverie.

"You trying to tell this jury you no longer work there?" It was a guess, but I figured a pretty safe one.

"Yes."

"When did you cease working there?"

"About two months ago."

"Did you resign?"

"Yes."

He was getting more nervous now.

"If you had not resigned, was there a pending threat that the Center would fire you?"

This time he licked his lips before answering. "I respectfully refuse to answer the question based upon the Fifth Amendment right against self incrimination."

Not well spoken, but exactly what I expected.

Gotcha now sucker. I'm going to bleed you for a while. Hope you like it as much as you liked screwing Judith and your built in harem.

"Mr. Greely, would you please look at what has been previously marked as plaintiff's exhibit #14 and tell me if you recognize it? May I approach the witness, Your Honor?"

"You may approach, Counselor."

I handed Red the three page document and he swallowed, knowing what was coming.

"Do you recognize the document, sir?"

"Yes."

"And would you tell the jury, what is the document in your hands?"

"It is my former resume."

"By former, you mean the one you were using before the Center hired you and the one you submitted to the Center for consideration when you applied for a position with them?"

He swallowed again, thought for a moment and said, "Yes."

"The document has a yellow marker on one part, do you see it sir?"

"Yes."

"And what does that highlighted part say, please?"

"It says Masters Degree in sociology/psychology."

"May I publish the document to the jury, Your Honor?"

"Certainly, Counselor. The jury will take the document and pass it around. Please do not take too long with it ladies and gentlemen. You will be able to see it later, in the jury room with all the other evidence. You do intend to introduce it, Counselor?"

"Yes, Your Honor, in fact, I will do that right now?"

"Any objections, Mr. Handell?"

"No, Your Honor."

"The document is received into evidence as plaintiff's exhibit #14. The jury will now examine plaintiff's exhibit 14."

It took about four or five seemingly long minutes for the jury to pass the document along. When they signaled they were through, I retrieved it and held it in my hand.

"Mr. Greely. You do not have a master's degree, do you?"

"No."

"Why was this title and certificate submitted if it was not true?"

"I respectfully decline to answer based upon the Fifth Amendment."

"Your Honor, I request that the witness be designated as a hostile witness for examination purposes."

"Mr. Handell?"

"I would object, Your Honor. An adverse witness, maybe, but he has done nothing hostile."

"The rules are quite clear, Your Honor," I said. "This witness is refusing to answer questions that are material and relevant to my case, and it is obviously done to benefit the witness. I am entitled to have the witness declared hostile."

"The witness is found by this court to be hostile to the legitimate interests of the plaintiff and is therefore subject to examination under the rules regulating examination of a hostile witness. You may proceed, Counselor."

"Thank you, Your Honor."

"Isn't it true, sir, that you lied on your application, and submitted a forged Masters certificate in order to gain a position of authority and compensation you otherwise would be neither qualified nor entitled to?"

"I refuse to answer based on the Fifth Amendment."

"You worked with Judith Hoople, did you not?"

"Yes."

"You were her supervisor, correct?"

"Yes."

"You also treated her for psychological problems, did you not?"

"I treated her all right, but not the way you are suggesting."

Whoa, what the hell was that! He should have pleaded the Fifth. What's going on?

Even Bill looked puzzled.

I continued, "Isn't it true, sir, that you approached Judith Hoople about hypnotizing her, and, based upon your position at the clinic, you convinced her to let you hypnotize her?"

"No, she actually came to me with a plan to have a lot of fun and get paid for it."

"No sir," I almost shouted. "Isn't it true that once you had her under your hypnotic control, you abused your trust as a counselor and attempted treatments which were unproven, untested, unprofessional and harmful?"

"I will admit, what we did was unprofessional in the normal sense, but it was a lot of fun. This lady knows more sexual positions than a monkey and she is good at all of them."

The Burl Ives smile was wide and evil looking and I wanted to smack him in the face, but instead I continued to practice law.

"Objection" I screamed to the judge while almost spitting on the witness. "The witness is not answering the question but making self-serving, derogatory, mean spirited and nasty statements to hide his own wrongdoing!"

The courtroom was buzzing, Red Greely was smiling and I was almost apoplectic. Bill Handell was open mouthed but gathering his thoughts fast.

"Your Honor, the witness has answered the question, albeit not the answer counsel wished," Bill finally spoke.

Judge Midder was clearly perplexed, but in true judicial fashion he opined, "Mr. Greely, please confine your responses to the questions asked. Counselor, continue."

My mind was spinning.

Damn. What the hell is going on? This son of a bitch is willing to lie under oath and clearly risk perjury. Who has he been talking to?

"Isn't it also true, sir, that you further abused your trust by physically abusing Mrs. Hoople, and having unsolicited and unauthorized sexual relations with her and her child alters while she was in your hypnotic trance and unable to resist your advances?"

"I believe she was the one to first bring up childlike foreplay, but as I said, it was fun."

This time, instead of blowing my top, I stood back and looked at this evil little man and recognized that having gone this far, he was committed. He would continue to lie. He had to. Not only that, but he was enjoying himself in the process. I had to come up with a new plan, but what?

He's breaking out in a sweat and he looks exactly like the pervert you would expect to see in a dark shadow outside a porno flick. He even keeps running his hand down his pant leg! He may be killing me, but I need to see where this is going. If I stop now, he clearly wins. In for a penny…

"Isn't it true that you engineered trysts throughout the days and weeks in which you hypnotized Mrs. Hoople and while in your hypnotic spell, you had her provide you with oral sex, vaginal sex, and any other kind of perverse sexual acts which you desired in order to satisfy your own sexual urges, in complete violation of all ethical, moral and legal rules and regulations of your profession?"

Red actually licked his fat lips with his disgusted little pointed tongue before replying. "I believe you mentioned several things that happened, but not through hypnosis. Hypnosis was merely an excuse, a way out if we were questioned. We both wanted it and this was a way we could have it all."

Red Greely was sweating openly, now often wiping his brow and upper lip with his shirtsleeve. But, I recognized it was not the sweat of fear, but lust.

You rotten son of a bitch. You plead the Fifth anywhere it can kill you even without witnesses, but all the rest is your word against hers. You're trying to avoid criminal prosecution by a bad verdict in this civil case. Some lawyer has clued you in and you're willing to take the chance. What's a little perjury against rape, etc?

That's it, you pig. Let me try to set this up so the jury can see just what a sorry son of a bitch you really are. I'm not letting you sink my case, you bastard.

Changing my tone and trying to look far more relaxed and confident than I felt, I continued.

"You really enjoyed your sexual tryst's with Mrs. Hoople, didn't you, Red." I asked in a not too aggressive tone.

"Oh yeah, she was the best." Still licking his lips my despicable, fat little pig continued, "She was insatiable. One minute a five year old and the next, a knowledgeable pro. I couldn't satisfy her as much as she wanted, but I sure gave it the old college try."

As I looked at the jury, some of the men looked as though Red may be making a few points, but the women just looked disgusted.

What a hole I have dug! This should have been open and shut and now I don't know how to shut it down.

"Please take a moment and think back to the time you can remember when you and she had the most sexual fun on company time, Mr. Greely.

"Objection, what kind of question is that?" Bill was on his feet. He didn't know where I was going, but he didn't like it.

"Counselor, approach." Judge Midder didn't care for it either.

Only Red seemed to enjoy the question, and as I glanced at him, I could see he was actually thinking back to the question and the possible answer.

"Counselor, this court clearly is lost. Where are you going with this question?"

"Truthfully, Your Honor, I hadn't planned anything like this round of questions. It is my sincere belief that the witness is lying under oath and I'm merely trying to find a way to end my questions without letting him poison the well, so to speak."

"Judge, he has admitted this is nothing more than a fishing expedition—"

"Both of you be silent." Judge Midder was not liking the moment, but he apparently didn't like the witness either. "Counselor, you are on a very short leash. Watch it. Now get back to your positions."

I don't think Red paid any attention to the sidebar. He's still thinking about the question! What a truly dirty little man.

"Well sir?" I intoned.

"There were so many. It's a very difficult decision, you know, which was the best."

At this point Red was openly wiping his hands on his pant legs and sweat beaded his brow and upper lip. Before each statement he licked his lips with that pointy little tongue and his expression was glazed.

This bastard may get off right here in court! How did he ever pass for a professional? I have never been so disgusted in a courtroom. I've got to get this over, but how?

"Mr. Greely let's forget about the episodes themselves and get straight to the point."

"You passed yourself off as a professional, took Judith under your wings and allowed her to think of you as her savior and then used that power to satisfy your own urges. In other words, isn't it true, sir that you deliberately induced a dependency state in which to hold Mrs. Hoople under your spell so that she would satisfy every perverted sexual desire you requested, whenever you wanted that satisfaction?"

Before he could answer, I cleverly continued.

"And isn't it also true, sir, that when you had satisfied all of your perverted desires and used Mrs. Hoople until there was no desire left in you for her sexual favors, you dumped her without even attempting closure, knowing, even with your limited education and forged credentials, that this would result in a complete breakdown and potential life threatening psychological crisis to Mrs. Hoople?"

Pulling himself away from his perverted reveries, Red's answer was one of the best curve balls ever thrown: "I'll tell you what's true, Counselor. Judith Hoople is a virtual sex maniac who wanted to screw twenty-four/seven. She can take it anywhere—"

"Objection Your Honor, move to strike as non responsive!" I literally screamed at the court, red faced and mad as hell at this fat little pervert.

"Sustained." Judge Midder was as red faced as I was. "The jury will disregard the witness's statements." Then, turning straight at the witness. "And, sir, you will refrain from any self-serving comments and hold your testimony to answering the questions put to you. Do you understand me, Mr. Greely, sir?" The last, although in question form was an unmistakable threat which no one could miss.

"Yes, sir," was all Red offered, seeming pleased with what his comments had caused.

Dear God, now what. Nasty as this foul man is, at least two of the jurors are giving his testimony way too much credit. I may have lost them. If they believe it is even possible for the sex to have been consensual, that's it. The pervert walks, no criminal prosecution and we all go home broke and Judith, broken.

All right, think. What can I do to turn this around? God, for the first time since this trial started Bill looks happy. Think.

"Mr. Greely, I only have a couple questions left; however, before I ask them I wish to remind you, you are under oath and subject to prosecution should you decide not to answer truthfully."

"Objection," Bill was out of his seat. "Counsel is badgering the witness."

"Sustained. Counsel, the Court will admonish the witness, if it feels it necessary. Please continue."

That wasn't too bad. Midder went light so I can guess he agrees with me in principle.

"Isn't it true that after treating Mrs. Hoople like dirt, abusing your trust, sexually satisfying all your perverted sexual desires and dumping her, you then sent her a bill for over two thousand dollars to cover the part of your "services" that the insurance company would not pay?"

"Objection, calls for more than one answer," Bill quickly shot out.

"Sustained. Rephrase the question, Counselor."

Taking the insurance billings in my hand I asked, "May I approach the witness, Your Honor?"

"Go ahead, Counselor."

"Do you recognize these, sir?"

"I refuse to answer on the grounds of the Fifth Amendment".

Good, you bastard. Let's see if I can get a little something before I close.

"Your Honor, I move to enter as evidence, these papers previously marked as plaintiff's number six."

"Any objection?"

Bill merely nodded.

There being no objections, the plaintiffs six are admitted into evidence."

Request permission to publish to the jury, Your Honor."

"Permission granted. Ladies and gentlemen, please take a look at the exhibit and pass it along. You will have plenty of time to examine it closely in the jury room."

With that I handed the packet to the first juror and waited while everyone had a chance to read the billings. When the Forman passed the billing on to the clerk, I continued.

"Once again, sir, after you finished all of your treatments and all of your admitted trysts, isn't it true that you sent Mrs. Hoople a bill for over two thousand dollars for your services?"

"I refuse to answer, based on the Fifth Amendment."

That hit home. I think some of the jury would lynch you if they could you sorry substitute for a human being. But I'm still worried about the look of the men, earlier. That hurt.

With a look of disgust and contempt on my face that took no effort to produce, I looked away from Red Greely and said, "I have no further questions of this witness, Your Honor."

Judge Midder was looking at Red Greely as if he was a pile of dog doodoo.

"Any cross-examination of this witness, Mr. Handell?" The contempt was clear in Judge Midder's voice.

Bill was far too good a lawyer to jump in to try and defend the indefensible, especially such a cowardly appearing one. "I have no questions of this witness, Your Honor."

"Very well, Counselor. The witness may step down. Gentlemen are you both through with this witness, or do I need to keep him on call?"

"I have absolutely nothing further of this witness, Your Honor," I said.

"Nothing from me either, Judge." Bill said.

"O.K. then. Mr. Greely you are excused from this courtroom and released from your subpoena. The court will notify the State Attorney of your testimony here today and it will be up to the State to see if criminal prosecution is warranted. Good day, sir."

"Mr. Newton, I think this is a good time to break for lunch. Have your next witness ready to resume when we return."

"Ladies and gentlemen, the court admonishes you once again, not to talk about this case among yourselves nor with anyone else. We will be in recess until 1:30. Bailiff."

As the bailiff went through the motions, I thought, *I was sure thinking of a better ending than that. Did not expect Red to lie. The Judge helped when he mentioned criminal prosecution, but the jury might think that only applies to the billings and hiring. Greely made some points. Son of a bitch. So much for a good ending and quiet lunch.*

CHAPTER TWELVE

"Mr. Newton, is the plaintiff ready to proceed?"

We were back in the courtroom. Over lunch I had explained to Joe and Judith that I intended to call no more witnesses. I did not believe that I could do any better than what I had already done, and this would surprise the defense at least a little. Bill would not have the evening to go over testimony with his expert. The less he was prepared, the better it was for us.

"Yes, Your Honor."

"Mr. Handell?"

"The defense is ready, Your Honor."

"You may call your next witness, Mr. Newton."

"Thank you. Your Honor. May it please the court; the plaintiff has no more witnesses to call, so, at this time, the plaintiff will rest her case."

Judge Midder was holding back a smile as Bill turned apoplectic.

Jumping up, Bill nearly shouted "Your Honor—"

"You have an objection, Counselor?"

There was nothing for Bill to object too. He was caught with his proverbial pants down and he knew it.

"Your Honor, the defense was not prepared for this early a conclusion of Mr. Newton's case. Of course, we have a motion to dismiss, based upon a lack of a *prima facie* case having been established. Then, we could be ready to proceed in the morning, assuming that the Court denies the motion."

"Mr. Handell. You may assume whatever you wish about your motions, but you will be ready to proceed with your first witness following your motion, assuming you have one. You have 15 minutes to prepare your motion. Be ready with your first witness following the hearing."

"Ladies and gentlemen, I will have to ask you all to go back to the jury room for a few minutes. These lawyers have some arguing to do outside your presence, and then we will resume the trial. Thank you for your patience. I will call you back in as soon as we are ready. Meanwhile, remember; do not talk about this case among yourselves. Bailiff."

As the Judge and jury left the courtroom, Bill shot me a dirty look and almost bolted out the back door. He needed to get his number one witness over here, fast. He was back in five minutes, red in the face and pulling out case law and notes from his briefcase.

Bill and I both knew that his motion was nothing more than an exercise to preserve his earlier motions for appeal. Any chance of an argument against my having established a prima-faci case against the Center had died with Lofton's testimony. However, it would give Bill's witness time to arrive and get ready to testify.

* * * *

"Mr. Handell, are you ready to proceed with your motion?"

"Yes, Your Honor."

"Get on with it, then."

Bill brought out all his earlier arguments and added the new posture that even if his earlier motions had been denied, based upon all the evidence presented at this point, the plaintiff could not prevail in her case. Ignoring Dr. Lofton's testimony, Bill pointed out all the flaws in our case, and concluded that we had not established a *prima facie* case and therefore the case should be dismissed with prejudice, no defense being necessary.

It was an admirable effort, taking almost 45 minutes in the process. But it was pure B.S. and we all knew it, even the Judge. Judge Midder didn't even ask me to rebut the argument.

"Thank you Counselor. Your motion is denied. Are you ready to call your first witness?"

"Your Honor, my witness is Dr. Charles Krauff; however, I respectfully request that I have a few minutes to confer with him prior to calling him to the stand."

"Very well, Mr. Handell. The jury is still out, so you have 15 minutes until I call them back in. You may talk to your witness in the witness room. Be back in 15 minutes."

Judge Midder went to his chambers. Bill went to the witness room, and I headed to the restroom. I figured I had the most enjoyable break.

* * * *

"Are you ready to proceed, Counselor?"

"Yes, Your Honor," Bill said.

"Bailiff, bring in the jury."

When the jury had been seated, Bill called Dr. Krauff to the stand. After he was sworn in, Bill began his examination.

"Good afternoon, Doctor. Would you tell the jury your name and occupation, please?"

"Hello. I am Doctor Charles Krauff, and I am a psychiatrist."

"And where do you practice, Doctor?"

"My office is in the Sun Trust bank building, downtown Tampa."

"Now Doctor Krauff, you said you are a psychiatrist. Will you please tell the jury about your credentials, starting with your education in high school, and continuing until your doctorate?"

"Your Honor, the plaintiff will stipulate to the Doctor's licensing as a psychiatrist and his expertise in that field." I said, hoping to cut off the flow of attributes designed to boost the Doctor's status in front of the jury.

Bill immediately cut off that avenue. "We thank the plaintiff, Your Honor, but I think it important for the jury to understand where the Doctor is coming from."

"Please continue, Mr. Handell."

"Thank you, Your Honor. Doctor Krauff, you were about to tell the jury of your education?"

"Yes sir. I attended high school in Roanoke Virginia, graduating with honors and a scholarship to Yale University…"

It took Bill the better part of an hour to wind his way through the credential phase of his witness. He covered book writings, articles, peer review positions, *etc.* He stopped just short of sainthood and tendered the Doctor to me for cross-examination of his credentials. Since I had already stipulated as to the Doctor's expertise, it was futile to do much, but I needed to insert some reality into this bloated ego.

"The defense tenders the witness as an expert in the field of psychiatry, Your Honor."

"Mr. Newton, would you care to examine the witness?" Judge Midder asked me with a smile, obviously expecting me to decline.

"Yes, thank you, Your Honor."

The Judge and Bill both looked puzzled as Bill backed away from the stand to allow me to question the witness.

"Doctor Krauff, you have been tendered as an expert in the field of psychiatry. I just need to clarify a few points in my own mind before you continue.

"You indicated in your answers to your counsel that you attended Yale as an undergrad and Johns Hopkins for your M.D. and then went on to be Board Certified in the psychiatric profession, correct?"

"Yes sir, that is correct."

"Now, at both Johns Hopkins and Yale, classes in psychiatry are offered which use the DMSO as a primary reference book, isn't that so, Doctor?"

"Yes, that is true."

"In fact, you used the DMSO in psychiatry with about the same credence as you used the Merc's Manual in medical school, correct, Doc?"

"Well, I hadn't exactly compared them, but I guess you could say that; yes."

"And isn't it true, Doctor, that you had assignments in your psychiatric classes that required you to use the DMSO, not just as a source, but as the ultimate authority on the answer to the assigned question?"

I was setting him up for my own purposes, and he knew it. But I wasn't allowing him any room to maneuver.

"Yes, I suppose that's true."

"Sorry Doc. I don't want you to suppose. I just want a clean answer, yes or no."

"Yes, that is true."

"Thank you. Now, this case involves a person with diagnosed Multiple Personality Disorder. You already know that, correct?"

"I did not diagnose—"

"I did not ask you what your diagnosis was, Doctor. I asked you if you knew that this case involved a person with a diagnosed case of MPD. Please answer the question. Your counsel will ask you all about your diagnosis later."

"Yes, I am aware that your client has a previous diagnosis of MPD."

"Thank you Doctor. Have you ever treated anyone for MPD?"

"You already know the answer to that, Counselor."

"Yes sir, I do, but the jury does not. Please answer the question, Doctor."

The anger was just beginning to show in his face as Dr. Kraut answered.

"No, I have never treated anyone for MPD."

Good, I'm finally beginning to rattle your cage, Doctor.

"Matter of fact, you don't even believe in MPD, do you Doc?"

"I understand it is a recognized..."

"Doc! Just answer the question, please. You can do all the explanations and dancing later."

"Objection."

"Sustained. Counsel, watch it. Doctor, kindly answer the question as it is put to you."

"Well Doc? Do you believe in MPD or not?"

"Personally, no."

Turning to the court I started before Bill or the Judge could see me coming.

"Your Honor, I move to disallow the witness as an expert on the subject of Multiple Personality Disorder. His own bias, as shown so clearly here, will not allow him to exercise his expertise in an unbiased fashion. He has openly admitted that—"

Now reacting and trying to cut off my little jury speech, Bill hollered,

"Objection"

"Sustained. Counsel, approach the bench. Mr. Newton, you know the proper procedure. I told you I will not allow speeches to the jury. What the hell are you doing anyway? You already agreed to accept the witness as an expert. Now you want to reverse that. No way will I allow such a reversal."

"Your Honor, this is not a reversal. I agreed that the witness was an expert in the field of psychiatry, but not in the field of MPD. He has already demonstrated that he is unable to use his expertise fairly or with any honesty when it comes to MPD. He admits that the DMSO is a known and accepted authority in psychiatry and he still refuses to accept the legitimacy of a diagnosis that takes up three full chapters, over 200 pages of that same authoritative publication. Under the circumstances, I don't think he can stand as an expert in the field relevant to this case."

Judge Midder was red in the face, and looked like he was sucking on a lemon, but he was thinking. Bill couldn't let this go any further. Without his witness, he had nothing.

"Your Honor, this is ridiculous. In order to exclude this witness, you would have to assume that he had no expertise to evaluate and diagnose a dozen other illnesses, including MPD. No matter treatment, diagnosis is the key to expertise. You would also have to assume that the plaintiff has MPD. One of her own treating physicians disagreed with that. She did not like his diagnosis, so she went elsewhere. That doesn't make him wrong nor does it mean he isn't an expert in his field. Doctor Krauff is an extremely well recognized expert in psychiatry and to disallow him to testify in this case would be reversible error."

"Mr. Newton, you have posed a unique argument, but one that I think will not prevail. I believe it best to let you demonstrate to the jury the witness's bias. They can then use their own sense to give him the credibility they think he is entitled to. If I prevented him from testifying based upon his prejudices, the appellate court would have us all back here repeating this trial for a second time. I don't want that, and, neither do you. Motion denied, objection overruled. The witness may testify."

After we had resumed our places Judge Midder asked me, "Mr. Newton. Do you have any other questions for this witness pertaining to his expertise?"

"Not at this time, Your Honor."

"Very well then, proceed with your witness, Mr. Handell."

"Thank you, Your Honor. Now, Doctor. Would you tell the jury how you came to first see the plaintiff, Mrs. Hoople?"

"Certainly. According to my notes, Mrs. Hoople was first seen in my office as a referral from your office. She was sent to me for an independent medical/psychological evaluation."

"Excuse me, Doctor, but would you explain to the jury what you mean by an independent medical/psychological evaluation?"

"Yes sir. This is a term that is used when a physician such as myself is asked to examine an individual who is not a patient and render findings of the examination to the referring party. This is usually in the context of a law suit, an insurance application, job qualification or something of that nature."

"These are routine types of exams then?"

"Oh yes. We do several each year."

"Do you or your staff have any financial interest in these exams or their potential outcome?"

"Absolutely not. I receive my remuneration by the type of testing performed and the time I spend on the case, nothing more. I have absolutely no interest in the outcome of the case."

"Now Doctor, would you please tell the jury about your examination of the plaintiff?"

"Yes. Let's see here. Mrs. Hoople presented to my office at approximately 10: AM and was tested for about three hours. She then broke for lunch, and upon returning to the office, I personally examined her for over an hour. In that way, I was able to use the results of her written exams as well as her demeanor to enhance my ability to evaluate her responses to my questions."

"Were there any specific traits or peculiarities of Mrs. Hoople that stood out during your examination, Doctor?"

"Oh yes. She was obviously a willful and manipulative person."

"What exactly do you mean by willful and manipulative, Doctor?"

"I mean that Mrs. Hoople will do anything, whatever it takes, short of hard labor, in order to get her way."

"Would she lie?"

"If she felt it necessary, yes."

"Would she cheat?"

Time to cut this garbage off!

"Objection, Your honor. Assumes facts not in evidence—"

"Sustained. Mr. Handell."

"Sorry, Your Honor."

"What else did you notice, Doctor?"

"Mrs. Hoople is intelligent, well read and very opinionated. She keeps up with everyday affairs of a broad nature, and is able to converse intelligently on a wide variety of subjects. She is capable of using this knowledge and her innate intelligence and manipulative personality to provide herself with the creature comforts she craves."

"What else, Doctor?"

"Although at first blush she seems like a loving person, she actually is incapable of sustaining a loving relationship. Her personality will not allow her to seriously care for others, as it detracts too much from love of self. She is truly quite cold inside."

"She is an extremely self centered person. Her whole world revolves around self. Other things matter only to the extent that they add or detract from self. If it adds to self, it is embraced. If it detracts, Mrs. Hoople will discard it rapidly."

"Doctor Krauff. Mr. Newton asked you earlier about MPD. What is MPD, Doctor?"

"MPD is an acronym that stands for Multiple Personality Disorder. Multiple Personality Disorder is a mental state where one apparently believes one has more than one personality, often in conflict with one's real self."

"Proponents of MPD believe that the MPD victim, for lack of a better word, usually has no direct knowledge of his or her other personality."

"You don't sound as though you put much faith in a diagnosis of MPD, Doctor?"

"True enough, Counselor. I believe that MPD is nothing more than psychiatry trying to come up with alternative diagnoses to various mental problems that already exist, but are too harsh to want to label someone with. We don't like to say she has schizophrenia, or is manic-depressive or any number of offensive sounding psychological illnesses. It is a reflection on the trend of modern do-gooders, who can't abide with garbage collectors when a garbologist sounds better. Just as people went from being labeled handicapped to physically challenged individuals, psychiatry has joined the politically correct generation and altered it's labeling of illnesses. MPD is one of those unfortunate generic terms that sound impressive and less offensive than a genuine diagnosis."

"Then you don't believe that Mrs. Hoople has MPD?"

"Obviously, I don't believe she has that acronym. She does, however, have a problem. She suffers from a lack of self worth that she believes money can resolve, and she will therefore continue to suffer from her imaginary psychological problems until she has been financially rewarded."

"Then you believe that Mrs. Hoople's psychological problems are all money oriented?"

"Not one hundred percent, no. She also craves attention. She loves to be in the limelight. Currently, MPD assuages that craving. However, when the financial gains are realized from this phony MPD act, the act itself will no longer be necessary, and she will magically recover. Like Lazarus, she will be instantly healed."

"Let's get away from MPD and Mrs. Hoople for a minute, Doctor. Lets talk about Dr. Greely.

"Have you read the records of his treatment of Mrs. Hoople?"

"Yes."

"Do you have an opinion as to his qualification as a doctor?"

"Yes. I do."

"What is that opinion, doctor?"

"Red Greely is no doctor. If he was, he would be a disgrace to whatever discipline he had his doctoral degree in. Veterinary technicians are far more advanced in the treatment of their patients than Red Greely was with his."

"Red Greely worked for the Crisis Center, did he not?"

"Yes, according to my information, at one time he did."

"This was during the period that he treated Mrs. Hoople, correct?"

"Yes. Before, during and after his treatment of Mrs. Hoople, that is correct."

"Should Red have been treating Mrs. Hoople?"

"Red should have never treated anyone, Mrs. Hoople included."

"Do you have an opinion as to whether or not the Center should be held responsible for Red's actions in his treatment of Mrs. Hoople?"

"I do."

"What is that opinion, Doctor?"

"The Center cannot be held responsible for something they had no knowledge of. Red lied on his application to the Center and even went so far as to submit a phony degree to support his qualifications. All the treatment of Mrs. Hoople was conducted in secrecy and out of the direct line of knowledge of the Center. Much of it was even off the Center's property. Mrs. Hoople voluntarily abetted Red in this deception and withheld knowledge of this treatment from the Center. She cannot now hope to blame the Center for something which she herself hid from their scrutiny."

Son of a bitch!! He snuck that in over his deposition testimony. If I object, it only drives the opinion deeper into the brains of the jurors. Damn, damn, damn. That hurts.

"Thank you, doctor. I have no further questions, Your Honor."

"Thank you Counselor. Mr. Newton, do you wish to cross?"

"Yes, Your Honor."

"Proceed then, Counselor."

"Thank you, Your Honor."

I took Dr. Krauff's deposition and openly carried it with me to the podium. I wanted Dr. Krauff to know I was ready for him. I only wished I felt that way myself.

All right, Doc. You're good and we both know it. Now we'll see if I can bring you down a peg or two.

"Doctor Krauff, you told the jury that your connection to Mrs. Hoople was as an expert, conducting an independent evaluation, correct?"

"In so many words, that is correct. Yes."

"And you also said that you do several of them a year, correct?"

"Yes, they are routine in my profession. That is correct."

"About how many independent exams a year do you conduct, Doctor?"

"I'm sorry, Counselor, but I don't keep records of the number of exams I give per year."

"Come now, Doctor. You must have some idea. How about I help you narrow it down. Would it be a number greater than 100?"

"I hardly think it would be that high, Counselor."

"Greater than 50?"

"Maybe 50, but I don't think it is that high."

"Well, in fairness then, let's just say forty, O.K., Doc?"

"That sounds about right."

"Now, of these forty, how many of them would be independent exams conducted at the request of the defense bar as opposed to the request of the plaintiff's bar, Doc?"

"I don't keep those records, Counselor."

"Oh come on now Doc! How about I help you out again. Can you name one case, only one, in the past year in which you examined a person at the request of the plaintiff's bar, Doc?"

"Obviously, I can't reveal the names of my patients. It would be a breach of ethics for me to do so."

Several of the jurors nodded in agreement with this statement.

Nice going Doc, but all wrong.

"Believe me, Doc, I have no intention of asking you to violate a privilege. But you and I both know that the privilege only applies to patients. None of the independent exams you conduct are upon your patients, Doc. If they were, they wouldn't be independent, now would they?"

"Well, I guess I misspoke."

"Thank you Doc. Now please answer the question."

"I can't remember a name at this time, Counselor."

"Isn't it true, Doc that the reason you can't remember a name is because there is no name to remember? All your IMEs are done on behalf of the defense bar. Correct?"

"I guess that might be true for the last year." This admission was so grudgingly given that I did not even challenge the guess word.

"Isn't it true, Doc that the reason the defense bar comes to you on a regular basis is that they know they will get a favorable response from your office to their needs?"

"Absolutely not!" The good doctor was looking every bit the wounded and outraged innocent.

"Wait a minute, doctor. Are you telling this jury that the defense bar would spend hundreds of thousands of dollars each year to hire your office to give them results that hurt their cases? Is that what you expect this jury to believe?"

"You know perfectly well that is not what I mean, Counselor."

"I don't know anything perfectly well, doctor. And for that matter, neither does this jury. That is why I asked the question."

"Objection."

"Sustained. Keep it to questions, Mr. Newton."

"Sorry, Your Honor.

"Isn't it true, doctor, that if you repeatedly gave unwanted results to the defense bar in response to their requests for I M E s, these attorneys would quit coming back for your expertise?"

"I guess you could say that."

"And if that did happen, your office would stand to lose several hundred thousand dollars a year, correct?"

"I suppose so."

"Then, doctor, contrary to your earlier testimony you do have an interest in the outcome of this case. Isn't that true, Doc?"

The doc's face was red and his anger was showing.

"Absolutely not! You have twisted what I have said into something it is not. I never indicated an interest in the outcome of this case, never!"

"I guess we'll just have to let the jury decide what you meant by what you said, Doc. Meanwhile, let me ask you this. Why do you keep a copy of the DMSO in your office?"

"Obviously it is there as a tool to my profession."

"What does it do for you, Doc?"

"It is a ready reference to diagnoses and treatment of mental illnesses."

"Kind of like a department store catalogue, right Doc?"

"I don't quite understand what you mean, Counselor."

"What I mean is that you can open the catalogue and pick out what you want and order it. Pick and choose, so to speak."

"Certainly not. This is not a game. You have certain signs and symptoms, and you match them up with known responses and arrive at an accepted diagnosis. It promotes uniformity and assistance in recognizing and treating illness."

"Well, Doc. If you can't pick and choose, then what allows you to reject the diagnosis of MPD? It is an accepted psychological phenomenon, is it not?"

"I do not 'pick and choose' as you call it. I merely choose not to accept the diagnosis of MPD."

"Semantics, Doc. Nothing but semantics. How many other diagnoses listed in the DSMO do you choose not to accept, doctor?"

"I don't recall, at this time."

"All right then. Just name three others for the jury please, Doctor Krauff."

"I can't think of three right now."

"Two? How about one Doc? Not even one for the jury, Doc?"

"No."

"So you just don't like MPD. Strange coincidence, ain't it, Doc? I mean Mrs. Hoople being diagnosed with it and you doing the IME and all. Kind of makes you wonder, doesn't it, Doc?"

"Objection!" Bill was getting tired of his chief witness being roasted.

"Overruled." Maybe the Judge wasn't?

"Answer the question, Doctor Krauff."

"I don't remember the question, sir."

"Let me rephrase it for you, Doc. Don't you think that your non-belief in the psychological illness that affects the plaintiff is the real reason that you were hired by the defendant to do the 'independent' examination of my client?"

"Absolutely not. I have a reputation as a qualified psychologist and I assume that is the sole reason I was hired."

Well Doc, I don't believe you and neither, I expect, does the jury. You've still done a lot of damage, but now there are some chinks in the armor.

"Let's change the subject for a moment, doctor. How many employees do you currently have in your office, Doc?"

"Objection, Your Honor. Relevance." Bill did not know where I was headed, but he wanted to cut me off, if he could.

"How about it, Mr. Newton? What has the number of employees in the doctor's office got to do with this case?'

"Sorry, Your Honor. But if the court will bear with me for a few moments, it will become clear."

"All right, sir. But only for a few moments. Then you better make your case or get off it."

"Thank you, Your Honor."

"Well doctor. How many?"

"I have six others. One doctor, three nurses, a receptionist and two office workers."

"The doctor. That is your partner?"

"Junior partner actually."

"When you hired this doctor, did he offer you a resume, doctor?"

"Of course. He came highly recommended."

"And he had doctoral certificates?"

"Certainly."

"Did you check out his credentials?"

"Certainly. I have no desire to be held accountable for someone else's unqualified blunders."

"Prudence dictates that you check him out before you allow him to practice in your office, correct?"

By now the doc knew where I was going, but there was little he could do without looking like a fool.

"That would be true, yes."

"What about the nurses? You check them out too?"

"Yes, of course."

"Ever let the nurses practice without a license?"

"Of course not."

"Are you aware of any qualified medical or psychological practice in the Tampa Bay area that hires doctors or other practitioners and allows them to commence practicing medicine in their office without first checking to ensure that the new practitioner is qualified to practice?"

"No, I am not aware of any."

"Would it be fair to say then, doctor, that it is a standard in the field of medicine for an employer to ensure that his medical employees are qualified to practice in the field in which they are hired?"

"Yes."

"When you researched the materials supplied to you by the defendant regarding the hiring of Red Greely by the defendant, Crisis Center, did you find any evidence to support a thorough checking of Red's credentials by the center?"

"Not if you put it in those terms, no."

No, you don't get off that easy.

"Well, Doctor Krauff. Put it in any terms you like. Did the Center check out Red's credentials? Yes or no"

"No. Not at first."

"Not at first! Hell Doc. Isn't it true that they never checked him out until after this lawsuit was filed?"

"Objection!"

"Overruled. But watch your language, Mr. Newton. Doctor Krauff, you may answer the question."

"Yes, Judge. I guess that's true."

"No, Doctor Krauff. Don't waffle. Yes or no. True of false. One or the other!"

"Yes. Based upon the information I had access to and reviewed, yes."

"And still you find no negligence on the part of this defendant?"

"You're taking this all out of context—"

"Yes or no, Doc. Yes or no."

"No negligence."

"No wonder they hired you. No further questions, Your Honor."

Bill was fuming. But if he objected to my oratory, it would only drive the point into the minds of the jurors. Knowing he was still far ahead, he elected to fume in silence.

"Any re-direct Mr. Handell?"

"No, Your Honor."

"May the witness be excused?"

"Yes, Your Honor." Bill and I both chimed in.

"Doctor Krauff you may step down from the witness box. You are released from your subpoena and free to go about your business. Thank you for coming."

"Mr. Handell. Will your next witness be a long one?"

"Yes, Your Honor. Two or three hours, I expect."

"Fine. I believe this is a good time to break for the evening. Court will be adjourned and we will re-convene promptly at 8:30 in the morning."

* * * *

Back at the office I pretended everything was fine. I told Judith everything was going well and I sent her home for a good night's sleep. I also let Joe go home early. There was nothing I could do about what would happen in the morning.

Bill Handell had only one witness left. Judith. It would not be pretty. His whole case was built on her being a fraud, and he would do everything in his power to shake her up tomorrow. He was good and I knew he would make several points with the jurors. He already had poked several holes in our case and at least three of the jurors thought Judith was not what she presented herself to be. It would only take one lost juror to lose the case and Bill was determined to get at least that one.

I poured a stiff Crown Royal and left off the ice. It would be a long night.

CHAPTER THIRTEEN

"Mr. Handell." Judge Midder intoned, "Are you ready to call your next witness?"

"Oh yes, Your Honor. I certainly am." Bill replied to Judge Midder's inquiry with a wolfish smile.

It was 9:10 in the morning, and the impaneled jury was ready to get to the end of the trial. From the look on Bill's face I knew this was going to be a rough inquiry. However, I wasn't prepared for the intensity of Bill's obvious dislike of my client.

I whispered to Judith. "Remember, stay calm, listen to his questions carefully, and absolutely *no* switching. O K? Are you ready now?"

Judith nodded just as Judge Midder said, "Mrs. Hoople, will you please take the witness chair? I will remind you that you are still bound by the same oath you took before."

Once Judith had been seated Judge Midder looked at Bill Handell and said, "Your witness, Mr. Handell."

Bill nodded. "May it please the court; I would like the witness to be declared a hostile witness. I have the case law right here."

"Objection!" I damned near knocked over my chair, I was so mad. We had already been there.

"Your Honor. As I started to say before I was rudely cut off—" Bill began again.

"Objection!" I shouted again. I was still standing from the first objection.

"Sustained. Counsel approach the bench."

Judge Midder sat stonily and red faced as he waited for counsel to approach and the court reporter to set up.

"Your Honor," Bill began, but the Judge cut him off before he could continue.

"Mr. Handell. I will not allow speech-making requests or objections in front of the jury. I am sure that the record will reflect that I have already ruled and made myself clear on that point. Additionally, I have already ruled on your request and explicitly laid out the method and manner in which you are to examine this witness. If you wish to address this court, you will request as bench conference. Then, if I allow it, you will then address this court out of the hearing of the jury. Is that perfectly clear?"

I was trying not to smile. Judge Midder's face had progressed to a bright crimson as he addressed Bill Handell.

"Yes, Your Honor. Perfectly."

"Now, about your request to have the court declare your witness to be a hostile witness. That is denied. Mrs. Hoople is, as I have already ruled, an adverse witness. Therefore, you have wide latitude with which to question this witness. You may use leading questions, *etc.* However, this court will note for the record that at no time has your witness shown a scintilla of hostility in her answers to this court or to your client."

"But Your Honor! If the court will allow me to cite these cases," Bill began again.

Judge Midder had had enough. "Counselor, I have denied your request. If you wish to examine the witness, I suggest you do so. *While you still may!*" Judge Midder seriously emphasized his last four words.

"Now, both of you gentlemen get back to your respective positions."

As soon as we had regained our 'respective positions,' I at my table and Bill at the podium, Judge Midder said, "You may proceed, Counselor."

Bill nodded and looked at Judith.

"Mrs. Hoople. What is the one common thread, the one diagnosis that every professional who has examined you has agreed upon? Every one?"

"I'm not sure that every single one of them has completely agreed upon a single thing. Especially if you include your doctor that you sent us to."

"No Mrs. Hoople! I did not send any 'us!' I sent you and you alone."

"Objection! Argumentative."

"Sustained."

As if nothing had been said, Bill continued. "Oh, Mrs. Hoople. Think hard. Isn't here one single thing they all agree upon? Just one?"

"Not that I can think of." Judith answered.

"Isn't it true that every single one of these treaters, doctors or counselors, no matter, each and every one of them has diagnosed and classified you as manipulative?"

Judith sat there for a moment, like a deer startled in the headlights before she answered. "I had never thought of that. I'm not really sure, but if you say so, then I guess it's true."

"It's not what I say, but what your treating psychotherapists say, Mrs. Hoople.

"Do you consider yourself a manipulator, Mrs. Hoople?"

"No, I do not."

"Why do you suppose all your doctors do?"

"Objection! Calls for speculation."

"Sustained."

"Mrs. Hoople," Bill continued, "Are you trying to manipulate this jury?"

"No. We're just trying to answer your questions." Judith shot back.

Easy, easy. Don't let him get to you!

"Mrs. Hoople. And I'm talking to Judith Hoople, not a 'we' or an 'us,' I believe you have told this jury that your father raped, no, repeatedly raped you while you were an infant? Still in diapers?"

Judith took a deep breath. Looking down at her hands and then up at the jury she said, "Yes, that's true".

"Yes, that's true. Yes, that's true? Do you seriously expect this jury to believe that you can remember things that happened to you while you were still in diapers?" Bill was almost shouting, evincing a tone of disbelief.

"Objection, badgering the witness."

"Sustained! Counsel, control yourself." Judge Midder began to look serious as he admonished Bill.

"Answer the question please." Bill went on as if nothing had transpired.

Before either the Judge or I could cut in. Judith began to speak. "Mr. Handell, as I explained earlier, I don't remember my earlier childhood any more than the next person. I only recall these special events that were so traumatic to me. This has been explained to me, and to you."

"Stop right there, Mrs. Hoople. I want to have your answers, not the answers of some counselor with fancy psychological overtones. My question was directed to you and your memory, independent of any explanations."

I could object, but I don't think he is scoring any points with the jury. So... I'll let him go, for now.

"How do you think it is that you can really think to when you were in diapers and that no one else can remember that far back?"

"I guess most women have not been forcibly raped by their fathers at that time," Judith replied.

Several jurors smiled at Judith's answer and Bill realized he had made a mistake. Violation of rule number one. If you don't know the answer, don't ask the question.

"Mrs. Hoople. With your father dead that only leaves three people who can address your charges. True?"

"Objection!"

"Sustained. Rephrase the question, Counselor."

"Is your father alive, Mrs. Hoople?"

"No, he died several years earlier."

"You hated your father. Didn't you?"

"No, at least not that I then realized."

"You've already told this jury that you burned all of his photos. Or had you forgotten that?"

"That was only after I had learned what he had done. I cried at his funeral. I even kissed his lips in the open casket at his funeral. I did not know." Judith lowered her eyes and her tone as she responded to this obviously painful episode in her life.

"And your mother? You hate her too, don't you?"

"No. Yes. Not exactly. I've—"

"Not exactly?" Bill interrupted, "You've what?"

"Objection" I shouted. "The witness has not finished her answer to the question."

"Sustained. Mr. Handell, please allow the witness to finish with her answer before moving on to the next question."

Bill smiled. "Mrs. Hoople, do you wish to complete your answer?"

Damn! I fell right into that one.

Startled, Judith nodded. "Thank you, Judge. What I was trying to say was that in my teenage years and forward, until I met Red, I loved my mother as well as the next daughter loved hers. That is one of the problems I have, right now. All these years I loved her dearly, and now I know what she did and what she allowed my father to do. It hurts, deeply. I haven't talked to my mother in over four years. I have no pictures of her. I couldn't even read her deposition."

Judith had tears in her eyes and a catch in her voice at the end of her answer.

"Well, your mother certainly doesn't agree with your recollections, now does she, Mrs. Hoople?"

"I believe she denied them."

"Your brother doesn't agree with you either, does he Mrs. Hoople?"

"I don't believe my brother was in the bedroom when my father raped me. I know he was not with us at the cult meetings." Judith was beginning to look somewhat haggard.

"In fact, there is no one in your family, of for that matter, anywhere else that can support your allegations. Isn't that true, Mrs. Hoople?"

"No. It's a dirty, hideous secret that no one cares to admit. I wish I did not know. I wish I'd never met Red Greely. I wish...." Judith's voice trailed off, eyes still moist and a face expressing deep felt remorse and regret she seemed to shrink in the witness box.

"You like to play games. Don't you, Mrs. Hoople?"

"I used to," Judith answered.

"Used to? Why you still do. Don't you Mrs. Hoople? I mean, isn't it true that you bought a brand new Nintendo game when you settled your case against Red Greely?"

"Objection! Your Honor, may we approach the bench?"

"Sustained," Judge Midder almost shouted. "The jury will disregard that last statement from Mr. Handell. Counsel approach...Now!"

As soon as the court reporter was set up I began. "Your Honor. We already agreed that it would be O.K. to mention the settlement between Red and my client. However, we also stipulated that nothing would be said about amounts. Nothing. This is just a sneaky way for Mr. Handell to back door his way into forbidden territory. It has no other relevance."

"Your Honor," Bill began "I was just—"

"I know what you were 'just' doing, Counselor. I wasn't put up on this bench yesterday. I don't intend to have you create a mistrial or an appeal that will be overturned. Nor will I allow you to circumvent my earlier decision. I warned you before that you were on the edge of a contempt citation. Do you understand me, Counselor?"

"Yes, Your Honor."

"Both of you return to your positions.

"Please continue, Counselor."

As if nothing had transpired at the bench, Bill began. "As I was saying, you do still play games, don't you Mrs. Hoople?"

"Yes, I do. But what I was trying to say earlier, not physical games. Nor any games that require figuring, like monopoly or cards. I just don't enjoy them any more. Not even with the kids."

"Isn't it true that this whole thing is really just a game to you? A big game for really big stakes?"

"No that's not true at all."

"Red Greely never volunteered to cure you of your smoking habit, did he?"

"Why yes, he did." Judith answered with a puzzled look on her face.

"Isn't it really true that in fact, you approached Red Greely with the idea, not the other way around?"

"No, that's not true. He app—"

"Tell the truth, Mrs. Hoople."

"Objection. He's badgering the witness and not allowing her to finish her answers."

"Sustained. Once again, Counselor, please allow the witness to complete her answer before popping another question." Judge Midder was clearly exasperated, but just as clearly, in control.

"Mrs. Hoople, you have something else to say?"

"Yes, thank you Your Honor. I was saying that it was Red who came up with the idea of treating us. We did not go to him. He asked us." Judith was beginning to wear under Bill's relentless attacks. Even though the Judge was ruling in our favor, I could see the strain in her face and the frightened look in her eyes.

I stood. "Your Honor. I know it's a bit early, but I could use a break."

Judge Midder looked at the courtroom clock. It was 10:10. Ladies and gentlemen, it is a little earlier than I had planned for our break, but I'm going to call a 20 minute recess."

"All rise, court is now in recess." The bailiff intoned, clearly as ready for a break as I was.

After the jury had left Judith came over and slumped in her chair. I attempted to perk her up. I told her that she was doing well and that Bill was not scoring any points with the jury by his highhanded manner. I worked with her for five minutes and then sent Joe with her to the ladies room to freshen up.

Despite what I had told Judith, even though the jury didn't like Bill's tactics, he was scoring some points. Some doubts were being ensconced in their minds. Bill's completely arrogant refusal to show any sympathy at all for Judith had to have them wondering why. What did he know that they didn't?

I was ready for this show to be over. Bill was highhanded, but he was not stupid. All he had to do was to convince one juror that Judith was a fraud. It would be close right now. Much closer than I liked at this stage of a trial.

* * * *

Back on the stand, Judith waited for Bill's next question.

"Isn't it true, Mrs. Hoople, that you really liked Red Greely? From the first day that you went to work at the center?"

"At that time, yes. I guess so."

"And you flirted with him, trying to get his attention?"

"No, I did not flirt with him. He's twenty years older than I am. I respected him."

"No Ma'am. You flirted with him. Came on to him from your first day on the job. But he rejected you're advances. Didn't he?"

"I told you. I did not make advances to him."

"And isn't it true that you saw this hypnosis thing as a con? A way to get alone with Red Greely so that you could advance your own agenda?" Bill was continuing with his questions as if she had agreed with him, and rapidly moved from one to the next.

"No, absolutely not. I wanted to quit smoking and he volunteered to treat me. Me and several others, I might add." Judith's tone betrayed exasperation.

"But you're the only one that continued with Red more than four or five times. True?"

"I don't really know. Maybe."

"When did you first see *Three Faces of Eve,* Mrs. Hoople?"

Totally surprised, Judith said, "Let's see. About 8 or 10 years ago, I think."

"How many times did you see it?"

"Two, three or maybe four times. It comes on late night UHF channels occasionally. I like a lot of the old movies."

"But this one more than most. Right?"

"I like it O.K."

"Have you ever read the book?"

"Yes, I have."

"In fact, you own a copy of the book. Don't you?"

"Yes, I do."

"Let's see now. You've been on Maury Povich?"

"Objection!"

"Sustained."

"May we approach the bench, Your Honor?" Bill asked.

"Approach, counsel. Both of you."

At the bench, Bill started. "Your Honor, I do not intend to go into the show itself, at least not at this time. At this point I am merely attempting to introduce evidence that this whole MPD episode is nothing but a sham to gain publicity for a future book and to reap illegal profits buy suing Red and the Center. It is all an act to promote her own agenda. I am entitled to pursue this line of questioning."

"Counselor?"

Judge Midder looked at me, clearly impressed by Bill's logic.

Arguing a losing battle won't gain me any points. As long as Bill isn't going into what happened on the show he is probably entitled.

"Your Honor, I have no objection to counsel mentioning the show itself. Obviously, the jury already knows about it. As long as the rules are clear that we don't go into the show itself without ample advance warning so that we can argue before any damage is done."

"Very well. Mr. Handell, you may continue, but within the scope you have indicated. Any change will be approved by this court prior to your questioning the witness. Understood?"

"Yes, Your Honor."

Back at the podium, Bill continued.

"Mrs. Hoople. You appeared on the Maury Povich show?"

"Yes, sir." Judith, whose chair at the witness stand was close enough to allow her to have heard most of the argument, knew where Bill was headed. That helped a little, but not much.

"And you appeared on *Alive at Five*?"

"Yes sir."

"And you appeared on the Cathy Fountain Show?"

"Yes sir."

"And you plan to write a book on this whole thing. After the trial is over. Correct?"

"Well, that's never been a sure thing." Judith hesitated.

Jumping in the gap, Bill continued. "Not a sure thing? Why, Mrs. Hoople. Shame on you. Isn't it true that you called Nicholson's Graphics and Covers to inquire as to how much it would cost to have them prepare a book cover for you?"

Where the hell did he get that?

With a stunned look on her face Judith barely nodded and said, "Yes."

"Nicholson Graphics. Isn't it true that Nicholson's is the same outfit that designed the cover for the book "Three Faces of Eve?" Bill was grinning and he pronounced the last as if he had just won the lottery.

Recovering her composure Judith nodded. "Yes sir. It is. And I did call them to see what it would cost if I did write a book and needed to pay for a cover. I called them about six months ago."

Well, at least she did not call them before she met Red.

"And isn't it true that you have inquired as to a book publisher regarding your book?"

"Yes. Actually I have contacted several publishers. I am a divorced mother of two who cannot hold down a job and is reduced to living below the poverty line. Mr. Handell, I was trying to find a way out of the hole that I find myself in. But nothing came of the inquiries. They all told me that I had to have a good portion of the book finished before they would consider it, much less advance any funds on it. By the way, I got the idea from the producer of the Maury Povich show."

The answer took some of the sting out of Bill's questions, and, put a little of the color back in Judith's face. I knew it wasn't completely true though. Judith had talked about a book from the first time I met her. But it sure as hell wasn't my job to point out my client's errors.

"But Mrs. Hoople. Don't you have any faith in your own lawsuit? Certainly you don't need the suit and the book both just to rise above the poverty level?"

"Objection. Calls for speculation."

"Sustained. Get on with it, Counselor."

"Mrs. Hoople. It is your position that now, after Red so to speak, that you can switch in and out of various personalities without hypnosis. Isn't that true?"

"Yes. We can."

"Would you like to switch right now? Show the jury some of these little kiddies the jury has heard so much about?"

Damn you!

"Objection! May we approach the bench?"

"Come ahead, gentlemen."

At the bench, I was scrambling. "Your Honor. I can't believe that counsel is attempting to have my client switch personalities. First, it is clearly outside the scope of direct examination. Second, it is not something that I think should be conducted without the presence of a trained psychotherapist. It can potentially be psychologically dangerous to my client. Counsel is clearly just trying to foster a dog and pony show to make a mockery out of a certified medical condition."

"Mr. Handell. Where are you going with this line of questioning?"

"Your Honor. I have no intention of asking this lady to switch personalities. I haven't asked that. I just asked if she wanted to. I have my motives, but they don't involve asking her to actually switch personalities."

"Very well, you may continue with your questioning. But only within the confines you have alluded to."

Back at the podium Bill continued. "Madam court reporter. Would you please read back the last question?"

"By attorney Bill Handell: Would you like to switch right now? Show the jury some of these little kiddies the jury has heard so much about?"

"Thank you, madam court reporter. Well, Mrs. Hoople?"

"No. I would not like to show the jury the children right now, Mr. Handell."

"Well, why not, Mrs. Hoople? Are you scared? Afraid? What?"

"No, Mr. Handell. I am neither scared nor afraid. As Mr. Newton advised us, we are here to tell the truth. That is the reason I am on the stand. Not to put on a dog and pony show."

It was a good answer. I was pleased. Judith had clearly been paying attention at the bench conference.

"You don't consider your previous performance with the whining, crying and whispering a dog and pony show, Mrs. Hoople?"

"Objection!" I was up so fast that I knocked over my chair. "Commenting on the witness's testimony in a derogatory fashion in front of the jury while the witness is still on the stand is an improper and egregious abuse of the system."

I just said a lot more than the judge normally allows, but damn Bill anyway! That's a cheap shot and Judge Midder just might allow me to get away with it.

I was right.

"Sustained. Mr. Handell you are an officer of the court. The court should not have to remind you how to conduct yourself. You will apologize to the witness. Now."

"If my question offended you Mrs. Hoople, then I ask that you accept my apology." While his mouth uttered the words, Bill's eyes were anything but apologetic. He knew he had made his point. Unlike the plaintiff, Bill only had to convince one juror Judith was not what she purported to be.

Judge Midder broke in before anything else could transpire. "Ladies and gentlemen. This seems to be a good time for the noon recess. It is now 11:50. Be back at 1:20."

* * * *

Back at the office, Judith was unusually quiet. I noticed that she looked very tense. I worked with her, trying to get her in a better frame of mind. I told her she was doing well and that Bill had not scored any major hits. I let her know that she only had a couple hours to go and then it would be over. That Bill was desperate and firing off his last salvos. I felt like Vince Lombardi at half time with the opponent ahead by three touchdowns.

Judith's response was to remain uptight. She did not take well to public criticism, especially when she couldn't fight back and Bill left few openings. She picked at her food, moving it around the plate while she sipped her drink.

So much for my pep talking skills. Guess that's why I'm a lawyer, not a coach.

* * * *

After the lunch break, Judith returned to the witness stand. She appeared quiet and reserved, pensive. She steeled herself, waiting for the next question. It wasn't long in coming.

"Mrs. Hoople." Bill opened the afternoon session. "You indicated earlier that Red Greely treated you both at the Center and at his personal office. Correct?"

"At the Center. At his office and at his residence."

"And all this time you had only two traumatic episodes. Correct?"

"No, Mr. Handell. That is hardly correct. I had numerous traumatic experiences at Red's hands. I assume you are referring to his two incompetent attempts at reversing my condition?"

"Strange isn't it, Mrs. Hoople, that both of these major traumas would occur at his office. Away from the Center and without any witnesses?"

"I don't really know what you are asking. We *never* had any witnesses. You don't conduct legitimate individual psychiatric sessions in front of witnesses, much less the kind of sessions I later became aware that Red was conducting. Once we began regular treatment, other than Red's trysts in the Center for a *quickie*, if you will, most of the sessions took place in his office."

"Tell me a little more about the video flashback treatment, Mrs. Hoople?"

Judith paled a little as she went back in her mind to answer the question. "As I explained before, it was supposed to place all these scenes in my mind at the same time, and I would be receptive to them. I guess it was supposed to create a condition or mental state in my mind that would show some nervousness and a little anxiety, but no truly overt reaction."

Judith was obviously having trouble, visibly having to force herself to concentrate on the past.

She continued. "It didn't work that way. I could see everything. I could feel everything, all over again." Judith was speaking very softly now, clutching at her handkerchief with both hands.

"All the thrusting, the pain, the drool." Judith drifted off, her soft voice trailing, her eyes full of tears.

"Come now, Mrs. Hoople," Bill began, trying to shake her out of this lethargic state. "You aren't going back into that baby-raping routine again? Please, no more of the diapers. I mean, you don't really expect this jury to believe that you feel pain that supposedly occurred while you where an infant in diapers? Do you?"

"It happened, Mr. Handell. That's all I can tell you." Judith was almost whispering and she had a frightened look on her face.

Bill's eyes squinted, emitting the menacing glare of a badger moving in on his next meal.

"And Red Greely brought all this out! Yes, yes. I know. And all the time that you are supposedly reliving these experiences, Red Greely is supposed to be molesting these young girls. Only it isn't young girls, is it? It is really you, Judith Hoople, isn't it?"

"I, I, yes. I mean no. I mean it wasn't like that. When the trauma was severe he wasn't doing these things." Judith was shaking now, crying openly with her voice catching in her throat.

"Red Greely never molested any children, did he Mrs. Hoople?"

"Yes, he did. Judy and—"

"Mrs. Hoople." Bill interrupted. Isn't it true that the only body you are aware of that Red had sex with was the body of a thirty-four year old woman? You, Judith Hoople?"

"Physically, that's true. But not mentally. Wait. I don't mean that the way it sounds. I mean that the child alters are not mentally mature beyond 5 or 6 years old." Judith was grasping now. Her answers were disjointed and lacking confidence.

Get it together, Gal. Bill's not doing anything that would be objectionable and any lost objections on my part would only focus the jury on your plight. Straighten up and get tough.

"Isn't it true that the only person Red had sex with was you, Mrs. Hoople? You alone and you wanted it, didn't you?"

Oh well, here goes nothing. Got to try to break this up.

"Objection, asked and answered."

"Overruled. The witness may answer the question." Judge Midder wasn't buying.

"Do I need the court reporter to read it back, or do you remember the question, Mrs. Hoople?" Bill asked the question with a slight smirk.

"He had sex with the children." Judith was almost pleading now, desperate to be understood. "I only had sex with him after he threatened to drop us all from treatment. After he ran off and left us for a month. I never wanted to be Red's lover. Never." Tears were now streaming down Judith's face.

"Oh come now, Mrs. Hoople. You wanted Red Greely from the very beginning. Isn't that true?"

"No. No I did not," Judith cried.

"These severe trauma episodes. Isn't it true that they were nothing more than a means of keeping Red from becoming disinterested? Leaving you with no man in your life?"

"No. That is not true. I had David. Even after our divorce we were friends. We loved each other. I did not want Red. I did not want him. I just wanted to be well."

"And the second traumatic episode, the integration I believe you called it, tell us whose idea was that?"

"It was Red's idea. I knew nothing about it." Judith was puzzled and hurt at the same time.

"Nothing about it?" Bill almost growled. "Isn't that the way Eve was cured in the movie you saw several times? In the book you have read and re-read in your home, and that you own a copy of?"

Judith drew back as if she had been slapped in the face. She looked at Bill Handell, pleadingly. "I guess that is what worked for her. But I didn't know about the treatment. Red is the counselor. He is the one who suggested it. I was his patient. It was his idea." Judith was losing it. I looked at my watch, but it was too early for a break.

Hang in there Judith. Only a few minutes to go.

"Correct me if I am wrong, Mrs. Hoople, but you still expect this jury to believe that there is a little baby inside you who remembers being repeatedly raped by your father. All while this little baby is in diapers. And that this little baby girl suffers from partial paralysis and arthritis. And that when Red tried to treat you, she, the little girl in diapers, became the ruler of the roost? The one in charge of all of these people, children and adults alike, who are supposedly inside you? Especially that she ruled over you, a thirty-five year old woman?" Bill's face and voice were showing nothing but pure skepticism, and, as I looked at the jury, some of the same skepticism was reflected in their faces as well.

"You make it sound dirty and false. It was not like that. That's not the way it was." Judith was crying openly now.

"Well then, how was it, Mrs. Hoople? I'm just trying to clear up the mystery. The truth is there never really was a rape of anyone in diapers that anyone remembers. Not you, not a crippled baby, not your parents, no one! It never happened, did it Mrs. Hoople?" Bill was openly contemptuous now in both his questions and his mannerisms.

"Yes. It did happen!" Judith almost shouted, her face contorted with anguish. "I was in the crib and he ripped off the diapers." Judith's eyes began to roll up and her lids began to flutter as her voice dropped into a low moan.

"He was there, his fingers poking and pushing. Then, pain. Searing pain and thrusting...thrusting...thrusting." Judith's voice slowly dropped to a whisper.

"Oh come now Mrs. Hoople." Bill was on a roll now and he wanted no sympathy from the jury from Judith's actions. "You don't really expect this jury to believe you can remember this so called rape from the mind of an infant?

Possibly if it was from the bum you said allegedly raped you in an alleyway, but in diapers?

"Objection, multiple question."

"Sustained. Get on with it, Counselor."

"Well then, Mrs. Hoople. Tell us about this bum. Was he big? Tall? A midget? What is on the agenda for this allegation, Mrs. Hoople?" The contempt and disdain were evident in each word and infliction in Bill's questions.

"No, please I don't want to do this. I don't want to go there." Judith had a very frightened look on her face.

"Mrs. Hoople. You're in a safe courtroom surrounded by people who can protect you. Do I have to ask the court to instruct you to answer the question, or will you answer it on your own?"

About one more smart-ass crack and I'm going to lose it myself. Come on, Judith. Speak up!

"It was after school." Judith began to remember and her voice took on the quality of a little girl.

Oh, shit!! What's going on?

"He was big, and filthy. His fingernails were dirty and his fingers had stains on them. His teeth were yellow, coated with scum. His hair was thin and matted. His pants were held up by a rope." Judith's face was white now. Tears and sweat mixed and her hair began to wilt. She seemed to sink into the witness chair. The jury was completely attentive, as were the rest of us.

She continued. "He pulled me into the bushes behind the dumpster, threw me on the ground and yanked off my little panties. Then he pulled down his pants, he had no underwear on." Judith's eyes began to glaze and her pulse was racing. Her hands were wringing the handkerchief in a forceful grip. "He hurt me. He pushed himself into me. It feels like a hot branding iron inside. Oh God, it hurts!! He is thrusting inside me, deeper and deeper. I'm going to rip apart! Oh God, please Mister. Please let me go. Don't hurt me anymore. Please. But he can't hear me. No one can because his filthy hand is over my face."

Judith was back to a whisper now. Every ear in the courtroom strained to hear her next words. Even Bill seemed somewhat taken aback.

Her voice choking, as if she were barely holding herself back from vomiting, Judith went on. "He's inside me now and on top of me on the outside. He completely dominates me with pain and weight. As he gets closer to finishing, he gets wilder. His drool is dropping on my face and on my neck. Oh God. He's shoving harder and harder now. Oh God. It hurts so much." Judith's face was now in an animalistic state, showing raw fear and pain, her head jerking and her lips pulled tightly around her teeth.

"The thrusting is getting worse. My insides are torn and raw. Each thrust is more painful than the last." Judith began rocking now, quick little jerking rocks that moved the witness chair back and forth. Her eyes went to the ceiling at the back of the courtroom. She tried to go on. "Nasty, so nasty. His slobber. His filthy hand on my open mouth. Inside me it is hot and in pain. I am bleeding. Oh God! It hurts! Gunhhh!" With an animal like grunt, Judith swayed in her chair. Jerking from that, she suddenly stopped swaying and rolled up her eyes completely into the top of the sockets. With a few small flutterings, her eyelids closed. Then, while the entire courtroom watched, mesmerized, Judith slowly curled up in the witness chair with her thumb in her mouth.

Son of a bitch!

Pandemonium broke out as I glanced at Bill. He was standing there with a shocked expression on his face watching as Judith snuggled her legs up to her chest like an infant, in a fetal position.

She let out a little whimper and then was out cold.

EPILOGUE

Judge Midder was the first to react. Getting no response from Judith, he cleared the courtroom.

Bill Handell immediately moved for a mistrial, which Judge Midder promptly denied.

After about 20 minutes, Judith recovered enough to be helped out of the courtroom and sent home to bed.

Dr. Felton Berry opined that Judith would need 24 to 48 hours rest before she could continue the trial and Judge Midder sent the jury home with instructions to call in the next afternoon to see when they would return for the rest of the trial.

Bill Handell, Tim Snead and a very unhappy claims adjuster left the courtroom arguing intensely.

Back in my office, the first offer for settlement came at 4:50 PM.

By 9 P.M. the case settled for $1,500,000.00.

At 1:00 A.M. Judith was drifting off to sleep, heavily sedated and wearing a silly smile.

At 1:00 A.M. I sat in my office with a watered down Crown Royal on mostly melted ice, still pondering the question I would never ask Judith. Sleep was still a long way off.

* * * *

Two weeks later Joe came running into my office. "Boss, you'll never guess what happened." Without waiting for a reply or even taking a breath, she continued.

"Judith sold her book. I mean it isn't even written yet but they gave her an advance and said they were sending her a ghostwriter to help her write it. All she has to do is give them the facts. She wouldn't give me the actual figure, but she said it was way into the seven figures."

"Great," I said. "Let's hope she tells them some good things about us."

* * * *

Two weeks after that, I came into the office and Terry was there. The look on her face told me I wasn't going to like what she was about to tell me.

"You'd better sit down, Boss." Terry handed me a large thick manila envelope.

Taking the envelope from her hands, I gazed at the return address—The Florida Bar.

I pulled out a thick packet and as I spread it out, I recognized the legal caption. It was the one thing a lawyer hates most to see. A full-fledged lawsuit by the Bar against a lawyer. Scanning the contents I could see that in an attempt to cover his own pathetic self, Red Greely had done it now. Through his lawyer he had filed a complaint that had gone well beyond the normal status and was now a full blown attempt to have me disbarred for joining with a client to embezzle from an insurance company by committing fraud with the filing of a false law suit.

Damn, damn, damn. I knew I never should have taken this case. Well, at least Bar complaints are normally confidential. Total garbage! Damn!

Wrong.

A slight movement of my door and Evie, my receptionist was scooting in my office, eyes furtively glancing behind her.

"Sorry Boss, but there is a hall full of reporters and cameras and God knows what else gathering from the lobby all the way back to the elevator."

Handing me a copy of the same complaint Terry had given me, she went on, "They are all holding on to one of these and asking for you."

"Son of a bitch! Someone tipped the media and set this up. What the hell is happening?"

Judith winds up a multimillionaire and I wind up defending my law firm and my license against a false complaint that will undo all the good cases I have handled and advertising efforts I have spent money on for the last ten years.

Damn it. I knew I never should have taken this case. Damn, damn, damn!!

"Joe, get your cute Filipino ass in here, right now!" I shouted, my mind racing as I began to formulate my next move.

www.ingramcontent.com/pod-product-compliance
Lightning Source LLC
Chambersburg PA
CBHW060105260626
47160CB00005B/1807
* 9 7 8 1 6 0 2 1 5 1 0 5 5 *